FIRE AND ICE

NORTHWEST ICE ROMANCE
BOOK ONE

CAROLYN MILLER

PRAISE FOR CAROLYN MILLER

Praise for *Fire and Ice*

"A delightful, laugh out loud romance that fans of hockey stories will love!" ~ *SUSAN MAY WARREN, USA Today bestselling author*

"With a strong hero and even stronger heroine, *Fire and Ice* combines tough issues with romance and laughter in such a real way. Miller is becoming masterful at both deep plots and well-rounded characters that keep you invested and turning the pages. Even better, she never fails to leave you with a smile and happy sigh when you reach the final page. This latest addition to her hockey romance series only cements that fact. A must read." ~ *SUSAN TUTTLE, best-selling author of Along Came Love series*

"Not only was I entertained by the engaging characters and well-written plot, I also loved the deeper explorations of faith, value, prayer and how women are treated in sports reporting. Hannah and Franklin's chemistry is full of fireworks and they might melt the ice with their can't-resist-any-longer kisses. Needless to say, *Fire & Ice* scores a big win with me!" ~ *CARRIE BOOTH SCHMIDT, Reading is my Superpower blog*

"Fire and Ice starts with a fun premise then digs deeper into the kind of relationships that last throughout this whole series and beyond. Sure to inspire." ~ *ANGELA RUTH STRONG, bestselling author of* Husband Auditions

"He's a hockey player trying to transfer smoothly into his hometown team, and she's a sports reporter trying to keep her job. Between the two, things are heating up on and off the ice in this newest addition to Carolyn Miller's "Original Six Hockey Romance" series! A great read for fans of hockey and romance alike, don't miss out on this Canadian getaway!" ~ *ANGELA K. COUCH, author of* A Rose for the Resistance

Praise for the Original Six series

"I loved the dialogue and the hero and heroine, the very authentic and real challenges they faced and the unique setting and hockey slant." ~ *RACHEL MCMILLAN, bestselling author*

"A touching romance set on the breathtaking shores of Canada's Lake Muskoka. Sarah and Dan are so vividly drawn they practically leap off the page! Their sweet, slowly evolving friendship deepens into the kind of lasting love Christians long for. A must read!" ~ *MEGHANN WHISTLER, award-winning author of* The Billionaire's Secret

"There is nothing like a wonderful redemption story where someone changes their life and becomes a better version of themselves. It is a good reminder to me that God offers incredible grace to all of us." ~ *GOODREADS review*

"Carolyn Miller keeps on turning out these beautifully written, tender hearted books!... There was humor and brilliant bantering conversations, heart stopping romance, as well as exciting descriptions (and sometimes dangerous passages of play) of hockey games. Well worth the late night/early morning read!" ~ *KAYE'S REVIEWS & NEWS*

"I am emerging out of my book hangover after reading *Checked Impressions* by Carolyn Miller....The romance, humor and themes of identity are so enjoyable and make for a great read!" ~ *BECKY'S BOOKSHELVES*

"Adrenaline, chemistry, romance, and lots of wooing!...You do not have to be a fan of sports or even knowledgeable in hockey and short track to appreciate *Love on Ice*." ~ *GOODREADS review*

"Carolyn Miller scores another win with *Love on Ice*, the second book in her Original Six Hockey series. I absolutely loved the faith thread in this story. It's message that success does not lie on what we do, but who we are is powerful." ~ *GOODREADS review*

FIRE AND ICE

CHAPTER 1

"They want me to wear what?"

Hannah Wade's stomach knotted as she stared at the Malibu Barbie-worthy dress, its hot pink color, short length and plunging neckline sure to make her look like the famous doll, especially given Hannah's own blonde hair and height. Nope. No way. How could she ever be taken seriously wearing something like that?

"Dirk thought it would be fun," Mandi explained, rolling her eyes. No, the station's sports executive producer wasn't exactly known for his twenty-first century views. "It's just for the interview."

"But if I wear that for my first time in front of the cameras then I'll forever be typecast as the ditzy girl who doesn't know what she's talking about. And I've worked so hard to get this job."

When her Olympic dreams had shattered along with her ankle, Hannah had thrown herself into her media communications degree with the aim of exactly this: becoming the first female sports reporter at Calgary's premier news and sports television station, CNSTV, and working in a job that meant she'd finally be able to pay back her mom for all her years of funding Hannah's sports career, a career that hadn't turned out how either of them had expected.

While CNSTV wasn't everyone's cup of tea, they'd been the only ones offering a pay check, as agent, Lisa Miller, had pointed out. The station had apparently succumbed to recent public pressure about inclusivity, even if inclusivity stretched only so far as including a woman as part of the sports team. It had been made very plain at her interview that this was a new "challenge" for the station, something Hannah thought should've been a challenge maybe fifty years ago. But hey, there were dinosaurs everywhere in these parts. Most were still waiting to be unearthed, but some made their status plain via their misogynistic comments on TV.

Mandi's lips rolled in as she nodded. "So, what do you want me to do?"

Hannah's nose wrinkled at the dress, even as appreciation grew for the understanding given by the station's lead stylist—actually, given CNSTV's patriarchal systems and tiny budget, their *only* stylist—for all things hair, makeup, and wardrobe. "Is there nothing else?"

Mandi's head tilted. "How committed are you to being blonde?"

Hope jumped. Hannah held out a long wavy strand. "Can you change this that quickly?"

"It won't be perfect, but we have a couple of hours until your interview, right?"

"Yes." Which would allow time to source other clothes, too.

The next ninety minutes passed in a flurry of hair dyeing, washing, and drying, during which she tried not to imagine what Dirk and the rest of the team would say. There wasn't anything in her contract demanding she look a certain way, was there? A quick scroll of her phone where she'd saved important documents didn't give any details pertaining to that.

So, they were just going to have to lump it if they couldn't like it.

Another glance at her phone as the hair dryer shrieked shifted Hannah's thoughts to the interview with Calgary's latest recruit. Franklin James. Her heart skipped a beat. Would he remember her? When she'd learned at today's production meeting that she was destined to meet him she'd been stunned. Sure, she kept abreast of hockey news as much as the next Canadian—okay, given her involvement in the sport maybe a *tad* more—but the fact she was going to be the first from CNSTV to interview him?

Judging from Drew Anderson and Bob Patresky's reactions they hadn't been too happy about it, but when Dirk had explained it was going to be a "soft" interview they'd calmed down. "Hannah is spunky and smart," Dirk had said, "and she needs to start somewhere. This will be a good opportunity to wet her feet with a soft toss of an interview."

Hannah's fingers tightened. Just because Dirk thought it was going to be soft didn't mean it would be. She had no intention to play things meek and mild just because she was the token female on the sports reporting team. Playing soft had never been her style. Nor would it have seen her win gold at World Championships, or be in the mix for Olympic selection. Regret soured her stomach. If only—

"So, are you ready?"

Mandi's voice drew her back into the here and now. "Let's go."

Mandi grinned then twirled the seat so Hannah could see her reflection in the mirror.

Her heart hitched. Was this a mistake? "I look so different," she whispered.

"You look like you're a natural brunette," Mandi said. "You look amazing."

And without Hannah's usual lazy ponytail or sloppy bun, she

looked three million times more professional. With her glasses on, she'd look studious, even.

Mandi flicked the brush through Hannah's hair a few more times, plumping out the curls. "It should hold its bounce, provided you don't get it wet."

"Thank you so much."

"Less of a Barbie bombshell now, huh?" Mandi winked, removing the hairdressing cape. "I think Dirk will flip when he sees you."

"It's a good thing he won't until after my interview then." Hannah wriggled from her seat, checking her phone. Good. She still had thirty minutes before the interview was scheduled.

"So what will you wear?"

"I'll stop at my apartment and get a shirt. These pants will do."

Mandi giggled. "I think I'm going to love working with you. Those guys sit here wanting all the trimmings to mask their late-night drinking sessions and bald patches, making sexist comments throughout, and you on your first day rock up and own your appearance like a boss. That's fire, girl." She high-fived Hannah. "Respect. They won't know what's hit them."

"I hope so." She grinned, and made a mental note to send Mandi flowers. It wasn't every day the sisterhood united like this.

Thirty minutes later she stood in a park overlooking Calgary's cityscape, tugging at the back of her pale pink silk shirt so it didn't stick to her back in the mild sunshine. It wasn't the weather making her sweat.

Royce, the cameraman, hoisted the camera on his shoulder as Jason, the producer who was also responsible for sound, listened to his earpiece and adjusted levels on his computer. "Love the color," Royce called.

She grinned, her nerves settling a little as she swiped on lip gloss. Okay, so she didn't want to look like an overly made-up doll, but neither did she want to tick off Dirk. The pink shirt was proof of her effort to demonstrate her femininity like Dirk seemed to want her to.

"Want to run through it again?" Jason asked.

"Sure." She tugged out her notes and scanned them quickly.

He thrust a microphone in her hand then stepped back beside Royce. "In your own time."

She shifted, planting her feet more firmly as she gazed at the camera and nodded.

"In three, two," *one*, Jason mouthed, before pointing at her.

"Hello, I'm Hannah Wade from Calgary News and Sports TV and I'm here today to meet with the newest member of the Flames, Franklin James."

"You could smile a bit more," Royce called. "Maybe it's the new hair color but you look a little too serious."

She lifted her lips high. "Like this?"

"Aim for something less Joker-like."

She dimmed her smile by half. "Better?"

"Think casual happy, not forced happy."

Her cheeks twitched as she worked to find something that felt natural. Then her breath hitched as a figure walked into view.

Franklin James. She swallowed. He wore a gray suit that looked like it had come straight from the expert tailors at Henry Singer, his broad shoulders filling it out to perfection.

"Are you Hannah?"

"Yes." He didn't recognize her? Maybe it was the new hair color. She held out a hand which he grasped. "Hi Franklin. Good to see you again."

"Nice to meet you."

His deep voice seemed to rumble right through her, carving a path for a spurt of disappointment that he obviously did not remember her. Okay, fine. No way was she going to admit to meeting him once upon a time. Maybe teenage her had truly been forgettable. She resisted the urge to fluff her curls, instead pasting on a smile. "Thank you for your time today. I hope this won't take long."

"No problem."

He smiled, and a shiver of…something…rolled through her. Oh, how unprofessional. Her clothes might make her look like a principled career reporter, but there was no hiding the truth. She was as much a sucker for this hockey player's humble charm as thousands of women across North America. Yes, she might've read some comments online about his "flaming hot" good looks—hello, it was called research—and she knew there were plenty of women who'd kill for a chance to interview him. So she had to play it cool, act professional, and tamp such feelings down. She'd done it before, after all.

She lifted her chin, glancing at Jason as he held up a finger as he listened to his phone.

"What is it?"

Jason nodded, murmured something then shoved it in his pocket. "That was Dirk."

Her chest squeezed. Had he heard about her altered appearance? She swallowed. "And?"

"We're doing this live instead."

"Live?" Franklin asked, glancing at her with wide eyes.

Just breathe. She tilted her chin higher. "It'll be fine," she assured, as if she'd done this a million times before. "Just think of it as like when you've come off the ice and have an interview straight away."

"Apparently they want it for the early news," Jason said. "They think doing it live will bring more energy. My guess is they want to get the first interview of Calgary's latest import and putting it on the Monday news will make a statement." He glanced at her. "And I wouldn't be surprised if Dirk is wondering whether you'd be a better fit for exactly that kind of interview, and is using this to test you out."

Breath constricted, and she wiggled her fingers in a vain attempt to release the tension. To actually be involved in real-time sideline interviews, rather than the soft fluff pieces they'd mentioned during the production meeting? She would pray it could come true, if she remembered how to pray.

"It'll be fine," Franklin murmured, echoing her words from before.

She nodded, heart easing a little at his encouraging smile. She might not have seen the man for ten years, but all she knew from what she'd seen in other news items and articles was that the man was as kind and unassuming now as he was back then.

"All right then." She straightened her shoulders. "Let's get this show on the road."

The next minutes saw them sorting out the best way to frame the shot as Royce insisted on capturing a sliver of Calgary's famous Saddledome arena in the background.

She glanced up at Franklin, appreciating the way the sun picked out his blond waves, his strong jaw, his smile. Her heels meant that Franklin wasn't too much taller than her, which actually made him kind of perfect for—

Seriously? She dragged her gaze from his lips. How could she be thinking like that when this was her most important moment in years? She had to make a good impression. On her bosses, on the viewers, not just the subject of her interview. And being the station's first female sports reporter added new weight to her shoulders. This was her chance to prove women were equally worthy of owning an interest in sports, that a woman's voice should be heard as much as any man's. Her focus had to be on that, not on impressing Franklin.

"We've got two minutes, Hannah," Jason called.

Two minutes? Nerves tingled along her skin. Nausea sloshed within.

"Don't worry, you'll be fine," Franklin murmured.

Hannah glanced up sharply at him. Did he know this was her

first time doing live reporting for CNSTV? She might've done so for college, but never had the stakes been as high as this. She wiped her sweaty hands on the sides of her pants.

She pulled out her questions again, and just the action of reading over them again helped settle her stress. Normal things. Questions about his family, his career, about Franklin moving back to the province of his birth. Normal questions.

"Hey, you've got this," Franklin said again.

"You bet your sweet mama I do." She turned to face the camera, ignoring a sound from him that gave stifled-chuckle vibes, and touched her earpiece. Drew Anderson, the station's sports anchor for both the afternoon and evening news, was talking.

"...and now we have an interview with Alberta's own Franklin James, newly recruited to the Calgary lineup, here talking with CNSTV's Hannah Wade. Take it away, Hannah."

Here went nothing. She lifted the microphone and smiled at the camera. "Hello. I'm here with Franklin James who has just been signed with Calgary after a long stint of playing for Boston in the NHL. Welcome back to Cowtown, Franklin."

He grinned. "Thanks for having me."

Oops. She should've placed the microphone in front of him. Rookie mistake. Her smile wavered. "So, can you tell us how you felt upon hearing the news you'd been traded to Calgary?" This time she remembered to point the microphone in his direction.

"I'm super pumped, as I've wanted to play here for years. And now to be here near my family, playing with people like Mike Vaughan again, is awesome."

"Your family live nearby?" she asked, as if she didn't know.

"My parents and sisters live near a small town just outside the city limits."

On a ranch that had its own movie set consisting of a real western town and backlot. She'd never forget when Franklin's sister Cassie had first told her about it. "They must be excited to have you back."

"It'll be great to see them way more often than I could before."

She nodded, trying to ignore his blue gaze that seemed to bore into her as she struggled to remember her other questions. Family? Nope. Just asked that. "You mentioned you'd played with Mike Vaughan."

He dipped his chin. "In Boston. He's a great player, a quality defenseman and teammate, and I'm stoked he's just been made captain."

"He'll make a good change." Wait. She hadn't meant to say it quite like that. "I mean yes, we all know Mike is stable and steady. Not that Alex Kapaulenyuk wasn't, except in his home life of course, so really it wasn't a surprise he was stripped of the captaincy." She froze. *Kill me now.* Had she really said that out loud? Could this get any worse? Maybe nobody had heard it. Or they could somehow suddenly kill airwaves and prevent her last comments from being heard. She cleared her throat. "But anyway, yes, you're right, Mike will be a good captain."

"Uh, yeah."

Judging from Franklin's stunned expression, and the dropped jaws of Royce and Jason, her hope that she'd just imagined her overshare was a dream that hadn't come true.

Quick, what were her other questions? "So, are you looking forward to meeting the rest of the team?"

Too late she realized she hadn't passed over the microphone, so she did. Only, the sweat slicking her palms made it slide from her grasp to land on the ground. She gasped, then bent to pick it up, reaching for it at precisely the same time as Franklin.

"Here—"

"Let me—"

She snatched the mike and jerked her head upright, only to crash into something solid. Or not so solid, as a grunt was followed by a wheezing sound, and her hair grew sticky. She touched it, glanced at her fingers—was that blood?—then turned to see Franklin pinching his nose as blood spatters decorated his beautiful suit. A non-PG word escaped, and she covered her mouth. Then realized Royce was still filming—had filmed the entirety of this debacle—spurring her into new frantic mode. What could she do?

"I'm so sorry, Franklin." She faced the camera, gritting out a smile. "Wow. What can I say but that's not quite the welcome home any of us anticipated today. But hey, it's probably good that Franklin knows we like to play tough here in Calgary. And with that, it looks like it's back to you in the studio."

And it looked like that was the end of her TV career.

FRANKLIN DREW BACK his hand and gazed at the blood smearing it with horrified fascination. He wasn't a stranger to bloodied noses—a life playing hockey didn't allow for that luxury—but never had he received one from a pretty brunette. The past two minutes felt surreal.

"I'm so, so sorry, Franklin," Hannah said, her eyes glistening, her hand rubbing her head where he'd bumped her. She wore his blood on her cheek. Had that been there during the last of the television interview when she'd crossed to the studio? If she didn't look like she might cry and if he wasn't in so much pain he might laugh at the ridiculousness of it all.

"Here." Jason, the dude who'd set up this interview and was doing sound, passed him a box of tissues, before drawing Hannah to one side where he began an urgent, low-voiced conversation.

"It's not the first time I've busted my nose," Franklin offered, his voice sounding weak and clogged as he leaned forward to reduce the blood draining into his throat.

"But the first time in an interview, am I right?" the camera guy—Royce?—said, chuckling quietly. "Sorry man, but that was epic."

Epically awful for Hannah. Had he ever had such a bad interview?

"Sorry we don't have any ice," Royce continued, shaking his head. "I didn't figure her for such a klutz. She seemed so switched on before."

"It was an accident," he muttered, wiping away the blood as best he could. He stole a look at where Hannah stood with the other guy, one hand over her mouth, the other clasping her elbow as she shook her head.

"I can't believe they hired her," Royce said. "She only got the role because the boss has a thing for blondes." He laughed out loud again. "And then she dyes her hair brown!" He chuckled as he packed away his equipment. "Don't worry. After this episode she won't be back to bother you again. She won't be bothering anyone again, so you'll be safe."

"It wasn't her fault," Franklin insisted. "If I hadn't bent down at the same time—"

"Because she dropped the mike." Royce swore. "Amateur hour if you ask me. But then, it was her first day on the job, so I guess that counts. First and last, probably."

Aw, man. Now he felt bad for her. And truth be told, he'd enjoyed talking with her, her green eyes sparkling as she talked. It was hard to imagine her as a blonde—he'd always preferred brunettes anyway. Although there'd once been a blonde who had made an impression...

"Sorry, man," Royce said. "I hope you didn't have big plans after this. You were looking so sharp too."

Franklin winced. Truth be told he'd been planning to meet Mike and his wife Bree at their house for a welcome-to-the-team dinner. "I'll make a detour via my apartment and get cleaned up."

Hannah broke off her conversation and rushed to him. "Franklin, truly, I'm so, so sorry about everything. I can take you to a doctor or the hospital if you prefer. And please, let me pay for your dry-cleaning. I really didn't mean—"

"Hey, stuff happens. And honestly, I've broken my nose more times than I care to remember, so I know what to do." He carefully wiggled the cartilage and felt it shift into place. "See?"

Her jaw sagged. "Doesn't that hurt?"

"We play tough in Calgary, am I right?"

"You heard that?" She shook her head. "I really didn't mean to sound so glib. I just didn't know what to do, and I knew it was such a bad interview, and I—"

"It's okay. I'll be fine. And so will you."

Her lips pressed together as if she tried to hold back a million words of doubt. Then her head tilted, as her earpiece squawked. Her eyes widened, her chin wobbled, and she glanced at him with a whispered "I'm so sorry" and pulled out her phone and shifted back to where Jason stood, his arms crossed, forehead plunged into misgiving, mouth pulled into a frown.

She winced, listening on the phone to whoever was berating her—even he could tell as much from the angry screeches—with a downcast head, her lips in a flat line, all vivacity from earlier drained away.

Poor thing.

He was tempted to stay and try to help her but knew he needed ice to stop this swelling into Elephant-Man proportions. With one hand on his nose he lifted the other and offered a wave. "Thanks."

"Thanks for nothing, right?" Royce grimaced. "Sorry, dude. Welcome to Cowtown."

"See ya, Hannah," Franklin called.

She glanced at him, and the distressed look in her eyes punched him in the gut. Still, he had to admire her grit as she managed a wobbly smile and mouthed a "So sorry" at him again.

"It's okay. Sorry about all…that," he tried to reassure her, although he knew his appearance wasn't helping.

Jason shifted closer. "You got my number. Send me the dry-cleaning receipt and we'll take care of it."

"Sure," he said, more to put an end to it than because he would. His salary was likely at least ten times what these guys were making.

Back in his truck he studied his face in the mirror. Yep, it was swelling already. With any luck he'd have two black eyes like what had happened before, which would mean avoiding contact sports for the next few weeks—not exactly ideal when he was supposed to be jelling with a new team.

Still, he couldn't blame her. Stuff happened, after all.

He drove to his apartment, shocking one of his new neighbors as he exited the elevator on his floor. "War wound," he said, pointing to his face.

"Thank you for your service," she called, forcing him to stifle a chuckle as he rounded the corner and unlocked his apartment door. Five minutes later he was lying on his leather sofa, head tilted with a carefully positioned ice pack on his face, as he texted Mike. SORRY, GONNA BE A LITTLE LATE.

A few seconds later came the reply: JUST CAUGHT THE INTER-VIEW. YOU OKAY? CAN POSTPONE IF YOU LIKE.

A MAN STILL HAS TO EAT, he tapped back. JUST GONNA BE DELAYED A BIT.

REMEMBER WHERE WE ARE?

Nope, but Mike seemed to have figured that might be the case as he re-sent his address. Good. Siri would know where to guide him.

An hour later he was knocking on the big wooden door of Mike and Bree Vaughan's home in their gated community. From the outside it seemed a nice place, modern with its clean lines and angled roof lines, but with homey touches, like the use of honey-colored wood and stone, and tiny shoes scattered near the front steps.

The door opened. "Franklin, you made it." Mike held out a hand.

Franklin gripped it. "Thanks for having me."

"Good to see you. Although that looks like that hurt," Mike pointed to his nose.

"Yeah, not the way I'd planned the day to go, but what can you do?"

"Is he here?" a feminine voice called. Seconds later, Bree Vaughan's dark hair was swinging around her shoulders as she peered around her husband. Her mouth fell open. "You poor thing!" She winced. "I saw it on TV and it looked so painful. Please, come in."

Bree led him into the living room, the black-and-white wedding photo over the mantlepiece showing the joy of Mike and Bree. He still remembered the day from six years ago, and it had set the benchmark for what he wanted in life. A partner who cheered him on and whom he cheered on too, whose life blended with his, and who shared similar goals, values, and faith.

It was funny, but faith hadn't been a big priority until lately when a return to his native province had seen a return to his roots in other ways as well. As soon as he got settled he'd have to find a church.

"Have you seen a doctor yet?" Mike asked.

"No need. I'm an expert these days in putting things back where they belong."

"You should probably get it checked over by the team doctor, Dr. Willis, tomorrow, anyway."

Franklin nodded. "I won't say no to any ice if you've got some spare."

Bree hurried away, returning soon with an ice pack not

dissimilar to the one he'd used earlier.

"Thanks."

He took a seat on a leather sofa, and gingerly placed the pack on his nose. He probably looked like a fool, but Mike had seen him looking worse, and the times he'd met Bree before made him feel comfortable to be real.

"You poor thing," she sympathized again now.

He peeked at her, caught her looking at him in a way that reminded him of Hannah earlier. "It must've looked pretty crazy on TV."

"Definitely not what that poor reporter expected, I'm sure."

"Hannah." The name suited her. Unpretentious, honest, hardworking. It reminded him of something...

"I rarely watch CNSTV, but when Mike mentioned you were going to be on it, and then when I heard they finally had a female reporter, well, I knew I had to see it for myself." Her smile was wry. "I don't normally enjoy watching those men on that channel's sports shows—they can seem pretty immature sometimes—and I have to admit I was surprised when they finally got a woman in. She seemed nervous, but nice."

He started to nod, but the pain in his head put paid to that, and he winced. "She was nice."

"Oh, do you need ibuprofen?" Bree asked.

"I wouldn't say no."

As she went away to collect it, Mike checked everything the team had promised had been undertaken.

"Gotta say I was impressed. I didn't expect the apartment fridge to be filled, so that was classy."

"They're a classy organization."

"Especially now they got rid of Alex as captain, huh?"

Mike blew out a breath. "It wasn't a popular move with everyone, but some of us felt it was overdue."

"I know that I'm the newbie here, but even on the east coast we could see things weren't right. He always came across as a selfish player, then what he did to Todd Devin."

Mike shook his head. "Poor dude. Such a mess."

"They did the right thing in promoting you."

"It's been a bit of a learning curve, but so far so good."

"Here you go, Franklin," Bree said, returning to the room, and handing him the medication, a fresh ice pack, and a glass of water.

"Thanks." He swallowed, then placed the glass on the side table, next to a photo of Mike and Bree with a bunch of grinning Asian kids and a handmade sign that said Mission Possible for Future Generations.

Bree sat on the arm of Mike's chair. "So, what are you two talking about?"

"Your husband's captaincy."

She beamed. "I'm so proud of him!" She pressed a kiss to Mike's blond hair. "You're the right man for the job, babe."

"You're biased, but I'll take it."

Franklin's chest tightened. He wasn't jealous, but there was a sweetness between these two he wanted.

"Mommy!" A little boy wandered into the room, rubbing his eyes. He glanced at Franklin and his face puckered. "Who are you?"

"My name is Franklin. I'm a friend of your dad."

"He plays hockey with me, Ethan," Mike said, rubbing a hand over the boy's tousled fair curls.

"Why do you have that on you?" Ethan pointed to the ice pack.

"I hurt my nose."

"How?"

For some reason, trying to explain to a little kid who couldn't yet be four years old seemed hard to do. "I, uh, had an accident."

"It looks hurty."

"Yeah."

Fortunately, Ethan didn't seem to require any further details as he nodded, then wandered off to a bookshelf filled with kids' books and toys.

"Have you seen the interview yet?" Bree asked, pulling out her phone.

"Nope." And he had no intention to.

"I think—oh dear."

"What?"

Bree glanced at him. "I'm afraid you're trending on social media."

"You're kidding, right?" Franklin drew his phone from his pocket and saw #HockeyHunkHammered and #ReporterFail climbing. His heart sank. "Man. It wasn't her fault."

He clicked on a link that showcased the interview in its entirety. Just as he remembered, Hannah had looked sparkly and excited, and yeah, she'd forgotten to give him the microphone, but that wasn't a biggie. He tensed, watching the back-and-forth, waiting for the moment when—

There! Ouch. Even though he'd already gone through the collision he felt secondary pain just watching it again. But he hadn't seen the look of shock on Hannah's face. The way she'd winced as if the impact had hurt her too. And he'd never asked if she was all right.

"Ugh."

"What is it, hon?" Mike asked his wife.

"I can't believe the people demanding she get sacked." Her violet-gray gaze met his. "Sorry, Franklin, but it looked like an accident to me, and yet there are all these people saying all kinds of horrible things about her."

"One of the crew with us thought she'd get fired." Or had Royce only wished it?

"That's so unfair!" Bree exclaimed.

"Come on, honey. You know you need to not get upset." Mike clasped her hand.

Bree placed a hand on her stomach. "You're right."

Whoa. Was she pregnant? He knew better than to ask personal questions. Three sisters had taught him that. She could tell him if she wanted.

Mike and Bree held a wordless conversation then glanced at him. "You're a praying man. I was going to tell the guys on the group chat tomorrow, but seeing you're here, well—"

"I'm pregnant," Bree announced. "And it's a bit of a surprise, because it came soon after little Ellison was born last year. We found out yesterday that it's twins."

"Bree is a twin," Mike said. "Brent Karlsson is her brother."

Franklin nodded. "Congratulations. On the babies, I mean."

Bree's lips twisted. "Yeah, I'm pretty sure at times that brother of mine would think I should be congratulated for sharing his gene pool."

Mike draped an arm around her shoulders. "We're still coming to terms with things, as there's been a lot to wrap our heads around. So, I might end up leaning on some friends a little more this year."

"Anything I can do to help, you only need to ask," Franklin assured.

"Hey, that reminds me, are you interested in joining the group chat tomorrow? It's for Christian hockey players, and because there's a few of us now we've started a new one for those of us in the northwest." Mike rattled off some names, and Franklin recognized a few of them. Ryan Guillemette from Edmonton—they'd played together a million years ago. Luc Blanchard from Winnipeg. Chris Thomas from Vancouver. Jai Mullins, an alternate captain at San Jose. "You mentioned last time that you might be looking for a church too, so we can help you out. Or not." Mike grinned. "I know this is not exactly your first rodeo in Cowtown."

"You're so funny." Bree rolled her eyes. "Anyway, enough of that. I bet the man is hungry, right? Mike will get the barbecue started, so come on out to the patio, while I get the salad and things ready."

"Let me help," he said, pushing upright. "I can carry something."

The next minutes passed in cooking, conversation, and more catching up, as he and Mike shared over their time together at Boston. "But you're enjoying being home?" Mike asked.

"It's awesome to have Mom and Dad and the girls nearby."

"You've got three sisters, right?" Bree asked.

"All younger than me."

"What do they do?"

"Cassie manages part of the ranch that deals with movies and stuff."

"Movies?" Bree asked.

"Yeah, our ranch has a western town attached to it. We've had a number of movies and TV shows filmed there. Lincoln Cash did a western movie, and Ainsley Beckett did the historical series *As the Heart Draws*."

"Oh, I love both of them. Wow!"

"Jessica is in her last year of vet medicine and Poppy has been studying dance in Winnipeg."

"Three sisters must've kept you busy growing up."

"I've always been the protective older brother, so it's been fun to reconnect and find out what's going on in their worlds."

Bree sighed. "I have two older brothers—Dean lives in Vancouver, and Brent is older by only fifteen minutes—and it wasn't easy being the only girl. They were always looking out for me."

"You've done okay for yourself though, haven't you?" Mike teased.

"Only just." She winked at Franklin. "Once we convinced a

certain someone that his best friend might be an acceptable match for his sister."

"More than acceptable," Mike said, clasping her hand and kissing it. "The best."

Bree grinned. "I bet having all those sisters means you're a gentleman."

"I try to be."

She nodded. Her phone buzzed, and she winced. "Poor girl."

"Who?" Mike asked.

"Hannah. One of the Calgary WAGs just sent a message to our chat group, calling for the team to blackball Hannah from further interviews."

"What?" Mike's brow lowered. "Let me guess: Alex's girlfriend."

"Yeah. Not his wife." Bree shook her head. "How Kristen thinks she has any right to criticize when she broke up a marriage I don't know. Poor Hannah. It's so unfair. I feel like I should do something to help but I don't know what."

"If Franklin isn't blaming her then I don't see how anyone else can get upset," Mike said.

Bree's forehead furrowed. "I can't believe the horrible things people are saying about her."

"Pray for her, honey," Mike advised. "It sounds like she needs all the support she can get."

Protectiveness surged. Maybe he should reach out and ask for an interview redo. But only with Hannah. That might show them. And help her. Maybe it was the old-fashioned gentlemanly traits his mom had instilled in him, but it seemed time the "Reporter fail" label changed.

CHAPTER 2

"...*A*nd I'm afraid this has proved to be an experiment gone wrong." Dirk folded his hands. "I really can't see any way of coming back from such a debacle."

Will Sanchez, the station's media manager, shook his head. "The comments on our social media are calling us unprofessional, and are nearly all negative." He arched a shaped eyebrow as he glanced at her. "One simply doesn't want to become a meme on one's first day on the job."

Hannah gripped her knees under the table. How had things escalated into this? She'd barely slept a wink last night, running over the failed interview in her mind, fielding concern and cruel comments on her social media—including featuring in several awful memes, one that had her looking wild-eyed and open-mouthed as she stared at her bloodied hand like a crazy lady— and rehearsing her defense in today's meeting. But the icy reception and frosty remarks tossed her way since her arrival this morning had diminished her to mouselike behavior. So much for Mandi describing her as fire yesterday.

Lisa, her agent, had reminded her several times in their phone call last night that it was something that could have happened to anyone, that the station needed her more than she needed them, and that Hannah needed to remember her worth. Lisa's pep talk ran through her mind, reminding her to find courage as much as any time she'd faced a screaming puck. She regathered battered emotions and lifted her chin.

Drew Anderson shook his head. "You should've seen the messages on my socials. I've even had Alex Kapaulenyuk message me saying he would refuse to have anything more to do with our station if we keep her."

Hannah froze. No, they couldn't do that, could they? Lisa had reassured her that the terms of the contract stated she couldn't be fired unless for "professional incompetence." Did this count as that? Oh, if only Lisa was here instead of halfway across the country talking to the next Serena Williams wannabe! And anyway, Franklin had seemed so good about it. Had he had a change of heart? She swallowed, and finally found her voice. "Franklin didn't seem too upset yester—"

Dirk held up a hand, stopping her. "I cannot think of a worse outcome. How could Calgary's premier sports TV station operate without direct interaction with Calgary's top sports team?"

The room filled with loud complaints. Bob Patresky, who co-anchored *Hockey Hour* with Drew Anderson—the station's top-rated program and a show known for its caustic observations as much as the sexist personalities of its upper middle-aged anchors—shot her a glare. "It can't."

But it wasn't her fault! Sure, she perhaps shouldn't have announced her opinion of Alex's loose morals on TV, but she'd only said what most of the chats and blog posts had been saying since news of his affair first broke. She glanced at Dirk. "Of course Alex is not going to be happy about having his personal inadequacies mentioned, but that message was from just one person," she pointed out. "Have you heard anything from the team themselves?"

"'One person,' she says." Bob's teeth glinted as he smiled without humor. "Only the captain of the team."

"Former captain," Jason muttered, from where he was studying his phone.

Drew rolled his eyes. "Who still would be if it weren't for one mistake."

Heat rose, along with memories of her own father's betrayal. "One mistake? You mean a married man sleeping with a teammate's girlfriend, and then carrying on a secret affair for six months is just 'a mistake'? Excuse me for having a different understanding of what a mistake is." Her fingers clenched. "We're not talking about a onetime thing, like 'oops, I accidentally kissed someone I'm not married to,' although how anyone can do that and excuse it I don't know. Instead, we're talking about a person in a position of influence, whom thousands of people look up to, who should've had an awareness of his responsibility to his team as much as his fans, who then deliberately lied and manipulated others and deceived Todd Devin and the rest of his teammates in order to protect his selfishness. That's not a mistake. That's a character flaw."

"Sheesh." Bob hissed out a breath, eyeing her like she was a leper. "You don't need to get hysterical."

Hysterical? "I beg your pard—"

"Look," Drew interrupted her again. "We knew it was a risk adding a girl to the lineup—"

A *girl*? Excuse me?

"—and we were proved right."

Jason cut her a look then faced Dirk. "To be fair I don't think she intended to belt Franklin in the nose, did you Hannah?"

Her frustration at being talked about instead of included faded. "Of course not," she snapped. "And Franklin knew that. He even apologized—"

"It's such an awful—"

"He apologized to me!" she finished loudly, cutting off Drew.

The men all reared back in their seats, their expressions ranging from dismay to disapproval to disdain. A whispered "See? Hysterical" wafted around the room.

Will sat back in his seat and mouthed a "wow."

"There is no need to raise your voice," Dirk said primly.

"Except when it seems nobody is listening to me, or letting me finish my sentences." Frustration gripped her, and she shifted in her seat, her shoulders back, chin up, as she eyed Dirk, her agent's words singing faintly in her head. "You told me that the station needed to be seen as inclusive, that it was way too white-bread and chauvinistic, and that viewers were tired of the same old antics."

Drew swiveled a look at Dirk. "You said that?"

Dirk held up a hand, cutting him off. Well, maybe equal opportunities existed in some measure, at least. "Go on, Hannah."

She drew in a deep breath she hoped might calm her. "Yesterday, my first day, was supposed to be a normal interview, but someone somewhere decided to make it live, and we all know a live interview has way more potential for mishaps."

"In hindsight, that perhaps was not the wisest course," Dirk admitted, with a glance at Drew.

Her chest tightened. Wait. Did that mean Drew had pushed for the live interview? Indignation rose, but it probably wouldn't help to pursue it, not when someone here was finally taking a degree of accountability. She scanned the room. "If I'd had the chance to do the interview as originally intended, all of those mistakes could have been edited out. But it's like someone was trying to hijack my opportunities before I'd even had a chance."

Someone seated opposite wearing a sports coat and a sneer. "If you can't handle the heat, stay out of the kitchen," Drew said.

"Or maybe stay in there," Bob's mutter was edged with growl.

"Do you mean to sound so sexist?" she demanded.

Judging from his smirk it seemed he did. She returned her attention to Dirk. "If you don't want this station to be regarded as sexist then you need to do something about comments like that." She pointed at Bob. "I'm sure a TV station with a reputation for misogyny wouldn't want to be seen as undermining and then firing someone, when it might appear that they are trying to make a woman look bad. That sure wouldn't look good on your socials."

"She's got a point," Will said, brow furrowed.

Dirk looked thoughtful.

"It doesn't change the fact that she is clearly not up to the job—"

"I am sitting right here, Drew. You don't need to speak about me as if I'm not in the room. My name is Hannah, in case you've forgotten."

He breathed out a foul word, and sent her a look that if looks could kill was no doubt designed to pulverize her.

She forced herself to meet Drew's gaze, raising her eyebrows, and reminded herself of the many times when others had tried to shut her up or shut her down. And while some might question why she might want to continue to work in this environment, she was not about to let him intimidate her. She'd never been a fan of letting bullies win.

"Dude," Jason murmured.

"Yes, that is not how we speak when ladies are in the room," Dirk reprimanded Drew.

Drew bristled, shooting her another scathing look.

It shouldn't be how people spoke *ever*, but now was not the time to mention their unprofessionalism.

"What I want to know is why you changed your look without telling us," Will said. "We shot all this promo with you as a blonde and then you're brunette." He crossed his arms.

"You're gonna cost the station a lot of money if we have to redo the promotions."

"I'm sorry I did not make my objections to being objectified more clear," she said stiffly. "But the outfit someone chose for me made me uncomfortable, and I'm not prepared to lower my personal moral standards when what I wore was clearly professional and appropriate."

"But your hair—"

"I did not like feeling like I was here to be a stereotype. However, I see your point about the advertising, and I'm sorry I did not think that through more." She glanced at Dirk. "Truly."

His chin dipped, then he glanced at Will. "How much of that is released?"

"We froze it after the interview, when we weren't sure what would happen with her."

She blinked. They really thought they'd get rid of her so quickly? "I'm sorry Dirk, but I didn't want to look like a ditzy blonde, which again is how I felt I was being set up to be portrayed."

"Instead you looked like a ditzy brunette," Drew muttered.

She clenched her fingers. What she wouldn't do to smack that smirk off his face. "Well, it's not like people here are all free of mistakes live on air, is it?"

Drew blustered. "Well, I really must take exception—"

"How about a different nose incident?" Jason murmured.

Tension eased a fraction as subtle smiles and smothered chuckles of amusement rippled around those assembled. Drew's nasal hygiene habits caught on camera had caused a media frenzy two years back.

"How many times do I have to tell you it was just a bad camera angle?"

Sure it was.

Drew glared at Jason, then at Hannah. "And a bad camera

angle is a heck of a lot different to a girl who drops a mike, swears on TV, then belts a hockey star in the face."

"Excuse me?"

Drew guffawed. "What? Are you denying it?"

"Yes."

Mouths swung open.

"What part? That's all true. You can't deny it."

"I can." She angled her chin higher. "I'm not a girl. I'm twenty-six years old. The term you're looking for is woman."

Will chuckled and glanced at Dirk, who wore his own look of bemusement. Jason's phone buzzed, and he glanced at it, eyebrows pushing up.

"I don't care what you are," Drew snapped. "You're not right for the job."

"Actually, for a newbie, I thought she handled the situation as well as she could," Jason said, his gaze on his phone. Now it was her turn to feel stunned. That certainly hadn't been the impression she got yesterday when he'd chewed her out.

"What do you mean?" Dirk asked.

"Well, she was able to think pretty quickly on her feet. That line at the end about being tough in Calgary, that was kinda cool."

"Cool?" Bob scoffed. "That was—"

"And she did seem to establish a rapport pretty quickly with Franklin," Jason continued smoothly, glancing up, his dark eyes flicking to her then back to Dirk.

Her chest tightened. There was a reason for that. It helped when she had met the guy before.

"She better not start thinking she's gonna steal my rinkside interviews," Bob grouched, refusing to look at her.

"Or my features," Drew added with a frown.

"Actually," Jason held up his phone, "I just got a message from Franklin, asking for an interview do-over."

"What?"

Her question joined the others.

Jason pushed up from a slouch in the chair. "Apparently he only wants to speak with you, Hannah. As an exclusive."

"Really?"

"He must be a glutton for punishment," Bob scoffed.

Or a genuinely good guy. She lowered her head, blinking back an unfamiliar sting. What was happening to her? Only a couple of days on the job and she kept wanting to cry like the little girl these men obviously thought she was. But showing her emotions had never got her anywhere. Mandi might call her fire, but Hannah had to appear as cool as ice.

Another phone buzzed, and Will glanced at Dirk before picking it up. "Huh."

"Yes?" Dirk asked.

Will looked at Hannah then back at Dirk. "Looks like she's got some fans."

"Hannah is here in the room with us," Jason murmured.

Will glanced at the ceiling then back at her. "Hannah, it looks like you've got some fans. Instead of 'Reporter fail' and 'Fire Hannah' there's a new catchphrase trending."

"Which is?" Dirk prompted.

"'Keep Hannah' and 'Hannah keeps it real'." Will shrugged. "And my assistant just sent a message saying Bree Vaughan wants to do an interview with you too."

"Who?" Drew asked.

"Mike Vaughan's wife. You know, the captain of Calgary's top sports team," Jason said.

"There's an official request from the club as well for Hannah to do a series of behind-the-scenes interviews with some of the families, too."

"They want Hannah to do that?" Drew frowned.

"Yep." Will's mouth curved slightly.

Bob shrugged. "Behind the scenes with WAGs is more soft

material, so who cares? It's not like real journalism or what we're about."

Truth be told, doing interviews with hockey's wives and girlfriends wasn't the summit of Hannah's journalistic aspirations either, but if it meant she kept her job…

"How did that happen?" Drew demanded, shifting to face her. "Does she even know these people?"

She pushed up her brows, waiting.

"I think Hannah is waiting for you to address her properly," Jason murmured.

Drew sighed, and finally shifted to face her. "Fine. Do you know these people, Miss Wade?"

"Hannah will do fine, thanks, Drew. And the answer is no. I've never met them before in my life."

"Then why?"

She shrugged. "I don't know. Maybe they're nice people." She glanced at Will. "But I'd be very happy to schedule something with them as soon as possible. And with Franklin, too," she added for Jason's sake.

He nodded. "We'll set something up."

She faced Dirk. "I promise that the next interview will go far more smoothly."

"It couldn't get any worse," Drew muttered.

She ignored him. It looked like these meetings were going to be times when she'd have to learn to pick her battles. And ignoring Drew—and Bob—was just going to have to be part of her life.

Dirk nodded slowly, his thoughtful gaze shifting between her and Drew. "I wonder."

"Wonder what?" Drew asked.

Dirk shook his head, seeming to snap to decisiveness again. "Schedule the interviews for Hannah, and redo any of her promo material that you can't photoshop."

Jason and Will nodded and made notes on their tablets.

"You're going to keep her?" Bob asked.

"Hannah has a contract, and we don't want to be accused of being sexist now, do we? Besides," he rubbed his hands together. "As long as it doesn't hurt the advertising dollar, a little controversy never hurt ratings, did it?"

She was here for the ratings? At least she was still here. "Thank you, sir. I won't let you down."

"I know you won't."

"Unbelievable," Drew muttered.

She pressed her lips together, tweaking up a corner of her mouth as Jason nodded. She appreciated his support, even if he had torn strips off her yesterday. Maybe she could find a way to work with this team, even if she'd be very happy to not speak to Drew or Bob again.

Thank goodness for Bree and Franklin. She owed them big time. And would make sure their interviews proved to be her personal redemption round.

She tilted her chin, glancing around the room of nonbelievers. Just watch her.

"FRANKLIN! WELCOME. COME ON IN." Bree held the door open and gestured inside. "Mike is in the study and we'll eat in just a moment. The group starts in half an hour, but I'm gonna guess you've already learned the art of eating fast."

He chuckled, then winced. The pain might be less intense than yesterday but the swelling had only increased.

"How is your nose feeling today?" she asked, leading him to the dining area.

He waved a hand to Ethan who was coloring in pictures on a brightly-colored plastic kiddie table. The boy glanced up, smiled and waved, then resumed his artistic endeavors.

"It's letting me know that it's there. I saw the team doc and he didn't have much more to offer in the way of instructions." Apart from telling him that even though Franklin might have broken his nose many times in the past, that was still no reason for him to attempt to fix it himself. "Just as I don't try to do your job and block pucks neither should you try to do mine and fix faces," Dr. Willis had said.

Franklin had agreed, the advice much the same as what his horrified parents had said last night when they'd finally caught the TV footage. In his excitement at moving here, he'd forgotten what it might be like having them so close they could scrutinize his every move.

"So just keep icing it and being careful, huh?"

"That's it. Hey." He stood and shook hands with Mike, who was carrying a tiny baby in his arms. "And who's this?"

"This is little Miss Ellison," Mike said.

"Aww, so sweet."

Bree sighed. "I do love a man who says sweet."

"Hon, you just met him," Mike complained.

Bree laughed. "I think he knows I'm a one-man woman. Speaking of, do you have a girlfriend, Franklin?"

"Nope."

"Anyone on the horizon?"

"No, ma'am." He'd dated casually plenty back in the day, when his schedule allowed, but now he was looking for something—someone—more permanent, something his new recommitment to God encouraged.

"Come on, babe. Let the man be. You don't want to scare him off with such questions."

Bree mock-pouted. "Fine. You two can serve yourselves while I feed these two." She placed a hand on Ethan's head. "I know Mike is raring to find out what the others have been up to lately."

"Raring," Mike said, glancing at Franklin. "You're raring too, right?"

"Born raring."

They served themselves plates of pasta and salad, and discussed team things while Bree fed the children.

Franklin had just scraped his plate clean when Bree said, "Oh, I just remembered. I got a message back from the team's media department. They agreed." She grinned at Mike.

"Remind me?"

"They've agreed to my idea to do a series of specials on the families of the team."

"Great." Mike's forehead furrowed. "I thought they already did something like that."

"Yes, but I especially requested that they use Hannah Wade."

Hannah. Franklin resisted the urge to touch his nose.

"And they agreed? Well, good for you." Mike picked the last slice of cucumber from the bowl and ate it. "How many families are involved?"

"A few. Well, they're starting with ours. I hope that's okay."

"It's cool." Mike grinned. "We'll have to see if we can mention MPFG—"

"Ooh, yes!" Bree smiled at Franklin. "That's the mission organization for kids in the Philippines that Mike is a spokesman for."

"Always plenty more to sponsor," Mike said with a wink.

"Sign me up."

"I'll send you the deets now. Thanks, man." Mike tapped on his phone, and a notification popped up on Franklin's phone.

Half a minute later Franklin was sponsoring two kids. How easy to make a difference in the world. "Love technology."

"When it works," Bree said.

"It's awesome to think we can shine a spotlight on important things," Mike said. "Hey, maybe we can get them to focus on some of our Jesus décor."

Franklin glanced around, but there were no life-size cutouts of a bearded Middle Eastern-looking man in robes. Then he saw the sign that stated some of the things this family believed in. Huh.

"Did you really just look around for a photo of Jesus?" Bree asked him.

"No." Franklin drank his water. "A cardboard cutout, maybe."

She grinned. "You're funny. Maybe that'd be better than the one of Mike stashed in the hallway closet." Her laughter rippled. "That reminds me. One day I'll have to tell you something that Allie told me she once did. I don't think she meant to tell us, it might've been an overshare at Dan's wedding last year."

Franklin nodded, not sure if she was talking to him or Mike. He suspected Mike, because he didn't know who Allie or Dan were. Although it might refer to Dan Walton, who played defense for Toronto. He was pretty sure he'd gotten married last year.

"We better get ready," Mike said, pushing back his seat. "I got a message from Chris earlier. He's eager."

"Thanks for dinner," Franklin said. "And for reaching out to help Hannah like that. I asked CNSTV if I could do another interview with her too, so I hope it means she keeps her job."

"I'd think they'll have to." Bree smirked. "I might've reached out to a few friends of mine and got them to post to their followers about the need to keep Hannah around."

"Stealth tactics, huh? Remind me not to get on your bad side."

Her baby fussed, and she waved a hand at him. "Go, have fun. And meet your new best friends."

"Yes, ma'am."

He followed Mike to a small room off the living area. Inside were a desk, computer, and shelves filled with books. A calendar with pictures of kids and tropical scenes reminded him of the Philippines kids' sponsorship project Mike was involved with. Mike was pulling up another chair.

"Hey, I know you can do this from your own place, but I figured you'd appreciate meeting the guys with me."

"Sure." He sank into the leather office chair Mike pointed to. "Remind me what this is about?"

"A group of us gathers together online and encourages each other in God things as well as hockey and other parts of life. It's a great reminder that helps keep things real."

"Cool."

Mike tapped the keyboard and the screen filled with a face. "Chris."

Chris Thomas played goalie for Vancouver. "Dude." He peered at the screen. "And new dude. Franklin, right?"

Franklin lifted a hand. "Hey."

"Wow, what a welcome you got in Calgary, huh? How's the face?"

"Sore."

Chris chuckled. "Sorry man, but it was funny. She looked kinda dainty and then walloped you a good one."

"Nothing dainty about that one." He got the impression she was far tougher than all her apologies and near tears.

The screen split into several more squares, and the introductions and welcomes continued: Luc Blanchard, Ryan Guillemette, Jai Mullins, and an older man named Josiah Abrahams.

Josiah introduced himself—apparently he was Jai's former church minister who had started the original online Bible study group several years ago—and then people shared about their vacations.

"Me and the wife took the kids to Disneyland," Chris said. "That was awesome."

"Love Disneyland," Ryan agreed. "I went hiking with my brother near Jasper. That was fun. We saw a couple of bears."

"What sort?"

"Grizzly. Got the adrenaline going for a bit."

"I bet."

"I went hunting for the first time," Luc announced.

"Hunting for a girlfriend?" Chris asked.

Luc shot him a scowl that said this wasn't the first time that joke had been made. "Please. I'm not ready to settle down."

"Can't leave it too long. You're getting on, bro," Chris teased.

"I've got a few years until I'm thirty, and don't have any gray hair yet. Unlike some."

"Low blow, dude," Jai said, putting a hand to his shorn dark hair.

"I didn't mean you," Luc said.

"It's what being an alternate captain does, so Allie tells me."

Was that the Allie that Bree had mentioned before? Franklin leaned in.

"So, you better watch yourself, Mike. Leadership has a lot to answer for," Jai said, winking.

"Hey, congratulations again on being promoted to captain," Josiah said. "That's really something."

"And well deserved," Ryan said. "You'll be great."

"It's an honor, that's for sure," Mike admitted.

"Aww, he's blushing," Franklin said, which scored a round of laughter.

"Dude, I invited you in and this is how you treat me?" Mike complained good-naturedly.

"This'll be good having an insider who can give us the lowdown on Magic Mike," Luc said.

Franklin coughed. "Magic Mike?"

Now Mike's face really was red. "There's nothing to see here, definitely no dancing or anything of that nature."

Luc chuckled. "I just meant he's like the golden boy. Got the hot wife, got the kids, got the house and now he's got the captaincy. He's like Captain America, except Canadian."

Mike shook his head as the others laughed.

"Yeah, pretty sure Captain America wasn't married," Chris said. "Or had kids."

"Speaking of," Mike said, "I wouldn't mind if you guys would pray for us. Bree is expecting."

"Again?" Chris asked. "Whoa, didn't mean it to sound like that. But didn't you guys just have a kid? Don't you have a TV?"

"Hey congrats," Jai said. "That's exciting."

"Thrilled for you both," Josiah said with a big grin.

"It's going to be doubly exciting," Mike said.

"Doubly?" Luc blinked. "Are you having—no. Are you saying you're having twins?"

"Yep."

"Congratulations, Mike," Josiah grinned. "Children are a blessing from the Lord. You'll have almost a quiver full."

"Quiver?" Luc asked. "Is that five?"

"Life will be busy enough with four, thanks," Mike said.

Ryan laughed. "Well, it's game on. Looks like you're gonna need all the babysitting help you can get. Franklin and I are closest, so I guess we'll get honorary uncle status, huh?"

"Any time any of you want to swing by, you know you're welcome," Mike said.

"How is Bree feeling?" Jai asked.

"She's okay. She gets tired sometimes and has to watch her iron levels," Mike admitted. "She's talked about inviting a friend she used to work with in Toronto out to stay with us, maybe help with the kids once the season picks up."

"She's in our prayers," Jai promised.

"Thanks."

Other assurances of prayers followed, then the spotlight returned to Franklin, and he was asked to share a bit about his testimony.

"Okay." He thought back. "So, I grew up in a Christian home, went to church, but hockey soon took over my life and then when I moved away for juniors I didn't go to church anymore."

"It's often the way," Josiah murmured.

"I knew Mike was a Christian when we played together in Boston, but I didn't really think about faith too much. I missed home, though."

Mike nodded. "I remember a conversation we once had about that."

"Yeah. I've never liked the big smoke, and don't do too well in big cities, so when I found out I was traded here it felt like an answer to prayer. Then I discovered that my parents had been praying for me, my sisters too, and I realized that this was where God wanted me to be. A few weeks ago, I was in church," in the chapel on their family ranch, "and recommitted my heart and now I'm here."

"Awesome stuff," Josiah said.

"You've found a church then?" Ryan asked.

"I'm going to go with Mike this weekend. Of course it'll be different once the season starts, so I want to make the most of it while I can."

"Good plan. And hey, at least if you're connecting with us then you've got some good support around you," Jai said.

"Good to have you here, brother," Chris said.

"Are your sisters single? Luc wants to know," Ryan asked, with a wink.

"Yeah, pretty sure Ryan is 'asking for a friend,'" Luc said, making air quotes with his fingers, to another round of laughter.

"Last I heard, yes. But not living near you, so I don't know if that'll work for you, Luc."

"At least they're in the same country," Ryan said.

"Hey, we've all seen long-distance relationships work out, even when they live on the opposite sides of the planet," Josiah said.

"That's right. Brent and Holly did long distance, and they're very happily married," Mike said. "Holly is from Australia," he explained to Franklin.

"And Dan married an Aussie girl too, so it can work out," Jai said.

"How about you, Franklin? You're not married, are you?"

"Nope. Still looking for the one."

Ryan's nose wrinkled. "Do you think there really is only one girl that you're destined to marry?"

"How many do you want to marry?" Chris teased.

Ryan rolled his eyes. "I don't mean to sound like we should be marrying multiple people, but man, I hear all the time that your true love is out there, and sometimes I wonder what happens if they get hit by a bus, or they die before you meet them. What happens then? Do you think there's only one right person for us?"

"Nope." Chris's voice was flat. "I love Disneyland, but I think that company's movies have a lot to answer for."

Josiah nodded. "I'm afraid I agree. I think we can be happy with any number of people, so I don't ascribe to the 'magic dot' theory that you must walk a certain path and there is only one right person and if you slip up then you get it wrong and you miss out. That doesn't say much about God's ability to redeem things."

"Exactly." Chris glanced over his shoulder. "I mean, I love my wife, but I think it's not about the person you marry so much as the person you are to them. Tom Cruise was wrong. Loving someone isn't about someone completing you. It's about you loving them completely. And I think you can only do that when you really understand how completely you are loved by God."

"Whoa." Luc crossed his arms. "Look who's ready for Bible college."

"Hey," Chris held up his hands. "I'm just speaking from my many years of marriage."

"How many years have you been married?" Franklin asked.

"Six. Maybe seven?"

Luc chuckled. "Don't let the missus hear you don't remember how long you've been married for."

Jai nodded. "I've only been married for three years but I've learned love is more about actions than feelings."

"Dude! TMI," Luc joked, clamping his hands on his ears.

"I didn't mean—! Man." Jai shook his head as the others laughed.

"Do you guys always talk so much about relationships?" Franklin asked.

"Exactly," Luc said. "How many times have I said the same thing? Come on, I need the season to hurry up and start so we can talk about manly things, like hockey."

"So when can you play again, Franklin?" Jai asked. "You look like you're getting a couple of nice black eyes."

Chris laughed. "So epic to watch."

"The doc said in a week or two. Hey, it was an accident," Franklin said. "She was mortified. It was supposed to be a regular interview then it got changed to a live one, which is why she was a bit flustered."

"It was her first day, too, huh?" Chris said.

"Yeah. Now there's talk she might lose her job."

"What? No way. That's unfair," Ryan said.

Jai nodded. "Allie told me Bree had sent out a message to her and some friends trying to round up some support. Apparently there's a conspiracy theory that people were gunning for her to lose her job, that some people don't think women deserve to work there."

"That's so wrong," Ryan said.

"I don't know why she'd want to work for such a sexist bunch of goobers anyway," Luc said.

"But maybe having her input can help change the conversation," Franklin said.

"Ooh, sounds like someone's made an impression," Luc joshed. "And not just with giving you a new nose job."

He shrugged. "I gotta admit, that even despite everything, I found the way she kept her cool kinda impressive."

"Ice queen, huh?"

More like fire.

"I've heard that an impression can happen when someone hits you," Chris teased.

Franklin lifted a shoulder, not sure how much further he should press the point. It seemed some of these guys appreciated a joke more than getting to the heart of things. Although what his heart really was saying he didn't really know.

"I liked her line at the end about being tough," Jai offered. "She used to play hockey, right?"

She did?

"That's what Allie said," Jai continued. "That she almost made the Olympic team until an injured ankle forced her out."

Really? Huh. As soon as he got a moment he'd look that up.

"Well, that puts a different spin on things, hey Franklin?"

The smile Chris gave contained a glint Franklin wasn't sure what to do with. It wasn't like he and Chris had ever exchanged more than a few words before, and yet the man somehow was reading him like a book. Because maybe this new piece of information had ratcheted up his interest in her a little more. Hannah Wade seemed to hold an equal measure of sassy fire and ice, and he found it intriguing. His pulse increased, as the thought of a redo interview grew more appealing.

"That'd be tough, getting to that elite level then losing out. Then to have something like this occur," Josiah said.

"We're doing what we can to help Hannah keep her job," Mike said.

"Good luck with that," Chris said.

"Hey. It's good to see you again, Franklin," Ryan said. "It's been too long, eh?"

"We'll have to get together sometime. Maybe in Red Deer," Franklin offered, before adding, "We used to play together a lot, back in the day."

"And you still will, given the Battle of Alberta clashes are legendary," Mike assured.

"Can't wait," he said.

And neither could he wait for the next time he came across the fascinating Hannah Wade again.

CHAPTER 3

Two days later, Hannah was being welcomed inside the Vaughan residence. The past days had been spent doing research and offering voice-overs for sports reports deemed "soft" enough for a woman. In other words, the less important pieces, like tennis, rugby, and cricket. Her sports-loving heart had welcomed delving into these sports that received little airtime in comparison to some. But her first love was always hockey, so she'd been thrilled when the chance to set up the interview with Bree Vaughan had come about relatively quickly. She might like to think herself strong and tough, but she welcomed the chance to escape the office and Bob and Drew's poisonous glances, and visit Bree at her lovely spacious home instead.

"Thank you so much for the opportunity," she said to Bree, as soon as they were inside and seated. "You don't know how much this means to me."

"Oh, I have some idea," Bree said, offering her a coffee or tea, which Hannah refused, holding up her bottled water. "I couldn't believe what people were saying about you. I might not be able to do much, but I wanted to do what I could to show my support. I think it's so important that women support each other instead of tearing each other down. There's far too much of that that we see these days, especially on social media."

"I appreciate it."

"I mean, I have been called judgy in the past, but I'm doing my best to remember that we're all on this planet trying to do the best we can. Well, most of us anyway." Bree winked. "Is it judgy to say I'm not sure if some of those men you work with know how to speak about women? Or is that just the truth?"

Hannah chuckled. "Let's just say they might be on the journey to discovering women's lib is a thing. Or they might not."

"Ha! I've seen some of what that horrible Bob has said in the past, and I honestly don't know how you manage working there."

"To be completely honest, it's not been easy, but you've got to pay the rent somehow, right? I needed a job," after her accident, and the scholarship funds ran out, "and while I'm happy to help break CNSTV's glass ceiling, it's easier when I'm able to get out of the office and do things like this." Hannah shrugged. "As long as I don't have to have too much to do with Drew or Bob then I guess it'll work okay."

"I can't believe those two with their overinflated opinions of themselves, despite neither of them having played professionally."

"Weirdly, I suspect neither of them would appreciate having that pointed out to them."

"I'd love to see someone try!" Bree laughed. "Whereas you, you did play hockey, right? I got a message from a friend who said she looked you up and realized you were going to play at the last Olympics until injury forced you out."

"Yeah, that had been the plan since I was a little girl." She'd competed at World Championships, even winning gold for

Canada then, but the dream had always been the Olympics. Her stomach knotted.

"I can't imagine how devastating that would've been. Actually, I can imagine it. My best friend Holly was a short-track skater, and had a bad accident several months out from the Vancouver Games, and hurt her knee and got a bad concussion. She stayed here for several months and, now I look back on it, I think she was really struggling with depression as well as all the challenges of recovering from major injury. She ended up making it—she even won Olympic gold—but going through the uncertainties is a hard place to be in."

Hannah nodded, the memories still too raw. The accident during training, when a wayward stick had seen the bones in her ankle smashed into pieces, the surgery to correct it meaning she'd never fully regain the support she needed to reach the heights of athletic prowess again. She knew about depression, about the hopelessness of a lost dream. But her get-up-and-go attitude had soon seen her channel her energies into finishing her studies, then working to secure a position that still allowed her to pursue her love of the hockey world.

"Anyway, I'm sorry that happened to you. And hey, you've probably talked to professionals about it, but if you ever want to talk to someone else, I'm sure Holly would be happy to talk to you. She's retired from short-track now, she married my brother and is now a mom, and she's just started studying sports psychology."

"She'd have a lot of good perspective, given her history."

"That's what I said. I think she's amazing, juggling motherhood and studies and Brent's career, but then, some people are great at juggling responsibilities like that, aren't they?"

"I think we can underestimate what people can manage," Hannah said.

Bree sipped her tea. "Anyway, all of that to say I am happy to do whatever to help you out. I don't think it was fair the way you were judged, especially now I know you were so talented in that area yourself. So it seems ridiculous that people have judged you for being a young and pretty woman."

"Thank you. I have to admit it's not the first time I've come across prejudice." Hannah held out a strand of her hair. "I'm actually blonde, so all my life I've been used to people calling me dumb."

"What? No way. That's so wrong."

"Right?" She shrugged. "But what can you do when there are a million jokes that get made about dumb blondes? Ever noticed that they're all about women, never about men?"

"You're right."

"Uh-huh." She sipped her water. "All my life I've been treated a certain way, just because of the way I look, so it's made me work harder and try to be smarter to prove myself."

"I think we all find it easy to judge others on external appearance."

"Exactly."

Bree nodded. "I have several friends like that. Holly can appear very focused and forthright, but she's also warm and sweet. You might be a bit like her, having to put on a tough facade to make it in sports."

"Holly? Your sister-in-law?"

"Yep! Married Brent four years ago. Mike calls her a firecracker."

Hannah smiled. She'd been called the same.

"I have another friend back in Toronto that I worked with," Bree continued, "and to look at her you'd think she's this Goth who is all about hard-core metal bands and an arachnophobe's worst nightmare, but actually she's super sweet, would do anything for you, and is a good friend."

"An arachnophobe's worst nightmare?"

"Sylvie wears spider earrings, has a cool spider web bag, and she's got a pretty unique fashion sense."

"She sounds fun."

"She is. I'm actually hoping she will come and visit soon. Maybe you can meet her."

"I'd like that." She could do with more friends. The years of sports and studies and intense focus had stolen a lot of the friendships she once treasured. People like Cassie, their friendship fizzled to one of happy birthday wishes on Facebook. Teammates who had fallen by the wayside as life pulled them in different directions. Real friendships felt necessary, even more so in this fragile space of needing to feel assurance in the face of male outrage.

Bree's head tilted, and she studied her. "Well, I'll let you know when she's around. And I'll talk to Holly and see if I can link you up too."

"I don't know why you're being so kind to me, but I really appreciate it."

Bree shrugged. "It's what Jesus would do."

"Jesus?" Uh-oh. Was she a God-botherer?

"I'm a Christian, just trying to shine some of God's light and love in this world. I don't always get it right, so forgive me when I get it wrong. But regardless of what you believe, I want you to know I'm supporting you."

Emotion welled, and she glanced away. Why she was acting like she was anti-God she didn't really know. She wasn't, really. Just felt like God was anti-Hannah. But maybe He hadn't quite given up on her yet, for there was deep kindness here, kindness she hadn't experienced in so long. Since her parents' divorce, the past fifteen years had been all intensity and drive, leaving little room for softer emotions. Maybe in her pursuit for achievement she'd missed out on some important things.

"Thanks," she finally managed to croak out. "Wow, I certainly didn't expect to be delving into my personal beliefs and challenges when you asked to meet."

"Sorry, but not that sorry." Bree grinned. "But I can take a hint. Now, the brief was to have a behind-the-scenes interview with the families of the hockey players, or something like that, right?"

"Yep." Hannah smiled. "So I guess we can consider some of this background work."

"Yes, we can, and we will." Bree winked.

Amusement rippled through Hannah's chest. "Okay, so let's talk about what you'd like to share about. If we plan a few locations, coming to the front door like we're just meeting—"

"Ooh, but not with a camera in the background, like I open the front door and act surprised when really the camera person has been there for ages. I always think that looks so cheesy. Like, 'oh, I totally didn't notice this camera person standing behind me!'"

Another chuckle escaped. "Noted. No cheesy fake surprise shots," she said, pretending to write it down. "Does that mean we can do real surprise shots?"

Bree's nose wrinkled. "I don't know how real I really want to be. Like if you see me yelling at Mike or dealing with a diaper or stuff like that, I don't think that's what people really want to see."

"Or maybe it is. Maybe you can be showing the other side to all the glamor and glitz people seem to associate with being a hockey WAG."

"Oh my gosh, okay, that's a really good point. I'll admit there is a degree of pressure to look a certain way. Like, I've been in restrooms with some of these women and totally not recognized them because they haven't had all their hair and makeup done. Yes, I know I'm not supposed to be judgy but I really am so grateful that I knew my husband back when we were kids and he got to know me instead of a version of me that wasn't really real."

"See? This is the kind of stuff I think would be good."

"But is it hockey-related enough?" Bree asked. "They're not into empowering women too much on that station."

"Hmm. We might need to see how we can work that in, but I think it's an important thing that needs to be shared." Hannah scribbled some notes—for real, this time—and admitted, "I was told this was going to be a soft interview, so maybe that plays into what they consider soft journalism."

"I just don't understand why they don't ask the person who has played elite-level hockey to be the one who's calling the games and things like that."

"I can't imagine people like Drew and Bob taking kindly to me muscling in on their turf, can you?"

"No, but I think it'd be good for them. And honestly, they might get more women watching sports if there was a woman on the panel."

"Yeah, I can't see it happening. You should've heard them trying to shut me down, talking over the top of me and inter-rupting when we had our last production meeting. I'm pretty sure Dirk, the executive producer, was happy for me to do my own thing and avoid all the egos and testosterone."

"It's so weird they're like that. Most major networks have female panelists and treat their female reporters with respect."

"But women have always struggled to be recognized, to have their voices heard and paid attention to as much as their looks. And even today female reporters get treated badly sometimes. Like, there was someone who had hot dogs thrown at her just a few years ago, simply because she was reporting on sports."

Bree's eyes widened. "That's insane."

"I know it's insane, but it shows how far some people need to come. Women might be able to play pro sports in many countries around the world, but there are still Neanderthals out there questioning why women should be allowed to report on sports."

"Well, thank goodness for places like ESPN, right? Maybe you'll have to see if they can take you on."

"I can't see ESPN calling me up anytime soon, can you?"

"One day, maybe. You never know. But you probably need a few more interviews under your belt before they come calling."

"And probably ones where I don't end up clonking someone on the head, right?"

"That might help, too."

The morning passed with setting up several scenarios; Hannah jotting notes on what Royce could film, including family time, scenes from the Saddledome, splicing footage of Mike's skating from previous games, and home videos of the kids sponsorship program in the Philippines Mike and Bree were involved in. Excitement picked up. She would still have to run all of this by Jason, and there was no way of knowing what he would deem acceptable or not, given his mixed responses in past days. But still. This was being a real reporter, putting together a news story that would not only entertain but hopefully inspire a little, too.

They talked and Bree made more coffee and offered cake, which Hannah refused. "I don't exercise nearly as much as I should these days, and sitting around a lot means I put on weight a lot more easily."

"Just wait until you've had babies," Bree groaned.

"I'll be waiting a while."

"No man in your world?"

"Footloose and fancy free."

"Just like Franklin, then," Bree said, winking.

Her heart stuttered. She tamped it down. Emotions just made things messy. "Yeah, I really am trying to stay focused on my career right now."

Bree's lips curved to one side. "I remember Holly saying something similar, once upon a time."

"Besides, I can't see him going for the girl who broke his nose, can you?"

"I think the fact he mentioned he was wanting to do a redo interview with you suggests you can't have made too bad an impression."

Hannah shrugged. So the fact he had reached out to her via Jason had been both a surprise and nice validation. Jason had urged her to do something as soon as possible, so she'd set that up for tomorrow. She wondered just what he might want to say in this next encounter. Her lips twisted. At least nobody could say she'd left him without a memorable impression this time.

"Well?" Bree teased.

"Well what? He's a nice guy, I think everybody knows that. It doesn't mean he'd be interested in me."

"Sorry. I shouldn't get involved."

"No, it's okay. It's just tricky, especially as—" She closed her mouth with a snap. She really needed to get better at not over-sharing.

Bree studied her, amusement playing about her mouth. "Look, I can pretend I didn't hear that and not ask you, but I'm also *very* happy if you want to finish that sentence and tell me whatever it is that you clearly want to tell me."

Hannah laughed despite herself. "Do you treat all your friends like this?"

"Pretty much," Bree admitted. "And hey, if you don't want to tell me, that's okay. But if you do want to talk to someone, then I hope you consider us friends enough that you would feel comfortable to share with me."

Strangely enough she did. She might not have known Bree very long but there was an authenticity and a sense of genuine friendship that she felt from her.

Hannah drew in a deep breath. "Okay, here's the thing. I actually knew Franklin before this."

"You did?"

She nodded. "His sister and I once were close when we were playing hockey at high school together and she invited me back to the ranch where he was living at that time before he moved east. We got to know each other a little bit, and I thought he liked me, but nothing happened. And then when we met again he obviously didn't remember me, so I wasn't about to admit that I once had a crush on him. And that's all. Lame story, I know."

"Not lame at all," Bree breathed. "So you had a crush on him."

She winced. See? Overshare. But there was no backing away from this now. "Almost ten years ago. I hadn't seen him since."

"And his sister?"

"Haven't seen her for years either."

"But you could," Bree said thoughtfully. "Especially if you're doing these fun interviews with Calgary players' families."

"I am not using an interview to try and get a guy interested in me."

"Which guy don't you want to get interested in you?" a deeper male voice asked.

And she turned to see a grinning Mike Vaughan had entered the room, and was standing beside a bemused Franklin James.

"Hey honey." Mike kissed his wife, forcing Franklin's gaze back to the pink-cheeked reporter, staring at him with wide eyes.

"What are you doing back so soon?" Bree asked Mike.

"Franklin left his jacket here last night and thought he'd swing by to get it." He smiled at Hannah, held out a hand. "Hey, I'm Mike."

"Hannah Wade," she said. "Although I suspect you know that, seeing I'm interviewing your wife."

"I didn't see any cameras, so I wasn't sure."

"I'm avoiding live reports for a while." Her attention finally returned to Franklin. "Hi again."

"Hey."

"Your nose is looking better. How is it feeling?"

He touched the bandage the team doctor had strapped on before the on-ice session, the strapping and a visored helmet the only way Franklin had received the okay to participate in the team practice skate. "It's still tender, but it's attached, so that's the main thing."

"I'm so sorry."

"Don't." He held up a hand, softening his tone at her look of shock. "I mean, please don't apologize any more. I know you're sorry, but I don't want to keep living in that moment and I don't think you do either. There's enough other people living there for us both, don't you think?"

"Yes."

"So, let's agree to never mention that again and we both move on, okay?"

"Sure."

"Speaking of moving on," Bree said, her gaze flitting between Hannah and himself, "maybe you should show people just how much you mean that."

"What do you mean, hon?" Mike asked.

"Just that it might be good for team morale if we had a party, you know, to welcome Franklin, oh and Chad—he's the other new guy, right?—to the team. I mean, I'm sure Franklin has met various people at various times but especially now you are the captain, it's probably good to set a different tone to what tended to happen before, and it would be a great way for them to get to know others as well."

"Sounds good," Mike said.

"Uh, sure," Franklin agreed. "But what does that have to do with moving on?"

"Well," Bree said brightly, "if we could get Hannah here to

film it, especially as she's doing behind-the-scenes interviews with the players and their families, it could be great PR for the team. And for you too," she said to Hannah kindly. "I think people would like to see what happened next between you two."

Hannah's mouth swung open, her cheeks remaining pink. "Bree, what I said before, I didn't mean—"

"No, nothing like that," Bree rushed to say. "It's just that it would be good for people to say that you and Franklin have no hard feelings between you both. That's all."

Franklin held up his hands. "Hey, I've been saying from the get-go it was an accident, so there's no hard feelings from me."

"I've been saying the same, but still." She gestured to his nose. "Viewers would see your nose and make their own assumptions, wouldn't they?"

"Assumptions that would get challenged if they see us getting along and doing that interview."

"Which we've already scheduled for tomorrow," she reminded him.

He nodded. "At Steak and Majors." Hey, if he was doing an interview, he wasn't opposed to eating well—and healthily— while at one of Calgary's top steak houses.

"That's such a nice place," Bree approved. "And there you can be as public or as private as you like."

Franklin shot her a glance. Did she mean to make it sound like it was a date?

Something Mike seemed to recognize too, as he murmured, "It's an interview, hon. That's all."

"I know." But Bree's smile held a touch of mischief. "Oh," she straightened. "So when do you think we should have the party? I think it should be soon, before the season kicks in and every-one's schedule gets really busy."

"I'm available to do whatever whenever my illustrious captain commands," Franklin offered.

"Well, Hannah, what would work for you? Would a party sometime in the next two weeks work?"

"I don't know how many of the guys will be back from their vacations," Mike pointed out.

"They'll have to get back soon, because preseason starts in three weeks. I think we could easily make it work in that time frame."

"But only if you get some help," Mike said softly. "I don't want you overdoing things, okay?"

"I promise," she whispered, eyes on him.

Franklin glanced at Hannah, saw she looked as awkward as him. Did she know Mike wanted Bree to take things easy because she was pregnant? Bree and Hannah obviously had some rapport in sharing personal details like what he'd heard before. Had she really said she was interested in someone on the team? He knew he was the new guy here, so it couldn't be him. The way she barely looked at him only made that more clear.

"So that's arranged then? We'll aim for two weeks, and Hannah can bring her film crew and do interviews with the players here. That could be fun! Who knows what you'll capture?"

"As long as it's nothing like Alex making out with someone else's wife or girlfriend again then that'd be great."

"Ugh. Kristen won't like it." Bree wrinkled her nose. She glanced at Franklin. "She's Alex's new girlfriend, and didn't like it when Hannah mentioned that the other day."

Hannah sighed. "Sorry. I probably should've thought a little more about what I was saying, but obviously I was nervous and feeling under pressure, especially because it was live. And while what I said was true, I probably shouldn't have said it quite like that. I find that sometimes my mouth runs away with me, which can prove problematic, as I think we all know."

"You get an Amen from me," Bree said, lifting a hand. "I need to be more careful with what I say, too."

Hannah nodded, and turned to Mike. "Having said that, I am so honestly glad that we now have a captain who is someone I think is worth looking up to. It's so important that the kids have a role model who is actually worthy of respect. Too often we see people in high-profile positions not live up to the expectations that fans have of them, and I'm glad that in you we have someone who is loyal and hardworking and honest."

"I do my best," Mike said, wrapping an arm around Bree. "It's easier because of this woman. I'm so thankful to God for her support, her generous heart and care for others. I'm grateful that we have a solid marriage built on friendship, and that we've known each other for years. It helps to know that we're both committed to doing things God's way, staying faithful to each other."

Hannah nodded, the light in her face draining away.

Franklin's chest twinged. Was it the mention of God that had done that?

"Are you okay, Hannah?" Bree asked.

"My parents divorced when I was eleven," Hannah said softly. "So I have a lot of respect for people who can find a way to make a marriage work. Not everyone is so lucky."

"I'm sorry," Franklin murmured. "That must've been rough."

She stared at him, her mouth twisted as if she was trying not to say something, then she nodded, and glanced away. "Okay, well, I better be going."

"Oh, you don't have to leave, do you?" Bree pleaded. "You could stay, Franklin could too, and we could get to know each other some more."

"I really have some work to do, and I'll need to square up with the others what the date is for the party to make sure I can be here."

"But—"

"And Franklin and I will be getting to know each other tomorrow at the interview anyway."

"Again," Bree said with a little smile.

Again? Hannah shot her a reproving look. No way did she want to make things with Franklin more complicated than it already was.

"Well, have fun with that," Bree said.

Mike glanced at his wife. "You okay?"

"Just dandy."

Judging from the wide-eyed way she was looking at Mike, Franklin figured he needed to let her say whatever she was clearly bursting to say in privacy. "Right, well, I'll be off too. Thanks for the session, Mike. Good to see you, Bree. Hannah." He nodded.

Hannah's gaze lowered as if she wasn't too sure what to do with him. Man, what did he have to do to convince her that he didn't hold the accident against her? Maybe he could convince her in the interview tomorrow.

He waited until she made her farewells then followed her outside. She had a small blue Mazda that had seen a few years, which made his shiny Ford Ranger look too big and new by comparison. But when a man was gifted a car as part of the team's sponsorship, what was he to do?

"Nice ride," she said, gesturing to the vehicle.

"It gets me from A to B."

"That's Alberta to New Brunswick, right?"

"That'd be A to NB, but yeah."

"Oh, look who knows his alphabet," she said with a slight smile.

"Look who knows how to pack a verbal punch," he teased back. At her widened eyes, he hurried to reassure her. "That wasn't meant to reference the other day."

"I know. That was a headbutt, not a punch."

He grinned.

"Anyway, we agreed to not mention that anymore, right?"

"Mention what?"

"See? I've got no idea what you're talking about anymore."

"That makes two of us."

She laughed, and the sound triggered another memory. He studied her.

"What?"

"Nothing. I just keep thinking I know something, then it slips from my mind."

"Hmm. That sounds like something someone who might've recently suffered a blow to the head might say."

He smiled. Then realized, "Hey, I never asked you if you were okay."

"You mean about my blow to the head?"

"Yeah. I mean, I got all the glory and sympathy, but you still got hurt too, didn't you?"

"Not anything like you." She touched the crown of her head. "That spot is still a little tender, but at least I'm not needing to wear plaster on my nose."

"It's not plaster, just a bandage."

"I'm sor—so glad that it's not going to be permanently affected."

Amusement spurted at her attempt to swap her apology for something else. "I'm waiting until my hockey days are done before doing permanent surgery. I figure a bent nose is just going to be my weakest link until then."

"Some people do broken teeth but you do nose, huh?"

"Apparently." He shrugged. "I'm grateful I don't need to wear a plate like some guys." Like TJ Woletsky, the enforcer-turned-Christian who Mike had explained had had a God encounter a year or two ago. Definite proof God was real.

"It's a good thing we're not talking about the incident-that-shan't-be-named."

"It is."

Her lips curved, curling into his heart until he was sure some subconscious part of him recognized her. But where, when, he couldn't figure out.

"Why do you keep looking at me like that?" she asked. "Are you worried I'm going to do you another injury?"

"Hey, I thought we weren't talking about headbutts or noses?"

She nodded, head tilted, as she studied him still.

There it was again. Something in the lines of her face that beckoned a memory that still bobbed beyond reach. Maybe he should just ask.

"Do I know you somehow?"

Her face blanked.

"Hey, I know that sounds like a bad pickup line, and that we met a few days ago, although that day was just insane so I didn't notice it then. But now, I can't help feeling like you remind me of someone, but who it is I don't know."

Her lips pressed together, her gaze falling to somewhere around his left shoulder.

"What is it?"

She shrugged. "Clearly the fact you even ask that means that you don't."

But that wasn't really answering the question, was it? He watched as she moved to her vehicle, opened the door and got in.

Maybe he could find out more in the next interview tomorrow.

And he suddenly couldn't wait.

CHAPTER 4

"*D*o you have a booking?" The maître d' studied
Hannah, his glance sweeping her up and down.

She lifted her chin. "There should be a booking
under Wade."

"Wade?" He drew a finger down the book again then tapped
it twice. "Ah. I see. Table for two. Very well." He summoned a
waiter to take her to a table, who gave her his own haughty
once-over, before inclining his head and murmuring "This way."

Hmm. Was he another sports fan who had recognized her
name? Another person who blamed her for ruining the good
looks of Calgary's new hockey star? Wouldn't he be in for a
surprise when he saw who her lunch companion was.

As she followed the waiter she saw people glance her way. It
seemed her attempt to dress up in a flowy green dress she'd
thought said professional-but-friendly had not quite been the
right attire for a place that appeared filled with suits. Or maybe
it was the new hair. She'd hoped yesterday afternoon's session
at the hair salon to bring Mandi's rushed dye job to something
more resembling the promotional posters might be helpful in
keeping the peace with Dirk and Will. The stylist had called the

look bronde, the blonde highlights through her hair looking natural, although it felt very unnatural to have spent so many hours on her hair in the past week. She was normally more of a wash-and-go woman, but apparently appearances mattered, even to snooty waiters in top restaurants. She wondered what Franklin would think. She shrugged. He probably wouldn't even notice.

The waiter pulled out a chair at a table in a quieter section of the busy restaurant, and she thanked him and sat down.

Businessmen and couples nearby glanced at her, then away. So far it didn't seem she had been recognized. Had her new hair color altered her looks that much? Maybe the fact she'd pulled it into a sleek ponytail had helped. Or was it the black-framed spectacles she wore that kept her disguise? She didn't normally wear glasses; contact lenses were her preference, something she'd grown used to in a lifetime playing sports.

She breathed out, adjusted the linen napkin, accepted the cloth-bound menu, and pretended to scan it as she wondered for the hundredth time how she was going to face him.

Why had she run away from Franklin yesterday? Why hadn't she admitted that yes, she knew Cassie, and knew him, and had once floated down a river with him holding her hand while they were tubing, and actually had thought he might want to kiss her! Trying to find the words to explain all that without her sounding like some crazy stalker person had been too much. Put it down to her own personal impact after bumping her head but she simply hadn't been able to find the right words. Which was *terrible* for someone employed in a job where thinking on her feet and being quick with words was literally what she was paid for. And equally frustrating because she'd always prided herself on being strong and brave, yet one question from him had the power to make her run away. Bold, brave, fiery her had *run away*. She groaned.

A glance from a nearby middle-aged man suggested her

groan had been too loud. She offered a wry smile then ducked her head and pulled out her phone. She'd come early, as much because she wanted to own the space and feel comfortable without that flustered feeling she often felt in Franklin's company, as it was to avoid the rudeness of being late. She just hadn't figured him to be tardy.

Her phone held no apologies for being delayed, and the time had definitely ticked into meeting time. So where was he?

"Excuse me."

She froze. Glanced at the man from the nearby table. Had he recognized her? "Yes?"

"If you're not using the salt would you mind passing it to us."

"Oh! Uh, sure." She passed it to him and smiled.

"Thanks." He frowned. "Hey, you're not that sports reporter chick, are you?"

She swallowed. His frown and tone didn't appear too friendly. "Why do you say that?"

His gaze narrowed. Then dropped as he pulled out his phone, and showed something to his dining companion, then glanced back at her.

Sweat dripped down her back, and she hastily averted her eyes. Awesome. Was he one of those people who had written horrible things? Lisa had begged Hannah not to look at her social media. And she'd killed the commenting option, but not before she'd seen a death threat. A *death* threat. Because she'd accidentally hurt a hockey player? What kind of person did that? She'd known she'd need a thick skin in this business. Just hadn't expected she'd have to grow one quite so quickly. And now, she lived in this weird space of not knowing who might be out to hurt her, because they thought she'd deliberately tried to hurt someone. Maybe she should call Franklin and arrange they meet somewhere else—

"Miss?" The snooty waiter's face wore boredom as he placed

a carafe of water on the table. "Is your dining party joining you?"

She nodded. "He'll be here soon." She hoped. Where was he?

"Very well. Can I get you something to drink?"

"No, thanks. The water is fine."

His lip curled, as if thinking of her as a tightwad who'd probably only eat and run after taking a picture in the Instagram-worthy surroundings. She glanced away and poured herself a glass of water, noticing several others were looking at her, then murmuring quietly to each other.

She took a breath and released. She didn't need to be paranoid. This was probably just something she would need to get used to. A sports reporter on TV had to get used to being in the public eye. Even if she didn't like the way she had been portrayed, or the rumors people made up about her.

She peeked across at the table where the man had borrowed her salt. He caught her looking, and opened his mouth and glanced at his hand just like she'd looked in the meme, before laughing.

Her breath hitched, and she glanced away, all words of defense shriveled. People might think they were just being funny, but did they have no idea that it simply came across as cruel?

The seconds ticked by, a basket of bread was unceremoniously dumped on her table without a word. Looked like that waiter had figured out who she was too, and wasn't wanting a tip anytime soon.

She sipped her water, ripped her bread roll in half, eating some—the French butter made it extra tasty—and shredding the other half into remnants she rolled into small balls. Look at her being so classy. She rolled her eyes at herself, then glanced at her phone. Still no word. Glanced around the room, avoiding the smirks that suggested her disguise wasn't as effective as she might've hoped.

"Hannah?"

Her gaze snapped up, and was instantly snagged by Franklin's blue eyes. He smiled, and a fluttery feeling shot through her chest.

"Sorry I'm late. You'd think I'd know better by now but I got stuck on a one-way street, then found it hard to find a parking spot. I hate being late, too."

"It's okay."

"The maître d' said you were here but it took me a bit to recognize you. You look different."

She touched her hair. "It might be this. Or the glasses."

"Maybe." He took his seat. "I didn't know you wore glasses."

"But you don't really know me though, do you?"

His expression grew thoughtful, and she panicked as she wondered whether her barb would see a resumption of his gentle probing from yesterday. She didn't have time for that. Especially not in front of all these people. "Let's just call it my disguise."

His lips tweaked. "Woman of mystery, huh?"

"Exactly."

"You look great, anyway."

There it was again, that same fluttery feeling. But no, what she'd said to Bree yesterday was correct. She had no desire to try to have a relationship with a man who clearly thought she was forgettable, and who had made zero effort to contact her all those years ago. Besides, she had her career to focus on. "Thanks."

"So, is anything on the menu looking good? It's been a while since I ate here, but I remember it as delicious, and—"

"Hey, are you Franklin James?" the nearby diner from before interrupted.

Franklin glanced at her, then at the diner, shrugged, and held out a hand. "Hey."

"Oh man, I can't believe it. Can I get a picture with you?" the man said.

"Uh, sure."

He posed for a selfie with the man, and she had to admire Franklin's easy willingness to meet the fans. Some people would prefer to be left alone, but over the years she learned the players with the biggest fan bases were the ones who made the effort to connect, even when it might be personally inconvenient.

It seemed various others also noticed they had a celebrity in their midst, and the next minutes passed in several other requests for photos, along with a couple of not-so-very-surreptitious snaps, and a few dropped jaws as people seemed to put two and two together and realized who she was too.

A titter of laughter drew her attention, and she saw two men studying their phones. They weren't looking at her memes, were they?

"Hey," Franklin drew her attention. "Ignore them."

She gritted out a smile. "That's easy for you to say."

"Hannah!"

She turned instinctively, then blinked as someone took her photo and laughed.

"Hey," Franklin objected.

She should never have arranged this. People were laughing at her, pointing at her, smirking. Her fingers clenched. Why had she thought meeting in a public space was a good idea?

"Hannah." Concern etched Franklin's face as he studied her. "We can go elsewhere if you like."

And be chased away by bullies again? She tilted her chin. "I don't mind."

His lips pulled to one side. "You don't have to pretend to be brave for me."

"Who says I'm doing this for you?"

She winced as the words came out, all sharp and spiky, and the way Franklin blinked, then nodded slowly. She was about to apologize, even though she felt like she'd apologized a million times to the man already, when the snooty waiter from before drew up to their table again.

"Mr. James, I did not realize you were dining with us today. Welcome. We're so pleased you could join us today."

Well. That was a far more gracious welcome than what she'd received.

"Thanks."

The waiter gestured to the nearby diners. "Are these people bothering you?"

Franklin glanced at her, and she shrugged. It wasn't really okay, but objecting would steal their opportunity to photograph Calgary's new hockey star, and would only make people hate her more. "It's fine," she muttered.

"Can I get you some appetizers?"

"Can you give us a minute?" Franklin asked.

"Certainly."

He moved away, and Franklin leaned forward, his hands on the table, his gaze intent. "Hey, really, if this is a problem, we can go somewhere else. I don't want you feeling like you're a goldfish in a bowl."

"I don't think you can do my job without feeling like that," she confessed.

His hand reached across the table and touched hers. Her fingers jerked, nearly knocking over the glass. "Sorry."

"It's okay," she whispered.

"Really?"

She nodded, unable to speak. Why did this man have such an effect on her?

He smiled, slouching back in his chair as he studied her. "You know what would be funny?"

"What?" She took a sip of water.

"If we pretended to be going out."

She choked.

"Hey, are you okay?"

No. She cleared her throat. "Yes. And no. That would be a terrible idea."

"Why?" He grinned. "If I hold your hand it'd give people something else to talk about."

Sure would. But messing with her heart wasn't wise. "I don't think you'd really want to do that."

"Why not?"

"Because everyone would think you've lost your marbles because I hit you on the head."

"But if they see I don't hate you, maybe it could stop some of the haters."

"Yeah, but then I'd get hate from all those who weren't dating you, so I don't think that'd work, either."

"Hmm. Maybe."

What?

He chuckled. "Maybe we should just discuss how to do this second interview instead."

The second interview. Of course. "That's exactly right."

As if her brain caught the reminder she snapped into professional mode. What was she doing wondering what others thought of her? She had a job to do. "So, about that, when I was speaking with Bree yesterday we talked through various ways we could do the feature on her family. Now we could do something like that with you, and piece together an interview at home with snippets from your games, or do a more formal sit-down interview where you could talk in more depth about your hockey plans, or we could do something else completely."

"Excuse me, are you ready to order now?" a new waiter asked.

"I'm hungry, so yeah." Franklin held up the menu, and quickly ordered.

She did the same, and their menus were collected, their

water glasses refilled, and the waiter moved away, leaving them to face each other again.

She sipped her water, conscious of Franklin's perusal, the way his attention seemed to dim the notice of others, and the way she couldn't hide behind her menu anymore. "So."

"So." He smiled.

My goodness, the man's grin was magnetic, tipping her emotional equilibrium off balance. She forced herself to refocus. "So, what kind of interview do you want to do?"

As soon as the words escaped, her pulse increased. *Please don't say with your family.* How would she pretend she'd never met them before?

He took a bread roll from the freshly delivered basket and cut it, smearing half with the fancy butter. "Well, from what Bree says, maybe it would be good to do something similar."

"Like?"

He shrugged. "Like, it could be good to help viewers relate to me if they get to know me a little more. See where I grew up and stuff."

No. "I think Bree meant more families of the players, like their wives and kids and such."

"But my folks and sisters are my family," he objected.

"Sure, but whether they can be said to have the cuteness factor of a little baby, well, I don't know."

His lips pulled to one side. "I think most people would think where I grew up was pretty cool."

"A ranch, right?" she asked, like she didn't already know.

"You've done your research."

Yep. By actually visiting that ranch with his sister. "Um, sure."

"Have you seen pictures?" He drew out his phone, tapped the screen a few times, then showed her, flicking through picture after picture of sunset-lit hills, cows and horses, and the wooden buildings used in film and TV productions.

"It's beautiful," she murmured. She'd thought so on her visit before, too.

"I think it's the most beautiful place on the planet. I mean, I haven't been everywhere, obviously, but I've done some travel to Europe for hockey, and gone to the Caribbean for vacation. Hey, you can keep your Paris or tropical islands. I love the ranch most of all."

"The Three Creek Ranch," she murmured.

"You know it?" His eyes brightened. "Of course, you've researched me, haven't you?" He grinned. "That sounds arrogant, doesn't it?"

Hey, she was happy for this turn in the conversation. The more rabbit trails the better, if it meant avoiding the truth. "I don't think of you that way."

"Well, I appreciate it. My folks taught us to remember our Lord and our roots. I did better on the second than the first."

"You're a Christian."

"Yep. I've only recently got back into a relationship with God though. I walked around in the wilderness a little too long."

His words tugged at her. She'd made a commitment in high school, not long before Cassie had invited her to visit that summer, but family dramas, hockey and studies had proved effective distractions. That, and her broken ankle meant it didn't seem like God paid much attention to her these days.

"Anyway, I think it'd be fun to show it off a little. We're a working ranch, but we can always do with more visitors."

"I see. So this interview is about free advertising for the ranch, is it?"

"You bet your sweet mama it is."

She blinked, then laughed in memory of what she'd said to him the other day.

Before she could ask about it their food arrived, which demanded their attention.

She relaxed, the food, and okay, the company too, making

her feel comfortable. Maybe it was silly to not admit she'd visited the ranch, especially given the increasingly likely possibility she might end up visiting again, but she didn't worry about that, happy to go where the topic of conversation flowed, as they traded stories, and even bites of food like they really were the couple he'd suggested they pretend to be.

"So what made you want to be a reporter?" he asked, once his plate was clear.

"I've always loved sports, so when I had my accident which meant I couldn't compete at the same level anymore, I needed something that would still allow for my passion. It was easy to switch a few courses around and change my major into a journalism degree, so that's what I did."

He nodded. "And how are you finding working at CNSTV?"

"It's been okay." She wrinkled her nose. "But maybe that's because I haven't had much to do with Drew or Bob in recent days."

"I've seen how they talk about women. To be honest, I'd be really happy to never speak to either of them."

Her heart clenched. "I don't know how well that would go with all your commitments to media, but I appreciate the support."

"You got it."

She sipped her water, trying to cool the flicker of pleasure his words had provoked. "Anyway, I think there's something special about getting to know the reason behind what makes a person choose what they do. It's those reasons that really make the story." She tilted her head. "Like I could ask you why a rancher's son plays in the NHL."

"And you should."

She chuckled. "Okay. Tell us, Mr. James, why does a rancher's son play in the NHL?"

"Because hockey is awesome," he said promptly.

"It is, isn't it?" She grinned.

FRANKLIN'S HEART gripped a little tighter. Or maybe that was the effect of Hannah's smile. It seemed to have him in a choke hold, one he really didn't want to do a thing about. The more time he spent in her company the more he realized she was exactly the kind of woman he enjoyed being with: relaxed, easy to talk to, with an edge of tease. And her sparkling eyes and pretty features didn't hurt, either. Nor the fact she obviously loved hockey as much as he did, without the weirdness of worrying if she was a superfan.

"May I clear your plates?" the waiter asked.

"Sure." Franklin joined Hannah in pushing his plate closer to make it easier for the employee to move away.

He settled back in his chair. "So, when are we going to do this?"

"The interview?"

He nodded. "I think it'd be fun to go to the ranch. I could introduce you to my folks, you could meet my sisters, get all the background gossip on me."

Her lips pressed together. "Actually—"

"Now, may I interest you in our dessert menu?" the waiter asked.

"I don't need anything," Hannah said.

Franklin declined as well. "So, Hannah, you were saying?" he prompted.

"Nothing." She sipped her water and watched as the waiter moved away.

Around them, interest seemed to have died away, and he could only hope it meant his presence meant Hannah would be safe. He might've done a little close-to-midnight scrolling last night, and seen a few death threats against her. That fact, as much as anything else, had pushed him to further degrees of protectiveness. For how could anyone treat a fellow human being like that?

"Are you okay?" she asked. "You keep looking at me."

"Sorry. I was just thinking."

Her eyebrows rose, but he couldn't reply. How could he admit to this feeling of protectiveness? He had no right. And he got the vibes that she was like his sister, Cassie, and plenty liberated enough to not need a man to stick up for her. But it didn't stop the fact that he did want to help her. And that perhaps he hadn't been completely joking about wanting to hold her hand earlier.

"Want a coffee?" he asked instead.

"No. I should probably go soon. I'll need to get back to the office to check our schedules and figure this out a little more."

He nodded. "Doing much this weekend?"

"Not really."

"I don't suppose you want to show a newbie around the city?"

"I thought you weren't such a newbie."

He shrugged. "I still need to know good places to eat." He gestured to the restaurant. "This place is good, but a little stuffy with all the suits."

"I agree."

He got the feeling they agreed on a few things. It was all part of what made her intriguing.

"So, you're not going to see your family, then?"

"I hadn't planned to. But now you mention it, I probably should. Hey, you could come. It's not far, and then you could figure out what sorts of shots you want and where it would be good to film."

Her eyes widened. "I don't think we actually agreed to do the interview at the ranch."

"Well you should. It's awesome."

"I know that, but…"

"But what? How can you not want to come visit the ranch?"

She studied him. Then her gaze fell. "That's the thing. I actually have—"

"Sorry to interrupt, but are you Franklin James?" a woman asked.

"Um, yeah."

"Oh, my boyfriend didn't believe it was you, but I said it had to be because of your bandage. How is your nose?"

"Um, it's fine. Thanks for your concern but I'm in the middle of something here, and—"

"Oh! I'm sorry. I know you're very busy, but would you mind taking a quick photo of us?" She smiled at Hannah.

"Sure." Hannah took the photo then passed the phone back.

"Oh, thanks so much." The woman beamed at Hannah. "Wait. Aren't you the reporter chick who hurt him?" She peered at her more closely. "You are! Huh. Is that your disguise, is it? Those glasses won't fool anyone."

Hannah's lips pressed together, her body language suggesting she wanted to be anywhere but here.

"That was an accident," Franklin said. "You can't seriously imagine that anyone would want that to happen."

"Hmph. Well, I guess it's true then," the woman continued, before beckoning for someone to join them.

"What is?" He was struggling to hold onto his patience.

"What they say about female sports reporters."

Hannah froze, her eyes meeting his for a second before darting away.

His chest tensed. He'd heard enough locker-room banter over the years to know this was something he did not want Hannah to hear. "If you'll excuse us." He pushed to his feet, then moved to help Hannah from her chair, effectively forcing the other woman to shift aside.

"Is everything okay?" The head waiter hurried to them.

"Yeah. We'll pay at the door." He tilted his head to the gossip woman. "If this lady would let us leave, that is."

"Excuse me, ma'am, but if you could kindly move so the gentleman and his partner could leave."

"We're not—"

"Thank you," Franklin said firmly, cutting off Hannah's protest.

The nosy woman gasped. "So it is true."

"What?"

"You're together?"

"What's a little headbutt between friends?" he joked. "Come on, Hannah. Let's get out of here."

She nodded, gaze averted, and he paid, overcoming her protest when they got outside.

"Look, I'm sorry but I didn't want to stay stuck there with a woman who kept making nasty comments about you."

"But I was going to pay. Or the station was, anyway. It's the least I can do after wrecking your suit the other day."

He shrugged. "You can pay next time."

"Next time?"

"Yeah. How about you buy the coffees tomorrow when we head out to the ranch?"

"What? No. I'm busy."

"Doing?"

"I don't need to tell you."

All at once he realized how he must've come across. "Okay, okay. Fine." He held up his hands. "I'm sorry if I was pushy."

"You were."

He grew aware they had a crowd. "Where'd you park?"

She mentioned the same parking garage as him, and they fast-walked there, soon escaping the onlookers as they hurried up the concrete stairs.

"Look, Hannah, I don't want you to feel threatened when you're out with me."

"I'm not out with you," she insisted. "This is just an interview."

He glanced at her, saw her creased forehead. So she knew what the other woman had been implying too. He shook his head. It was crazy what some people out there thought. He stopped, touched her shoulder, his tone soft. "I just thought this would be a good chance to show others that we are friends, and that they should not judge you harshly, because I don't see you that way."

She swallowed. "I don't think what you do will matter to some people. There will always be someone wanting to blame the woman."

"I'm sorry."

"Thank you," she whispered.

"Hey."

He didn't know what came over him, but he felt an insane desire to hug her. So he did. And he reveled in the feeling of her in his arms.

Then realized she'd frozen.

His arms dropped.

She stared at him, eyes wide. "What are you doing?"

How to explain the surge of compassion that had prompted this impulse? "I thought you needed a friend."

She exhaled, hand on her chest, as she stepped back, open-mouthed.

He was about to explain when he saw a couple of teenagers, holding up their phones, as if filming. Man. "Where's your car?"

"Over there," she pointed.

"Mine is just here." He beeped it unlocked, managed a tight smile for the teens. "Hey there."

"What are you doing?" she hissed, as he directed her to get into his truck.

"Saving you from being harassed," he gritted out.

"I don't need you to save me," she said. "I'm plenty capable of that myself."

"You're tough, I get it. But do you really want to have your car license plate up on social media for all kinds of trolls to find?"

"What?"

He opened the door for her, gestured for her to get inside. "Those two kids with the phones are filming us," he said quietly. "And they'll keep filming us, whether you get in your car or mine. At least with my car I can take this to the dealer tomorrow and get a new one. They won't blink an eye. But I don't know if you can do the same."

She sat in the passenger seat, and he closed the door, then hurried around to the driver's side. "Have a good day!" he called to the kids.

Her lips were tightly pressed as he drove from the space. Then she sighed. "And just what am I going to do about my car? I've got to get back to the office."

"Well, I can either drop you off at work, or I can double back in a minute and you can collect it shortly."

"I think you should do the latter. I don't want to pay overnight parking charges."

"Fine." He executed a sharp turn, then started up the nearest ramp to ascend the floors he'd just driven down.

"You know some people might regard what you've done as kidnapping."

"I didn't see you running and screaming."

"Because you gave me no choice!" She blew out a breath, and he caught how her exhale tickled the hair over her eyes. "Don't you think you're being paranoid?"

Had she read the threats being made about her online? "I think it's best to be cautious."

Her gaze flicked to his. "I hardly think someone is going to car bomb me. We're talking about hockey fans, not terrorists."

"Look, I can't help it. I'd hate for something bad to happen to you when it was partly my fault. Hey, I'd do exactly the same if you were my sister."

Her shoulders drooped, her lips pressing together, and she nodded.

He drew closer to her blue Mazda. Fortunately, it seemed the teenagers had now gone. "Don't you think so many of those comments will go away if people know we're friends?"

"Is that what we are?" she asked, looking him straight in the eye.

"I sure would like to think so."

Her head tilted, then she nodded. She opened the door and got out, using her key fob to unlock her vehicle.

"Is that it then? We're friends?"

"You said it." She sat in the driver's seat and powered down her window.

"So, when will I hear back from you about the interview?"

"Tomorrow."

"Yeah? Great." He shoved his hands in his pockets. "And when will I see you again?"

She sighed. "At the ranch. Tomorrow."

"Really? Awesome. Hey, let me give you the address."

She shook her head and started the engine. "You don't need to."

"That's right. You can look it up online."

"I can, but that's not it."

It wasn't?

"I visited with Cassie ten years ago." She shot him a look that could only qualify as a smirk and then drove away.

CHAPTER 5

This was such a dumb idea. Scratch that. This was such a *terrible* idea. Why had she admitted the truth to Franklin? Her knuckles whitened as she gripped the steering wheel, as her car turned off the highway and passed along a wide avenue of poplars, the faintest tinge of gold burnishing the leaves. Not that she'd admitted the whole truth to him, having ignored his phone calls and texts last night, apart from sending him a message to say she'd be at the ranch at ten a.m.

Not that it mattered, anyway. He didn't know she'd once had a crush on him. And it wasn't like he had x-ray vision and could see inside her heart now. Even if he did he'd see nothing but professionalism there. She'd make sure of it.

But her professional reporter hopes seemed to drain away the closer she drew to the ranch, the drive igniting memories from a decade ago. Her bruised heart that had embraced Cassie's easy friendliness. The warm welcome to the James family ranch. Her only-child awe at meeting Cassie's parents— still married!—and the sudden yearning to have sisters. Her marveling at the ranch's size and surrounds. Then the way her heart had skipped more than one beat when she'd met Cassie's older brother.

She exhaled, tamping down a fresh spurt of emotion, forcing her thoughts to other things. Would Cassie be there? If Hannah had been cleverer and thought this through instead of freaking out last night, she would've sent Cassie a message on Facebook, just a simple hello and a heads-up she was visiting today. Because she had a feeling if Cassie found out that Hannah was to visit without telling her—

Her phone buzzed. She glanced at the number and recognized it as Franklin's. She pressed answer, thankful the call could go through the car's audio system. "Hello?"

"Hey, it's me." Nervous-sounding laughter. "Franklin, that is."

"Franklin?" She smiled.

"Franklin James." A pause. "Hey, is this Hannah, or did I—?"

She chuckled.

He exhaled loudly. "Are you almost here?"

"Depends where 'here' is."

"At the ranch. Hey, is that your car I can see on the drive? Man. Never mind." The call ended.

Amusement escaped in quiet laughter. If she didn't know better, she'd almost suspect the man of being as nervous as she. Although what he had to be nervous about, she didn't know. Except…

What if he *had* remembered?

Her chest tightened again, and she had to force deep breaths. It was okay. She could do this. Prep for the interview, meet— okay, re-meet—his family, and if anyone asked then she could easily pretend to have forgotten all about old times or simply laugh over reminiscences relating to her younger foolish self. She lifted her chin. And she would one hundred percent keep her tongue in check and *not* overshare.

The two-story ranch house drew into view, its deep angled roof lines reminding her of Green Gables from the 1980s film of LM Montgomery's classic novel. Cassie had said the James family had owned this farm-turned-ranch for over a hundred years, and everywhere she looked she could see the way they had preserved and improved upon their heritage. But that was the mission of the James family's Three Creek Ranch, outlined on their website: building on the past to create a sustainable future for the next generation.

The road veered to the side and she followed, ignoring the sign that pointed ahead to Western Town and Backlot. The grass was long, suggesting the rains over the summer had done their job well, and that the reddish-brown cattle grazing nearby would be well provided for with feed until the snows hit.

She steered into the gravel parking area and killed the engine, just as a jeans-clad figure stepped onto the wraparound porch. She swallowed. It wasn't fair that someone could look so good in both a suit and a pair of nicely fitting jeans.

Franklin moved down the steps, and she almost got the impression he was disappointed not to open her car door, but she was well and truly able to do such things herself. She didn't need his assistance. She *did* need to keep professional distance between herself and him, and preventing his gentlemanly actions might help her heart to get the memo.

She stepped out, and he held the door open for her. "Hey."

"Hey there, cowboy." Tease would help her maintain proper boundaries. And might tamp down a heart all too quick to leap at his smile. Like he was doing now. Quick, she needed a distraction.

She turned, shutting the door carefully then locking it, willing her face to portray calm.

"You don't need to worry about locking it. We don't see too many car thieves out here," he drawled.

"Are you talking more slowly because you're trying to sound like a cowboy?" she asked.

He grinned, and her heart danced a little faster. "Are you nervous or something?"

"No. Why would I be nervous?"

"No reason."

But judging from that blue-eyed twinkle and lone cheek dimple there was a reason. She hefted up her laptop—she suspected she wouldn't need it, but it didn't hurt to be prepared, especially when it acted like a shield. Or at least she hoped it might. Just what had been said about her here? Or had nothing needed to be said, because she'd said—and done—it all on TV? If his folks and sisters blamed her, then a laptop shield was better than none.

"Come on in." He gestured to the steps. "Or do you remember the way?"

"It's been a while," she said, ignoring his tease. Okay, so he did remember something about her previous visit. But just what? Swimming with her and his sisters? Holding hands? More? Her heart skittered.

She walked up the steps, across the wooden porch, and through the open door. Down the central hallway she could hear voices, coming from the living room at the back, where Franklin was leading her, voices which now included—

"Woah." Cassie pushed her hands on her hips and stared. "So that's why he didn't tell us who was coming to visit."

Did that mean her former best friend wasn't glad to see her? Hannah pushed a smile past the inner disquiet. "Hey Cassie. It's been awhile."

"Sure has."

Regret squeezed her chest. "I'm really sorry—"

"Come here." Cassie stepped close, arms wide, and Hannah sank into them as her friend held her tight. "I'm so glad to see you."

"I'm sorry I didn't keep in touch better," she murmured.

"It takes two, remember?" Cassie drew back, studying her. "Wow. You look different."

Hannah touched her hair. "It's a little different—"

"No, I don't mean that. You, you look different." Cassie's hazel eyes held warmth and curiosity. "I read that you'd hurt your ankle, but that was a while ago now. Is everything okay?"

Maybe there'd be time to share honestly later, but Hannah was very conscious of the large blond man standing in the kitchen, arms crossed as he leaned against the counter, his gaze equally interested, next to—

"Oh! Mrs. James. I didn't see you there."

Franklin's mom smiled. "I'm not surprised when my kids are demanding all the attention. How are you, Hannah?"

The warmth in her voice and expression chased away all concern that Leonie might blame Hannah for her son's black eyes. "I'm good."

"Are you?" Cassie peered at her, frowning. "You look like you haven't slept well for weeks."

"Cassie," Franklin protested.

"What? I haven't seen her for years, except on TV or in a newspaper article, and then she turns up with shadows under her eyes that almost rival yours, so yeah, I'm gonna ask questions." She faced Hannah. "Are you okay? Or is this just the aftereffects of dealing with my lame brain brother?"

"Hey, don't call me—"

"I honestly never meant that to happen," Hannah said to Mrs. James. "It was an accident—"

"As anyone with an ounce of commonsense could see," Cassie interrupted.

Hannah's nose wrinkled. "So you saw it then?"

"Saw it. Read the blog posts. Saw the memes. I didn't know there were so many people out to savage female reporters."

"It's the state of the world we live in," Leonie said. "People are so quick to blame, and find it hard to excuse."

"Which is why I thought it'd be good to have Hannah come and visit us here, and clear things up via another interview, that it might help change people's minds," Franklin said.

"That's what you thought, huh?" Cassie smirked.

Why were his cheeks turning pink? If Hannah didn't know better she might suspect he did remember what happened all those years ago, and that Cassie somehow knew.

"Well, I'm glad you're with us," Leonie said, "and I will gladly do all I can to show people you are welcome here anytime."

There it was again, that blessed sting of emotion she never liked to admit to. "Th-thank you."

"Aw, Mom, now you've made her cry."

"I'm not crying," Hannah said, blinking hard. "It's just really good to see you both again."

"It's been too long, hasn't it?" Leonie drew her to the pine table and chairs. "Now sit, I'm going to make us a cup of coffee, and we'll catch up and then figure out this interview."

"Yes, ma'am."

Leonie swatted her hair. "Don't you 'yes ma'am' me like I'm an old woman. Sit. Tell us all your news. You've had a bit going on in recent times, haven't you?"

So Hannah obeyed, and shared a little about her skating and how her injuries had drawn her to studies. "So that's why I'm doing what I'm doing."

"That must've been devastating," Cassie said, a wrinkle in her brow. "I remember how that was all you ever wanted, was all you ever talked about."

"Yeah, it wasn't fun." Her heart was tight. She didn't dare look at Franklin.

"I'm really sorry that happened to you." His deep voice plucked at her emotions again, forcing her to blink hard again.

"And you can be sure we'll do all we can to make this interview the best," Leonie assured her.

That's right. She was here to do an interview. Not get

stupidly emotional over things in her past that could never be changed. She sipped her coffee and pushed the mug away. The sooner they got this show on the road the better. Then she could leave.

"I know Poppy and Jess will be so bummed they missed seeing you," Cassie said.

"How are they?" She might be itching to start so she could escape but manners meant she should ask at least.

"They're doing well. Jess is in Red Deer doing a vet school internship, and Poppy is back working locally as a dance teacher after helping run a studio in Winnipeg," Leonie explained.

"Poppy is back, huh?" Franklin said.

"See? Lame brain. He's only been told a million times," Cassie said.

"Your brother has likely had his mind on other things," Leonie reproved.

"I bet," Cassie said, with another disconcerting smirk at Hannah.

It was now *really* time to start that interview. "Well, I know you're probably all busy, and I don't want to take up all your time—"

"We've got all the time in the world for you, Hannah dear," Leonie said.

"You're like family," Cassie assured her. "Really distant family, but you're still family."

Now she had to look away, and rub a hand over her eyes.

"Hannah? Are you okay?" Franklin asked.

Cassie hushed him with, "Hannah doesn't have much family."

She sucked in a deep breath and got her wobbly emotions under control. "My mom often seems more concerned about her college students than me, and Dad left when I was eleven, to start a new family. I haven't seen him again." She glanced at

Leonie, then at Cassie, but still couldn't meet Franklin in the eye. "I guess that's why I appreciated coming here. But hey, I really didn't mean to be emotional like this. Do you mind if we concentrate on the interview now?"

"Sure," Franklin said, his assurance echoed by Cassie a second later. Leonie patted her hand.

"Right." Hannah drew out her laptop, more because it gave her something to look at than because she needed the prompts she'd written down earlier. "So, you'd be happy to do something here, yes?"

The next minutes passed with planning out the style of interview and types of questions she could ask. They discussed and decided a "home on the range" focus would prove a nice point of contrast to the other more urban-based hockey players' families she'd be interviewing in upcoming episodes.

"How do you feel about horseback riding?" she asked him.

"I enjoy it."

"No, I mean you being filmed doing some in the interview."

"Sure." He grinned. "If you'll come horseback riding too."

"Me? I haven't ridden a horse since..."

"Since the last time you were here, right?" Cassie said.

"There just wasn't much opportunity," she mumbled, not looking at him.

"Well, you know what they say."

Her heart tensed. "What do they say?"

"It's just like riding a bike. You've got to get back in the saddle again."

Her gaze narrowed at him. "I don't think people are going to need to see me bouncing up and down on the back of a horse."

"Oh, yes, that'd be perfect." Cassie clapped her hands. "It'll make you relatable, and people will love seeing a glimpse of the ranch." She glanced at Franklin. "In fact, you should probably take her out to see the horses now."

"I really don't think that's necessary," Hannah protested.

"*I* really think it is. Besides, don't you want to figure out which film shots you could use? If not riding, then you should definitely take her on the ATV and see all the ranch."

"But—"

"You could go too," Leonie said to Cassie.

"I would, except I've got stuff to do here. And besides, I'm not the one Hannah is interviewing. She probably needs to spend more time with him than with me."

Franklin glanced at Hannah. "I'm game."

"Well, after you do that you could come back here and have lunch," Leonie said. "I know Derek will be back by then and he'd enjoy seeing you again, Hannah."

"He would?"

"I think Dad wants to know about Drew and Bob, and what they're like in real life," Cassie stage-whispered.

"Don't get me started," Hannah warned.

Leonie smiled. "Well, that sounds like that's settled. We'll eat around one, if that works for you. Derek will be back from the cattle sales then."

"Uh, sure." Hannah glanced at Cassie, swiftly moving from her smirk to Franklin.

"Shall we go?"

Why did those words uttered in that deep voice make it sound like a date? "Let me grab a jacket."

"HANNAH? ARE YOU READY YET?"

Franklin stared as Hannah exited the house and grinned.

Oh. His heart thudded as she tipped up the brim of the borrowed cowboy hat he thought belonged to Cassie. The hat completed the picture of Hannah as a cute cowgirl, with her tight jeans, cowboy boots, and plaid shirt.

"What's the matter?" she asked, her expression fading into uncertainty.

"Nothing." His voice sounded raspy. He cleared it. "Want to say hello to the horses first?"

"Sure."

He took her to the barn, and tried not to be enchanted by her enthusiasm, the way her face lit up as she patted Rex the Australian kelpie, and crooned to the horses, and said hello to old Daisy, whom she'd ridden the last time she was here.

"I can't believe she's still here," Hannah said, caressing Daisy's mane. "Do you think she remembers me?"

How could anyone forget Hannah? How had he? Now it seemed almost obvious, he could kick himself. But why hadn't she said anything that first time?

"Franklin?" Her head tilted.

"Uh, sure. Hey, do you want to go for a ride on horseback or on the ATV?"

Her nose wrinkled. "I feel like the ATV will be easier, and less work too, right?"

"Yeah." Truth be told he didn't mind missing out on getting a bruised backside either. "Come on."

Her long legs matched his stride as he took her to the section where his dad and Cassie stored the ranch equipment. "It's so good to be here again. I forgot just how pretty the scenery is, and then seeing the animals."

"It's like you can breathe better, right?"

"Exactly." Her eyes sparkled.

Except when he got on the ATV and she got on behind him and wrapped her arms around his waist, her curves pressed against his back, he might've forgotten how to breathe.

"We gonna go, cowboy?"

His fingers clenched. "Hold onto your hat, pilgrim."

Her laughter was drowned out by the engine as he gunned the machine, and she clutched him tight. He smiled as she squealed like a little kid as he drove down a gully then roared up the next slope. This was fun. He drove to the top of the hill which overlooked the ranch house and barn, as the Rockies gleamed in the distance.

"You want to have a go driving?" he asked, when he paused at the top of the hill.

"Sure."

They shifted positions, and he instructed her on what to do. And yes, he wasn't above putting his arms around her to show her exactly where to put her hands on the controls.

She wriggled, and he eased away. "It's not like I've never been on one before," she said.

"I remember."

She glanced back at him, her eyes wide, then her gaze slipped away to study the view. "You didn't say anything before."

"Because I wasn't sure until today. Then when you and Mom and Cass were talking I knew."

"Knew what?"

"Knew you were the blonde who got away."

He heard how her breath hitched. Had she heard that comment as holding more than regret? He didn't know what exactly he felt about her, except that with her he felt comfortable and at ease to be himself, and that there was a steady hum of attraction simmering between them, as tangible as the ATV they sat on.

His heart wavered, wondering what she'd say...

"Do you mean to make that sound like I escaped a serial killer?"

A spike of regret she'd resorted to humor was smothered by relief his words obviously hadn't gotten too deep to create an issue between them. "See? That's something else I remember."

"What?"

"Your wacky sense of humor."

She pushed him. "That's mean."

"And the violence," he said, chuckling. "I remember the violence." He patted his nose.

"That's a low blow. What happened to not talking about it anymore?"

"Hey, you were the one mentioning it to my mom. I don't know how many times now I've heard you apologize, and—"

"Franklin, shut up about it, please?"

He laughed again, then directed her to drive them to a nearby hill that overlooked the movie set. She killed the engine and they walked to another viewpoint that showed the movie set in all its glory.

A ragtag collection of houses and shop fronts lined a dusty street that looked like it had come straight from the 1800s. Because it had. Granted, some of the buildings, like the schoolhouse and the saloon, had been shipped in from other parts of Alberta, but the main parts of the town were all that remained of a tiny settlement that had existed here, before the hardships of the 1930s meant it became a place of ghosts and dust.

His great grandfather had extended the ranch in the fifties, swallowing the town as the ranch grew to become one of Alberta's largest, its ten thousand acres allowing for thousands of cattle and 360-degree vistas of the Rockies, prairies, woods, ponds, and creeks. When location scouts in the early 2000s had knocked on Mom and Dad's door, saying it was incredible to find a location without sight lines of any modern-day trappings, it had been an easy yes. That first historical film had led to a spin-off TV series, then another, then a Hollywood blockbuster that had really set the Three Creek Ranch on the map. Ranches needed to diversify or die. Cattle couldn't pay all the bills.

"It's awesome," she whispered. "I remember coming here with Cassie and being stunned to find people had their own town in their backyard. We lived in an apartment growing up and didn't have a single tree, let alone all this."

"It's pretty special."

He caught the wistfulness in her words, and again that surge of protectiveness came over him. He knew that Mom had already said it, but he hoped Hannah would take up the invitation to visit as much as she pleased. But would saying so take this relationship to a place he wasn't sure it should go?

"It's pretty cool," he said instead. "Lincoln Cash did a western here a year or two ago and said he loved the place."

"That's so awesome."

He nodded. Having a major Hollywood star rave about the Three Creek Ranch on social media had been the highlight of Cassie's year. "Cassie has been managing things here for my folks for a while now, so she's the one to talk to if you want to find out what's been going on with the movies and stuff."

"I've been such a bad friend to her," she murmured, her gaze on the buildings.

"She mentioned she'd fallen out of touch with you."

She shook her head. "It was me who stopped staying in contact. I got so focused on other things, and it just…happened."

"It does," he said, scuffing the ground with his boot.

He glanced at her, tracing her profile and comparing her to the girl who had stolen his heart long ago. Maybe his sister was right and he was a lame brain, because why else would he have failed to recognize her? Now, the longer he looked at her, the more apparent it was that she was the blonde from ten years ago, in that summer before life had picked him up and dropped him east. Back when he couldn't make promises, especially to a girl he barely knew. Did she remember holding hands with him on the river? How could he even ask that without sounding dumb?

"I'm glad you're reconnecting now" was safe to say. And true.

And judging from the way her eyes slanted back to his, she might feel the same way too. "Thank you for insisting I come."

"My pleasure," he said. And it was.

He held her gaze, smiling a little as pink danced along her

cheeks. And, judging from the way her blush deepened and she dropped her gaze, maybe she did remember a thing or two from when they were both teens.

"So, do you want to do some of the interview out here?" she asked.

He blinked at the sudden redirect, and shaded his eyes, pretending to look over the town as he worked to hide his disappointment. "Yeah, sure. Why not?"

His gaze fell on the church, and his skin prickled. He'd always been glad it wasn't just some put-together movie set, but had been a consecrated place of worship, where once upon a time people had been baptized, married, and buried. He still felt the place was filled with prayers, which was why it had proved the perfect place to recommit his heart to God several weeks ago. His commitment to doing things God's way, not his own anymore.

His heart twinged. What would God say about Franklin's feelings toward Hannah? Maybe it was too early for him to be thinking about chasing a woman, when truth be told, he wasn't sure where she stood in matters of faith. He'd done a lot of Bible reading lately, and stuff he'd read a dozen years ago seemed branded on his heart as much as the Lazy J on any nearby cow's backside: *Don't be yoked with an unbeliever.*

Man. He rubbed a hand through his hair. But doing things God's way meant more than a prayer in an aged chapel. It meant pushing past fickle emotions, meant seeking God's direction in this moment. He knew he had to ask her, even if it made him sound lame.

"Hey, um…" The rest of his words failed him as she glanced up at him and smiled.

"Hey, um, what, cowboy?"

Man, he was a sucker for her tease.

But the question of her faith niggled at him, the weight of it, the very momentous consequences of her answer, wrenched his words far away. How could he ask such a thing? *Lord, what do I say?*

"Has the cat got your tongue?"

More like the brunette reporter. Brunette. Not blonde. "Why did you dye your hair?" he blurted.

Gosh, he was smooth. Not.

"I beg your pardon?"

"You were blonde, right? I remember you that way," he added, when she looked at him with a tilted-head smile.

She opened her mouth as if to speak, then closed it, like she'd had second thoughts. Had she been about to ask him what else he remembered from years ago? Or was that his wishful thinking? She exhaled. "I knew that if I were to look like the Sidelines Barbie that CNSTV wanted, then I'd be pigeonholed as such forever. I didn't want to start off my career like that, so I dyed my hair."

His hand moved without permission and touched a curl. "So soft."

She stared up at him, her expression wondering, and he realized that such an action was hardly that of a man not wanting to lead a woman on. Especially one who was struggling to hear what God might be wanting him to say.

He swallowed, stepped away. Pointed to the other side of the hill where the Rockies gleamed with their ever-present cap of snow.

And suddenly the words were there. "Isn't that just beautiful? Don't you just love this world God has created?"

"Um, yeah. I guess. It can be really beautiful."

"Right? I look at the Rockies and just see proof of God's existence, don't you?"

She glanced up at him sideways.

He kept his face benign as he glanced at her then away. A man could get lost in those eyes, and having just come back to faith, he didn't want to lose his way again.

"Are you a Christian too?"

"Too?" he asked softly, heart drumming as he hoped against hope. Did that mean—?

She sighed. "Bree Vaughan was practically forcing it down my throat. And judging from the plaques around your mom's place, she still believes too."

"Does that mean you don't?"

She shrugged. "I don't know what I believe anymore."

Disappointment crowded his chest, so hard and sharp he found it hard to breathe.

He lifted his gaze to the hills. *Help, Lord.* A shaky exhale later he managed to turn the conversation with a fake surprised "look at the time. We'd better get back otherwise Mom will have my hide."

But questions about Hannah's faith niggled at him during lunch. Then continued as he didn't prolong conversation afterwards, simply agreeing when she said she needed to return to the city. She shook hands with his dad and hugged his mom and Cassie, but only gave him a nod.

"See you around, cowboy."

He fought the tension inside and shoved his hands into his pockets, wanting to seem normal, casual, so his family didn't suspect his feelings ran as deep as they did. "Probably when we do this interview on Wednesday next week, eh?"

"Um, right."

She thanked his mom and Cassie one more time, then got back in her little blue car, and he had to fight the urge to follow. He planted his booted feet more firmly as she drove away.

"You okay, son?" his mom asked.

"Sure thing," he said, as blithely as he could.

"She's pretty," his father said.

"But hurting," his mother murmured.

"You saw that too, huh?" Cassie wrapped an arm around him.

"What are you doing?" he asked her.

"Just giving my big brother a hug."

"Why?"

"Because I thought you might be needing one. Especially since, you know, you didn't get the hug you wanted."

His dad moved away, but not before Franklin caught the creases at his eyes that suggested he was hiding a grin. "You're annoying, you know that, don't you?" he said to Cassie.

"It's a good thing you're obliged to love me," she said.

Maybe this was why he enjoyed Hannah's tease. It reminded him of home.

"She's not ready for you, Franklin," his mom said.

"Excuse me?" He shrugged off Cassie's arm. "I don't know what you're thinking, but—"

"Oh puh-leeze." Cassie rolled her eyes. "How dumb do you think we are? It's always been obvious how you two feel about each other."

"I don't know what you mean," he said stiffly.

"Come on. You and Hannah had a thing for each other ten years ago. The only reason nothing happened was because you took off east. I've wondered sometimes if that's why she never called," she added softly.

"God needs to work in her some more," his mom said.

"I know."

His mom patted his arm. "Pray for her, Franklin. I've always liked the girl but I sense she's in for some more battles yet."

"I will. But just so you know, given the potential for conflict between her work and mine, I don't think anything could happen, even if I did want it to," he added for Cassie's benefit.

She shot him a look of scorn. "You're not fooling anyone by pretending you don't want something to happen."

"Let God have His way in her," his mom advised. "And guard your heart so you can be the friend she's going to need." She drew a thumb down Cassie's cheek. "And you do the same."

"Yes, Mom," Cassie said, before shooting him a cheeky look. "But I guess I won't be quite the same friend as Franklin would like to be, huh?"

"Have I ever told you that you're a brat?"

"Many, many times, brother dear," she said, scooting off out of arm's reach.

He glanced at his mom. "Don't worry. I'll guard my heart."

"I think you need to, although I fear poor Hannah doesn't know how to do the same."

He swallowed, then nodded. "I'll pray for her, but that's it. I promise."

"You don't need to promise anything to me," she said. "Just remember Who you're living for now, and do what pleases Him."

He drew in a deep breath and released it slowly. Guess this was what was meant by denying himself, picking up his cross and following his Savior. But his chest ached at the thought of those green eyes and those pink lips.

CHAPTER 6

"It's looking good, Hannah," Jason said, as he watched the rushes.

"I think we captured something of the behind-the-scenes world of Mike Vaughan." Flashes of past games were interspersed with to-camera moments when Mike and Bree talked both individually and together about hockey, family, his kids program in the Philippines, and more.

"I think you've got all the right elements."

One of the knots in her chest since Saturday's visit to the ranch eased. That visit had left her second-guessing so many things, not least of which was her ability to capture what fans really wanted to see.

"And your time with the little kids looked pretty fun." He glanced at her. "It should help your image."

She nodded, but his words had snuck inside. She didn't want to be the person always worried about her image, but how could she not be? Her job depended on it.

Jason nodded. "I'll get the team to splice and dice and we'll have it ready for tonight."

"Great."

She managed a smile and he left her to return to her desk and computer, where footage from yesterday's visit to Franklin's family ranch awaited attention. Her stomach tensed again.

That second visit had felt so different to Saturday's. Part of that was her focus on professionalism—she wasn't about to be led astray by emotions again. It had helped knowing Royce was there, recording everything, so nothing was allowed to creep into flirty land again.

She winced. How had she allowed herself to relax to that extent? She should've known better. Should have kept her guard up, but no. Franklin had to stare at her with those deep blue eyes. He had to smile at her, and hold her tight, and touch her hair, and say things like he remembered her, didn't he? She'd thought everything was going so well, then in a split second it had changed.

She shivered, stomach sick as she remembered feeling all too aware of the awkwardness that had chased the ease she'd felt with Franklin on the ATV. What had she said to make him draw back? For one moment she'd been sure he'd wanted to kiss her. The next, he was talking about God. God? She rolled her eyes, tapping her pencil on the desk. What did God have to do with anything?

Her phone buzzed with a message. She glanced at it. Bree was asking when the interview might be shown.

They said tonight, she typed back. The Vaughan interview was taking pride of place in a special news item before the station's flagship show, *Hockey Hour,* returned next week.

Excellent! Bree responded. *Don't forget the party next Wednesday.*

Looking forward to it.

She studied her phone, the swirling dots indicating Bree was still composing a message. Then the swirl disappeared.

She let out a frustrated breath. Glanced at the computer screen. The parts of Franklin's interview needed to be edited, and she wanted to make sure there was no footage of her looking enamored by a man who clearly wasn't enamored by her. Heaven forbid she looked like she had hearts-eyes going on, even though she was pretty sure that was what she'd displayed on Saturday. She groaned.

"Everything okay?" Dirk said, pausing by her desk.

She straightened. "Just fine."

He nodded, lingering, and she wondered what he wanted. It was rare for the program's executive producer to visit this part of the open-plan office. CNSTV's first female sports reporter certainly didn't have the luxury of a glassed-in office like Drew or Bob. "Jason mentioned he was pleased with the Vaughan interview."

He had? "I'm glad he liked it."

He pointed to her screen, which had stilled on an image of Franklin smiling at the camera. "The redo interview, huh?"

She nodded. "I'm planning to give this to Jason soon, then it's onto the next one."

"And who is that with?"

"I'll be talking with Kurt Matthews, the goalie, and hope to set up some more interviews when I attend a party at the Vaughans' next week."

"A party?" He frowned.

"Bree Vaughan invited me to film a preseason party with some of the players," she said quickly. *Film* sounded so much better than attend. "She thought it might be helpful to build connections." She shrugged. "I'm hoping it will help build their trust. She also has spoken about setting me up with a few other wives of NHL players, people like Detroit's Brent and Holly Karlsson, and Jai and Allie Mullins from San Jose. I hoped I could perhaps conduct interviews with them, too, which could prove a great way of building viewership, especially when we're talking about people of Brent's caliber and fame." The man had a dozen endorsements with everything from watches to sports drinks, and a rabid fan base. "Anyway, Bree has proved to be a useful contact."

"Sounds like it. Huh."

From the way he was studying her, she didn't know if he was pleased or not. "Sir? If I've done something wrong—"

"No, not at all. I guess I just didn't expect that you would build such rapport quite so quickly."

"I think they're glad to talk to a woman, especially someone who understands hockey."

"That's right. You played, didn't you?"

How could he have forgotten? She'd been sure her sports career had been instrumental in helping her get this job. Whatever. "Anyway, like I said, it's mostly Bree's doing." And from what Bree had said it was partly fueled by Hannah's mistreatment at the hands of others. But saying so might not prove wise. "I'm just grateful to have the doors opened for me."

He nodded. "I suspect those doors wouldn't have opened for Drew or Bob."

Her smile was tight. "I suspect you might be right."

"Hmm." He nodded again. "Well, keep up the good work."

"Thanks."

He moved away, and she slumped back in her desk chair, but not before she caught Drew's scowl from across the room where he waited to speak to Dirk.

She looked away, but casually, to not give the impression he intimidated her. She'd found the best way to deal with the unrelenting tension between Drew, Bob, and herself was by pretending they didn't exist. She suspected they felt and did the same concerning her.

Truth be told he did intimidate her, but she'd rather die than give that impression.

Her attention returned to the screen, to Franklin, to yesterday's interview.

It had gone well, mostly. Leonie and Derek had sat at the

kitchen table talking about Franklin's skills on ice from an early age. They'd shown photographs from when he was six, skating on a frozen pond at the ranch. Then pictures taken during Franklin's tween and teenage years, local clubs, as Leonie talked about taking him to events and balancing that with running a ranch.

Royce had captured footage of Franklin on a horse, the ATV, and more of his boyhood bedroom complete with old jerseys, trophies and medals. She'd barely needed to do a thing as she let his story do the telling for her. But she'd loved getting a peek inside the life of the boy who had become this man she now knew. Who he was today had been forged through the hard work and ethics of his family. And while part of her was tempted to cut the part where Derek and Leonie talked about faith, another part felt a tug to keep it in. Cutting out the expression of one's beliefs and how that had shaped and impacted a person felt as disingenuous as denying her right to sports reporting simply because she was a woman. So she kept it in.

She tapped her finger and the film stilled on another image of Franklin staring at the camera, a small smile on his face. She swallowed. He'd looked at her on top of that hill with that same expression on Saturday. Then yesterday, he'd been pleasant, but almost distant, with none of that warmth from Saturday. What had she done to turn him off?

"I DON'T KNOW what it is but something about this one feels a little off." Jason leaned back in his seat, studying the screen where Franklin's behind-the-scenes interview was paused. She'd given him the footage last Friday, and he'd messaged on the weekend to say he wanted to discuss it with her before Monday's production meeting, which was due to start shortly.

"I thought the ranch stuff would be interesting," she said, trying to tamp down the defensiveness begging to escape.

"No, that's a good spin, and definitely will be interesting—I don't think viewers expect to see too many cowboys who play in the NHL. No, it's just something else."

She tensed. Had something of her own personal feelings towards Franklin come across? She'd tried hard to keep it balanced, to appear engaged and interested and as perky as any celebrity interviewer, but still, there was always a risk she might have worn too much heart on her sleeve.

Jason clicked his fingers. "The part with the parents talking about church. It feels a little forced and makes the rest of it drag. You should cut it."

"But it's who they are."

He cut a look at her. "And you say that having known them for five minutes?"

"Actually, I've known the James family for ten years."

"What?" He sat upright. "And you set up this interview knowing that?"

"Well, yes. I didn't know I wasn't supposed to do something with people I know."

"It just puts a different spin on things, that's all. You can be accused of bias."

"Only if people know, which they don't. It's not like we've been really close that whole time. Truth is I've barely seen them in recent years." Regret panged. She should have made more of an effort, though. She cleared her throat. "Does this seem biased to you?"

"No. Actually it seems fairly well-balanced. Apart from the God stuff. You know we don't allow that kind of thing to air."

She pressed her lips together. The references to faith in Mike and Bree's interview had apparently been subtle enough to avoid being called into question. Christians often seemed to have a target on their back, which seemed unfair. "But don't you think that helps to give some understanding for why he's like he is today? He's known as one of the good guys of hockey, has never lost his temper, and I think a lot of that has to do with how he's been raised and what he believes."

His brow furrowed. "Are you and he a thing?"

She coughed, and did her best to appear incredulous as he raised his eyebrows. "Please. Do you remember this is the man I gave two black eyes?"

His lips twisted. "I do."

"Then you can rest assured he has zero interest in me."

"Uh-huh."

"And I have none in him," she fibbed.

He studied her seriously. "Because you know there mightn't be a clause in your contract forbidding such a thing—CNSTV probably haven't had to consider it until now—but it could be deemed a conflict of interest if there was."

"Well, there isn't."

"Just keep it that way, okay?"

"Why? What makes you even ask me that?"

"You seem a little too invested in this family."

"They're nice people, Jason."

"By all accounts so are Mike and Bree Vaughan, but I didn't see you looking quite so bright and sparkly with them."

"Bright and sparkly?" Uh-oh. How enamored had she appeared? "I was trying for perky and interested. Anyway, surely that's got to be better than being boring and critical."

"We definitely don't want boring around here."

She jumped, turning to see Will holding a folder. "I didn't hear you come in."

"We're getting ready for the production meeting. Are you two ready?"

"I am." She pushed back her chair. Glanced at Jason. "I think you should keep it in."

"Fine. But don't make a habit of it."

She nodded, and followed Will from the room.

"Don't make a habit of what?" Will asked.

"He thinks I'm letting personal things get in the way of real reporting. Which I'm not."

He shrugged. "The way I see it is the more personal the better. Feature interviews are about bringing color and filling in the details of people's lives. I don't think you can do it without getting personal."

"Thanks, Will."

He nodded, and opened the door to the conference room, then gestured her inside.

For once she didn't take umbrage, knowing if she did then she would have to accept the "one of the boys" treatment in other ways too. But it was a fine line balancing between expectations of how she should be treated. She just wanted to be respected.

Dirk took his seat, and was followed by Bob (on a phone call) and Drew, Jason, and others. Dirk clapped his hands which got Bob off his phone, and proceeded to tell people about the highs and lows of the week's broadcasts. "We're heating up now, especially as we head into preseason, which will mean needing everyone to pitch in." He glanced at Hannah. "That includes you."

Hannah nodded, conscious of Bob and Drew's sneers.

Perhaps Dirk was aware of their derision because he said, "It seems Hannah has been hitting it out of the park with her ability to get exclusive interviews."

"What interviews?" Bob asked.

"Exclusives with Detroit's Karlsson, and Jai Mullins from San Jose, is that right?" Dirk asked her.

She dipped her chin. "And possibly Dan Walton from Toronto, and some others too."

"Walton's married to that singer with a huge Instagram account, right?" Will asked.

"I believe so."

"Then we want that." Will tapped his folder. "I got the stats from last week's behind-the-scenes interview with the Vaughans. You got some nice numbers, Hannah. Good feedback in socials, too."

Dirk smiled. "I knew we were right to take you on."

It didn't seem the place to say thank you, especially with Bob scowling at her from across the table, so she did her best to look humble but pleased.

Dirk cleared his throat. "Okay, so what have you got for us?"

Bob and Drew talked about the start of their program, *Hockey Hour*, which was launching its new season on Friday night. Dirk nodded. "I think you should keep some room for another report from Hannah."

"Hannah?" Drew frowned. "What report?"

She glanced at him, then at Dirk. "Which report did you mean, sir?"

"How many reports have you got?" Bob asked.

"I'll have one about Franklin James," she said, catching Jason's nod, "and the preseason player party from this coming Wednesday."

"What party?" Bob asked.

She kept her face impassive. "The Vaughan welcome-to-the-team party."

"I've never heard of that."

"It's a new initiative."

"I think we'll definitely want both," Dirk said. "And because it's pre-preseason, there won't actually be much else to report on. The following week we'll have more content when we see tryouts and scrimmages and fan reactions, but for now, this will work well." He nodded. "Make it happen."

"Yes, sir," Drew said, exchanging a look of resignation with Bob, as Hannah fought to keep the smile from splitting her face. Things with Franklin might be confusing and in the friend zone, but Dirk's directions were clear enough. And now she couldn't wait for this party on Wednesday night.

"COME ON." Hannah beckoned to Royce as she smiled and introduced herself to Kurt Matthews, Calgary's mammoth-sized goalie. Music was pumping, competing with the shrieks and splashing from the pool area and a dozen conversations. It seemed many of Calgary's players were happy to gather again after the summer.

Everywhere she heard snippets of conversations, caught glimpses of strong men and tanned, toned women. It was a world she was familiar with, yet not. Here she was definitely seen as an outsider, none more so than by Alex Kapaulenyuk, who with his girlfriend Kristen, had refused to even look at her, let alone speak to her, pointedly ignoring her when she'd been within arm's reach.

Bree had seen and sympathized. "Don't worry about them. He's just sore you called him out on TV, and she doesn't like people thinking she's at fault for anything."

"I don't think any of us like that," Hannah had murmured.

She'd seen Franklin in the distance, but he'd always been surrounded by others, so she wasn't about to speak to him. Especially when she'd seen more than a few people look at her, then look at him, then grin. Calgary's other new recruit, Chad Pelley, whom everyone expected to be the third-line center, even had the nerve to ask her what Franklin had done to deserve a beating like that. She'd been trapped, not knowing what to say as all her words fled. Fortunately, he'd been distracted by a curvy blonde who Hannah hoped was his girl-friend. This team didn't need any more ructions between teammates.

"How are you doing?" Mike called across a group of women.

She shot him a grimace-smile and a thumbs-up, but really, she should've thought this through a little better. She hadn't counted on the noise and blur of bodies. What she really needed was a quiet space where she could ask questions and the players could be seen and heard properly.

"Hey!" Mike waved again, and pointed to the kitchen.

She nodded, and directed Royce to meet her there.

Mike offered her and Royce a drink. Royce refused, and Mike handed her a lemonade. "Sorry about all the noise. I don't think we expected to get this many people."

"No problem." She tilted her head. "Do you mind if we get you on camera now?"

"Sure."

"Okay." She glanced at the camera, nodded for Royce to film, then smiled back at Mike. "It must be exciting to see your team-mates after the summer break."

He grinned. "It's been great to catch up with guys I consider buddies."

"And how has the reception been to you taking on the team captain role?"

"Everyone has been great. It's gonna be an exciting year."

"Absolutely." She smiled, then glanced at the camera and sliced at her neck.

Royce lowered the camera. "That should be okay."

"Good. Hey, I was going to suggest if you want a quieter space to interview you could use the den," Mike said.

"Where is that?" He pointed to a room just off the dining area, and she saw it was the perfect space. Quiet, the plain cream wall would work well as a backdrop, preventing the visuals from being too busy. "Thank you. Now we just need to get the guys to talk to me." She grimaced. "I think some of them are worried I might give them the same welcome I first gave Franklin."

Mike laughed. "I got a solution for you then."

She followed him back to the living area where he whistled loudly. "Yo! Thanks everyone for coming, it's awesome to kick the new year off like this. Big kudos to Bree for all her hard work in pulling this together."

There was a round of applause and cheers.

"I wanted to say before we eat I need each of you to visit the den," Mike pointed to it, "and have a quick interview with Hannah here from CNSTV. Wave your hand, Hannah." She did. "Thirty seconds, that's all, and the best will make the cut. Speaking of cuts, I just talked with her and I did not get a bloody nose, and I guarantee you won't either, so do the team a favor and talk with Hannah. You know the fans love to see stuff like this. Also, if there's anyone else who is willing to do a behind-the-scenes interview with her please use this time to set that up with her too. And enjoy tonight!"

More cheers, and the earlier looks of wariness warmed to welcome.

Yes, she had to cope with some good-natured ribbing—she suspected Franklin had to cope with more—but it felt nice to be included, especially when she and Royce moved to the den and was able to ask the players about more than just the usual concerning vacation highlights and offseason training work-outs, and relate to it as well.

"Quad work is the pits, right?" she asked the goalie, her first interviewee.

Kurt nodded. "I forgot you played."

She willed her smile not to waver. "I played forward, so didn't ever have to do the insane training I've heard some goalies have to do."

"Like Beau Nash. That dude is incredible. I've seen some of his workouts that Montreal have posted, and it's like he's made of rubber."

"Gotta admit I don't miss insane workouts," she said with a grin.

"That's cruel, girl."

She laughed, he chuckled, and the next player came for his thirty seconds.

In fact, nearly all of the team obeyed their new captain, except for Alex who flat out refused, even when she saw Mike point in her direction.

Royce excused himself for a moment, and Hannah moved to the door of the den, peering out at the crowd in the living room. Bree came over, balancing little Ellison on her shoulder. "How is it going?"

"Great." Now. Thanks to Mike. "How are you doing?"

"It's going well. Ethan is playing in the sandbox under another parent's supervision, so I'm headed out there next. But I wanted to tell you that I tried reminding Kristen that it'd be good for her social following to do an interview, but she declined."

Hannah shrugged. "It's okay. I've got nearly everyone else."

"Who else hasn't done it?"

"Franklin, but he's been busy, and it's not like I haven't done an interview with him recently."

"Franklin!" Bree called.

His blond head swiveled, then his blue gaze slammed into Hannah's. She lifted her chin, ignoring the increase in her pulse. "Hey."

He smiled as he walked over to the den, but it lacked the warmth of that earlier visit to the ranch. "Hi Hannah."

She tried to speak, but the teasing "cowboy" comments of earlier wouldn't come.

"How have you been?" he asked politely.

"Fine, thank you." Ugh. The stiff formality felt like they were meeting for the first time.

"Is everything okay?" Bree asked, glancing between them as they moved to where Royce had returned and now watched them curiously.

"I'm good," Hannah assured, even while her heart questioned why he was being so awkward. She held up the mike and smiled. "So, Franklin, are you enjoying yourself tonight?"

"Yes."

"It must be nice to finally meet many of the guys you'll be playing with this year."

"Sure is."

Ugh. Could her question be more lame? Open-ended questions, that's what she needed. They'd never be able to use this. "So, um, what's been one of your favorite things about this summer?"

He glanced at her, then at the camera. "It's been great reconnecting with people."

She swallowed. Did he mean her?

"Like Mike," he continued.

She blinked, mentally staggering. "O-of course." She lowered the microphone, her smile. "Thanks, that should do."

He nodded, and moved away, but not before his lips twisted into an almost-smile.

"You good?" Royce asked her.

She nodded. "Yep. I think that's pretty much everyone." Everyone who wanted to be interviewed, anyway. "Feel free to grab some more shots of the party and outside, then grab something to eat. I'm just going to take a breather for a moment."

"Sure."

He left and she closed her eyes, replaying that last stilted interview on her mind. How had things grown so awkward between them? What could she do to repair things? She blew out a breath, her emotions suddenly wobbly. But no, she didn't have time to indulge in self-pity. She had to fake it until she made it, for a little longer at least. She had to—

"Well, well. Look what we have here."

She turned to see Alex eyeing her with a look she imagined

the Big Bad Wolf gave Grandma, and her heart tensed in fear. She pasted on a smile. "Ready to talk, Mr. Kapaulenyuk?"

"Oh, I'm ready. But not in front of your camera. Just to you."

"Okay." She willed steel to her spine. "What about?"

"About your self-righteous comments about me on TV, let's start with that."

FRANKLIN SERVED himself from the caterer-supplied salads, the array amazing and complete with little placards announcing the names and appropriateness for those who needed to be gluten- or allergy-aware.

He side-eyed the plate Kurt held, then realized that the goalie would forever be destined to eat more given his height and breadth was at least two inches more than Franklin.

"How you doing?" Kurt asked him.

"It's fun."

Kurt nodded, gestured to a stone table and bench near the pool unclaimed by anyone else. They were shaded by a large cream-colored umbrella.

Franklin dug in, the explosion of tangy deliciousness on his tongue nearly drawing a moan. "So good."

Two of the team's first line forwards, Tom Chavez and Jake Hooper, joined them, and conversation about vacations interspersed with comments on the general deliciousness of the food. Maybe the tease would stop and people could focus on the future instead of unfortunate accidents from the past.

"I see you found a few good places to eat," Kurt said.

"Huh?"

Kurt drew out his phone, tapped the screen a few times. "You and reporter girl." He nodded to inside. "You got a thing going on, huh?"

"Nope." Franklin shoved in an overlarge forkful of Caesar-dressing-drenched lettuce.

"She's cute."

"Yeah, but not really my type," Franklin said. She couldn't be, not when she wasn't a Christian.

Kurt laughed, and slugged down his drink. "Yeah, I guess a girl who clocks you in the nose like that would take some getting used to."

Franklin withheld a sigh. Would this ever go away?

A raised voice snagged his attention, and he glanced behind. Through the window he could see a shadowed someone—it looked like a woman—putting her arms out, as if trying to prevent someone from getting too close. He frowned.

"I said get away!"

He stood. He recognized that voice.

"What the—?"

Franklin ignored Kurt's question and muscled past people chatting in the door. Quick. Where—? A glance around. He couldn't see—

"Ah!"

He reached the door to the den at the same time as Mike, to see Hannah rubbing her knee, as Alex bent slightly, grimacing.

"What happened?" Mike demanded.

"Nothing," Alex wheezed. "We were just talking—"

"Is that right, Hannah?" Franklin asked, his attention sliding back to her.

She glanced at him, then at Alex, then back at Mike. "I think Alex has made it obvious he's not wanting to do an interview with me." She straightened. "Which is his right."

"I won't talk to anyone at CNSTV except Drew or Bob," Alex grouched, standing upright.

There was still something off in the dynamics here, but he guessed the way Hannah and Alex barely looked at each other, whatever had just happened was going to be off the record.

Alex muttered something to Mike that Franklin didn't hear, then left the room. Hannah's shoulders instantly eased down an inch. "Are you sure you're okay?" Mike asked her softly. "He didn't try anything?"

"Nothing I couldn't handle."

"So he did?" Franklin asked quickly.

"Nothing I couldn't handle," she repeated firmly, looking him in the eye.

He saw determination there, along with something else. Fear? "You know if someone tries to hurt you, there is no shame in admitting it."

"That's right," Mike said. "If a guy tries to threaten or intimidate you, then I want to know."

Her smile held no joy. "If you wanted to know every time a guy has ever threatened or tried to intimidate me, then you'd be here a long time. But hey, I appreciate the support."

His heart twisted. How many times had this happened to her? But then he remembered the disgusting things he'd seen posted online, calling for "the witch" to die.

"I'm really sorry you have to face stuff like that," he said.

She shrugged. "It goes with the territory. And that's the thing. You have to face it, face the bullies, otherwise you just end up having it beat you into submission, and put you back in the kitchen like some of these men seem to think women belong."

"Has someone said that to you?" Mike asked.

"It doesn't matter."

"So, someone did?" Franklin pushed.

"Look, we all know Bob is a dinosaur. It's not unexpected."

"He's probably threatened by you."

She rolled her eyes. "As if."

"Why wouldn't he be?" Franklin asked. "You're young, pretty, fun and funny, and you know your sports, you're everything he's wishing he could be."

He caught the way Mike glanced at him, then looked back at Hannah, who stared at him too. Wait. Was Hannah's ability to overshare contagious? What had he just said?

"You're still in here?" Royce appeared in the door with his camera. "I thought you were done."

"I am now." Hannah flashed a smile Franklin didn't buy. "Well, I think we have enough footage, so we'll get out of your hair so you can go do more team bonding things. Thanks again, Mike. I really appreciate you opening up this opportunity for me."

"You're welcome. Make sure you catch Bree before you leave."

"Sure." She nodded to Franklin. "See you around."

He only dipped his chin as she left with Royce, conscious of yet more weirdness floating between them. He didn't want to appear needy, but he still wasn't convinced by her denial from before. But it wasn't his right to appear overprotective. She wasn't his sister. And after being convicted of how he'd treated Hannah on her first visit to the ranch two Saturdays ago—or not-first visit, as it turned out—he hadn't wanted to raise hopes or speculation when there could be no future until he knew their faith aligned.

But still. It kinda hurt to have her glance away, having obviously read his earlier reserve correctly, something he longed to address. But how could he when it was obvious, for a multitude of reasons, that they couldn't be together?

He exhaled, glanced at Mike, and forced a smile. "A bit of extra drama I bet Bree didn't plan on."

"That's for sure." Mike's brow lowered. "Do you think Alex did try something and she's just covering it up?"

"Hard to say," he admitted. "But she's always appeared honest to me, so I don't think she'd have a problem admitting the truth if there really was something shady to be concerned about."

"We should keep an eye on him, anyway."

"For sure."

Mike nodded, studying him. "You like her, don't you?"

He shrugged. "I wouldn't say that." His heart pinged at the lie. But was it a lie when he knew saying it aloud would lead to all kinds of drama nobody needed? "Look, I don't know where she's at with God, so you don't need to worry. I know there's no future there."

"Have you talked with her about faith?"

"A little."

"Hmm." Mike glanced at him again then gestured to the door.

Franklin took the hint and exited the den with him.

"Keep praying for her. She's obviously got lots she's dealing with. You never know what God will use to break down someone's walls."

"Ain't that the truth?"

"Come on." Mike clapped a hand on his shoulder. "Let's get this party started."

CHAPTER 7

The TV flickered, and she swallowed her cold pizza, digesting trepidation as she waited for *Hockey Hour* to start. The past two days had been insane, working all hours of the day to get the interview and party scene prepped in time for tonight. But she'd managed it. Jason almost seemed pleased too, calling her work polished.

She thought back to Wednesday night, shivering at how Alex had spoken to her, tried to grab her before she'd kneed him, his vile threat which she'd tried to shrug off. But still couldn't. She might've become used to people making threats online, hiding behind their keyboards and screens, but rare was the time when she felt such hostility from someone face-to-face. And yet Alex had done that. Threatened her.

Her stomach heaved. Even Bob and Drew hadn't been quite so direct in their contempt. And even then, she could almost understand where they were coming from, feeling threatened by someone younger than them. But Alex's denial of all wrongdoing was a different beast, and while she was fairly confident he'd never actually carry out his threats, she also didn't want to go out of her way to provoke him. And yes, she might be an independent woman wanting to prove herself, but she had also been a smidge glad when Mike and Franklin had barged through that door.

Franklin's concern had been almost overwhelming, her relief at having people she felt were on her side chasing away the hurt from earlier when it appeared he wanted nothing to do with her. She couldn't figure him out. He'd been almost flirty at the ranch, then cold the next time she'd seen him there, then concerned, then distant. She couldn't get a read on him at all. Why act so concerned on Wednesday then not even say goodbye? Was he conscious of this strange, strained vibe between them, too?

She slumped in her sofa, the TV screen a blur. But for all his mixed signals and complexity, he'd then had the decency to send her a text yesterday to check she was okay. Which she'd replied to as blithely as she could. For how could she be seen to do her job if she caved at the first challenge?

Her phone flashed a message. She snatched it up. Read the name.

Cassie. Hey, Mom wanted to make sure the interview is tonight.

Sure is! She typed back.

A few seconds later: Cool.

Hannah sent back a smiley face, then glanced at the TV again. *Hockey Hour* was supposed to begin in ten minutes, and she was as eager as Cassie's family to see how her interviews came across. Not just how Drew and Bob spoke about it and her, but also how viewers responded. She wasn't sure it was a great idea to read her social media comments, but at least she'd have a gauge on how things were being perceived.

Her phone buzzed again. Bree. Party on tonight?

For a second she wondered if Bree had sent this to the wrong person. What party was Bree going to? Then it was clarified at the same time as her next message.

I meant is the party interview on tonight. Facepalm emoji.

Hannah smiled, and tapped back *Yes.*

Great! Next time I'll be more organized and you should come here and have a viewing party. If you want to. No pressure.

Her heart leaped at the offer. I'd love to. Because truth be told, it was a little lonely doing this. It would've been nice to watch this redo interview with someone.

The shrill tone of her phone drew attention. Cassie was calling? "Hello?"

"Hey, just me again. I'm in town and was wondering if you'd like some company."

How did she know that? "It's been a big week so I'm watching *Hockey Hour* at home, but if you want to call in that'd be awesome."

"Great! I'll be there soon. With food. Just remind me where you live again?"

She told her the address, cleaned up—put away the cardboard pizza box, anyway—and put her hair up in a messy ponytail. Cassie would understand the sweats and lack of makeup.

The apartment entry buzzed, and Cassie's voice came over the speaker. Hannah buzzed her in, taking a moment to glance around the room. It had been a busy week, and her washing remained to be put away. But she was too tired to bother. It wouldn't matter anyway. It wasn't like Cassie didn't wear bras too.

A knock came at the door. She opened it. "Cassie, hey. Oh!"

Her eyes widened as she took in the sight of Cassie's brother. "What are you doing here?" she blurted.

He held up a plastic bag that smelled like it held Chinese takeout. "Food delivery."

"Nice digs. Come on, the show's about to start," Cassie said, rushing past.

Leaving Hannah to stare at Franklin, conscious she certainly did not look her best self. She put a hand to her messy hair, then dropped it. All her words had fled.

"I, uh, don't have to stay if it's a problem."

She blinked. "Um, sorry. I just wasn't expecting you."

His mouth tweaked. "I'm getting that impression. Cassie called in at my place earlier, and then she wanted food, then she suggested coming here. But hey, I get that it's awkward, so I'll just leave this with you," he thrust the bag at her, "and—"

"No, it's fine." She ignored the bag, and stepped aside and gestured him inside. Then winced at the pink bra sitting on top of the laundry basket. She sidled past him and snatched it off, stuffing it inside the back pocket of her sweats.

A glance at him revealed his smothered smile. Darn. Maybe she hadn't been as quick as she should've been.

"Hope you don't mind," Cassie said. "But I've found some plates and utensils."

"Make yourself at home."

"I knew you'd say that. Okay if we eat in front of the TV?"

"Sure."

"Quick, it's about to start."

Hannah joined them in sharing the food then took a seat next to Cassie. The bunched-up bra in her pocket made it uncomfortable, so she took it out and tucked it down the side of the seat. She'd wash it again. Some day.

Familiar trumpet music from the TV accompanied an equally familiar red, gold and black logo as it swiveled through animated versions of a burning mask, flaming skates, and glowing hockey sticks before settling with a swoosh in front of the Saddledome.

She peeked at Franklin in the floral fabric armchair that used to belong to her grandma, and smothered her own smile. That was a look. His gaze was riveted on the TV, but he glanced at her, and she pivoted to focus on the TV again. Drew and Bob were at the glass desk, both of them slouched in their chairs, leaning to either side.

"Good evening, folks, yes we're back for the first *Hockey Hour* of the season, and it's safe to say we've missed you."

"And you've missed us, apparently," Bob said with his trademark smirk.

Cassie shouted, "No, we haven't."

Hannah chuckled, and choked on a dumpling.

"You okay there?" Franklin asked.

She nodded, sucking down water and clearing her throat. "I'm fine."

"Well, let's get into it," Drew said. "I think it's safe to say there have been some changes over the past few months while we've been away. In fact, I think there is no team who has had such a crazy offseason as Calgary, who lost two stars in Todd Devin and Bryan Jones, but added top-tier talent in Franklin James and Chad Pelley."

"Ooh, look who's top-tier talent, huh?" Cassie teased her brother.

He shrugged, but the upward quirk to his lip suggested he appreciated the praise.

"Add to this the captaincy drama, which saw Alex Kapaulenyuk relinquish the role to alternate captain Mike Vaughan, and we have a new leadership team in place which will make life interesting, if not challenging," Bob said.

"And it's not just the team who have had some challenges. You got sick there for a while, didn't you Bob?"

"Pneumonia isn't fun at my age," Bob said.

"It's not fun at any age, I imagine, but it meant poor Bob had to take some time off, which opened the door for the powers that be to take on a new reporter, and when I say new, I mean *really* new." Drew chuckled, as the shot pulled back to display a screen with a still of Hannah and Franklin's incident.

Hannah's gasp was smothered by her mouthful of fried rice.

"You've probably all seen this by now, huh?" Bob said.

"Old news," Cassie said, shaking her head. "I can't believe they're showing this still."

Hannah shrugged, working to appear unaffected, but she suspected she knew why. Any attempt to undermine her would be one they'd take, especially as they were the show's producers.

"That's right. Our very own Hannah Wade certainly made an impression a few weeks ago when she took on Calgary's latest recruit, Franklin James. And when I say take on, she certainly did that, didn't she Bob?"

Bob chuckled. "It's fair to say that's one first impression that's gonna be extremely hard to forget. But hey, we'll soon be back with more from Hannah so stick around and watch round two of Hannah taking on Franklin James."

"Ugh. Why'd they have to make it sound like that?" Cassie complained.

"Ratings," Hannah said, before scooping up some of the sticky chicken. "It serves their cause if I seem dumb."

"That's so wrong."

Warmth trickled through her at Franklin's deep voice. She pressed her lips together, refusing to look at him. Why on earth was he here? Especially today, on a day when she looked like such a mess?

The music and logo drew attention again, and Drew and Bob talked about the recent signings. "I really think James and Vaughan would be good together, and with the signing of Pelley we have a center for the third line that gives a solid one, two, three down the middle."

"He's a player who applies tremendous pressure on his opponents, so it'll be good to see him boost that line, which will help make this team better."

She nodded. Drew and Bob might be misogynists, but they did know their hockey.

They continued with more of their preseason commentary,

including speculation about the Flames and what Mike Vaughan's new captaincy would mean for the club.

"I mean, he's known as a stable defenseman, but will he be too steady?" Bob asked. "And one can't help but wonder what Alex is making of all of this, and how the off-ice dramas will affect his playing ability this year."

"A situation made more challenging with commentary from people who perhaps don't understand all the ins and outs of what it's like to play professionally," Drew said, before another clip of Hannah's own infamous comments was played.

She winced, sneaking another peek at Franklin who was glancing back at her with his own wrinkled nose. Did that mean he agreed with them? Or felt sorry for her? Either scenario was not really okay.

"Says the man who has never played a professional game of hockey in his life," Cassie complained. "Seriously, how long do we have to listen to him for?"

"Look, all I know is that we want to see hockey, not just hear other people's opinions on it," Bob said.

"Which describes you to a T," Cassie yelled.

"Sis, calm down—"

"It's okay," Hannah said, glancing at Franklin before placing a hand on her friend's arm. "Maybe you shouldn't watch this if it's going to get you upset."

"I don't understand how you can't be upset, when they're saying these kinds of things about you."

"They're just words," Hannah said. "It doesn't need to mean anything more than that."

"Words can still hurt, though," Franklin said quietly.

She pressed her lips together. Sure.

"Well, I'm not convinced you're getting a fair shot in their coverage so far," Cassie said, getting up as the program cut to a break. "But at least this chow mein is good."

"That's the important thing." Franklin rolled his eyes.

"So, tell me why you're both here again?" Hannah said, joining brother and sister at the dining table where the various containers of takeout were.

"Try that one, it's really good," Franklin said, gesturing to something with dark-sauced strips of meat and broccoli.

She dumped some on her plate as Cassie scooped up some fried rice.

"I was in the city already and took a chance my brother here might like some company," Cassie explained. "Then we obviously needed food and while we were out getting some I thought it would be fun to see what you're up to. It is okay for us to be here, isn't it?" Cassie checked.

"Sure. I was just surprised, that's all." She glanced at Franklin. "I'm surprised you didn't have plans."

He shrugged. "I'm making the most of downtime while I can. Once the season starts it's hard to get the chance to relax at home. I've never been too much of a partier."

"He's always been a homebody, this one," Cassie said.

Franklin shot her a mock glare. "You make me sound so lame."

"Only if you care what Hannah thinks of you," Cassie retorted.

Hannah turned back to her seat, not willing to risk another peek at the man. Cassie obviously didn't mind sharing her opinions. But did Hannah feature in his thoughts like he did hers?

The logo and music appeared and she settled back in her seat as Bob and Drew returned.

"Thanks to our sponsors. Okay, earlier we promised you round two of Hannah wading into Franklin James—"

"Ha ha."

"—and here we have a special report from her, direct from his family's ranch."

The screen cut to footage she'd worked so hard on, the shot of the drive to the ranch and her voice-over. "Many people know Franklin James as one of the NHL's strong defensemen, but some might not realize such strength has been honed over a lifetime of working with his family at their ranch right here in the foothills of the Rockies, just thirty minutes from Calgary."

The video switched to an aerial shot from the drone Royce had used that showed the ranch in all its loveliness, with its mix of hills, a pond and three creeks.

Then it cut to a picture of him, smiling at the camera.

"Ooh, it's you." Cassie pointed. "Oh, and me! Oh, and hi Mom," she waved at the screen.

Hannah's chuckle was echoed by Franklin's.

"The James family have ranched this property for over one hundred years and the same care that has seen this land flourish is evident in how Franklin approaches his game with hard work and integrity."

"Oh, someone has some nice things to say about you," Cassie teased her brother.

Hannah's cheeks heated. She refused to look at him, even though she felt his gaze swing her way again.

The interview continued, and just like the last dozen times she had watched it, she watched how the video morphed from him standing with his parents and sisters to the stables, an image of him riding his horse, and even a shot overlooking the western town. She drew back in her seat, watching it with a more analytical response, her senses attuned to each flicker of surprise or enjoyment from her guests. It must be funny watching the interview and seeing their lives on display like this. There was footage of her talking with Franklin, and just like she said in that earlier production meeting, it was amazing how much more could be edited when it wasn't live. She looked way more calm and poised than that first interview indicated. She peeked over at Franklin again, catching the tweak of his mouth that suggested he was enjoying this.

"And what do you credit as some of the keys for your success?" on-screen Hannah asked him.

He offered a humble half-shrug. "I don't know if success is the word you're looking for, but I definitely think my family and their values have helped me become the person I am today."

"We've always instilled in each of our children the values of faith, honesty, and hard work," Leonie said.

"And it's safe to say that this is one cowboy who will bring that notion of integrity and commitment to his game and the blue line here in Calgary," on-screen Hannah continued, as film played of Franklin's hits and defense plays. "Stay tuned, Cowtown. Franklin James is here to play."

Satisfaction steamed through her as the end reel played, before cutting back to the studio.

"That was excellent," Cassie said.

"Thanks, Hannah," Franklin said. "You made me look better than I am."

"She did, huh?" Cassie said with a smirk for Hannah.

"Well, that was certainly an eyeopener about our new recruit," Drew said from the studio.

"Sounds like someone has lassoed our reporter, huh? I wonder if each player will get the gold-star treatment," Bob said snidely.

"Hey, it had to improve, right? She could scarcely have been as bad as the first time," Drew said.

Hannah's jaw clenched, and she glanced at her phone. Notifications and messages were popping up, she was glad she'd kept it on silent.

NICE INTERVIEW! Bree.

THANK YOU, HANNAH. THAT WAS LOVELY. Cassie's mom.

A couple of taps on the screen confirmed that her social media was blowing up. She read a few comments.

He seems so nice!

Franklin sure puts the hot into Flames.

What? No headbutts? Disappointed.

Bob's right. She obviously has a thing for him.

I bet they're sleeping together.

She's so fat and ugly.

Her heart shriveled, and she put away her phone.

"You okay?" Cassie asked, peering at her.

"Um, sure."

Cassie's gaze trickled to her phone then back. "What are people saying?"

"Nothing much. They liked it." Most seemed to. She hoped.

"Uh-huh." Cassie took out her own phone, and a few taps later, was staring at the screen, her forehead wreathed in wrinkles. "Man."

"What?" Franklin asked, pulling out his own phone.

"No, don't you look," his sister said. "I mean it. It'll just get you mad."

"Whoa." He straightened in his seat. "You can't say something like that and not expect a man to look. What have people said?"

Cassie exhaled. "Dumb things. Which is why you shouldn't look. And that goes for you too, Hannah. Your interview was good, in fact your interview was *great*. You showcased the ranch so beautifully. And my brother should get you to do all his PR. Honestly, you made him appear so much nicer than he really is in person."

Hannah chuckled despite herself. "I could only work with the material I was given."

"And put a shiny spin on everything," Cassie said winking. "It's okay. I know how you really feel."

Whoa. She did *not* just say that. "Cass—"

"Hey, look, it's an ad for the dealership where I got my car," Franklin said.

She glanced at him, meeting his gaze and mouthed a "thank you" for the change in topic.

He nodded and she dragged her gaze away, tempted to look at her phone again but knowing it probably wasn't wise.

"I don't know how you thought you could manage watching this by yourself," Cassie said in a soft voice. "People can be brutal."

"People are entitled to their own opinions," Hannah said.

"But not when their opinions are based on a lie," Cassie objected.

The advertising ceased and it was back to Drew and Bob, who began their summary of other teams and offseason gossip. Hannah listened without paying much attention, her heart still stinging at some of what she had read online. Why did people care more about what she wore than what she said? How could people assume the worst, or wish her ill? All she could do was her best, and if some people didn't like that or misinterpreted or misunderstood then that was okay. It said more about them than it did about her.

But while logical she might know that, it didn't change the prickle within. She'd been wrong before. It might just be words, it might just be people's opinions, but they actually did hurt her. And she knew she should be bigger than this. She *knew* that. But despite her best efforts it felt like a sliver of poison had crept past her defenses and got to her heart. A moment of discouragement washed through her quickly followed by the thought she should just give up.

She blinked. No. This was what she wanted to do. What she felt born to do. If she couldn't play hockey herself then this was the next best thing. And she wasn't going to let a few anonymous keyboard warriors stop her from doing what she knew she could do well.

"You okay, Hannah?" Franklin asked.

She nodded, gratitude at his thoughtfulness curling fresh warmth through her heart. "I'm going to have to get better at managing my expectations of others," she admitted. "I was used to seeing people's comments about how I played but this is next-level. And while I think it's still important to be aware of what the general public thinks, it's also apparent that I need to put some filters on my social media to weed out those who have a vendetta against me."

"People can be dumb, eh?"

"So dumb," Cassie agreed.

"But not everyone," Hannah clarified. "Just a tiny fraction."

"But unfortunately it only takes a few germs to infect a lot of others," Cassie continued.

Which left Hannah wondering what the general public opinion would ultimately be.

Another break for commercials was followed by Drew and Bob's last segment.

"So, we mentioned before that Mike is now the captain of Calgary and we see that he is wanting to shake things up a little," Drew stated. "It may surprise some to know that even though preseason is about to start he was recently hosting a party for the team at his house."

"And a very nice house it is too," said Bob. "Not that I'd know."

"But Hannah Wade managed to score an invite," Drew said, "Here she is at Mike Vaughan's house with some interviews with members of the team for your summer recaps. Have a listen."

Hannah watched herself grin at the camera. "I'm here at the house of Calgary's new captain Mike Vaughan and his wife Bree, and we're talking with the players about their summer highlights and hopes for the season ahead." The shot cut to a series of her interviews with Mike, Kurt, and top forward Tom Chavez.

Again, she watched it critically, looking to see what she could've done better, gauging the response of Cassie and Franklin as they watched too. Cassie wore a big smile whereas

Franklin seemed more contemplative, or at least that's what the crease in his brow suggested.

"And Franklin," on-screen Hannah asked, "what are you looking forward to?"

His answer felt as cold as on Wednesday night. Her stomach swooped at the contrast between that snippet of interview with him and what had happened just minutes later at the party. She glanced at him, saw him looking back and she pivoted away.

Bob smirked from the screen. "Rumor has it that not everyone was happy to talk with Hannah. In fact, she was seen exchanging harsh words with Alex, who probably didn't like being called out on TV without the chance to defend himself. Which is why we thought the fans might like to hear from the man himself."

What?

The camera angled back to show there was now another person seated at the desk.

Drew grinned. "Let's welcome Alex Kapaulenyuk. Thanks for joining us tonight."

"Pleasure," Alex said.

"What on earth?" Cassie said. She swiveled a look at Hannah. "Did you know about this?"

"Of course she didn't," Franklin said. "Look at her face."

She instantly blanked her expression but obviously it was too late. She collected her phone and saw that Jason had left a message for her to call him. She would, as soon as she listened to whatever it was that Alex was about to say.

"—hard when people deliberately misunderstand and are not privy to all the facts," Alex said. "And yeah, I admit I made mistakes, but I don't think it's fair to have complete strangers passing judgment when they know nothing about me all my life. So yeah, it's been hard to deal with a private matter in such a public way."

"I can't believe this," Cassie said, fuming. "How dare he try to blame you."

Hannah refused to look at Franklin, even though she could sense his concern for her. Her phone buzzed again, as the interview continued. Another message from Jason. *Call me ASAP.*

She sighed.

"What is it?" Franklin asked.

"I have to make a phone call."

"Want us to leave?" Cassie asked.

"No, you can stay. I'll just go to my bedroom."

"We'll clean up," Franklin promised, moving to collect the sauce-smeared plates.

She nodded and moved to her room where she shut the door and answered the now-ringing phone. "You saw that?"

"I just got off the phone with Dirk. He wasn't made aware that Drew and Bob would be approaching things in this way," Jason said. "I think it's fair to say that they will not be in the good books and you might do well to consider how you want to respond."

"Respond to what? Sorry, but I've gotten used to Drew and Bob sneering at me."

"But the station can't be seen to be having this divide between its reporters and I think Dirk will have a few things to say about that. Man." Jason swore. "I can't believe they got Alex on. It's like they're setting themselves up against you."

"Welcome to my world."

He sighed. "I'm sorry. I don't know what to say except I am not okay with this and I want you to know that I'm on your side."

Her eyes blurred. "Thanks, Jason. That means a lot."

"Don't mention it."

"I didn't think you liked me much," she admitted.

"You didn't exactly give the best first impression in that first interview, but what I'm seeing now is what people have been asking for. It'll be interesting to see what the viewers say."

"Yeah, not all of that is good," she admitted.

"Don't read it," he advised. "We've got people who can take care of that for you, so for now turn off your comments and delete the apps off your phone if you need to. We'll talk more about this on Monday, okay?"

"Okay," she promised.

The call ended, and she stared at her phone, before she slowly disabled the comments and put her phone on her bedside table.

But her heart felt tipsy. She wasn't okay. Not really.

"Do you think we need to go and see if she's okay?" Cassie asked Franklin as *Hockey Hour*'s closing music filtered through to the kitchen as they cleaned up.

He shook his head, even as he wondered the same. Hannah had been in there a long time.

"At least your interview was good," his sister continued. "Well, the first one, anyway. At the ranch. You seemed pretty distant in the second."

He bent to place more plates in the dishwasher, glad for the excuse so she couldn't see his face.

"What was that about?" Cassie pressed, her voice hushed.

He shrugged. He barely knew himself, but now, having glimpsed something of how hard Hannah had worked just to see it tossed aside in mean-spirited comments, he felt renewed regret for not trying harder. No, he didn't want to make things difficult for her, which is why he'd done his best to not make it look like they were an item. Heaven forbid he do something that might stir up her feelings. But neither did he want it to seem like she'd done something wrong, which is maybe how some people might perceive this. He stifled a groan.

"What?" his sister hissed.

"Just leave it, okay?"

"Have you done something shady?"

"No!" Man. "Why do you have to get in my face all the time?"

"Because I'm your sister. And I love you."

He grimaced, and she laughed.

"And I know you love me too, deep, deep within your heart," she continued.

He exhaled loudly. "Fine. Yes. Deep down. And maybe a little higher up, too," he added, holding his fingers a half inch apart.

Her chuckle broke off as movement drew their attention to where Hannah stood near the dining table. Her face was pale, her smile tight, like it was glued on.

"Everything okay?" he asked.

She shrugged. "It will be."

But the way she didn't meet his eyes suggested it wasn't really.

"Sorry about that." She moved to the coffee table. "Oh, you cleared up already."

"We loaded the dishwasher with what we could find," he said.

"Thank you."

"Hey, you didn't expect us to show up uninvited, invade your house, make a mess, and leave, did you?" Cassie asked.

"Well…" The lift to Hannah's mouth held tease.

He dropped his gaze. He really shouldn't be focused on her lips.

"Who was that on the phone?"

Trust his sister to be direct. But he was thankful, as he wanted to know too. Maybe he'd misread everything and she already had a boyfriend. That Royce guy had seemed interested…

"Just someone from work."

His chest tightened. Royce?

"What did they want?"

Hannah shrugged. "They wanted me to know I might need to expect some fireworks in the meeting on Monday."

"But you were great," Cassie protested.

Hannah's nod showed more of the confidence he'd come to know. "Apparently some people weren't happy with how Bob and Drew spoke about me. But hey, we'll see. A lot can change over the weekend."

"Well, I think anyone who doesn't appreciate you and see the excellent work you are doing should be ashamed of themselves." Cassie opened her arms. "Come here."

She hugged Hannah, and he turned away, unable to ignore a savage internal tug that wanted to give Hannah a hug too. This was messed up, this trying to keep emotionally distant while his heart and senses hungered to be close. He pretended to wipe down the counter, giving them privacy.

"Thanks." Hannah's voice sounded wobbly. "I think I'm just really tired, and it's not exactly been the reaction I was hoping for."

"Hey, it's going to get better," Cassie soothed. "I'll be praying for you."

Franklin's head whipped back to watch Hannah's reaction. What would she say to that?

Hannah blinked, then glanced down. "Th-thanks."

Hmm. Not a dismissal. Maybe there was hope. She had believed in God before, hadn't she?

"Hey, do you want to come to church with me on Sunday?"

Huh? Cassie was supposed to attend church with him on Sunday instead of her usual church. He'd arranged a return visit to Mike and Bree's church after enjoying the service there last weekend.

Hannah shook her head. "Thanks, but I have plans."

Disappointment flickered within, despite himself.

"Okay, maybe next time," Cassie said easily. "And just you wait and see. God's got good plans for you, and He wouldn't have brought you into this role without it being important and lasting more than a few weeks."

His sister's words evidently bolstered Hannah's spirits as her chin lifted. "Thanks, I needed that reminder." Her gaze finally met his, and her smile was small but seemed more assured. Then her attention returned to his sister. "Thanks for coming. I didn't realize how much I'd need a friendly face tonight."

"Any time," Cassie promised. "And if I can't come, then you can always ask this dude here." She slapped him on the arm.

He coughed. "Uh, sure. Except with the season starting," and his desire to not stir up speculation—in Hannah or anyone else, "it'll be pretty busy soon."

"It's okay." Hannah's face drained of animation. "I don't want to be accused of nepotism or unprofessionalism, which is what will happen if I'm seen with you. There's enough of that floating around at the moment, anyway."

He dipped his chin, conscious of the way Cassie glanced between them, and straightened his shoulders. "Yeah, it's probably best if we don't talk to each other or look like we're friends."

She blinked, as if his words struck hard, but then her chin tilted. "Exactly."

Huh. So his words hadn't bothered her as much as they had him. But how could he say he wanted to be friends—more—without it getting tricky? And no way could he say anything like that in front of his sister. "Okay, I gotta go. Thanks for tonight." He moved to the door, held it open as Cassie gave Hannah one last hug.

"Praying for you," Cassie reminded her.

Hannah nodded. "I appreciate it."

When it was apparent she wasn't going to meet his gaze he

muttered a "bye" and closed the door, refusing to look back as he and Cassie descended the apartment block's stairs, nodding to a sharp-featured gray-haired woman instead.

His heart churned. Did she mean that about appreciating Cassie's offer to pray? What would that mean for the possibility of a future? But how could he even consider anything about a future now they had both agreed to keep their friendship strictly professional? It wasn't what he'd meant, but his tongue was tied, along with his hands. For how could anything happen if she didn't want to be accused of favoritism and seemed determined to keep him at arm's length?

CHAPTER 8

"I hear someone's not happy," Mandi said as Hannah passed her in the hall on Monday morning.

Hannah's feet paused. Gossip wasn't her thing, but neither was walking into a scenario without being prepared. Jason had cautioned her already, but maybe there was more. Forewarned was forearmed, after all. "What have you heard?"

"Dirk is apparently not impressed with the smear campaign from Bob and Drew on the weekend."

"I wasn't impressed either," she said dryly.

Mandi nodded. "Don't take it personally. Change is hard, especially for those who feel entitled. Just hold your ground, act classy, but don't take no bulldust from nobody. Remember, they need you." She squeezed Hannah's arm. "You've got this, girl."

"Thanks, Mandi." Her chin lifted. "I believe I do."

Mandi's chuckle followed her as she made her way to the conference room. Sure, it might be partly bravado, but Mandi had basically echoed everything her agent had said to her on Saturday. Lisa had been as shocked as Hannah about Bob and Drew's unprofessional behavior, but reminded her that it was in

CNSTV's best interest to deal with this. "For they aren't going to keep paying someone who they don't use."

Fear had arrowed through her. "You think they want to sack me?"

"They can't. We have an ironclad contract that will not allow that to happen. I think it far more likely they are going to be displeased with Bob and Drew and demand an apology from them at the least. If we play our cards right, we might even get more. Leave it with me."

The rest of the weekend had passed in cleaning and washing —including that pink bra—and wondering whether she should take up Cassie's invitation to church, before figuring it would only fuel rumors about Franklin if she was seen with him there. So instead she'd stayed home, binged hockey games on TV as she read online reports about other hockey teams and took notes, and tried to not wonder just what Lisa had in store. Her agent had connections with a multitude of female athletes, and her bulldog tenacity got results. Mom might teach about women's rights at university, but Lisa fought for them.

Disappointment panged at her mom's failure to return Hannah's call on Saturday. You'd think a mother might take time out for her only child but no. Not this one. The sting was less sharp these days, as history had taught her who her mother valued. At least some people had her back. Lisa, Cassie, Bree, who had messaged her over the weekend to see how she was doing. Gratitude warmed her chest again as she swung around the corner and entered the office space, beyond which lay the glass-walled conference room.

"Hey Hannah." Royce lifted a hand, offering her a doughnut from the box on his desk.

"Thanks, but—" She hesitated, her refusal paused on her tongue. If she truly wanted to be part of things here, then she needed to make an effort to not reject the overtures of friend-ship. And the situation with Royce had been mixed to say the least. She sensed he hadn't initially liked her, thought she was dumb, so his offer of a doughnut felt like a peace offering of sorts. "I shouldn't, but today I'm sensing I'll need all the sugar and fat I can get."

"Not too much," he warned. "The camera adds ten pounds."

She ignored the offense. It was true, after all. "I'll bring the doughnuts next week, huh?"

"Uh, sure."

She thanked him, ate it quickly—funny how it proved an instant mood lift—then wiped her hands carefully on a tissue snatched from her desk.

"Hannah?" Jason clicked his fingers from the door to the conference room.

"Coming." She grabbed her phone, laptop, notepad and pen and weaved between desks as she moved to join the others. Around her, she was conscious of people glancing away, refusing to meet her eyes, which redoubled the trepidation. Which was stupid. She shouldn't be the one in trouble here, and she wouldn't be made to feel like it.

She nodded to a production assistant. "Hey John."

He coughed. "Hannah."

She paused at his desk. "You redid this year's graphics on *Hockey Hour*, didn't you?"

"Yeah. Why?"

She shrugged. "Looks sharp. Nice job."

"Okay. Uh, thanks."

Hannah nodded, not smiling lest she come across like a brownnoser when she truly did mean it, and strode into the room.

She nodded to Jason who pointed to a seat next to him, which she took, taking care to seat herself before she glanced across the table. Her chest knotted. Seriously? He'd wanted her across the table from Dirk?

She managed a small smile for her boss then sat straight in

her chair as Bob and Drew wandered in. Last, as usual. She clenched her hands as fire rose within. How dare these two men treat her in such a way?

She sucked in a deep breath, ready to let rip when Jason murmured, "Hold it. Let Dirk speak first."

Hannah nodded, pouring a glass of water with an unsteady hand so some of it sloshed onto the table. She caught Dirk's frown as his gaze dropped to the puddle, and her agitation rose more. What was going to happen?

Dirk rapped the table, which prompted Bob to sit down quickly. She glanced at Bob and Drew, keeping her face expressionless. They both looked away.

"This meeting is something I never thought I'd have to do," Dirk said, his voice tight. "In all my years of producing television, I have never seen anything so arrogant as that performance on Friday night." He stared at Bob and Drew. "I want—I need—an explanation. Now."

Hannah kept herself still as the two men glanced at each other, shifting in their seats as if uncomfortable. It didn't sound like Dirk was playing nice today.

"I'm sorry, boss," Drew began. "But I'm not sure what you—"

"Don't give me that—" Dirk described Drew's failure to understand in a pithy way she'd heard more than once on the ice. "We hold these meetings for a reason. To give direction and bring accountability and make sure everyone is on the same page. So what were you thinking by getting Alex on the program? It was too much. Instead of a big-ticket item like the Franklin James interview, it got diluted by the Alex drama, so everyone was talking about that instead of Franklin. Calgary isn't happy."

"But sir, the opportunity came up—" Drew began.

"I know exactly how it came up. You and he are friends, he had a gripe with Hannah, and you accommodated that for your own selfish interests." Dirk's gaze could sharpen skate blades.

"Never have I seen such unprofessional behavior, treating a colleague like that." He pointed a finger at Hannah. "The way you spoke about her, belittling and laughing about her, was the height of unprofessionalism, and not something we condone in this place. I would normally deal with this far more privately, but you made a public spectacle of Hannah, and this station, which is why I'm discussing this in this manner here now."

Hannah's cheeks grew hot, but she remained motionless, her eyes lowering from Dirk's red face to the water jug on the table. She didn't want to—couldn't—appear weak or needy in this moment, so wouldn't give anyone the satisfaction of seeing how much she'd been hurt by these two men.

Dirk continued with his damning assessment of the character of the two sports anchors, before saying, "You owe her an apology."

Two mumbled apologies followed. She nodded, but still refused to look at them, keeping herself rigid.

"I've had some people calling for you both to be sacked—"

"What?"

"Don't interrupt me, Bob," Dirk put up his hand. "I'm so angry I've been looking at your contract this morning."

"Sir, I agree we pushed things a little far—" Drew began.

"A little?" Jason muttered.

"But it was just harmless banter, like what any guy might hear in a million locker rooms around the world," Drew continued, as if emphasizing her deficiencies because she lacked a Y chromosome. "Nobody meant anything by it."

"Yeah, we're sorry if your feelings got hurt," Bob said to her, in a voice that sounded anything but apologetic.

Way to go with an honest apology. Finally she looked at him. Then looked at Dirk. "May I say something, sir?"

"Please." He sat back and gestured for her to go on.

She turned and faced Bob and Drew more directly. "My feelings were not hurt," she said slowly, the tightness in her chest leaching out in her voice. "What got hurt was this station's reputation in your attempt to be funny. I don't care if you don't like me, but I do care when you seem to be making deliberate attempts to make me look foolish, like I should not be part of this team. Because that speaks about the management of this station, and you're basically suggesting they don't know what they're doing in hiring me. Did you mean to make it sound like the station's management is incompetent?"

Jason cleared his throat.

Had she pushed it too far? She didn't want to get Dirk offside, even if what she said was basically what he'd said too. "Now I don't make a point of having more experience than you in playing high-level sports—"

Bob blew out a noisy breath.

"—and I thought my recent efforts should at least have earned a small measure of respect. But the way you belittle me, it's like I've done something to make you dislike me." She paused, conscious that last statement could sail past without landing. "Have I done something to make you dislike me?"

Drew's jaw clenched, as Bob glanced away.

"Apart from being a woman, that is?"

"Well?" Dirk pressed, when it seemed neither man was going to answer. "Has Hannah done something to tick off either of you?"

"No," Drew muttered.

"No, sir," Bob said.

"You should be addressing that to Hannah," Dirk instructed.

They turned and repeated the same to her this time. She fought an inclination to roll her eyes.

Dirk sat back in his seat, then tilted his head at the man seated next to him who had been taking notes throughout the meeting. "Most of you know Peter Wills from HR. While Hannah has not made a formal complaint about your behavior I have instructed him that this will be recorded in your files, and if ever such a thing happens again it may be used against you."

"But sir, our contract—"

"Right now I have little desire to hear what you have to say, Bob. You are on thin ice as far as I'm concerned. Let's not forget your contract is up for renewal next year."

Drew's mouth sagged. "But *Hockey Hour* is what makes this station."

"And that's exactly why I am so incredibly angry right now. It should be about hockey and you made it about Hannah, and further exposed the frailties of this station for all the world to see."

"All the world?" Bob scoffed.

"Will?" Dirk gestured for the media manager to speak.

Will Sanchez straightened a stack of papers. "The story got picked up on networks across North America, Australia, the UK, Germany. There's a lot of comments about how Hannah was mistreated, that certain people should be fired."

There was?

Will glanced at her, as if sensing her surprise. "On the flip side, there was a lot of support for you, the interview with Franklin saw a ratings peak—"

Her shoulders eased as she permitted a small smile.

"—and people want to see more of you."

Her eyebrows rose, but she pressed her lips together, conscious any look of joy would be taken as a threat by the two older men at the end of the table.

"You probably didn't know that if you avoided social media like I told you to," Jason murmured.

She dipped her chin. That explained it. Maybe all wasn't lost after all.

"The upshot is, viewers want more Hannah," Will concluded, glancing back at Dirk.

Dirk nodded, like they had rehearsed this. Hannah's palms grew clammy as she wondered what would come next.

"Which is why we have decided to do things a little differently." Dirk pushed back in his seat, his gaze falling on Hannah once again.

Her skin prickled. What was going to happen now?

"After some lengthy discussions, we have decided that Hannah will be the one to do some of the in-game reporting—"

Her heart leaped. Was Dirk saying what she thought he was?

"—and conduct the player interviews, both between periods and postgame—"

"What?" Bob's shriek could summon dogs.

"—as well as filling in as studio host when the team plays away." Dirk glanced at her. "I'm assured you would be up for the role."

By whom? Lisa?

"Say yes," Jason murmured.

She closed her mouth. Nodded. "Yes, sir."

"But sir—"

She swallowed a spike of amusement at Drew's addressing him as sir, not Dirk.

"—she's so new," Drew protested.

"*Hockey Hour* is live, and we all saw how she messed that up before," Bob complained.

"Hannah will prove to be a breath of fresh air," Dirk said. "And I've been watching how she carries herself. She's not afraid to offer her opinion, and I think the program will benefit from that. Especially considering we have sponsors wanting to pull their support unless the misogyny stops."

"It's what viewers want," Will said.

"And sponsors," Jason added.

"What gives you the right to say anything?" Drew snapped.

Jason stretched out his hands with a click, click, and he looked at Dirk.

Dirk's fist thudded on the table. "The fact that Jason will be your new program producer."

"What?"

"Obviously you and Bob can't be trusted to not bully your way into doing your own thing, so we need someone who can be trusted to do what's right for the program."

"I can't believe it," Drew muttered.

"You better start," Dirk said. "Jason, when is your first meeting?"

"Right after this one." He glanced at Hannah. "You better come too."

"Sure."

"Right." Dirk exhaled. "Well, that's done. This is not how I planned for things to progress, but I will not have the station's reputation shredded because two men can't keep their opinions about women to themselves. Hannah? Before you go to Jason's meeting I need to speak to you privately." He glanced at Peter. "You better come too. The rest of you, get on with it. And do all you can to mitigate the mess these two have made."

Hannah collected her things and followed, then spent another fifteen minutes listening to Dirk's own apologies for letting things get out of control, before checking with her that she would be ready and willing to take on these new assignments. She agreed, signed new papers with Peter, and returned to her desk, this time catching a few more nods and glances as if others were pleased for her.

Then she remembered she had a new meeting to attend. She tilted her chin and moved to where Jason beckoned. It still seemed unbelievable, but it appeared redemption had arrived. Maybe God had answered Cassie's prayers after all. And maybe, just maybe, He still cared a little about Hannah, too.

~

"You look less like a panda these days, dude," Luc said, as the Tuesday night Bible study got underway.

Franklin touched his face. "It's still tender, but I'm glad the black has gone now."

"Don't have to wear makeup now, right?" Chris teased.

"No makeup here." Or ever.

"Yeah, eyeliner doesn't exactly jell with his macho cowboy image," Luc said.

"Eyeliner? This coming from the man who's always complaining we talk about feelings too much," Chris said.

"You're getting soft, dude," Jai teased.

Franklin chuckled at Luc's look of frustration. "I'm just glad he recognized my innate toughness shines through enough and doesn't require any glamming up."

Josiah and Mike joined them as the others laughed.

"So when is training camp starting for you all?" Ryan asked.

"We start Thursday," Mike said, and others said the same.

Thank goodness. Given recent preseason drama, Franklin needed more time to get his head in the game. The past week had been insane.

"How you doing, Franklin?" Josiah asked. "You've been in the spotlight a little lately."

"Hasn't he ever?" Luc chuckled. "First the nose, then the interviews with the girl who beat you up."

"She didn't beat me up," he protested, to the others' amusement.

"She's pretty," Ryan said.

"She's not a believer, so that's that," Franklin said flatly.

He caught Mike's head tip in the video, as if wondering just what Franklin was thinking. Yeah, he didn't know either.

"You mean she's on the journey," Josiah said. "God is working in the hearts of all people to draw them to Himself. It just takes some people a little longer to respond than others."

"But some don't respond at all," Luc said.

"Hey, don't underestimate the power of prayer. Our God can do anything."

"Yeah. That sounds like a song Sarah Maguire wrote for Heartsong Collective," Jai said. "Sarah Walton now," he added. "I've just been corrected by Allie."

"Is she listening?" Luc asked.

"Hi Allie," Josiah called.

"Hi Jo." A blonde ducked into Jai's screen and grinned and waved. "Hey guys. Don't worry, I'm going now." She ducked out again to a chorus of "bye."

"Hey, in Allie's defense, she only does it occasionally. She says we're more entertaining than some of the crew she works with at the art museum."

"How many others of you have your wife listening in?" Luc asked.

"Hey, my wife is Sarah's biggest fan," Jai explained. "Allie is always playing her music or choosing her songs when she leads music at church."

"Speaking of church, how did you go finding a place in which to worship, Franklin?"

"I went to Mike's and liked it. It's bigger than the one I attended years ago, but it felt friendly enough. They preached the Bible in a practical makes-sense-to-me way, and the music was good." He shrugged. "I'll get there when I can."

"We get a few Sundays off when we're not training or on the road," Mike said. "You should be able to get there more than you think."

He nodded, flattening his lips to hide the gut-deep desire to attend church with a certain someone. But Josiah was right, a stubborn thought persisted. God *could* do anything.

"Okay, let's get into it," Josiah said. "Ryan, want to open in prayer?"

Franklin bowed his head as Ryan prayed, forcing his thoughts heavenward as he refocused on what the meeting was really about. Yeah, catching up with the guys was good, but he needed this moment of stillness, the time to remind himself what was important. They might have a lot of Sundays off, but Tuesdays were looking pretty full, especially later in the season. The online Bible study group would still gather, knowing playing schedules would make it a challenge for everyone to always attend, which meant making the most of the chance to meet with the guys like this while he could.

Josiah led a study on prayer, and it reminded him of Cassie's words last Friday night as they'd arrived back at his apartment complex from Hannah's. She'd grabbed his hand and prayed aloud for Hannah, and he'd found himself agreeing with an Amen.

And prayers for her had continued off and on all weekend. On Saturday, while he'd gone jogging and later met Kurt and Tom for a meal. On Sunday, when he'd met Mike and Bree at church with Cassie, then joined them for lunch. Then today, in between phone calls with his agent and a weight training session in the morning, and an interview with a local newspaper.

Previous seasons had taught him that pressure started to hit during training camp, so to carve out this bit of time was good. Then he remembered that training camp meant a possibility he'd see her again. His heart kicked.

"What do you think, Franklin?" Josiah asked.

"Sorry, my head's been all over the joint."

"We won't hold that against you," Josiah said. "There is a bit to get used to."

Mike was looking at him in that way again. Franklin glanced down as if studying his Bible.

The study continued, then they shared prayer needs. Franklin was tempted to ask for prayer for Hannah but figured that would only invite more tease. Besides, prayer wasn't about how many people prayed, like the more people who did it could twist God's arm. Instead, it was about faith.

"Amen."

He echoed it a second later, then there was more tease and banter before farewells and sign-offs, when various players said they'd be back for next week. "Then the following week we have a back-to-back with you guys in the Big E," Mike said to Ryan.

"Can't wait."

Franklin signed off, and stared at the blank screen. Josiah's reminder to pray without ceasing was timely. It was all too easy to let the distractions and worries of the world creep in, and given his newly reaffirmed faith, he wanted to stay close to God.

His phone flashed. Cassie. *Guess what?*

He rolled his eyes. He loved his sister but hated these games. *What?*

Guess who just saw a breakthrough?

You? he tapped back.

No! I just got a message from Hannah.

His pulse picked up. *And?*

You'll never guess.

He closed his eyes. Then just called her. "What?"

"Ha! I knew you'd be interested in this."

"Hey, don't tell me then. See ya."

"Wait! She just messaged me to say she's kept her job, the guys apologized, and her job now comes with an upgrade."

"Which means?" Pride pinged at how well he stamped the excitement from his voice. Any flatter and he could grow wheat there.

"I don't know! I asked but she didn't respond. Maybe it's a secret or something. Anyway, I thought you'd like to know."

"Why?" he asked suspiciously.

"Because we were praying for her, right?"

"Sure."

"It's good news, isn't it?"

"Yeah." As long as his admission didn't result in Cassie being too in-his-face about prodding him to pursue Hannah. Because try as he might, the more he thought about Hannah, the more he prayed for her, and the harder it was to remain in the emotional neutral zone. Which had to be what God wanted. Right?

His phone buzzed again. Mike. "Hey, I better get this. Catch you later."

"Dinner, Friday night."

"Yep. Bye." Two taps on the screen and he switched calls. "Hey Mike. Ya miss me so much already?"

"You know it." Dryness lined Mike's voice. "Just wanted to check on you."

"Regarding?"

"A certain reporter. You know you have to tread carefully there."

Resentment spiked. "That I do."

"Look, I don't mean to sound heavy-handed, but just be careful."

"I know she's not a Christian so don't worry—"

"I didn't mean that." Mike sighed. "It's just I got word today about some changes at CNSTV, and what it means."

"I just heard she got a promotion or something."

"You've spoken to her?" Mike asked.

"Cassie mentioned it. I haven't seen Hannah since last Friday."

"Friday?"

Franklin winced. He'd managed to avoid any mention of the surprise dinner at Hannah's when he and Cassie had lunch with Mike on Sunday.

"What happened Friday?" Mike persisted.

"Nothing. Cassie dropped in to see me, then wanted food, so we went to get some. Then she wanted to see Hannah and we ended up at her place. We ate food and watched that stupid

Hockey Hour show." Man, explaining like this, like he was needing to justify himself, sounded so lame.

Mike sighed. "I knew it."

"Knew what?"

"Despite what you said before I think you do have a thing for her."

"No, I don't." Well, it was *mostly* true. He was trying not to have a thing for her anyway. And shouldn't intentions count for something? "She's Cassie's friend. Not mine."

Except it kind of felt she was becoming his friend. Praying for someone did that to a person.

"Look, I know you're wanting to be careful because of that whole equally yoked thing, but be careful, man," Mike said.

"There is nothing going on," Franklin assured him.

"From where I'm sitting, it seems you're a little too interested, and it won't be a good look for the team if she's known to be playing favorites when she's reporting. It could be seen as a conflict of interest, and affect her career."

Oh. If Mike was saying the same thing as Hannah had said on Friday night…"Point taken."

"Look, I just know of people who have been fired for similar things, and you don't want to add fuel to people wanting to get rid of her."

He sure didn't. But still, he needed clarity. "Are you saying I can't ever talk to her?"

"No." Mike sighed again. "Sorry, this is sounding harder than I meant it to be. I just don't want you screwing things up with her and having it affect her career or your game. And there's already been some rumors thrown around you both."

Like what? All at once his memory sparked: The restaurant. The hug filmed by the teenagers. His stupid comment about pretending to go out to convince people he didn't hold the nose job against her. Thank God she'd said no, otherwise this would be even more of a mess. But feelings could be controlled.

"There is honestly nothing to see here," he said. "But give me a straight answer, do you want me to not see her? If that's the case, I can tell Cassie to avoid her and not go near her again," yes, he sounded petty, "and—"

"Look, nobody is saying avoid her. Keep it friendly, but keep it professional, okay? I know you'll both have a lot to prove in these upcoming weeks, so just be careful in how your actions can be regarded by others, okay?"

"Aye, aye, captain."

A pause. "Don't be like that."

"Sorry." Sometimes it was hard to know where the line between tease in friendship and respect for his captain blurred.

"I just want you both to succeed. I consider you friends, and I know Bree does, too. It's just complicated, that's all. But it doesn't need to be. Not if you're careful."

"Sure. Thanks, Mike. I hear what you're saying, and I'll take care."

"Catch you on Thursday."

"Yep."

The call ended, and he blew out a breath. Complicated? *Lord, help untangle this mess.*

And he wondered what it would mean for the media interviews this Thursday.

CHAPTER 9

$\mathcal{E}$xcitement rippled through Hannah as she joined the throng of media representatives trickling through the door. The team medicals and testing had started several hours ago, and media availability was due to commence at eleven. There'd been some last-minute shuffle of arrangements, when the question of media availability was shifted from the WinSport arena back to the Saddledome, and she'd joined Drew and Bob—who ignored her and spoke only to each other on the van ride over—in sitting in the media room's front row while Royce set up his camera and mike. Dirk had insisted they show up together in a "sign of unity," but the way they continued to pretend she didn't exist wasn't going to fool anyone.

"Drew, Bob." Various reporters, including sports anchor legend Anton Fletcher, acknowledged them but not her. She tried not to let it rankle. She didn't for a minute think they didn't know who she was, too. She'd felt dozens of eyes boring into her back. She clutched her laminated media pass, waiting for the team's media managers to take control of the meeting.

Sports reporting was a funny job, moments of deadlines and high-pressure intensity interspersed with times of sitting around waiting. Jokes and laughter filled the room, and she sat, feeling conspicuous in the fact nobody reached out to speak to her. And while this wasn't a popularity contest—reporters were all about exclusives and ratings, after all—the only way to have friends was to be one, so she'd need to make an effort.

She glanced around, saw some gazes slip away, while meeting smirks and smiles from others. Her heart grew tight. Awesome. She offered a small smile to Natalie Reynolds, who reported for the local branch of the national TV network, as she moved past, balancing a to-go coffee cup and an iPad. Natalie paused, brow knit. "I've seen you before."

Hannah nodded. "Hannah Wade, from CNSTV." She tilted her head to the men seated a spare chair away. "I've seen you on TV for years. Nice to meet you."

"Oh, that's right. The headbutt girl."

Hannah's smile froze, her heart icing over. What, was this how all these professionals saw her too?

"Sorry, I shouldn't have said that." Natalie sipped her coffee, her dark eyes holding an apology. "You poor thing, what an introduction to this world, eh?"

"How not to make a first impression. I know."

Natalie nodded. "How are you doing?" Her glance at Bob and Drew suggested she knew exactly what the main problem was.

"Okay so far."

"Whew." The blonde ducked her head. "It's a boys' club, isn't it? But hang in there, okay?"

Her sympathy—and the knowledge that she was a woman who'd faced similar battles to Hannah—encouraged her, as the team's media rep moved to the microphone and practiced the "check one, two" of sound technicians the world over.

"Hi there," she said. "I'm Andrea Cummins. Welcome to today's media launch. We're going to be starting in a few minutes. The general manager, Mr. Don Belisario, will speak first, followed by the coach, Hank Schultz, and there will be time for questions at the end. Just a reminder that players will be available for interviews following the on-ice scrimmages tomorrow and on Saturday, but we ask that you put in your request at the back of the room. Okay, Mr. Belisario is now here. Welcome, sir."

Hannah straightened in her seat, laptop at the ready, as the general manager moved to the black-draped table, in front of a board covered in the red, gold, and white sponsors of the team. His gaze flicked across the room, pausing for a second on her, before shifting to Drew and Bob nearby.

Her skin prickled. Had he recognized her? Would he want to answer any questions or would he blame her too for hurting his latest new recruit? She pushed her hair behind her ear. How ridiculous to be so insecure. He was a professional. He'd treat her that way too.

"Hey guys, thanks for coming." He seated himself. "I want to talk a little about camp, and provide some player updates. We'll do questions at the end. Okay." He glanced at his notes. "We'll have sixty-seven players in camp, medicals, physicals are taking place as we speak. We'll break into three groups, and for the first three days there will be some movement between those groups. Then on Sunday there'll be a split-squad game in Edmonton, with some activity likely after that."

She nodded. Split squad would see the training camp roster likely split into A and B level teams, in an opportunity to test the lines against Edmonton who were doing something similar.

"I have some player updates." He then went on to share about a backup goalie dealing with a family issue, who therefore wouldn't be attending training camp. "He has the full support of the organization, and we request that you give him and his family privacy at this time. We won't be addressing this again until there's anything to update."

Poor Doychek was in Europe with a mom in palliative care.

Another player had a tweaked muscle during summer skates, but was skating on his own, under the supervision of the medical and development skills staff, and would rejoin the group soon.

"And they're our player updates, and we're excited to get going. So, have we got any questions?"

There were a few questions about the depth of players, with players from the minor leagues competing at training camp with those on professional tryouts, those seeking contracts, and the seasoned NHLers under contract.

"We've got lots of bodies, but how well you play determines how much depth you have. Competition is good. We're looking to dress the best lineup going forward so we can win."

"And what about the logjam at defense?" Natalie asked. "How do you think Franklin James is going to fit?"

"Well, Natalie, he'll fit in well if he stays healthy." The ripple of laughter at this underscored the pointed stares slicing her back.

But Hannah couldn't show emotion. Wouldn't let them see how much this stung.

"I know he and Mike Vaughan have played together in Boston," the GM continued. "So we'll be trying them out together, just like we'll be trying other combinations, as we work to find those that have chemistry and play well together. We've got a lot of young players who are hungry, who want to push the door down and earn a spot. Everyone has to prove himself, captain and new signings included."

She had to ask something, if for no other reason than to show his comment hadn't bothered her. She raised her hand.

The GM nodded. "You don't need to raise your hand, sweetheart. What's your name again?"

"Hannah."

He cupped his ear. "What was that?"

"Hannah Wade, sir."

"There's no need for sir, either." He studied her, expression unreadable. "Huh. So you're the one who tried to KO my star signing. You've got some nerve showing up here, haven't you?"

She swallowed. She could feel the self-satisfaction oozing from Bob.

He pointed a finger at her. "Don't do it again."

Do what? Show up at a press conference again?

"Now, what was your question?"

What was her question? "I wanted to know how you feel about Mike Vaughan being captain."

"Well, he wouldn't be captain unless I okayed it, now would he?"

Shoot. This wasn't going well at all. "I just meant—"

"I know what you meant, and yes, Mike is a solid player, and has been a good leader for years, and it was time to acknowledge that in a greater capacity. I know after the past year's drama the captaincy is in a safe pair of hands."

Such a nonanswer. But then, her question had scarcely been better.

"How is the mood in the locker room with this change?" Drew asked.

"Well, Drew, it's early days yet. But I'm sure you can ask Alex yourself, or maybe get him on your show again."

Hannah cringed. So the GM knew exactly who she was and what had happened in that awful episode from last week. He didn't seem to like anyone from CNSTV very much. How awkward all of this was.

"But in all seriousness, that's water under the bridge, and we're focused on moving forward. That stuff with Alex is personal, and neither I nor the organization will be commenting on this publicly any further. The Canadian market is a pressure cooker environment, we all understand that, but I think everyone concerned would appreciate this being left in the past and for them to have privacy." He sipped from his water bottle.

More questions followed about the competition for roster spots. "I don't care about where you played last year, or how old you are, we want players to show up, and we don't know until we get into competitive situations and face live bullets just how well we'll go. Our group is still a work in progress, our top nine is still fluid, we're tinkering, we're evaluating, so we're trying to get a handle on what we can do to build our team so we can win. We want to be a playoff team, so people have to earn their right to be on it."

A few more questions, then he glanced around the room. "We good? Okay, good to see you all."

He left with a nod and she breathed again. Whoa.

But there was no time to lick her wounds as the coach now appeared, and the back-and-forth began again. By the time Coach Schultz had finished she was itching to leave. At least he hadn't made fun of her like the GM had.

She glanced across at Bob and Drew, but they were talking to several others, probably complaining about her, if the glances in her direction were any indication.

Okay, then. She stood, and moved to the back and put her name next to the players she wanted to interview after the on-ice scrimmages tomorrow. She didn't need to worry about interviews on Saturday. Given her new responsibilities, Jason had given her a half day and instructed her to focus on the public meet and greet. Meet and greets should be a little easier, and might allow room for another kind of work: time with her mom. A sigh escaped, as Natalie drew near.

"You doing okay, Hannah?"

"Yep."

"Hey, don't take what Don said personally," Natalie said. "He likes to tease. And look on the bright side."

There was a bright side?

"At least he'll remember you."

Hannah's nose wrinkled. "Yeah, I'd prefer it not be that way."

"Well, like he said, focus on moving forward, keep showing up, and they'll forget. One day."

"You sure?"

"Well, some may. Others…" She shrugged. "Don't let them win, okay?"

She nodded. If it was a fight these men wanted, she was ready to play.

"WHAT DO you mean my name isn't down?" she asked Andrea, the team media representative, the next day. "I remember writing it down and requesting to see Mike, Chad, and Jake Hooper." But not Franklin. Avoiding him was probably wise.

"Yes, and then you crossed it off."

"No, I didn't." Agitation rose. She sucked in a breath, released it slowly. Smiled. "Would you mind if I took a look at that, please?"

"Sure."

The sign-up sheet held a list of player names, and sure enough, where she'd written her name in black next to Mike, Chad, and Jake had been scribbled out in blue. She tapped the page. "I'm sorry, but you can see that someone else has done that. It's a different color, see?"

"Oh." Andrea peered at it. "Well, I don't know how that happened."

Hmm, but Hannah had a fairly good idea.

"Look, I'm sorry but Mike's booked solid now, so maybe you can ask some of these other players." Andrea pointed to other names.

She bit back a sigh. "Thanks."

She supposed she couldn't complain too much. It wasn't like

she hadn't had interviews with nearly all of the players already in the past week or two. But this job demanded hustle, and she couldn't rest on previous work. The station wanted new content. Viewers wanted it too. And just because Drew or Bob might think they could foil her interview attempts didn't mean she'd let them.

Andrea pointed to the hall where players were lined up at various intervals, team-logoed snapbacks on back to front, towels around their neck, their faces flushed as they answered questions about their morning skate.

"Who we got?" Royce asked her, hefting his camera to his shoulder.

She mentioned the names of the players she'd been assigned, following him as he led her to the far end.

A large crowd had gathered around Franklin, and she kept her gaze averted as she passed, overhearing his answer. "...been great. It's an older group, so straightaway the pace is there, the execution is there. You know this is a team that's ready to compete."

"And playing in the east, you wouldn't have seen much of the way these guys play, so what is your biggest adjustment coming here?" Natalie asked.

"I guess the biggest thing is jelling with the guys, showing them I'm committed to this team, and I want to win. Calgary is the team I grew up supporting, so I *really* want to win."

Hannah peeked across, caught his gaze, then she ducked her head, her thoughts scrambled as she moved to where Chad stood with just one interviewer.

She stood to one side, trying to remember her questions, to look unaffected by that quick look. It wasn't fair to Chad if she was distracted by a pair of searing blue eyes.

From the ice came whistle shrieks and the clatter of sticks as some of the younger forwards underwent more work with the development skills staff. She'd watched the earlier session along with other media and members of the public. Given the hotly interested market, there had been some cheers when Franklin had skated on the ice before. And yes, she'd paid attention, even as Royce had set up camera shots and asked for her input. She couldn't help but note—from a purely professional point of view, of course—that Franklin was definitely one of the speedier defensemen the team had seen. If he and Mike did pair up, they'd be formidable in defense.

"Hey Hannah."

"Hi Chad." She smiled, glancing at the other reporter who was shuffling across to catch the end of Franklin's talk. She turned so Franklin wouldn't be in her peripheral vision. "How are you feeling after getting on the ice this morning?"

"It's nice to finally be at it again. It's good to feel like we're starting to click, find some chemistry, which I hope we can take forward."

"And have you had any welcome-to-Calgary moments?"

"Yeah, I've had a few, it's definitely a bigger market here than where I was before. I've appreciated Mike Vaughan picking me up and taking me places I didn't know where they were. He's a real leader."

She nodded. "And what do—?"

"Hey Chad, welcome to Calgary," Anton Fletcher spoke over the top of her, his deeper voice drowning out hers. "How has the team made you feel welcome?"

Chad flicked a look at her then answered. "Yeah, they've been really good, gone out of their way to make us feel comfortable here."

"You guys doing fantasy football this year?" Anton asked.

Seriously?

Chad chuckled. "Yeah, I'm not great. I usually get out around the fourth round, and yeah, it's not really my scene."

"And what—"

"Do you think—"

"What aspect of your game do you hope to improve in this year?" she said, pushing past Anton's interruption.

"I'm always wanting to improve my offense. I think I have a fairly solid defense but yeah, I'm hoping to put up more points this year."

"Thanks." She glanced at Anton, brows raised, and he dipped his chin as if to acknowledge her right to interrupt the interrupter, before he asked his next question.

Hannah sucked in a breath. Why did it feel like she was battling all the men here? Natalie was right. She couldn't let them win. So if that meant working twice as hard and beating the men at their own game—whether that meant interrupting or whatever—she'd do it. She'd never win if she let herself be trampled on.

She kept that in the forefront of her next interview with Jake, continuing to push past the interruptions offered by others, which earned a couple of smiles from the players, as if they recognized the tactics and were willing to help her out.

By the time she'd finished her allotted interviews, only Mike and Franklin remained chatting to reporters. Mike was looking tired, so she left him to it, directing Royce to grab some vision as Mike shared—for no doubt the dozenth time already today—about his hopes for the new season. She didn't need to ask anything more—she'd spoken to him several times already—but having some new footage of him with a to-camera introduction from her would make it look fresh and intentional.

Her phone rang. She glanced at the number. Mom. She pressed to answer, but it had already gone to voicemail. She tried to call, but no.

A new layer of frustration swept across her. Why couldn't her mother just leave a message like a normal person? Instead she insisted on speaking directly, and then, only at a time that suited her. Well, two could play at that game, and it didn't exactly suit Hannah to talk to her now anyway. She was in the middle of a workday, something one would think her mother would understand. But no. This was how Mom rolled.

"...and yeah, I guess it wasn't the start anyone was expecting, but stuff happens, eh?"

She stilled as Franklin's voice carried to her. Was he talking about their infamous meeting? Ugh. How to creep past without it becoming obvious to everyone...

Another question was put to him, and she maneuvered around the back, studying her phone as if needing to check it, pretending to be oblivious to the player who still garnered so much attention.

"Yeah, Mike has been great, a real leader, making me feel at home. Of course, it helps by actually being at home."

There was a ripple of laughter.

She glanced up.

Met his intense gaze again. "And it's been awesome reconnecting with family and old friends."

FRANKLIN BLINKED, and snapped his gaze away. How had that fallen from his mouth just as Hannah walked past? And why did she have to look so cute in that black and red suit? If he didn't know better he'd think she was sponsored by the team. But he did know better, and judging from some of the things he'd heard staff say, Hannah wasn't exactly ticket-holder-number-one around here. That, and some of the comments that revealed media prejudice against her, had dug past his new resolve to keep her at a distance. How could he, a defenseman, not protect someone who had crawled under his own defenses?

Someone was talking, and he refocused, even as another part of him was conscious that Hannah was walking away. "Sorry, can you repeat the question?"

"I wanted to know what your hopes are about this season."

"You mean apart from winning a certain silver cup?"

More laughter. They'd probably stop laughing at all his jokes once he wasn't the flavor-of-the-day new guy.

"I guess I want to do all I can to help this team become the best it can be, and I'm willing to do anything to help make that happen." It sounded trite, but it was true. And hey, when a guy was asked the same question in fifty different ways, what else could he do but resort to a few clichés? "Thanks guys."

He pretended not to hear a couple more questions as he walked away. Some media personnel were like vultures, they kept picking away until there was nothing but weathered bones. And he was tired, and still had to shower and do the usual things before he could head home. And even though it wasn't a game, he still felt drained, the past few days demanding the most amount of energy in weeks. Just wait until their first game on Sunday. A preseason game, but still. He wanted to prove himself, prove the team had been right in paying him big dollars to move back west.

He got to the locker room, stripped off his sweat-stained practice jersey and threw it into the bin, showered, changed, and met Mike again. Poor dude looked weary too.

"How are you doing?" Mike asked, face lighting up as he clapped him on the shoulder.

"It's a little intense, but good."

"Yeah, you've got the spotlight on you, so run with it while you can."

They discussed some of the plays and pairings, but Franklin knew that such combinations were up to the coaching staff. But he'd felt the chemistry in the on-ice partnership between him and Mike, as sure as the whack to the solar plexus from a certain pair of green eyes.

"And you're good with other things?" Mike asked in a lower voice.

"Sure."

Judging from the way Mike studied him, he figured maybe he'd seen that look between him and Hannah before. But that's all it had been. A single look. Well, two, if you counted the earlier one as well. But somehow seeing her made him hungry to talk to her again. It was like his sisters said: the absence of chocolate only made them crave it more. Deliberately avoiding Hannah only seemed to fuel his hunger to see her, speak to her, be near her. Not that he'd admit any of that for the world.

He drove home, pleading tiredness as an excuse to not go to Chad's and hang out before dinner with Cassie tonight. Doing media was exhausting, and tomorrow he'd do it all again. Still, it had been fun to see the little kids come out, and sign a few autographs like they thought him a bigger star than he thought himself.

But later, after a nap and trying to figure out whether he really wanted to eat pasta by himself again, he knew a sense of loneliness. Cassie had cancelled, citing a production company issue that had kept her chained to her desk at the office on the ranch. He could drive out there, but he didn't want to face the evening commute. But neither did he want to face the night alone.

He stared out at the cityscape, the lights twinkling as the sunset bled away under a heavy storm cloud. This had certainly been an action-packed offseason, the most full-on in years, moving cities, finding new friends, jelling with a new team, wrangling his heart.

He rolled his eyes at himself. Why questions about this still pecked at him he didn't know. Except that it felt like it had been a long time since he'd had a girlfriend. And now he was signed here, with a no-move clause in his contract for another three years, maybe now was the time to start thinking about his future beyond hockey. For one day this would stop, and his body would no longer perform. He might've outrun and outlasted several younger people in the physicals, but one day he'd be slower, and he'd be the one cut, unless he retired. And he'd much rather retire than be forced out, like some of the guys who had played professionally and now were begging for scraps like a professional tryout. He didn't want to do that.

Dad had always said there would be room for him at the ranch, and truth be told that's what he wanted too. But now with Cassie often in charge, who knew how she'd take to that. He might be the older brother but she'd always acted like she was the boss. He grimaced. Look at tough him, always at the mercy of headstrong women.

Lightning cracked, splinters of white against black and gray. He pressed his forehead against the glass, fighting a groan. What was it about Hannah that attracted him so? There'd been that moment when she looked upset, or, if not upset, then discouraged at least, and he'd wondered who had been on the phone. Then he'd been forced back into answering more questions, with every answer a variation of the same. He'd been glad she hadn't stopped to talk to him, even though he would've enjoyed a conversation with her more than anyone else today.

But Mike was right. Chasing Hannah was like trying to mix fire and ice. It wouldn't work. It would only snuff her career, and possibly his, too. But the silence was a gnawing thing, eating into his contentment. For if he couldn't have her, then who could he have?

Lord?

Panic which had streaked high, like the fingers of lightning in the night, eased as he prayed some more. He still felt so new with the God-relationship thing, and it was the first time he'd consulted God before chasing a girl. But he sensed before letting emotion win that he should see what God might have in store. Better that than pleading with God to change a girl's heart after he'd well and truly fallen for her.

"Hey God, I really don't know what to say except I want what You have for me, even if it's not what I want for me. And I don't want to be alone, but I don't know what to do. Is there a girl at church waiting for a Christian hockey player?"

Faces flashed from the past two Sundays. Yeah, he didn't need an angel to tell him that answer. The eager interest had been there, all right.

But try as he might, there was no tendril of soft feeling, nothing that had piqued his interest as much as that girl whose hand he'd once held on a long-ago summer's day. That girl who spiked adrenaline to his heart more than any rush on the ice. But that girl, for all kinds of reasons, seemed destined to remain forever out of reach.

He glanced at the TV. He wondered what would happen on *Hockey Hour* tonight. And felt a sudden urge to pray for her again.

CHAPTER 10

"*I*n three, two," *one*, Jason mouthed pointing to the trio seated at the desk.

Hannah smiled and looked down the barrel of camera one, as the intro music for *Hockey Hour* filled the studio. Just relax, Mandi had said while making Hannah up in the chair earlier. Yeah, right. Easier said than done.

"Welcome to *Hockey Hour*. I'm Drew Anderson," said Drew.

"And I'm Bob Patresky," said his sidekick.

As Drew's previously recorded voice-over talked up some of the featured highlights on the accompanying reel being shown to viewers, the wrestling in her stomach suddenly eased. Cassie's earlier reminder that she was praying for her made her wonder if she just had, for she suddenly felt a new sense of confidence and peace. Jason pointed at her, and she nodded, her chin lifting a fraction. That's right. She could do this. She *would* do this.

"We're here tonight with CNSTV's very own Hannah Wade, our newest special correspondent who is joining us at the desk tonight. Welcome, Hannah."

"Thanks for having me, Drew. It's great to be here." She dimmed her smile back.

At the production meetings this week, Jason had made it clear it was imperative that Hannah be seen to be welcomed by Drew and Bob in order to rectify the bad impressions made on the program last week. And while she was tasked with looking happy with being here while delivering reports, she wasn't going to look like a grinning fool.

"So, some of you may be wondering why we have another panelist joining us. For those of you who don't know, Hannah Wade is a sports journalist whose passion for sports, and hockey in particular, led her to the women's professional hockey league and gold at the World Championships, until an untimely accident forced her to focus on her second love: sportscasting."

Bob murmured, "Gold, huh?"

Hannah nodded. "That's right. It was a fantastic experience," she said, just like her autocue said. Not "and how many hockey gold medals do you have, Bob?" like snarky-her might want to.

Drew continued. "Now it was clear that some of what Bob and I did last week was not in the best of taste, so I'm pleased that Hannah was willing to overlook that and deign to join us tonight."

And every Friday night Jason wanted her to. And what was with the "deign," like she was some sort of princess? She willed her expression to remain pleasant, and not look offended.

"Yes, we're sorry if our actions offended you or anyone else, Hannah."

If? That didn't sound like someone taking responsibility. Neither was it what was written on the autocue. If Bob was willing to go off script then so was she.

"I appreciate that, Bob." Even though it probably sounded as fake an apology to the viewers as it did to her. "But I'm a big girl. And clearly I do not need people making fun of me when I am well able to make a fool of myself all on my own." She smiled at them both then gazed at the camera. "So if we're all willing to let bygones be bygones, then let's focus on what we're all here to talk about tonight, and that's hockey."

"That's right," Drew took over. "This week saw the start of training camp for all NHL teams, including our own Flames. We heard Calgary's GM Don Belisario talk about their new recruits Franklin James and Chad Pelley…"

The conversation continued and they soon cut to an ad, and she exhaled.

"You're doing all right, kiddo," Drew said.

"Thanks." Although she rankled at the *kiddo*. But it wouldn't do to call him Grandpa, not when she was trying to prove herself a team player.

Jason sent her an upraised brow look and she nodded, sipping her water.

She glanced at her notes, as his voice murmured in her ear. "Okay, next up is Hannah with the interview sum-up. Are you ready?" She nodded. "Okay, and we're live in three, two," *one*, he mouthed, pointing at her.

Hannah smiled, as a spike of adrenaline speared through her. "Earlier this week we had the chance to catch up with a number of the players at training camp. These are some of their stories." *Dun dun.* She smiled, her words reminding her of an old *Law and Order* episode, as the footage played of her interviews.

She grabbed a quick drink, checked with Mandi that her lipstick looked fine, and was ready when the camera swung her way again.

"It sounds like they're all pumped and ready to go." She glanced at Drew. This was where the scripted section ended and they entered opinion land. At least until the next commercial break. Now was the time to prove herself and her opinions as worthy contributions on the show.

He nodded. "Just like all of Calgary. We can't wait for the

first game against Edmonton this Sunday. The Battle of Alberta is always a fantastic grudge match."

"It's a shame it's in Edmonton this year," Bob grouched.

"But only fair they get a turn," she pointed out. "And really," she continued, when Bob looked at her, as if surprised at her audacity at countering him, "when we're talking split teams, it's not like our fans are going to be missing much. The game to really watch out for is when preseason is done, the team is finalized, and running at full capacity. I can't wait to see how they match up against Vancouver on October 12."

"Who do you think will be hungriest this year, Drew?" Bob asked.

She sat and nodded along as the two men swapped opinions, waiting for an opportunity to contribute again. But they continued their own back-and-forth, which was understandable to a degree, as they'd done this for years. Yet leaving her out of their discussion gave her the choice to play polite, or dive on in.

"…really feel like Alex Kapaulenyuk also has something to prove," Drew said.

She froze. He sure did. Like how to be a human.

"Although some here might not agree. I bet Hannah has some thoughts about that," Bob said, finally turning to her.

She nodded, willing her expression to look pleasant, and not like the man gave her the heebie-jeebies. "You know it, Bob. I would imagine Alex is very eager to prove his commitment to the team. In fact, that's exactly what he expressed to me in our most recent conversation."

"He talked to you?" Drew asked, eyebrows aloft.

"Sure." Amid his threats and wandering hands. "I was pleased to hear he is focused on doing all he can to contribute to the team in a positive way. No team needs off-ice drama getting in the way of what they're paid to do, and we as fans want to see that energy and focus and drive again."

"Careful, Hannah, it sounds like you're saying you're a fan of Alex," Drew's words held an edge.

"I have always been a fan of this team," she said carefully, "and like so many others, it was disappointing when we didn't make the playoffs last year. Some attributed that to certain team dynamics that weren't helpful, and yeah, I'm sure I speak for many when I say we don't want to see a repeat of that getting in the way of the team producing good hockey. Am I right?" She directed her question at Drew.

"Uh, sure."

"I think the addition of Franklin and Chad will bring a new energy to the team, and under Mike's leadership we'll see a much stronger team this year," she continued. "I'm excited to see what this year will bring, aren't you Bob?"

"Yeah."

He didn't sound excited. But that was on him.

She focused on the camera and smiled. "I'm sure there are many fans out there who are pulling for the team, so if you're a fan, make sure you jump on our socials and let us know who you're most excited about seeing play this year."

"Who are you most excited about, Hannah? Franklin?" Drew goaded.

"Well, sure. As a defenseman who likes joining the rush and isn't afraid to put his body on the line he's an exciting player to watch. I mean, who isn't a fan of a player who doesn't always play it safe?" She shrugged. "But I think it's fair to say that there will be many people eager to see what he and Chad will bring. How about you? Are you looking forward to seeing what Franklin will bring?"

"Well, I suppose so."

"You only suppose so?" She smiled. "Come on." She looked at the camera. "Anyone else get the feeling he's excited but just doesn't want to say so?" She turned to Bob. "Got someone you're keeping an eye on?"

He shrugged. "I gotta admit I think it'll be interesting to see what Mike brings in his new role."

"Exactly." She noticed Jason doing a wind-it-up gesture. "Hey, looks like it's time for a break. We'll be back after these messages from our sponsors."

She smiled, focused on the camera until the cameraman gave the thumbs-up.

Jason applauded her. "Good job. Now that's what we're talking about."

"But Hannah basically took over," Drew complained.

"Hannah provided energy and zest. It was especially noticeable when you compare that segment with before when you two looked like you were excluding her. Don't do that again."

Bob frowned. Drew looked away.

"And Hannah, good job with mentioning the station's socials. Will sent a message to say thanks."

"If it gets the conversation happening in a positive way, then that's great."

By the time they finished she was exhausted, but elated. It seemed her first live-to-air *Hockey Hour* cohosting opportunity had gone way above anyone's expectations—and certainly above what Drew and Bob thought.

Jason did a quick run-through of points to consider before next week's show, and she took notes. Drew and Bob did not.

Later, Jason drew her aside. "Hey, I meant it before. Good job. I know they're not the easiest to work with, but it'll get easier. And I can't wait to see what the viewers think. Now go home, get some rest. You're attending the last day of training camp tomorrow, right?"

She nodded. "In the morning for the public meet and greet, yeah."

"Then go to sleep. Don't check your socials, we'll take care of that, but I think it would be fair to say you will do pretty well with all of that."

"Thanks, Jason. I really appreciate your support."

He pointed to the exit. "Go."

She saluted and exited. In the parking lot, she could see Bob and Drew talking, and she waved at them. "Thanks guys. That was fun."

Judging from the terse nods in response they mightn't have had quite the same level of fun as she had. Oh well. Her heart danced as she drove home, pulled into her apartment complex, fielded elderly Miss Petty's queries in the foyer—she knew loneliness could make people nosy—and took the elevator to the fifth floor.

She unlocked the door, switched on lights, threw her bag on the side table, and slumped into her chair. Clicked on the TV recording of tonight's *Hockey Hour* and watched it through again. Smiled. Then sighed. Closed her eyes. And finally relaxed.

That had been awesome. The adrenaline that had kicked in during the show still swirled, but was slowly ebbing away.

That had been three million times better than what she'd expected. Someone—and not just Jason—seemed to have been looking out for her. Which was enough to make her wonder if maybe God Himself had had a hand in things. Which seemed ridiculous. But then, there had been a number of little things lately that made her consider His role in her life. Like, maybe He wasn't out to get her after all. Like maybe He had blessed her with good things. Like tonight.

"Hey God," her voice sounded loud in the quiet, "I don't know if You had a hand in any of that tonight, but if You did, thank You."

She didn't hear any great rumbly voice from on high, but it felt like something shifted inside, a little like a sense of something clicking into place, bringing a feeling of peace.

Maybe God wasn't finished with her yet.

Her phone buzzed, and she cracked open her eyelids and glanced at the screen.

Awesome job, girl. You were fire! Mandi.

She smiled, and typed back Thanks. All due to the fierce efforts of a super stylist I know.

That earned her a smiley face in reply.

Another message came from Cassie, then one from Bree, and a few others. She should probably eat, but she was too tired to move, so replied to them instead. Jason had told her she needed to go to sleep, catch some z's, but there was something nice about sitting here in the dark, with just the fake Tiffany-style lamp switched on, adding mellowness to the room.

Her phone buzzed again.

She glanced at it. Blinked. Franklin had sent her a message? Hadn't they agreed last Friday not to talk to each other? Good job it read.

Thanks, she typed back, wondering if he'd respond.

When no reply came for several minutes she pursed her lips and exhaled. Oh well. She wasn't trying to build her esteem on the opinion of one man. Especially a man she knew was dangerous for her peace of mind.

Besides, other people had messaged too. Dirk. Even Lisa. Her mom hadn't, but that was no surprise. Sports had never been cerebral enough for her mother, and seeing Hannah hadn't told her about her appearance tonight, she doubted whether her mother even knew about her win today. They'd arranged to have lunch tomorrow, so she could tell her then.

She scrolled through, tempted to look at her social media but refraining. Jason had said he'd get the station's HR people to look at some of the trolls, and until that was sorted she'd be better off not knowing what some people said. Which meant not knowing what good things people might be saying too. But that was just part of the challenge in this weird balance of producing content for the public that they felt they had the right to comment on, but also somehow protecting her privacy, and thus protecting her heart from the slings and arrows of people's bitterness.

A yawn escaped. She'd have to get to bed soon, as tomorrow would see another round of reports from the Dome. She heated and ate her meal-for-one, then glanced at her phone one last time before putting it aside to charge tonight.

You looked good.

Her heart fizzed. He'd responded? Thank you.

Much better to look at than Drew or Bob.

Oh. Her heart drooped. So he didn't mean she looked good herself. Hey, she'd recorded it, and even ultra-critical she thought she'd looked about her best. Good to know.

Wait, that didn't sound right.

She started to reply when his next message came through.

I mean, it wouldn't be hard.

She winced. So what did that make her? A three out of ten on the scale of attractiveness?

Her phone pinged with another message. Man, I'm so bad at this.

He'd typed that fast. Maybe he was using voice-to-text or something. Which made her wonder why he didn't just call. But there was something about texting that felt safer, a less personal way of connection than listening to the inflections and breath spaces of someone's voice. Although, if he just called maybe he could've said what he actually meant instead of these vague insults.

No, you're actually pretty good at lowering a woman's ego.

Ouch. Sorry. :(I just meant you look good all the time.

Her heart skipped a beat. Even with blood smeared on my face? She'd seen the footage. How could Royce have let her continue that first interview with Franklin's blood on her cheek?

Low blow, but yeah. Even then.

A thrill rippled. Okay, so these flirty-sounding messages weren't exactly screaming arm's-length friendship but right now she didn't care. There was something rather delicious about being told she was pretty by a man she liked. That was what he was saying, wasn't it?

WELL, THANKS. AND IT WASN'T MEANT AS A LOW BLOW. I'M OBVIOUSLY TOTALLY OVER THE INCIDENT-THAT-SHAN'T-BE-NAMED. (CAN YOU TELL?)

His reply came a few seconds later. HA HA. I JUST MEANT NOT ONLY DID YOU LOOK PRETTY BUT YOU LOOKED COMFORTABLE, CONFIDENT, LIKE THAT WAS WHAT YOU'RE MEANT TO DO.

I'M GLAD, she replied. I WAS FEELING NERVOUS, BUT THEN JUST AT THE START I FELT THIS GUSH OF PEACE FALL ON ME AND FELT SO MUCH BETTER. IF I DIDN'T KNOW BETTER I'D ALMOST THINK SOMEONE MIGHT'VE PRAYED FOR ME OR SOMETHING.

HE STARED at the screen in the dark of his apartment. Traffic noise from six stories down was muted, the advanced hour meaning the night felt close. Should he admit to being the person who'd prayed for her then? It wasn't like he'd been the only one. He knew Cassie was, and he suspected that meant his mom had too. Probably Bree as well. Still, the fact that she'd experienced peace just as he prayed made his heart tingle. Like they shared a secret bond—super secret, as she didn't know it was him. But a bond all the same. Just like the one being formed by these text messages.

Uneasiness strummed. It didn't hurt to message her, did it? He was only being encouraging. And it wasn't like anyone else had to know. Sure, Mom had advised him to guard his heart, and Mike had said to be careful, but messaging was only being a friend. Even if texting like this in the dark made it feel like something more.

Maybe he shouldn't have told her she looked good. Even if it was true. The way she'd smiled at the camera, he almost got the impression she was smiling right at him. It had done something strange to his heart. For he'd seen her smile at him that way before, too.

ARE YOU STILL THERE? Her message flashed on his screen.

He forced his thoughts from the past and back to the here and now, scrolling back up to see what they'd last been talking about. That's right. Prayer.

He sucked in a breath. Should he? Man. He hated second-guessing himself like this. And he slowly tapped out his reply. I WAS PRAYING FOR YOU.

He hesitated. Leave it at that or be honest and admit that others had been too? Before he could respond, his screen lit. THANK YOU. THAT MEANS A LOT.

It did? More heart knots unsnarled. Still, he felt he needed to own it. I'M SURE OTHERS WERE TOO. I KNOW CASSIE AND MY MOM HAVE BEEN PRAYING FOR YOU TOO.

BUT RIGHT AT THAT MOMENT?

That he couldn't answer. Maybe God had answered his prayer for her at that precise moment. But her earlier comment held a thread he wanted to pull. SO DOES THIS MEAN YOU DON'T MIND PEOPLE TALKING TO GOD ON YOUR BEHALF? He pressed send, then waited, watching with his pulse loud in his ears as the swirls showed she was composing a reply.

NO.

Huh. What did that mean? That it didn't mean that? Or that she was on the road to restoring her relationship with God again? NO, AS IN...?

NO, AS IN I DON'T MIND. A second later a smiley face came through.

GOOD.

HOW CAN I MIND, WHEN I'VE STARTED TALKING TO GOD AGAIN TOO?

His heart leaped. "Yes!" He fist-pumped, then felt another urge to pray. He didn't want his feelings to be the reason he was encouraging her toward friendship with God, but he couldn't deny it, either. Somehow he was going to have to sort through what this would mean. But right now he was too happy for her, to pull back. THAT'S GREAT NEWS, he replied. GOD LOVES YOU AND HAS GOOD PLANS FOR YOU.

ON A DAY LIKE TODAY I CAN BELIEVE IT.

He studied the words. But just because she'd had a win today didn't mean it wasn't true even when life's circumstances were tough. IT'S TRUE EVERY DAY. READ ROMANS 8:28-39.

He wondered whether she would read it. Then prayed that she would. Everyone needed to know that God loved them and nothing could ever separate them from that love. Just like they needed to know that God was able to use all things for the good of those who believed in Him. And while Hannah might've walked some dark paths in recent years, it didn't change the fact that God had been walking beside her, even if she hadn't felt His presence.

PROUD OF YOU. His thumb paused over the send button as he stared at the words. Would she think them patronizing? He didn't mean it to sound like that. He genuinely was glad she'd chosen to think on God again, just like he was proud that she'd proven herself tonight like that. But whether she'd see it that way...

He deleted it, glancing back at the previous message. She still hadn't responded. Maybe it had pushed her to read her Bible. Or maybe she'd gone to sleep. Which was what he needed to do too. Even if texting her like this after days of avoidance in public felt as satisfying as scratching an almighty itch.

GOTTA GO, he wrote instead. BUT IF YOU NEED TO TALK MORE ABOUT GOD STUFF—

She really shouldn't talk to him. That could get complicated if she leaned on him rather than God.

—THEN I KNOW CASSIE OR MY MOM WILL BE SUPER GLAD, ANY TIME. GREAT JOB TONIGHT. SWEET DREAMS.

He pressed send before he could second-guess that last comment. Then second-guessed it anyway. Then switched off the phone, moved to the shower, then to bed and closed his eyes to sleep.

But his thoughts wouldn't switch off, as current pride in Hannah mixed with sweetness from long ago.

He had been eighteen, visiting home after talking with his agent and securing more details for his move east. He'd be leaving soon, and while he knew his mom and dad would be thrilled as he stepped into his most cherished dream, leaving them and his sisters and the ranch meant other challenges. So it was with mixed emotions he'd driven down the avenue of trees to the ranch house he'd always regarded as home.

"Honey, you're back!" His mom had wrapped him in a hug that was more around his waist than chest these days. "This is a surprise."

"How'd you go?" his dad asked.

Franklin told him, and his dad's weathered face split into the biggest grin he'd seen since the NHL Draft two months ago.

They soon allayed his fears, and told him his sisters were down at the river, taking advantage of the coolness there.

"Go say hi. They'll want to hear your news too. Oh, Cassie has a friend."

Of course she did. Cassie was as sociable as he was good at hockey. She'd likely get drafted first pick overall for friendliness. Still, he changed into board shorts and slides, grabbed a towel and drove the ATV to the bend in the river where his family had long loved to escape the summer heat.

He parked near a tree, catching sight of his two younger sisters splashing each other while Cassie and her friend lay on black tubes out of splashing reach. "Hey!"

"Franklin!" Jessica screamed and ran up to him, tackling him in a bear hug probably meant to push him on the ground.

His other sister, Poppy, glanced at him with mischief in her eyes then kicked a spray of water at him as delicately as she might do one of her fancy ballet moves.

"Don't you start something you're not prepared to finish," he warned.

She did it again, which meant it was his big-brother obligation to chase her into the freezing water and throw her into the deep. She screamed with delight—he'd always had a soft spot for her—then begged him to put her down.

Which left Cassie, who even now was sighing in her best sixteen-year-old way as she said loudly to her friend, "And that is my big brother. Of course, you wouldn't know it, acting like that. Franklin, this is Hannah."

His heart had stuttered as his gaze landed on Cassie's friend. And stayed on her as she smiled.

"Hi Franklin."

It was a good thing he was standing in waist-deep Rockies-fed water, because teenage him wasn't used to seeing girls who looked like her. All blonde hair and curves and legs and smile. How had Cassie found a friend like her?

"Cat got your tongue?" Cassie teased.

He blinked, as embarrassment heated his cheeks. He cleared his throat. "Hi Hannah." Man, why did his voice suddenly sound so squeaky-deep?

Cassie seemed to have picked up on that as she laughed. "I think someone has made an impression."

Hannah's head tipped as she studied him. "Cassie mentioned that you got chosen in the NHL Draft. Congratulations."

"Th-thanks." He cringed. He sounded like an idiot. Why couldn't he speak normally? But women who could front magazine covers never hung out on his ranch.

"Hannah is the smartest girl in our year—"

"She exaggerates," Hannah interrupted, rolling her eyes.

"—and she loves hockey too," Cassie said, with waggling upraised brows.

Okay, his sister might be annoying sometimes but he also knew she loved him. He grabbed a spare tube from the shore and dragged it back to the water near where Hannah floated. "Hockey, huh?"

He barely heard her words, too busy drinking in her animated face, her musical voice; he could listen to her for hours. She loved hockey, like him. Was determined to compete at elite levels, like him. Was a Christian, like him. Enjoyed hanging with his sisters, like him. She was obviously really smart, modest, and yet sassy, responding to Cassie's tease with wit and ease. She was perfect.

But giving his sisters fuel for mockery wasn't on his agenda, and giving a green-eyed supermodel hope for more wasn't his style either. Or so he'd thought until later, when the younger two had gone and Cassie had floated down the river ahead of them, leaving him and Hannah perched on their tubes, enjoying the sun and the cool water.

He'd also been enjoying the way the water droplets glinted on her tanned legs and sparkled in her hair, the blonde strands trailing in the water. She had her eyes closed, and he'd used the moment to trace her features with his eyes, her fine dark brows, soft cheeks, the curve of her pink lips. His heart thudded.

She wore a purple one-piece that didn't reveal too much, but enough that he knew he'd struggle with his dreams. He wasn't immune to desire, he was a teenage boy, and his friends had boasted of their conquests in recent years. But his Christian upbringing meant saving those things until he was married, which was going to be a long way down the track until he'd settled into his new NHL club all the way across on the other side of the continent, in Providence, as part of the farm team for

Boston. Yet being with her made him question how long he'd have to be away.

He reached out a hand to touch her hair, trailing behind her in the water. Just as he thought—like silk. The sense he was taking advantage of her strummed guilt within, and he propelled his tube away. And nearly overturned. When he glanced back she was looking at him again.

"Um, hey." Ugh. Could he sound more like the lame brain his sisters often accused him of being?

She smiled. "This is nice, isn't it? So calm and peaceful."

Except for the feelings ricocheting around his chest. "Yeah."

"You're so lucky to live here." Quick smile. "So blessed, I mean."

"God's own country."

"Yes." She studied him, and the slight current moved them lazily along.

Above, the sky was like a blue bowl, around them the trees were hushed, with just the slightest whisper of breeze. He didn't know where Cassie was—he didn't care. This moment was all about him and this beautiful intriguing person he hadn't known existed a few hours ago.

Ahead, near the bend, a few dozen rocks created a slight rapids effect, and he sat up.

And maybe flexed a little—subtly, of course—as he noticed her gaze drift to his pecs. Yeah, he'd been working out this summer.

Then the current picked up, and her eyes widened, her gaze returning to the water.

"It's our mini rapids," he explained.

"Fun."

Her smile wrapped around his heart and squeezed. But no, he couldn't pursue this, even as every pore within screamed to touch her, to somehow find a way to make this work.

And yet she was the first girl to really touch his heart. More than just her looks, he liked that she was driven, that she was focused, that she was really smart, that she followed God like he did, too.

Hey God?

It was hard to hear past the hormones raging around his body. Harder still, when her tube bumped into his and he caught her flailing hand and she didn't let go.

They stared at each other, the water pulling them along, and his heartbeat thundered in his ears. Call him crazy but she seemed so perfect that it was like God had placed her here. Not for Cassie's sake. But for his.

His grip tightened, and he shifted, drawing her tube closer, until their arms grazed and fire seemed to arc between them.

"Hannah."

Her eyelashes fluttered as she studied him from under half-closed eyelids, smiling lazily. "Franklin?"

"I—oh!" His tube hit a boulder and they broke apart, and his shift in momentum caused him to fall into the river. He scrambled upright, tall enough that his feet just managed to gain purchase on the moss-covered rocks below, to see she was struggling with her own balance before she, too, fell in the water. His breath hitched then she resurfaced, blinking, laughing, as she pushed her wet hair off her face. She shot him a grin before she hooked her arm around her tube and moved to the river bank.

Laughter from the shore drew his attention to his sisters. Awesome.

He followed Hannah. "You okay?" he called.

"I'm fine," she said, shooting another quick smile back at him.

The way his sisters were smirking suggested their little moment before hadn't gone unnoticed. Which meant shrugging things off and pretending it wasn't a big deal.

"Well." Cassie stood with her hands on her hips. "Someone looked like he was enjoying himself."

"Hey, it's hot," he protested.

"Yeah. You could say that." Cassie eyed him.

"I mean it's good to cool off." Man, he hoped Hannah couldn't hear this.

"You guys are so lucky to live here," Hannah said, as Poppy gave her a towel.

Huh. His sisters obviously liked her more than him, giving her a towel.

"Don't go playing with her heart," Cassie murmured. "She doesn't need another man to leave her."

"What? I barely know her. Come on. Give a guy a break." He bent to collect his towel, then grabbed his tube, and was careful to not indulge in too-long looks with Cassie's friend again that afternoon, doing his best to avoid her until it was time for her mom to pick her up.

He exhaled, watching the car leave from his bedroom window. It wasn't fair to start something when he'd soon be nearly three thousand miles away. But he had a feeling he'd never forget this golden day when he'd let the perfect woman slip away.

CHAPTER 11

Saturday morning passed in a whirl of work until she could finally meet up with her mom for a late lunch.

Her mom's choice of the steak house she'd visited with Franklin didn't exactly scream cozy catch-up time, something her mom's air kisses and almost-hug reinforced. Still, the fact she'd allocated time for her only child had to mean something, right?

Hannah settled back in her seat, choosing the New York–style fillet, and noticed a couple of the patrons nearby shifting as they glanced at her. Maybe they'd recognized her. Or was that arrogant to think like that?

"Well, it's good to finally see you," her mother said at last, flicking her blonde bob behind her ear. "How have you been?"

"Busy," Hannah began. "And—"

"Oh, I know. There has been so much going on at the university, it's why I've scarcely had a chance to breathe. But enough of that. I hear congratulations are in order."

"For—?"

"Last night, silly." Her mother's laughter tinkled. "All my friends were texting me saying how wonderful you were, and how good it was to see a strong independent woman on that show holding her own. I was so proud of you."

She was? Misgiving twinged. Or was that because she was proud of looking like she'd raised a feminist daughter?

"It means a lot to know I've raised you right, and it's something I think really helps give credence to my work for women's rights, and…"

Hannah listened as her mom continued with her usual spiel about her work and herself. She ate her food, noting her mom barely stopped for breath, as if she'd been saving up—or rehearsing—this conversation over the months since they'd last seen each other. How awful was it that they lived in the same city but barely spent time together? Did that make her a bad daughter or her mom a bad mother? Probably a bit of both. She drained her water.

An hour later—Mom had said she was proud, but her conversation had instantly switched to her new classes for the year, giving Hannah the impression she hadn't even watched the show—and Mom's busy schedule released Hannah to play catch-up with housework, while she fought the feelings of rejection. It wasn't that Mom didn't love her—she knew she did, deep within her heart—but that she had long prioritized her students over her daughter. And it was growing harder to pretend it didn't hurt.

She couldn't help but contrast it to how Cassie's mom had treated her children and wish that that could be her lot too. Maybe she could take up her invitation to drop by tomorrow. It would be safe. Franklin would be playing in Edmonton, and because it was only a preseason game she didn't think they'd be up there watching. And Leonie's invitation had felt genuine, at least. She could swing by after church.

Church? What was she doing thinking of going to church? But maybe it would be a good way to do more of that reconnecting with God, like she had last night when she'd dug out the old Bible and read the verses Franklin had recommended.

She shivered, remembering the way the words had struck her as clear as David's stone had sunk into Goliath's skull. God loved her. *Loved* her. *Her*. And just like she'd once known, it didn't seem to matter that she had walked away. God still loved her. Had *always* loved her. Just like the prodigal son's father held his arms open wide to receive his son, so she felt the same. God's arms were opened wide to all people. They just needed to know that, and accept His embrace.

Questions and emotions pursued her sleep, and again on Sunday morning, when she felt that prompting to go to church again. She suppressed it. But read a psalm instead, and again felt a renewal of peace. Which lasted for a few minutes, before that weighty unsettled feeling fell again, like a boulder in her chest. She needed to do something, but it was too late to go to church now. But maybe…

She texted Cassie, then realized she was probably at church.

Then was surprised when a reply came back immediately. Yes! Come for lunch. See you when you get here.

She replied with a THANKS, her heart churning. For some reason it felt like something momentous was coming her way.

The drive to the ranch showed winter was well and truly on its way. Poplars whose leaves which only a few weeks ago had held the first tinge of gold were stripped nearly bare now. There was more snow on the mountain ranges, too. The average daily temperature had dropped substantially since this time last month and would soon plunge into wintry bleakness. Yet the welcome at the ranch remained forever warm.

"You're here!" Cassie wrapped her in a hug. "I was so glad to get your text. You could've come to church with us, you know."

"I thought about it," Hannah admitted.

"You did? I've been praying you would."

"Franklin said that." Oops. Judging from the way Cassie's eyes lit, she shouldn't have said that.

"Oh, he did, did he? What else did that handsome brother of mine have to say?"

She shrugged, ignoring the tease. "He gave me a Bible passage to read. I did. It was good."

"Huh. Well, there you go. Franklin the evangelist. Maybe our last name should be Graham, not James." She gestured her to go inside. "Come on. The others are in the back."

Leonie and the others welcomed her in with hugs and encouragement. "It's our television superstar."

"You were awesome," Jess said. "I loved how you turned to Bob and basically told him to eat cow cakes."

Hannah smiled, even as her heart wavered. Unlike her mom, they really had watched it. "I was pretty nervous at first," until Franklin had prayed for her, "but it was actually kind of fun."

"You looked like a pro," Derek said.

"That's right. You were confident, articulate, and knowledgeable," Leonie said.

"Thank you. That means a lot." She glanced at the kitchen island where Jess and Poppy were grilling toast. "I hope you don't mind me dropping in like this. I know you're busy, and—"

"Oh, don't be silly. You never need to apologize for calling by. In fact, we want you to drop by whenever you feel like it."

Emotion clutched her, and she pressed her lips together and nodded. What a contrast to her mother who basically needed four months' notice before scheduling Hannah in her appointment book. "What can I do to help?"

A short time later she was seated at the farmhouse kitchen table, eating soup and cheesy toast, listening to the friendly squabble of the younger sisters, while Cassie and her parents discussed ranch things. This felt safe here, and after yesterday's formal family time, she felt loved and accepted.

Conversation turned to tonight's game. Franklin had invited

them to the first of the preseason split-squad games, but given the first few games were being played away because of arena renovations, their responsibilities hadn't allowed much time away from the ranch, work, and studies.

"We'll look forward to the first real game when they are here."

Which would be Thursday in two and half weeks.

"So are you looking forward to that game?" Hannah grinned. "Dumb question, I know."

"Yeah. For a smart reporter, it kind of is," Cassie teased. "Mom and Dad are beside themselves."

Hannah glanced at them as they quietly ate their meal, their matching twinkling eyes revealing their amusement at their eldest daughter's exaggeration. "You're both very proud, I'm sure."

"It's one thing to have my son make it all the way to the big leagues, it's another to finally see him play for the team I've supported since I was a boy."

Oh. Her heart melted a little at the obvious pride Derek showed. "I'm sure the team will do something special to honor that."

"They've been great. Franklin got us all tickets halfway along at the lower bowl."

She nodded. "Best seats in the house, huh?"

"He asked about suite level, but we wanted to be in the action."

"Are you going to be reporting on that game?" Leonie asked.

"Um, yeah. I am." Wow. "I'm supposed to be doing some of the pregame and mid-game interviews, so that'll be fun."

"Will you interview Franklin?" Jess asked slyly.

"Maybe." She shrugged. "It depends on what my bosses want." And she knew they'd definitely want her to interview Calgary's homegrown hero.

"Are Drew and Bob your bosses?" Poppy asked.

"Nope. Thank goodness. Otherwise they would've probably fired me by now."

"You made them look better than they are," Derek said.

"Hopefully they'll be listening to what the viewers and sponsors want and start changing what they say."

Later, after helping clear and clean, she accompanied Cassie on another visit to the western town.

"I find I have to make the most of checking things whenever I get the opportunity," Cassie explained. "It's such a big commitment, and the weather always makes it a challenge so I need to clean and fix things when I get a chance."

"I can help if you like."

"Thanks, but I'm really only fixing the tin cladding in the bar area of the saloon, so it'll be pretty noisy. Are you happy to hang out by yourself? I won't take too long," Cassie promised.

Was it bad that she was relieved for a moment to herself? "I'll be fine."

Cassie moved inside the saloon, so Hannah strolled the dusty streets, past the tobacconist, the telegraph office, the drapers, along the wooden boardwalk to the end of Main Street. She'd seen this street before in movies and a TV show, so it was fun to pretend to be a damsel from a different era, even if she wore jeans and a warm sweater now.

At the end of the street perched a small white steepled chapel. Her heartbeat pulsed. She pushed open the door, escaping the cool breeze and entering a hushed space. Inside was dim, the stained glass spilling muted light over pews that held a beeswax sheen and aroma. A rush of goosebumps tingled along her skin. You could feel the prayers that had filled this space.

She sank onto a seat in the second row and looked toward the altar. The altar, where hearts could alter. Hearts like hers.

She closed her eyes, forehead sinking on folded arms draped across the pew in front. This was why she wanted—needed—to come today. She'd felt unsettled for a long time, ever since she'd started ignoring God when her dad had basically stopped communicating with her not long after her sixteenth birthday. God hadn't answered her prayers to reunite her family, which had to mean He didn't care. But lately, all the little comments about God and prayer and Bible verses had massed into a giant snowball in her chest and she knew she couldn't live like this any longer.

She might've missed church this morning, but she didn't want to miss church now. And she didn't need music or preaching or anyone else except God. Her heart was preaching to her, same as the words she'd read in the Bible this morning, same as the words she'd read in her Bible on Friday night. God loved her, He wanted to be her friend, and in this sacred space that had once hosted sacred services she felt a similar sacred touch of God.

She wanted God. She *needed* God. She needed Jesus to once again truly be the Lord over her life. So she confessed her sins, confessed her pride in doing things her own way, in seeking glory just as much as her mother sought personal validation in her work.

"I'm so sorry, God. I don't want to live that way, so caught up in my own world that I forget that it's people who truly make life worth living for. Help me live for You, so You become greater, and I become less."

Tears pricked then fell, and she choked past clogged breath as she swiped them away. But it didn't matter what she looked like, only that within this moment she felt a realigning of her heart's purposes to line up with God's. Like the prodigal daughter had been welcomed home.

Home.

It seemed a foreign concept, something she'd not known for years, ever since her earthly father had left his family to start a new family in Florida. Her earthly father might've abandoned her, but she knew now, *knew* now, that her heavenly Father never had, and never would.

By the time she finished she likely had mascara stains under her eyes, but her heart felt cleaner, lighter than it had for a long time.

By the time Cassie entered the chapel, Hannah had wiped most of those stains away. She hoped.

"You okay in here?" Cassie asked.

"Yes."

"Hmm." Cassie studied her. "You are, aren't you?"

Hannah nodded, as stupid tears begged to make a second appearance. "Believe it or not, I am."

Cassie waited, eyebrows poised, a tender smile playing around her mouth. "And?"

"And, yes, I made a new commitment to God, if that's what you're wondering."

"Yes! We've all been praying for you for so long."

She wiped at new tears. Did that mean Franklin had too?

"I'm so pleased, and the rest of them all will be too." Cassie's face shone. "Come here."

A long hug later and Hannah pulled away. "Thank you for letting me come."

"Letting you? Girl, you heard my mother before. You're like one of the family and family doesn't have to ask permission to come home."

"Stop it," she said, wiping at her eyes again. "You keep making me cry."

"Hey, I think that's more God than me, but whatever. I'm *so* pleased for you."

Hannah nodded. Cassie's joy seemed to shimmer from her.

"Oh! And I needed to let you know that it's getting close to the first exhibition game starting, so if you want to come watch it with us, we need to get back to the house."

"Oh, but—"

"You're family, okay? Besides, let's not pretend you weren't going to watch it."

Her cheeks heated. "Of course I was. It's what my work requires."

"Uh-huh." Cassie's smirk said something else, but she wasn't about to enquire. "Come on, let's get back."

Hannah stopped by her car and retrieved a notebook, the latter to make it look like watching the game was for business and not for anything else. Definitely not pleasure. Or any other reason Cassie's side glances might imply. She also took a moment to hide her red nose and smeared mascara with fresh makeup.

By the time she returned to the living room, the family was seated around the large TV.

"Did you enjoy your visit to the movie set?" Leonie asked.

She nodded, peeking at Cassie.

"I didn't say a word," Cassie assured.

"A word about what?" Poppy asked.

Hannah glanced at Mr. and Mrs. James. "I had a good talk with God about doing things His way again," she admitted shyly.

"Oh, my dear, you don't know how happy that makes me," Leonie said.

There was another round of hugs, and she reveled in the love, soaking it in like perfume on skin.

"We've been praying for you." Leonie stroked Hannah's hair.

"Cassie mentioned you had. Thank you." So much gratitude filled the cavern of her heart she could almost burst.

"Now, can I get you something to eat? To drink?" Leonie pointed to the table lined with snacks. "We have a few things there."

"It looks like a party," Hannah said, taking her seat.

"It's a double celebration now," Leonie said, smiling at her.

New warmth gushed through her chest.

"What's the notebook for?" Cassie asked her. "You taking notes on how fine my brother is, are you?"

"Cassandra," her mother warned.

"How fine he is at playing hockey, sure," Hannah managed, pleased her voice sounded smooth. She ignored the way the sisters glanced at each other.

"Let's go, Calgary," Derek said.

After the emotions of the past hour or two it was good to finally have the spotlight off her and onto hockey. She drew in a steadying breath as the pregame commercials continued. As this was an exhibition game it meant that the proposed roster of contracted players had been divided into two sides. Edmonton had done a similar thing and split their squad too. The two team As were playing each other tonight, which saw Franklin partnered with Mike behind the top forward line of Hooper, Chavez, and Kapaulenyuk, with Matthews in net.

"What do you think of their chances, Hannah?" Leonie asked.

"Given their experience they should win," she said. "It just comes down to how well they've jelled during training." Which was the point of all the rigorous practice of the past few days of camp.

After some years of non-televised preseason games, this year the powers that be had decided to show all the games in full. CNSTV wasn't covering preseason games—their budget didn't stretch that far—but the other major sports channel was broadcasting. She watched Anton and his cohost's pregame introduction, making notes on what CNSTV could do to sharpen their coverage. It was all about being snappy and sharp and giving viewers what they wanted with pregame reports and insights and analysis. She'd long wanted to be a sports analyst but recognized the depth of knowledge these two on screen had. And while she appreciated that, she'd also really enjoyed the chance to sit in the chair and host. So she watched how Anton and his cohost exchanged opinions, making notes on what they could do better at CNSTV.

"…and this will be the first we get to see of Franklin James, now playing for Calgary after spending all of his previous career at Boston."

"Where he once played alongside Calgary's new captain," Anton said.

"It'll be interesting to see how they work together, paired on the same line. A big shout-out to Franklin's family if they're watching."

"Whoo!" Jess shouted. "We're watching."

"I'm sure they are," Anton continued. "Proud Albertans I believe, on a ranch not too far from Calgary."

"The Three Creek Ranch," the sisters said in unison, drawing Hannah's smile.

The teams skated onto the ice then the national anthem was sung, and the announcer said, "Well, here we go with the first Battle of Alberta game of the year. It might be preseason and an exhibition, but the intensity is real. Hold onto your hats, friends. Hockey is back!"

The puck dropped, and the game started. Hannah's pen poised as she watched intently. Franklin was playing strong defense, skating well as he and Mike protected the net. She peeked across at his mom who was biting her lip. Leonie glanced at Hannah and winced. "I always get so tense whenever I watch him play."

"He's strong," she said. "He knows what he's doing."

Leonie nodded, her attention returning to the screen.

Hannah didn't blame her. Even as a player it was easy sometimes to succumb to the tension, to focus on the negative what-ifs and maybes rather than what the team had trained hard for. That's why there was a big focus on mental training as well. And yet it was one thing to know that as a player; it was another to be a spectator willing your favorites to win. But that was what made sports so fun. Training and skill only went so far. There was often a degree of luck at play, even if it was luck a person had to make.

The first period continued, and she smiled as Franklin's checks and hits scored cheers from his family. Then bit her own lip as he was tripped, sending an Edmonton player to the penalty box. Her heart beat faster as she watched him scramble to his feet and get straight back into the action. And it continued for the rest of the game, watching with a tension-filled gut as the plays continued.

"How are you finding the game?" Cassie asked her.

"It's really weird, isn't it, when you personally know someone who is playing. You're so much more invested that it gets hard to see it as just a game."

"That's because there is no 'just a game' as far as Calgary is concerned," Derek said.

"True."

"And you know a few of them now, don't you?" Jess asked.

"A few," she agreed.

"It must be funny when you've played at such a high level too," Cassie mused. "I mean, I remember playing a bit in high school, but it was never anything like this."

Hannah nodded. "Yeah, it's fun because I can see some of the strategies being used and identify some set game plays, and part of me can almost smell what it's like to be playing. That's so weird, isn't it?"

"I don't think I'd want to be smelling that," Poppy said, as one of the players lifted his sweat-soaked jersey. "Gross."

"Ooh, look, it's Tom Chavez, he's fine. And, isn't that cute one Franklin's friend?" Jess asked, pointing at an Edmonton player with dark hair.

"Ryan?" Hannah asked.

"Yeah, they used to play in Juniors together, back in the day," Derek said.

"Now they're in the same online Bible study group that Mike introduced Franklin to," Leonie said.

Huh. "Nice to know there are some good guys playing in the league."

She remembered then what Bree had said about some of her friends whose husbands were Christians and played in the league. And she made a note to follow that up. Because for all that this was an exhibition match, it felt plenty real. And she'd love to know how these hockey WAGs coped with watching their husbands and boyfriends play hard and risk injury.

Her stomach swooped and she swallowed. No. She needed to remove herself from that particular scenario. It wasn't about her, and she had no right to feel this way. She might like Franklin but she couldn't afford to like him in that way. She pressed her lips together.

Cassie nudged her. "You okay?"

"Yep."

"What are you thinking about?"

She shook her head, then caught Cassie's smile. "Stop it," she whispered.

"Stop what?"

"Being annoying."

"Funny, that's what Franklin says too."

Ugh. She rolled her eyes at Cassie who only chuckled, then returned her attention to the screen. And as Franklin continued to play hard, she prayed for his protection, and for protection for her heart.

"Good game, boys." Mike congratulated them all, with side hugs, back and helmet pats.

Franklin scored a real hug, as befitting the best new defense pairing in the league. Alex scored a fist bump. His mouthy attitude with the ref had seen a penalty against them resulting in a goal.

He hadn't been sure Alex would even respond to Mike's encouragement, as he'd taken so long to meet Mike with his own clenched fist, but maybe he'd grown conscious of the hush of the rest of the room's celebrations, and maybe it was the fact that all eyes were on the interplay between old captain and new that had made him finally raise his fist. All of the rest of the guys were one hundred percent Team Mike, so maybe Alex sensed this too. It must be hard to have to feel like one of the regular guys again. Franklin's heart, hardened since witnessing the aftermath of Hannah's interaction with Alex, softened a fraction toward the man.

He joined the others in stripping off his sweat-soaked jersey, removing his pads, his skates and slipping into the special bumpy-soled massage sandals loved not just by old ladies but by some hockey players too. Instant relief.

Around him guys were preparing for showers, which meant some revealing more than he was comfortable showing, especially at a time when reporters might come barging through the door. He'd witnessed a few awkward—and yeah, hilarious—unexpected encounters over the years.

"Good job, Franklin," Kurt said, with a back slap. "Great save, eh?"

"Took it for the team." And he'd wear the bruise for a week. But winning was worth it.

His phone rang. Mom. He huddled back in his locker-room stall and pressed answer. "Hey Mom."

"You were great, honey. Hey, your father and the girls want to know if you can make this a video call."

"Sure." Franklin quickly tugged on a fresh Flames-emblazoned T-shirt then pressed accept on the video call. He grinned at his family. "Hey, you guys like the game?"

"Good job, Son," his dad said.

"You were awesome," Poppy said.

"Nice work," Cassie said. "Even Hannah agreed."

"Huh?"

"Hannah watched the game with us." The screen shifted to include a face he hadn't been able to forget. "Say hi."

Hannah raised her hand. Smiled.

"What are you doing there?" Whoa. Not how he'd meant to say that. "I mean—"

"I got invited to lunch."

"Then invited to stay to watch the game, seeing she had to watch it for work purposes anyway," Cassie said, with another annoying smirk.

"So, what did the expert think?"

"You looked great," Hannah said.

He fought a smile as his heart hummed with satisfaction, satisfaction that faded as Cassie chuckled.

Hannah's cheeks pinked, but she kept her gaze on his. "I mean you played great and looked comfortable, like you and Mike had been playing together for years. Was he happy?"

"Yeah. A win always makes for a happy captain. But yeah, he said it felt strong, and so did Coach Schultz, so it sounds like we'll be sticking together."

Movement in the room alerted him to potential eavesdroppers, and he figured it wouldn't look too good to be caught talking to a reporter like this. Even if that reporter was off duty.

"Hey, I gotta go, but it's great to see you all." He added that last bit as code for Hannah. He was really glad to see her.

"Take care of yourself, Franklin," his mom called.

The phone wobbled and his last glimpse of Hannah faded as the screen filled with an image of his folks again. "You know I always do," he said.

"Have fun in Vancouver, Son." The next of their preseason games.

"Will do." He grinned, raised a hand again. "Love you."

"Bye."

The call ended, but he stared at the phone. Mom often had trouble figuring out how to end a call, and this time was no exception, and the screen had glitched on an angled shot of the room, with Cassie in the background seated on the sofa next to Hannah. Hannah had one hand on her heart, as if capturing his last words and holding them close to her chest.

Love you.

He blew out a breath. See? This was the kind of stupid stuff that stole focus from games. He needed to stay focused, not let crazy thoughts like this distract him. They couldn't be together. Except, it kinda felt like they should. What other girl would be welcomed into his family like that, without him even needing to do a thing?

"You okay there, Franklin?" Mike asked.

Heaven forbid the man saw who was on his screen. "Yep." He quickly screenshotted the image then stood, pocketing his phone. "Just talking with my folks."

"Bet they were excited."

"Yeah."

"Shame they couldn't come tonight."

He shrugged. "Ranching doesn't make it easy to get away."

"Which is why it's good you'll be playing so much closer to home now."

"Yeah." His parents had only seen a handful or two of his NHL games, and only once in Boston, when he made his debut. Since then they'd only seen him play when Boston had played in Calgary.

"My dad travels for work, so couldn't get to too many games, either." Mike's smile twisted. "I think he saw more of me in Boston than he has in Calgary but that's how it goes sometimes."

"Yeah."

Conversation shifted to transport and travel arrangements. Their first road trip while the Saddledome underwent refurbishment following minor flooding this summer meant their first real game was the first they'd play at home. Not how most teams started the season, but it was how it would be. Preseason games meant they'd sleep at a downtown Edmonton hotel tonight, then tomorrow fly to Vancouver, then play the next day, travel to Seattle the day after that, then do it all again there and then in Winnipeg and Minnesota, before return visits to Winnipeg and Edmonton. They'd then have four days off before their first regular season game at home. Well, not off exactly, just not playing.

Later that night he worked to ignore Chad's snores as he scrolled through his phone, his fingers stilling when he came across the picture he'd screenshotted from earlier. Hannah, hand on heart, head tilted as she listened to him say "Love you." Yeah, he meant those words for his family, but Hannah seemed as good as part of his family these days.

His thoughts flicked back to the memory-dream he'd had Friday night, when he'd relived every second of that first time they'd met. How could he not have recognized her in that interview? Sure, her hair was different, and the circumstances were unexpected, but he should have known her. It seemed the height of cruelty that they had finally found each other again only to be kept apart due to his work policies and hers. His heart clenched. And, more importantly, just where was she in her journey to reconnecting with God?

Was there any way they could make this work?

CHAPTER 12

The high of Sunday buoyed Hannah through Monday's production meeting, her interviews with other Calgary families on Tuesday through Thursday, and dinner with Bree on Thursday night. The guys were playing in Seattle tonight, and Hannah had appreciated the invitation to eat and watch the game with someone not related to Franklin.

She might be trusting God again with her future, and reading her Bible and praying, but she still didn't know what this meant regarding Franklin. And maybe Bree would have some insights into what to do, and how to manage expectations.

The house was quiet, lights dim, except for the living room where the muted TV flickered with pregame action.

"I put the kids down so we could focus," Bree said, placing a platter of nachos next to the antipasto grazing platter on the coffee table. "Don't get me wrong, I love being a mom—it's what I've dreamed of being, but sometimes it's just nice to be an adult again."

"I bet." Hannah thought Bree looked wan. "How are you feeling?"

"Tired. Like, really tired."

"Have you seen a doctor recently?"

"Yeah. Yesterday." She placed a hand on her belly. "She's watching my iron levels as they've gotten pretty low in the past, but apart from that she says everything is going well, but I need to take it easy."

"And this is taking it easy?" Hannah gestured to the lavish spread. "I would've picked up food if I'd known—"

"No, it's okay. I love doing this. Entertaining and hospitality is one of my gifts, I think. But I might need to pull back a bit on the team's Thanksgiving preparations this year."

"What do you mean?"

"Oh," Bree waved a hand. "Mike and I have hosted Thanksgiving here for the past few years and always had an open house policy for any team members who can't make it home and have nowhere else to be. We'll still do that but I might have to ask my mom for some more help. She's coming this Saturday and will stay for the week and a bit until Thanksgiving, the Monday after next."

"I forgot it was that soon."

"Not a big thing in your family?"

"No." Mom hadn't bothered since Dad had left. It had just become yet another holiday where Hannah felt like she didn't belong.

"I'm sorry. Well, you're welcome to join us here."

"Weren't you just saying you were hoping to scale things back?"

"Adding another place setting is hardly a challenge. And I'd rather you be here than feel like you're not welcome."

"You're so sweet. Thank you. I'll let you know. I probably should check with my mom and see if she wants to do something together." It's what honoring her parent was about, right? And even meeting at a restaurant would be better than nothing.

"Well, she's welcome, too," Bree said.

"Bree, do you hear yourself? That's not how you pull back from overdoing things."

"I know, but it's what I think Jesus wants us to do."

"Yes, but I think God doesn't want you pushing yourself to your limits, especially when the doctor and Mike have both told you to be careful."

"And my mom," Bree muttered.

"Is that why she's coming? To keep an eye on you?"

"Maybe. She says she's concerned, and wants me to get someone to help. You'd think she thinks I'm a child and not the mother of two children."

"Four, if you're including those."

Bree placed a hand on her belly. "Wow. When you put it like that..." She peered at Hannah. "Wait, what were you saying about God before? I didn't think you believed."

"I believed, just wasn't following Him for a long time."

Bree's purply-gray eyes widened. "Does that mean you are now?"

Peace rolled across her chest and she smiled. "Yes."

"Yay!" Bree's previous tiredness seemed to flee as she clutched Hannah to her. "Oh, welcome back to the family, Hannah." She pulled back, beaming. "I'm so happy for you."

"I'm happy too. Much happier, actually. I've felt tense for so long, and now to be feeling peace, it's like something has clicked into place like it's always meant to be."

"It *is* always meant to be. I think that's what is meant by God placing eternity in the hearts of all men. And women." She winked. "It's a God-shaped hole in our heart that people avoid, or try to fill up with trivial things, but those things are never going to bring the kind of peace that God can. Oh, I'm so happy for you!"

"Thank you," she said, feeling shy.

Bree said grace, adding a special thank-you for Hannah's recent faith recommitment, then pointed to the food and picked up a plate. "Help yourself. Now, tell me how this happened."

Hannah scooped up guacamole—it looked homemade—as she contemplated how to say this. Admit she'd gone to Franklin's family's place last weekend? How much did Bree tell her husband? She didn't want to cause any problems for Franklin or herself if people thought their friendship was anything but "professional," and Bree didn't seem the kind to keep secrets too well. But then, it wasn't like she'd gone there for him. She'd gone, wanting to visit the chapel, and knowing she had to do it for herself. "Um, I guess there's just been a lot of things that have pointed to that recently. Including what you have said."

"Really? I didn't come across too strong?"

She hesitated. How was she supposed to answer that honestly?

Bree winced. "I did, huh? I'm still working on that. But hey, if it ultimately helped, then I suppose it didn't turn you off."

"I think anyone who truly knows you would see the heart for others you have and respond to your kindness and generosity. And that's what God is about, right?"

Bree nodded, her eyes sparkling. "That's so lovely of you to say. It's all about God's kindness and undeserved mercy."

The muted TV showed the anthems playing, and she took a moment to thank God for His mercies. For renewed faith and hope for her future. For friends. Family. For her job, her house, for this country where she could live strong and free. So many blessings when one took time to truly see.

The puck dropped and the game started, and just as she'd done each game she took notes, scribbling down thoughts and impressions that would help her speak intelligently tomorrow night on *Hockey Hour*.

Jason had insisted she rejoin the panel—apparently the viewers had loved her, and they wanted to continue boosting ratings—and while part of her was as anxious about Franklin as

Bree was about Mike, she knew she had to keep some emotional distance too.

It was easier to do that, though, each time Mike and Franklin skated off the ice at the end of their shifts and she and Bree could relax and eat something else.

"It gets so tense, huh?" Bree said, popping in a grape. "You'd think I'd be better than this, but I still find myself praying so hard for him every game." She rolled her eyes at herself. "And this is only preseason. Ugh. I can't imagine what I'll be like when they get to the playoffs."

"I like how you say when."

Bree chuckled. "Yeah, I don't think the wife of the captain would be allowed to say if. Besides, they're definitely gonna make it, especially with that rock-solid defense from our guys."

Hannah coughed. She hoped by saying "our" that Bree meant the team's rock-solid defense and not anyone in particular. A peek at her showed Bree's tilted lips, so maybe she hadn't. Best to ignore that comment, then.

"They're doing so well, aren't they?" Bree said as Mike and Franklin skated off after another shift, the camera showing them grabbing drinks as they sat on the sideline.

"Yeah."

"Mike tells me that Franklin has really settled in well with the team. He's so glad to have a quality partner, who's also a quality man, too."

"He is that," she said softly.

Quality, inside and out. Willing to forgive, willing to work hard, willing to give second chances. He was a good, good guy. Someone she could fall for. Oh, who was she kidding? She *had* fallen for him. She'd long ago fallen for him. And it had taken until now to realize that her feelings ran deeper than mere like. Now that she recognized the quality of the man, and that his love for God and his family informed all he did, she recognized also that her tender feelings toward the man ran awfully close to love. She swallowed.

Did he always sign off with a "love you" for his family? The sweetness of that moment had touched her deeply on Sunday night. She'd had to fight for composure when his sisters' tease suggested it was a new addition to his farewell, before his mom had insisted he always said that to her. And regardless, the fact he did that for his mom showed him to be as kind and sweet as any girl could want. Imagine with what tenderness he'd treat his girlfriend. Or his wife. Shivers rippled up her skin.

"Are you warm enough there?" Bree asked.

"Uh, sure."

"I can turn the thermostat up. The nights are getting cool, aren't they?"

"Yeah."

She did her best to refocus on the game, glad when Bree kept the commentary on during the mid-game breaks so Hannah could take notes again on what they could improve on. She stayed for the end, overtime seeing a penalty shoot-out in which Alex—her stomach tensed—scored the winning goal, and helped Bree clean up as the postgame commentary continued.

"And another solid effort from Calgary's blue line," the sportscaster said. "This new pairing of Vaughan and James looks like a tough combination to beat."

"You know it!" Bree called. "Not that I'm biased or anything," she added, shooting Hannah a smile.

"Totally unbiased," Hannah agreed solemnly.

Bree laughed. "But it's true right? Their percentages mean they've let in fewer goals than nearly any other team in the league."

"It's early days yet," Hannah cautioned.

"It's good they're clicking, though."

"For sure." She put the last plate in the dishwasher, added the tablet, then turned it on.

"Thanks for all you've done." Bree clicked off the TV. "It was so nice to have a friend here to talk to."

"I'm sure you'd have lots of friends who'd love to come. I bet any of the other WAGs would love to come."

"Yeah, but I don't feel like I can fully connect with all of them. Some don't get hockey, or God, or me, so it's been nice to feel like I could do this with you."

"Even though I've only just gotten back in a God relationship?"

"But you were obviously already on the journey. Besides, some people you just feel at home with, right?"

"Absolutely." Like she now did with Bree. And Cassie. And Cassie's family.

Bree's smile drooped. "And to be really honest, as much as I love being Mike's wife and I'm so proud of what he's doing in the NHL, sometimes it gets hard too. I didn't realize just how full-on it would be with two little kids and being pregnant and having to do this on my own. I mean, I know I'm not a single mother but I'm so tired and the real season hasn't even begun." She sighed. "And when it does, I know I'll be responsible for making sure the kids are quiet so he can get his sleep and be in the right headspace on game days, and all the other things. It's going to be a lot."

Hannah rubbed Bree's upper arm. "Hey, you'll manage. Maybe there is someone you can ask to come help you, like a part time nanny, or something. In the meantime, you've got friends you can lean on."

Bree blew out a breath, putting on a smile. "I know. And I also know I sound like I'm complaining so I better stop."

"But isn't being honest what being friends is about? I might be a reporter, but I'm a safe space too. If you need to talk, I'll do my best to be here for you."

Bree's eyes glimmered. "You're so sweet." She sniffled. "I know I need to make the most of staying connected with my friends. It's not like I'm the only one going through this. I know Holly and Allie sometimes feel the same."

Hannah hugged her. "I'll be praying for you, and that you find the right person to come help you."

"Thanks so much." Bree pulled back, wiping her eyes. "Whew. Sorry about getting teary."

"No apology necessary. But hey, maybe some help is."

Bree nodded. "I might see if my friend Sylvie, she's the Goth preschool teacher I think I've mentioned before, is interested in moving west." Her lips curved. "She needs God, too, so if you're praying for me, then please add a prayer for her too."

"Will do."

"Oh, and if you want to come to church with me on Sunday, I'd love to sit with you."

"Thanks, but I've agreed to go with Cassie to her church."

"Good. As long as you're going somewhere." Bree hugged her again. "I'm so glad for you. Thanks again for coming."

"My pleasure."

"And I'll be praying things go well tomorrow night."

Hockey Hour. "Thank you."

She drove home, heart full, as she prayed for Bree, and this mysterious Goth friend of hers. Bree was so generous, but her big heart was perhaps a little too big for the responsibilities she now carried. She hoped—prayed—that God would help her ease back from overcommitting, and that Bree and Mike would be able to sort things out for their increasing household.

And that God would help her sort things out with feelings about Franklin. And help her do well tomorrow night.

"AND WE'RE BACK with *Hockey Hour,* coming live to you from Cowtown," Bob said.

Franklin's lip curled. He hadn't liked the way Bob had

looked at Hannah in some of the earlier shots. She sat, looking unmoved by Bob's obvious antagonism, looking as serene as a royal princess on tour.

A knock drew him to the hotel door. He opened it to find Mike. "Hey, come in."

Franklin jabbed at the remote control to mute it. How to explain to his captain and friend that he'd pulled out early from the team dinner because he wanted to watch the woman-who-was-not-his-girlfriend on TV tonight?

"*Hockey Hour*, huh?" Mike sat on the other bed. "How is she doing?"

"Hannah?"

Mike cut him a look.

"Holding her own."

"You talked to her lately?" Mike asked.

"No." Hadn't even texted. And that was killing him.

"Maybe you should."

"What?" He pivoted to see Mike's smirk. "Why do you say that?"

"Because she might have something to say."

"What do you know?"

Mike held up his hands. "Hey, it's not my news to share."

"But obviously someone has shared with you. Was it Bree?"

"Look, all I'm gonna say is that Hannah may have had dinner with Bree last night and they might have discussed some things."

"What kinds of things?"

"Again, not my place to share, but you can ask her yourself when she's off that." He pointed to the TV.

"Uh-uh." Franklin threw a decorative cushion at him. "You don't get away with saying stuff like that and not giving a man some kind of clue."

"Or maybe I do."

"Come *on*. That's cruel, man."

Mike chuckled.

"And I don't think that's what Jesus would do."

Mike snorted. "Wow. Pulling out the Christian guilt trip now, huh?"

"You better believe it."

"Yeah, well, let's just say you're on the right track." He threw the pillow back at him. "Don't stay up too late. We've got a game tomorrow."

"Yes, sir."

He barely noticed Mike's exit as his eyes remained glued to the TV, his heart tumbling over what Mike had just shared. Did he mean—?

No. Someone would've told him. Surely.

Had she—?

Hannah was talking, and he unmuted it, drinking in the sound of her voice.

"…obvious that the team dynamics are working well, and the blue line is looking really strong. If this partnership continues as they've started then I think it'll be a really good year."

His pulse increased. Was she talking about him?

Drew nodded. "It's like James has come to prove that big salary of his is worth it, and so far the answer looks like a yes."

So she *had* been talking about him.

"But it is just preseason," Hannah said, "and there's a lot more hockey to play still."

Breath hitched. Did she mean to sound disparaging, even if it was true?

"So we better hope and pray he and Vaughan keep clicking and stay healthy," Hannah concluded.

"Amen to that," Drew said with a laugh.

But Franklin's heart had snagged on her comment. Had she really said pray on TV? Did she mean it? Is that what Mike had meant?

He grabbed his phone, wincing. How could he ask without

sounding like a fool? Oh, hang it. *Have you heard from Hannah lately?* He pressed send.

A few seconds later: *Define lately.*

He groaned. Sisters. Fine. That's what a man deserved for triangulating and not going directly to the source. He should've known better.

His phone buzzed with a new message. *You watching HH?*

He was sorely tempted to ignore her, but after making it through an ad for Toyota then one for Tim Hortons, he finally gave in. *Yes.*

She's doing awesome, huh?

That deserved a thumbs-up. Cool, detached, unemotional.

The show resumed, with Hannah's report on Chad. He watched greedily, as his heart vacillated between gladness at seeing her and dismay at how easily she connected with Chad. He knew this had been filmed before Franklin and she had left the neutral zone and entered into almost-more-than-friends territory, but he still noticed spikes of jealousy whenever she smiled at Chad or they bantered.

The need to message her—better yet, call her—rose, and he had to fight the inclination to send a message right there and then. She couldn't answer now. And for all he knew she might have someone monitoring her phone while she was in the studio. But he wanted—needed—to talk to her, to find out about whatever this thing was that had got Mike excited and led Franklin to hope like he hadn't dared hope before.

Finally the torturous segment finished, and they cut back to the studio. Hannah was nodding as Drew and Bob did their between-them spiel, as if she was waiting to participate. But unlike last time, when it seemed she had been determined to jump in, this week she seemed more amused, calmly waiting for a break before offering her opinion.

"I think it's important to realize that such decisions as the league's permission of long road trips have an impact beyond the player," Hannah said. "It affects the families at home. And their well-being can have a further ripple effect on the player and their ability to focus. So it's important they take this into consideration."

"And yet sometimes decisions about road trips and schedules are out of the league's hands," Drew said, "like what's happened in Calgary with summer rain flooding the Stampede grounds and requiring more Saddledome refurbishments. I think you can't underestimate the intelligence of fans understanding that."

"I never underestimate the fans." Her mouth tweaked up slightly on one side. With wryness, probably. "Of course they understand things like that. But my discussions with family members have given me a new appreciation for the challenges of what life is like back home when these players are doing their thing on the road."

"It's what these women sign up for," Bob said, folding his arms.

"Sure, but it doesn't change the fact that it's important for teams to take into account the mental health not just of the players but of their immediate family too, as it can help or hinder the player."

"And who is going to pay for that?"

"The players' performance will be paying for that," she said, without missing a beat.

Franklin smiled.

"Happy wife, happy life, huh?" Drew said.

"If you want to see your players scoring then they need to be fully focused on that."

"I don't know," Bob said. "All this talk about mental health can be overdone sometimes. Like when a woman's upset. Is it mental health, or is it her time of the month and hormones?"

Hannah blinked, her mouth falling open. "How dare—"

"I guess what I'm really hearing you say is that they need to score on and off the ice, huh, Hannah?" Bob said.

"That is *not* what I—"

"And I think we're due to go to commercial break. See you after this." Drew pointed at the screen, and the program cut to more advertising.

Whoa.

His phone flashed. Cassie again. He pressed to answer her call.

"I can't believe Bob said that," she said without preamble.

"Poor Hannah."

"She looked lost for words, didn't she?"

"I think Bob will be in trouble." He hoped so, anyway.

"She was doing so well, too," Cassie said.

Yeah.

"Hey, what was it you wanted to know before?" she asked.

He played dumb. "About?"

"Hannah. You wanted to know if I'd heard from her lately. Why?"

That last word was asked in a slow but musical upwards inflected way that tugged at every one of his defense mechanisms. "No reason."

"Sure."

This was a bad idea. He should never have called her.

"What does my big brother want to know?" She sighed. "Are you going to give me the silent treatment now? Look, I haven't talked to her since we talked about going to church on Sunday."

"Church?"

"Yes! Isn't that great? Oh! But maybe—okay, I'm out. See ya."

The call ended, and he stared at his phone. What had happened? Did Cassie mean Hannah was talking about church in general or they actually were going to go to church together? His heart pounded. Because if it was the latter...

He called back, but Cassie wasn't answering. So he called Mike, but he didn't answer either. Clearly he was going to have to wait until the woman who consumed his thoughts was free to speak. He hoped it would be soon.

The program resumed, with an apology from Bob about his earlier comment. Hannah was stone-faced, her body language making it clear she did not like the man she sat next to.

He guessed whatever had gone down during the commercial break had not been easy, not for any of them, and he prayed for her, that she'd feel peace and regain the animation that made her so easy to watch. But she didn't, her comments a little slower, her tone flat, and her avoidance of Bob was becoming increasingly plain to see. His concern for her grew, so it was a relief when the end credits rolled, and he was finally free to message her, and hope nobody was there to see his name pop up on her phone.

You were great.

Simple, innocuous enough. Nobody could take issue with it. He hoped.

He spent way too long checking his phone, flicking between dumb programs on TV, wondering whether he should call Cassie again, or Mike, or even Bree. But he didn't want to miss a message, or the chance to speak with her if she called. And he hoped the fact this was his first message in a week wasn't a reason for her to ignore him.

He was being paranoid. She was probably still dealing with the fallout from Bob's comment in the program. She was probably still in a meeting with the producers and—

His phone flashed. His pulse increased then fell.

All good? Mike.

He sent back a thumbs-up emoji. No way did he want to worry the dude. He sighed.

The hotel room door opened again. Chad from the interview before. "Here you are."

"And there you are." Irrational jealousy spiked. He tamped it down. It wasn't Chad's fault Hannah had to interview him too.

"You okay, man? You look stressed."

"I need a shower."

"You do." Chad hurried to the bathroom. "But I need the can first."

Franklin spent the next five minutes willing his phone to ring, but maybe her meeting was still going or mind vibes wasn't a thing because she didn't answer.

Finally Chad escaped, the bathroom fan's loud whir suggesting it wasn't going to be pretty. "Sorry, man. That pork might've had MSG."

Franklin threw a cushion at him. "Thanks a lot."

"Any time."

Franklin glanced at his phone, half tempted to take it in with him. What if she messaged back while he was in the shower? But then…what if she did? He couldn't reply, could he? Best he just shower as quickly as possible.

By the time he returned Chad was in the other bed, earbuds in, scrolling through his phone. His eyes widened. "Are you not feeling well? That had to be the shortest shower I've known you to take."

Franklin shrugged, shoved his clothes in his bag, then glanced at his phone.

"Oh, some chick tried to call you."

"What?" He snatched up his phone.

"Cass someone."

Oh. His sister could wait. He checked his messages. Still no word from Hannah.

"You okay, dude?"

"Yeah." He got into bed, rolled onto his side, switched off the bedside light, stared at his phone. He should probably charge it but that would mean getting out of bed again, and—

His phone flashed. He glanced at the screen.

Thanks.

He pushed upright, glanced at Chad still scrolling through his phone, then pressed call. *Pick up, pick up, pick—*

"Hi."

"How are you?" he asked in a rush.

She sighed. "You saw it, didn't you?"

"I meant it before, you were great." He stole another look at Chad. He was keeping his voice low, but he'd really like to make sure his roomie didn't overhear this. "Can you talk?"

"Obviously."

He smiled at the bite in her words. "Give me a moment and I can talk too."

"You're in Winnipeg, right?"

"In a hotel room, with Chad. Your interview with him was good too." Franklin could afford to be generous now. It wasn't like she was talking to Chad now.

Another sigh. "I think that was the highlight of tonight."

"Well, my highlight is talking to you." Well, look at him being so smooth. He fist-pumped himself.

"Are you sure you should be talking to me?" she asked.

No. But he'd never say that. Not in a million years. "Let me grab a hoodie."

Chad glanced up. "Who's that?"

"Nobody" wasn't going to cut it. "A friend."

"Uh-huh." He smirked. "I think I can tell what kind of friend." He winked. "Didn't think you were the type, but hey, you do you."

"Dude, I'm not that type. It's a friend, not a booty call." He pointed. "Mind out of the gutter. I'll be back in a bit."

"Take as long as you need. No skin off my nose, bro."

Franklin pulled on a hoodie, track pants and massage slides, and put the phone to his ear. "You still there?"

"Yeah."

He grabbed his room key-card, pistol-pointed his hand at Chad, and left to his roommate's laughter. Technically he should be in bed, but this conversation felt too important for prying ears. "Sorry about that."

"I'm imagining what you're doing."

"Just had to put some clothes on." He winced. "I mean, I wasn't naked. Man. I mean—"

She chuckled. "It's okay. I won't imagine that."

He sighed. "Chad is my roomie, and he was saying all kinds of stuff—" No, she probably didn't need to know that either. "Sorry. I was almost asleep when you messaged, so I don't think my brain is working too well."

"I didn't get back until late. So, I'm sorry for keeping you from your beauty sleep."

"You think I need beauty sleep, huh?"

A beat. Then, "No."

He grinned. "Just for the record, I don't think you need it either."

He could just about hear her smile in the space of breath that followed. "You're sweet."

"Just telling the truth. You're the only thing worth looking at on that show."

"Ah, that show." She exhaled. "Jason was *not* happy."

"He's the producer, right?"

"Yeah. The guy you met that first day? He was seriously ticked with Bob."

"Yeah, not the only one. It's amazing the man still has a job."

"I don't know how much longer he will have one. But you didn't hear that from me."

"You still have your job, don't you?"

"Why? Did you think I was that terrible?"

"No, not at all. I meant it before. You were great."

"Yeah, Jason wasn't thrilled with my lackluster efforts at the end, but I felt blindsided, and couldn't pretend I was okay sitting next to such a man. Would you believe Jason had the nerve to tell me I should've smiled? Did he ask Drew to smile?

No. So I'm not about to smile and pretend my anger isn't justified and that everything is okay."

"How are you doing now?" he asked softly.

She made a sound which could have been a sniffle.

"Hannah?"

She gave a shaky-breath sound. "Stupid tears."

She was crying? His heart hurt. He longed to give her a hug. "I wish I could be there."

"Why?"

He swallowed. Admitting he cared for her—wanted to hug her—seemed dangerous and powerful at this time of night, especially talking on the phone like this, hidden at the end of a hotel corridor behind an ice machine. Heaven forbid anyone might need ice for their beverage tonight. "I wish there was something I could do."

"There's nothing anyone can do, but I appreciate the thought. It's amazing to hear your voice, let alone think you might actually want to see me."

"Of course I want to see you," he said. "It's just safer—"

"Not to," she finished. "I get it."

The fact she sounded as bummed about it as he was lifted his heart a little. Maybe this wasn't all one way, after all. He needed to change the subject. "Hey, a little birdie might've told me something."

"About?"

He arrowed his fingers into his hair. Clearly the playing of Games of Non Answer was genetic. "Cassie mentioned you were talking about church."

"Yes."

"Because?"

"Because I want to go with her."

She did? "That's awesome."

"Bree asked me too."

"Can I ask why the new interest in church?"

She hesitated.

"You don't have to—" he began.

"Because I—" she started then stopped. Chuckled. "You go."

"No, you go. Ladies first."

She drew in a breath. "Because I have a new interest in God."

His heart hammered. Had she taken the next step from their last conversation and gone from talking to God again to following Him? "Meaning?"

"Meaning I made a recommitment last weekend, and I'm wanting to do things God's way."

"Really?"

"Really." She laughed again. "You don't need to sound so surprised."

"I'm not surprised. Well, a bit maybe, but mostly I'm just so glad for you. Like really, *really* glad." So glad his heart might burst.

"I'm glad too. I've felt pretty stressed about a bunch of things and this just helped take so much of that burden away."

"Hallelujah."

"I mean, obviously not everything is perfect, like with this job and my mom, and—ah, other stuff."

He wondered what she was going to say but didn't. Did she mean them? Was *them* a possibility, after all? Suddenly Mike's earlier reaction made more sense. A future together could be an option if they both believed. Even if their work situations remained a challenge. Still, "God is into straightening our paths."

"Amen," she said softly.

His heart softened. He'd prayed for this moment, and to hear her own her faith like this made him feel a little emotional too. "I've been praying for you."

"I know." A beat. "I've been praying for you too."

Okay, that did it. This woman was gold. He had to see her ASAP. "I miss you."

"I miss you, too," she whispered.

His stomach swooped. Butterflies, others called it. "I can't wait to see you."

"Remind me when you get back?"

"We're another week on the road then we fly back after Edmonton next Saturday night."

"That feels so far away."

"Yeah."

"Bree mentioned how hard it was being separated when you guys were on the road," she said. "I guess I know a bit about how that feels."

His heart stuttered. "Are you saying—?"

She laughed quickly. "Not that I can see how this can be anything more than friendship."

"I'd like it to be, though."

A beat. Two. "Really?"

"Really." He blew out a breath. "So we're gonna have to pray that God can make a way for this to work."

"I already am," she admitted.

"Me too."

She laughed, and the sound tickled fresh joy to his heart. Then she yawned. "Sorry."

"No, it's late. Go to bed, and we'll talk more when we can. Okay?"

"Okay."

"Hey, but before you go, let's pray right now." He didn't wait for her assent, just closed his eyes and launched in. "Hey God, You straighten paths. Please work this out for us." *Us.* His heart tingled. "And help Hannah to sleep well, and bless her, in Jesus's name. Amen."

"Amen."

He opened his eyes. And saw Chad staring down at him, mouth agape.

The hope instilled by that phone call and prayer was further boosted by the Sunday service, where a sermon that felt like it had been written just for her encouraged Hannah to seek God and put His kingdom first, and all the other worries of life would be sorted.

It sounded simplistic, but as Cassie later explained, it was more about prioritizing and putting God first before letting other worries crowd in. So she was doing her best to do that. Each worry about her job or her mom or Franklin she would mentally place at the foot of the cross. And each time she did that she felt the worry ebb away.

Which was why she could sit here at the Monday production meeting and put her shoulders back and meet each man in the eyes. Bob, she noticed, looked away.

"It should come as no surprise that Friday's program was not our finest hour. In fact," Jason consulted his notes. "In fact, Bob single-handedly managed to tip at least one of our sponsors into pulling the pin."

Hannah's jaw sagged. She quickly closed her mouth, and snuck a peek at Bob. He'd slumped in his seat.

Dirk cleared his throat. "A local department store"—he named *the* local department store, where everyone who was anyone shopped—"has decided they do not wish to continue to partner with an organization they describe as, quote, 'misogynistic and anti-family values.'" He glanced at Bob, then Hannah, then nodded to Jason again.

She froze. This was all her fault. If she hadn't brought up that comment about families and wives—No. That was on Bob. There'd been plenty of ways to address that comment appropriately, and he had chosen none of them. *Lord, help me.*

"It appears that many of the complaints the station has received have said exactly that," Jason said. "Will? Care to expound?"

Will nodded, then began sharing some of the comments the socials had received.

Hannah cringed. How awful to be associated with something described in such ways.

"I don't need to tell you how embarrassed I am to be linked to this," Dirk said. "This has gone on long enough."

"Too long," Jason muttered, glancing up. His gaze met hers then swept around the room again. "As you can see, this leaves us with a problem. We have a show to produce for Friday, our last preseason episode before we start standard programming once the regular season begins. And with viewers and sponsors not wanting to see Bob then we need to consider what we're going to do. Do we take *Hockey Hour* off the air?"

What?

"That's obviously not an option," Jason continued, "given our contractual obligations to the team and various sponsors. Do we boot Bob and put Hannah in his place?"

"You can't do that," Bob protested.

"I think you'll be surprised at what we can do, Robert," Dirk said.

"Are you seriously thinking of ripping apart one of the best commentary teams in the business?" Drew demanded. "I have a contract—"

"That's right, and I'm sure you want to keep your sports job on the news, don't you?"

Drew blinked.

"We've thought long and hard about what we're going to do," Jason said, taking over from Dirk. "And after much deliberation this weekend the only choice we can see moving forward at this stage is for Bob to be suspended this coming Friday with Hannah taking his place, and we review things the following week when the regular season begins."

"But—"

"Don't interrupt, Drew," Dirk said. "Hear the man out."

Drew's mouth snapped closed.

"Obviously, if Hannah is going to still be doing the players' on-ice and game interviews, then we need to juggle that, which is where it gets tricky." Jason glanced at her. "You still want to do those, Hannah?"

"Yes."

"But—"

"Then we'll make it work," Jason said, ignoring Drew's attempted interruption. "The schedule is pretty kind to us, with only one Friday night game at the Saddledome that we'd need a contingency plan for, and even that isn't until December. So we can make it work, even if it means Drew hosts by himself."

"What about Bob?" Drew asked.

Hannah glanced at Bob. He looked pained, his features washed in gray.

"Bob's future is really up to him," Dirk said. "He's been informed, as has his agent, that he will need to undergo some counseling and be willing to have that announced in order for there to be any conversation about a return to work here."

Drew shot Bob a horrified glance. Bob nodded that it was true.

"I know this all comes as quite a shock, but it's not as if this has not been mentioned as a possibility before," Dirk said. "Now, are there any questions?"

"I don't see how she could manage all that and be on air for *Hockey Hour* too," Drew objected.

"You manage to do the news sports report and do *Hockey Hour*, don't you?"

"Yeah, but I've been doing this for years. She's just started."

"And she's very good," Dirk snapped. "As good as some people who have been doing the same job for years."

"Hannah?" Jason asked. "Do you have any questions?"

She shook her head. "Oh, actually, I do." She squared her shoulders. "What do we plan to include in Friday night's program?"

"AND I'M HOSTING, properly cohosting, with Drew this week," she said to Franklin later that night.

"That's awesome. Wow. What a turnaround."

"Right? If it wasn't so awful and people weren't so upset I'd be over the moon."

"God is working things out for good, huh?"

"For sure." She was coming to see this more and more each day. Even her mom had picked up the phone earlier when Hannah had called to tell her about the new role, and Mom had cheered her on. It was enough to make her lose her head and ask if she wanted to do something together for Thanksgiving next Monday. Maybe the question had surprised her mom so much she'd lost her head too, because she'd said yes. And Hannah had said she'd arrange something, ignoring the niggle of hope that maybe Cassie would invite Hannah to have lunch with them, which would mean Franklin might be there. And might meet her mom.

The silence stretched, and she didn't think it was due to tonight's loss against Minnesota. "Are you okay?"

"Yeah." His voice didn't sound it though.

"What's wrong?"

"Nothing."

"Are you sure?"

"I just had Chad look at me funny again tonight when I left to come talk to you." He blew out a noisy breath. "He heard me praying with you the other night, and knows I like a girl called Hannah."

She winced. "I'm not the only Hannah in the world."

"You're the only one for me."

Warmth gushed inside.

"And you're the only one he knows who is in my world, so the fact is he's a bit suspicious now."

Her smile faded. "What are you wanting to do? We can go back to texting if that makes it easier for you."

"But I love talking to you."

"Me too. But hey, texting can still work. And it won't be too long until you're back."

"Five days is too long."

"Look, maybe we just don't do phone calls in the next five days." She smiled. "Just think, it'll be like normal, because we never used to call until these past few days."

"I want this to be my new normal."

The raspy edge to his voice made her heart flutter some more. "Me too." She loved talking to him. "Then you're back, we can see each other, and that'll be fun."

"Hey, speaking of fun, what are you doing for Thanksgiving?"

Her heart squeezed. "Something with my mom, for the first time in what feels like forever. I haven't figured out what though. Bree asked me to their place. Apparently they do a team thing, but I'm not sure." She smiled, then asked coyly, "Why?"

"Come to the ranch with me and my family. Bring your mom too."

"But what will your family say?"

"They'll say it's about time."

She grinned. "I will, but only if I know it's okay with your mom."

"Come on, you know she loves you too."

Too?

The word hovered between them and for all her boldness she didn't dare ask him what he meant by it. Had he just said that he loved her? Her mother might've raised her to be strong and courageous but she was pretty sure it didn't extend to moments like this.

"Hannah?" he murmured. "Say you'll come."

Had he even heard what had slipped from his mouth? Maybe he had meant it, and her lack of response had scared him off. Or maybe he only meant it as in his mom loved Hannah like the way his sisters—or at least Cassie—did. It was way too soon to be talking about love anyway.

"Hannah?"

"Um." She blinked, trying to get her thoughts straight again. "I will, but only if your mom says it's all right for me and my mom to come. Okay?"

"Uh-huh." There was noise at his end, like murmured conversation. "Hey, I gotta go. I'll message you later, okay?"

"Sure. Miss you."

"Bye." He ended the call.

So she didn't want to be the girl who read into everything a guy said on the phone. But she did feel a degree of pique that he hadn't replied with a "miss you" to hers. Did that make her needy? Or simply insecure? Or was it just something guys did? Or maybe his roommate had been there and he needed to get out of looking like he was talking to her, and saying "miss you" would make it harder to deny.

Deny? She sighed. How long would they have to play this game of pretend and denial? Then she remembered. "Hey Lord, it feels like the hundredth time I'm praying about this problem, but I'm giving this to You..."

UNKNOWN CALLER.

Hannah glanced at her phone screen, debating whether to answer. She'd received a few unknown ID calls in recent weeks, and had learned after the first few whispered insults to not pick up. She'd found those promising to hurt or rape her were less likely to leave their threat as a voice message that could be traced. Still, she hadn't had one of those for a while. And it might be someone important.

"You've reached Hannah," she said.

"Hannah," a low voice said. "Hannah needs a spanner to the head—"

She pressed end, her hand shaking. Okay. That was on her. She shouldn't have answered.

"You okay Hannah?" John, the production assistant, stopped by her desk.

She started to nod, then shook her head.

"Hey, what's wrong?"

Royce was here too? "Nothing." She gritted out a smile. "I just got another phone call."

"What kind of phone call?" Royce asked, frowning. "You look pale as a sheet."

She pushed her phone away. "Someone trying to be a poet who thinks Hannah needs a spanner to the head."

Royce blinked. "Are you serious?"

She dipped her chin.

"That's messed up."

"You need to tell HR," John said. "Has this happened before?"

Hannah nodded.

"Then do it now. And get a new number." He patted her shoulder in a fatherly way. "I'm sorry there are people like that out there."

She pressed her lips together, unable to answer in case dreaded emotion returned. She blinked it back, pushed back the chair and moved to Peter's office, and handed him her phone. "I got another one."

His forehead furrowed. "Another phone?"

"Another threat. There was no caller ID but stupid me answered it anyway."

"I thought this had stopped."

"So did I, but apparently there are some people out there who still hate me." She hitched up her chin, feeling its wobble. Nope. She wasn't going to cry.

"Okay." He sighed. "I'll need you to fill out the report and I'm guessing you want to file another complaint with the police."

She nodded. "I don't know how much good that will do, seeing the last reports haven't done anything, but like you said before, at least if it's on file there's a record when something happens."

He shook his head. "I hate that it has to be that way, that we're even talking about the possibility of something happening, but I'm afraid it's the best we can do."

"Just another case of the victim having to take responsibility while the perpetrator remains at large."

"I'm afraid so, yes."

She filled out her report, spoke to her now-familiar police officer, and agreed to hand over her phone later that day.

"But I'm afraid it's unlikely we'll get anything from it. Burner phones are all too common these days."

"Is there any point in me handing in mine then?"

He sighed. "Probably not, in all honesty. Just don't go

answering any unknown callers until you've changed your number at least."

"Thanks."

Well, not having to lose all her information and contacts was one good thing at least. But still, the thought someone was out there wanting to hurt her made her skin crawl. She had a new appreciation for what her mom did, in doing what she could to redress the wrongs perpetrated against women and standing up for victims without recourse.

"Hannah?" Jason paused. "Everything okay?"

Be honest or deny? She was sick of lying. "Actually, no. I just got another phone call with someone saying they wanted Hannah to get a spanner in her head."

His eyes narrowed. "You've reported this?"

"To both HR and the police."

"I'll get Cindy to get you a new number. This is outrageous."

"Hey, at least I haven't had a hotdog thrown at me yet."

"A hotdog?"

"Yeah. Some of the stories out there about how people treat female reporters would make your hair curl. If your hair was long enough to curl," she added, glancing at his buzz cut.

"Good to see you still have a sense of humor. Do you need to leave? You don't need to see anyone?"

Was that last comment a question or suggestion? She shook her head anyway. The only person she wanted to see was playing in Winnipeg again tonight.

"Okay, well, let me know if that changes. And hey, you know the production meeting has changed to Tuesday next week, right?"

"Because of Thanksgiving Monday." When she'd finally see Franklin again. If his mom called her, that is.

"Doing anything?" he asked.

"Waiting on someone to get back to me," she hedged. "You?"

"I'm driving to Lethbridge to see my folks." He cleared his throat. "See Cindy, okay?"

"Yes, sir."

He smiled without humor, his furrowed forehead probably similar to hers, as she moved to speak to Jason's assistant. And prayed that whoever wanted to hurt her would keep their threats as just that. Words.

BANG!

Franklin shouldered Luc Blanchard into the boards and grinned.

"You're going down, dude," Luc called.

Sure he was. Like if someone tripped him maybe. But skating was what he was born to do, like Mike was meant to lead, and his dad was meant to ranch, and Hannah was meant to—

No. He gritted his teeth. He needed to focus, get his head in the game.

The puck slid to Mike who skated behind Kurt in the net and shot it to Franklin. He skated past the blue line, and shot to Jake who slap-shot it high, over the glass. A time-out was called, and he skated to the bench, sucked down an energy drink as the coach directed the next play. This. This was what he had to do. The rest of this game then one more, then he could finally resolve one of the biggest unknowns hanging over his head.

He'd asked his mom to call Hannah and invite her to Thanksgiving, but hadn't had time to check his phone this afternoon to see if there was any response. And not talking to her these past days had felt as agonizing as when he'd cracked a rib thanks to a hit by TJ Woletsky. But still, focus. He had to focus. There was less than two minutes on the clock, and unless

Winnipeg pulled out a hat trick then Calgary would win this game too, adding to their excellent preseason.

Franklin skated back on, stick at the ready as Luc took the puck for Winnipeg. He skated back, searching for where Luc might pass, knowing that Mike was ready to defend. Luc faked, forcing Franklin to rush, extending his stick in an almost-legal movement...

That wasn't quite legal enough, according to the referee, whose whistle saw Franklin sent to the penalty box. "But ref, it was legal."

"Not from where I was standing." He eyed him. "Want to make it more than two minutes?"

Nope. The door opened to the glass cage and he sat, fighting a smile at the insults being thrown his way. Hockey players weren't the only ones good at chirps in this place.

He watched the jumbotron tick down, winced as Winnipeg scored, knowing he'd get the blame for careless play. But despite the home side's name they weren't winning tonight, so he skated back on for the ten seconds before the game ended, and saluted the Calgary supporters in the crowd.

"James, that was careless," Coach Schultz admonished.

"Won't happen again," he promised.

"Better not."

He joined the others back down the tunnel, handed off his stick and gear, stripped, showered, and changed. He was glad he wasn't one of the names being called up to speak to the media tonight. That'd likely change once he got back to Calgary. He'd heard the team's media unit had planned some things.

"You okay?" Mike asked him on the bus later. "You've seemed a bit out of things lately."

If Mike hadn't hinted at a certain someone last week, chances are he'd still be in the zone. But because he had, it was like his world had turned upside down. "I'm good."

Chad turned from in front and smirked.

"What's that about?" Mike asked.

"Nothing."

"Nothing except…" Chad raised his brows.

"I'm good. Ignore him. He doesn't know what he's talking about."

"Except he's not said anything."

"Hey, I'm not talking about this here. Later." Unless he could distract Mike and get away with not saying anything at all.

But when he returned to his hotel room, Chad wasn't going to let go of things so easily.

"It's the reporter chick, isn't it?" Chad said.

"What is?" Franklin asked, playing dumb. Hey, his sisters had been accusing him of acting dumb for years. He could play dumb until the cows came home.

"Hannah. Your girlfriend."

"I don't know what you're talking about."

"Dude, I've seen your phone."

"What?"

"All the messages there. Your little lovey-dovey notes—"

"Lovey-dovey? Please."

"Whatever you want to call it. I've seen all your prayer stuff too. Way to go, cowboy. Acting like a Christian yet lying to the team."

"I'm not lying."

"Yeah? You're not exactly owning up to the truth."

Franklin folded his arms. "And what exactly is it that you think I've lied about?"

"She's your girlfriend, isn't she?"

"Nope. I've barely seen her. You've got a weird idea of what a relationship means if you never see the other person."

"You're still in contact though. I've heard you."

"Dude, I haven't spoken to her all week."

Chad looked uncertain. "But your messages—"

"Did you really look through my phone? That's an invasion

of privacy. Do I need to speak to the team about that or are you gonna let this rest? I don't see how any of this is any business of yours."

Chad frowned. "But if it affects the team—"

"It's not. She's my sister's friend, and yeah, that's how I know her." All true. "And if you're gonna go around stirring up trouble then I hope you have a good hard think about that because the last thing this team needs is any more drama between its players."

A knock came at the door. Franklin flung it open.

Mike. "What's going on? We could hear raised voices out in the hall."

Chad pointed at him. "Tell him, or I will."

"Gotta love a man who tries to give an ultimatum." Franklin glanced at Mike. "Can we talk?"

"Sounds like we need to."

He followed Mike to his room, then admitted it all. His joy at learning about Hannah's recommitment. His uncertainty about what this meant now. "Chad overheard us talking—"

"Us?"

"Me and Hannah, and he thinks it's sketchy. I think it's sketchy that he looked at my phone and read my messages."

"He did that?"

"Yep."

Mike sighed. "I didn't think he was like that."

Franklin shrugged. Apparently he was.

"Looks like someone needs a talking to about privacy."

Good.

"And someone else needs to remember what we've said before." Mike arched a brow. "Yes, it's awesome that she's a believer but it doesn't change the fact that if she's accused of favoritism then it will have dire consequences for her career. Or have you forgotten that?"

Maybe. "But it's not like anything has happened. Nothing

could happen anyway because I haven't even seen her since I found out."

"But you will next week when we return home. And if she's doing the reporting then what do you think will happen? Can she keep it professional?"

"Dude, we haven't even kissed, so I'm not about to start necking her on live TV if I'm interviewed, am I?"

Mike grimaced. "That's an image I really don't want to imagine."

But kissing Hannah was something Franklin was struggling not to dream about at night.

"I know you're probably praying about this, and hey, I will too." His nose wrinkled. "I bet Bree already is."

If she had a clue about what was going on, then Franklin would bet that too.

"Look Franklin, we've all had our struggles with figuring out relationships, but none of us have had to deal with this kind of conflict before. And like I said a few weeks ago, if you don't resolve this somehow, and things aren't kept professional, then it's only a matter of time before people find out and things turn badly. People have lost their jobs before, and they'll lose them again, or face suspension at least. And you're a brother, man," he placed a hand on his shoulder, "and I don't want to see things go bad for you."

His throat clogged. He cleared the emotion. "I appreciate that."

Mike sighed. "Don't make me regret this. And if I see anything that even has a whiff of non-professionalism, then I'll have to talk to Coach and management. You understand the position I'm in, don't you?"

He nodded. "She'll keep things professional, and hey, there will be nothing you need to worry about. Honestly."

"I mean it. I don't want to regret this. And I'll have a word with Chad about phones. Do you want separate rooms?"

"Yeah. I don't trust him anymore."

"Yeah, me either. Which is a shame. We don't need another Alex on the team."

No, they did not. He exhaled, praying as he returned to his room.

HOPES OF SEEING Hannah before she joined the rest of his family were dashed when she sent a message—on a new phone number, which might've explained why his mom hadn't been able to reach her easily—to say she was sick and couldn't make the church service with him and Cassie this morning.

He instantly parked in the church parking lot and called her back. "Where are you? Do you need to see a doctor? Want me to take you?"

She sniffled. "You don't want to catch my cold, and I sure don't want to be responsible for getting Calgary's new star on the sick list before the season even begins."

"But can you still come tomorrow?"

"I can if I rest today. Look, it's just a cold, but in the past when I haven't taken care of myself it's gotten worse so I'm just taking it easy."

"Do you need anything? Ibuprofen? A meal?" A hug?

"I'm fine. Well, I will be if I—*achoo!*"

He pulled the phone away from his now-ringing ear. "Whoa. That sounded like an explosion."

"It's the curse of my life. Loud sneezes. My mom says it's a family iniquity that I get from my dad. Apparently he was prone to bouts of seven loud sneezes at a time."

"Are you on seven?"

"Three, but—oh, no, *achoo.*" Then, "A-*choo!* Oh my goodness. I'm so embarrassed."

He smiled. "Don't be. We all have our little idiosyncrasies."

"Idiosyncrasies, huh?"

Yeah, look at him pulling out the big words. "Or you may prefer the expression gifts and talents."

"Pretty sure this is a talent nobody else wants."

She might be right. A glance at the church doors showed the last stragglers entering. "Hey, the service is about to start, but if you need me to swing by and bring you anything I'm more than happy to help out."

"I appreciate it," she said. "But I have everything I need here."

"Everything?" he asked softly.

"That I need," she said. "Not what I want."

His heart stuttered. It was probably a good thing he was about to go to church right now because he needed a dose of the Holy Ghost to be the cold water to douse this flame.

He exhaled heavily. "So tomorrow?"

"I hope to be there. With my mom. Your mom was so sweet about it."

"My mom *is* sweet. A sweet mama, if I recall right."

She laughed. "Go. You're going to be late."

"I wish you were going in with me."

"That's not a good look, either, is it?" she said gently.

No. Probably not. Not while they were trying to keep things on the down-low until some kind of future path could be determined. "I'll catch you tomorrow, then."

"Bye, Cowboy."

"Miss you," he said, but she'd ended the call, leaving him staring at the phone like a dummy.

Man. How had falling for this woman turned him so soft? Forget facing pucks faster than a speeding bullet. He wasn't Superman. More like the lamest hero out there, weak-as-grass Arm-Fall-Off-Boy, able to cope with…not much. She might call him a cowboy but he might as well be wrestling butterflies. Like the ones taking residence in his stomach at the thought of meeting her feminist mother tomorrow.

A shiver rolled over him. "Lord, you're really going to have to help me out with that one."

He glanced at the church. He could hear the music from here, but he still had one more thing to do. A quick scroll on his phone and he pressed a number that did same-day delivery, and voiced a note they'd add to his purchase. She might not want him to visit, but he hoped she liked this gift and would know he was thinking of her anyway.

CHAPTER 14

There were good ideas, and there were bad ideas. And taking her mom to meet the family of her not-quite-boyfriend-who-must-remain-a-secret surely had to top the list of dumb things to do. Especially when she hadn't exactly admitted to the real nature of her relationship with Franklin. What was the point when she hadn't seen him in weeks and they hadn't exactly clarified things and this was all new territory to her? And what was the point when he had to remain a secret, anyway? And her mom with all her networking friends wasn't exactly known for keeping quiet about things. But it was too late to turn back now, not with the ranch house sitting proudly with its lights aglow in the clouded midday sky drawing closer by the second.

She glanced across at her mom in the passenger seat. She didn't look fazed, but that might be because she hid it well behind makeup and expensive clothes. Her mom might be a feminist, but these days she didn't spurn those things that made her feel confident and strong. "You sure you're okay about doing this, Mom?"

"I wouldn't have agreed unless I was." Her mother pushed freshly highlighted hair behind her ear. "I remember this place now. I brought you out here one summer."

Hannah slowed the car, nerves rising the closer they drew. She'd called Franklin yesterday afternoon, when his gift of flowers had been delivered. She'd never received flowers from a man before, apart from a sweet sixteen bouquet her dad had sent her two weeks late, the last time she'd ever heard from him. That sure didn't count. But roses, red roses at that, suggested Franklin was taking this friends-to-more progression more seriously than she'd thought. She wondered if she hadn't had a cold if he might even want to kiss her.

She dragged in a slightly clogged-nose breath. She wasn't averse to looking better than she felt either, and hoped the makeup would hide the redness of her nose. It was probably a good thing Franklin wouldn't want to risk catching her cold by trying something like kissing today. At least it had only proved a mild cold, and hadn't hampered her finally seeing him today. But to see him, in front of his family, and her mother... This was such a bad idea.

"Hannah!"

At her mother's voice she jerked the car to a stop. Good thing they were wearing seat belts. "Sorry, Mom."

"Is something wrong? I know you've had a cold lately, but you're acting peculiarly."

And there were plenty of good reasons for that. Franklin was just one of them.

She swallowed. She still hadn't told him about the latest death threat. *Kill the witch.* Another brave anonymous person. "Sorry. I'm just a bit nervous."

"Is there something I need to know?" Her mother frowned. "This is Cassie's family, right?"

"Yes." She so should have told her mom the truth.

But before she could say anything more, the front door had

opened and Franklin was walking down the steps to the car, a big grin on his face.

"My, my, who is this strapping young man?" her mother murmured.

"Cassie's brother, Franklin."

"I see."

And Hannah rather thought she did.

She opened the door, and Franklin swung it wide. "Hi."

"You made it, after all." His grin could light candles. He bent down and spoke to her mom. "Hello, Mrs. Wade. Welcome."

"It's Ms. Bennett."

He nodded. "Ms. Bennett. I'm Franklin. Here, let me get your door." He winked at Hannah then moved around the back of the car.

Her mother shot her a look and murmured, "Is this just good manners or something else?"

Hannah carefully wiped her nose and prayed any cold residue would not travel further than the car. "He's a gentleman."

"Hmm. I didn't think they existed anymore."

No. Hannah was pleasantly surprised when her mother graciously took Franklin's outstretched hand and exited the car like some movie star from the fifties. She could wait for him to do the same for her—she could see he wanted to—but she exited herself, just in time for Cassie to sweep down the stairs and enfold her in a hug. "You're here!" She grinned at her mom. "Hi again Mrs. Wade."

"Ms. Bennett," Franklin corrected her.

"Of course. Welcome. We're so glad you came. Happy Thanksgiving."

Oops. She hadn't even said that to her mom yet. *Happy Thanksgiving*, she mouthed, to which her mom offered a wry smile as if realizing the same.

"Well, I sure am thankful," Franklin said, offering Hannah a wink. "I was beginning to think this day would never come."

"I understand you play hockey, is that correct?" her mother asked.

"Yes, ma'am."

"Oh, please," she fluttered a hand. "Please don't ma'am me. You make me feel as aged as a grandmother."

"One day, Mom, you may well be."

Her mother sent her a sharp look, as Cassie laughed, and Hannah realized just what she'd said. In front of Franklin, no less. How anyone could pay her to speak on TV was beyond her.

She peeked at him, saw his lips curled to one side as if amused. Then he winked again, and gestured for them to follow Cassie inside.

She moved to follow her mom and Cassie up the steps, but he stayed her with a gentle hand. "Hey."

"Hi." Her feet paused, one step higher than him. She wasn't wearing heels today—her boots were flat, in case another walk through the western town was on offer—and right now he was the perfect height for her to look deeply into his eyes. Or if she swayed closer, the perfect height to—

"Hannah? Are you coming?" her mother called.

"Yes, Mom." She mouthed a "sorry" at Franklin, who only smiled and nodded, and pivoted to join the others inside. She managed to slow her steps to speak quietly to him. "Does anyone in your family know?"

"Know what?"

She swatted his arm, but instead of a gentle swipe felt fire instead. "About *us*," she mouthed, pointing between him and her.

He leaned closer, so she could smell his aftershave. "I suspect all of my family have known I've had a crush on you for ages."

Ages?

"I think that's why my mom was so happy to agree," he

murmured, before quickly straightening as her mother turned around.

"Here you both are," Mrs. James said, with open arms. "Welcome to our humble abode."

"Thanks so much for having us," Hannah said, moving to give her a hug. "I really appreciate it."

Franklin's mom trailed a hand down her cheek. "You are more than welcome. I'm so glad you're feeling better. Someone," she added in a lower tone, "was getting quite anxious."

So she *did* know. Heat filled Hannah's cheeks.

"Now," she turned to Hannah's mom, and held out a hand. "I don't suppose you remember, but we met long ago when the girls were young."

"I do recall," Mom said graciously, like she was royalty. "Thank you for your kind invitation today."

Mrs. James said to Hannah. "Before I forget, I made my special cold-beating elixir, just in case. It's got ginger and garlic and all kinds of good things to help stamp out any cold."

"Thank you." But...garlic?

"Don't worry. I'll make sure Franklin drinks some too."

Could her cheeks get any hotter?

A mug was given to her with a yellowy liquid that looked and smelled kind of funky, but the taste of lemon and honey made it surprisingly tasty. "That's really good."

Leonie offered a cup for any other takers, and sure enough Franklin accepted, along with her hesitant mother. "That is much better than it looks."

"You can't always judge from first impressions, can you?" Mrs. James said.

The girls and Franklin's dad welcomed them too, and they were soon seated at the table, the three sisters and Franklin helping with the serving, Hannah's offer to help declined on account that she was a guest.

Her mother leaned close. "I get the feeling that young man is trying to prove something."

"Like the fact that he's a gentleman?" she whispered.

Her mom frowned. "Do you like—?"

"So, Hannah, are you feeling better now?" Cassie asked from across the table. "After your cold, I mean."

Gratitude at her friend's change of subject—deliberate, judging from the raised brows Cassie sent Hannah's direction—filled her. "Thank you. I'm feeling much better today."

"I was sorry you missed the church service."

"Church?" Her mother frowned at her. "What's this about church?"

Ah, another thing she should've mentioned before today. "Do you remember when I used to go, back in high school? Well, I've decided I'm going to go again."

"Yes, but isn't—?"

"We've long been church attendees," Mr. James said.

"And we even have a chapel on the ranch," Cassie said, "in part of the western town."

"The western town?"

"You remember, Mom. I'm sure I've mentioned this before." Maybe a decade ago. "There's a movie set of a western town that's on the property that's been used for all kinds of films and TV shows." She mentioned a couple of the more famous ones.

"Oh! Well, I have heard of that."

"I could take you there after lunch if you'd like, Ms. Bennett," Cassie offered.

"That would be nice. Thank you."

The meal was served, grace was said, and Mom managed to behave through that, bowing her head even though Hannah knew she didn't believe. But that wouldn't stop Hannah's prayers for her mom. She'd get there. One day, in Jesus's name.

"Amen."

Throughout the meal Hannah was conscious of Franklin sitting next to her, her mother on the other side, near Mrs. James. She wasn't sure how the seating arrangements had come to be but she was grateful, even if it meant she was seated opposite Cassie who was doing her best not to grin too widely each time she saw Hannah and Franklin glance at each other. Which, admittedly, was often. For how could she not stare at the man who looked so effortlessly charming with his Greek god-like physique encased in a humble cowboy-esque plaid shirt and dark jeans? Then to catch his stomach-tugging scent, or his smile, or have his arm graze hers sparking fireworks along her skin…

"Hannah, you did a great job on Friday night," Derek said.

Friday—? Oh, the cohosting gig on *Hockey Hour*, sans Bob. "Thank you."

"You looked like you were born to do the job."

She relaxed. "We've had a few challenges there lately so it was good to have it all run smoothly for once." And to feel comfortable, like she was finally respected and holding her own. Drew had been almost civil for once, even deigning to laugh at her jokes like he was actually amused and not just putting on a show.

"I'm loving your interviews, too," Poppy chimed in. "Are you interviewing all of the Calgary players?"

"All of those who wish for it."

"Who wouldn't want to be interviewed by you?" Jess asked.

Hmm, try Alex. But then, she had little desire to interview him, either.

"I don't think Alex is her biggest fan," Franklin said, stretching his arm to rest lightly along the back of her chair. "Sorry."

"It's okay. The feeling is completely mutual."

His grin arrowed into her heart, and she could've gladly

spent the rest of the day leaning back into his arm, marveling in the perfection of his features, except she was conscious the longer she looked at him the more smirks she'd be getting from across the table. So she dragged her gaze away. And sure enough, met Poppy's grin across the table.

"I'd think any player would want to be interviewed by you," Jess continued. "You're pretty, and twinkly—"

"Twinkly?"

"Yeah, she kind of does twinkle, doesn't she?" Cassie said. "Like flirty, but not."

"I don't flirt—"

"My daughter knows better than to waste her time leading on a man."

"Mom!" Hannah whispered.

"Well, it's true. I haven't raised you to be dependent on a man." She sipped her water, side-eyeing Franklin as she leaned forward. "Any man."

Kill me now. "Well, this is delicious, thank you Leonie," Hannah rushed to say. "I'm not much of a cook and don't eat baked dinners too often, so I really appreciate the chance for a meal like this."

"Can you cook pasta?" Jess asked. "It's about all Franklin eats these days. That and chicken."

Any second now, Hannah knew her mother was going to go ballistic for the suggestion that Hannah prepare a man's meals like some slave from the first century.

"I can cook my own meals, thanks Jess," Franklin said. He glanced at Hannah, amusement hovering around his mouth. "Maybe you should come visit me sometime and I could prove that to you."

Her heart double-thumped. In this world of cozy kitchens and possibilities, maybe she should.

She sensed his answer had pleased her mom—heaven forbid anything smelling of the patriarchy—and conversation drifted to the dancing careers of Poppy and her friend Bailey, in Winnipeg.

With the spotlight off her, her senses had time to tune in to Franklin and his nearness again. To admire his muscled forearms, still tanned from summer and dusted with light golden hair. To approve his hands, his long fingers with neatly trimmed clean nails. Where she sat she couldn't see his expression unless she kept turning to face him, which would only make things obvious. But with the attention on the other side, the other end of the table, she was very aware when his arm lowered, and his hand reached across and touched her knee, and, heart fizzing, she obeyed his invitation—and her instinct—and slipped her hand into his.

Goosebumps rippled as she reveled in his touch, in his care, in the slow caress of his thumb on the back of her hand. Breath suspended, and her chest grew tight. If mere hand-holding made her feel like this, imagine what kissing him might do? How glad she was that he'd also had some of what Cassie called his mom's "witch's brew."

Dessert was supposed to follow dinner but the girls complained they were too full and it was agreed to postpone dessert until people had time to walk off the meal, by a visit to the western town or a walk around the ranch. Her chest fluttered. Maybe this would allow time when she and Franklin could finally be alone.

She helped clean up, as Cassie and her sisters talked more to Hannah's mom about the movies they'd seen filmed here. For all her mom's reservations about pop culture she seemed eager to see the place, persuaded, perhaps, by the thought that a certain blue-eyed film star she had "quite enjoyed" in a western movie had once been there.

"Are you going to come, Hannah?" Jess asked. Goaded, really.

Hannah hesitated. While she was intrigued as the next red-blooded woman to know where Lincoln Cash had once slept, she really needed time with Franklin. "I, uh, visited not so long ago."

"I thought I'd show her the river," Franklin said easily, hands in his pockets.

"Well, have fun, you two," Cassie said.

"Hannah, are you sure?" her mom queried.

That would be one hundred percent "Yes."

"Come on, Ms. Bennett." Cassie gestured out of doors. "You want to come too, Mom?"

Hannah caught Franklin's head tilt and followed him out the back way. As soon as they were free from other eyes, he picked up her hand and held it as they walked to where he'd parked his truck. He opened the passenger door, and she was about to slide inside when with a soft "Hey," he shifted and moved to encase her in a hug.

She closed her eyes, and for the first time that day really felt like she could relax. His arms were warm and strong, his heart thudding strongly against her ear. For all she might be a twenty-first-century woman raised by a feminist mother, in his arms she felt safe. Secure. Protected. Like no one could ever harm her. She sank deeper in his embrace.

Laughter startled her, and she pulled away.

"Hey, they can't see us here," his deep voice rumbled.

Now she looked around, she saw he was right. Between the barn and his vehicle parked at an angle, they had this little pocket of privacy.

"Don't worry about them, or your mom." He smiled. "I just wanted to give you the hug I couldn't earlier."

"It's not exactly been on the down-low, has it?"

He gestured her inside, bracing himself on the door. "You can trust my family to not say anything."

She nodded, biting her lip. But whether the same could be said about her mother remained to be seen. "Hey, thanks again for the flowers."

"I hope you liked them."

"I loved them."

His eyes flickered. "They seemed to work anyway."

"What do you mean?"

"They were get-well flowers, and here you are, having gotten well."

She laughed, drawing in a breath of non-clogged air. "I'm wondering if that might be more due to your mom's special brew."

"It does the job," he agreed easily. "Better than taking medications."

"Well, the flowers were lovely, and your thoughtfulness was so appreciated."

His chin dipped. "I'm glad."

He drove to the bend in the river, to the place where they met all those years ago. "I didn't realize you could drive here now."

He glanced across at her. "Yeah, we graded it a few years back seeing we were coming here each summer."

She could see it now. Franklin helping his dad and Cassie run the ranch. He hadn't earned those wide shoulders and strong muscles by merely working in a gym. Hardworking. Humble. Down-to-earth. There was so much to like about this man.

He parked, they got out, and moved to the post-and-rail fence, the weathered timbers graying and cracked. He leaned against it and she did too, glancing down to where the river sparkled with long-ago precious memories.

"That was a fun afternoon," he said, as if stealing her thoughts.

"It was." She glanced at him. "One of my best memories from being a teenager."

"Really?"

She nodded. "My parents had broken up, and I loved coming here. Your family seemed so nice, so normal, and safe."

"Safe?"

How to explain those weeks, months, of uncertainty, of wondering where they would live, of Mom's tears every night that soon turned to steely anger that the husband she'd given the best years of her life to—had given up studies for—had traded her in for a younger model. Her mom's experiences meant she learned, just like Mom had said at the table, never to trust in a man. The only place that Hannah had felt any degree of certainty was in school, where she'd learned that by studying hard she could get good grades, and on the rink where by training hard she could succeed at hockey. Until she'd come here. "There's something special about this place. Maybe because it's been in your family for generations but it makes me believe that things can carry on, and carry on well, into the future."

"It's my favorite place on earth, partly for that reason." He angled his body to see her. "I'm glad you like it too."

"I love it." She inhaled, catching the scent of mellowed grass and bruised leaves.

"I plan to move here, or someplace like here, once hockey is done."

Her breath stilled. Did he mean to sound like he was having a "talk-about-the-future" conversation with her? If so, then he was treating this way more seriously than she'd dared hope. But then, he wasn't the kind of guy to do flings and one-night stands. He was a Christian. He loved family. She bet he wanted a family, too. Suddenly her joke earlier about her mom becoming a grandmother seemed to hold extra potency. Had he read in that comment that she was happy to settle down with a brood of kids too?

She exhaled, her mind spinning. She was reading *way* too much into this. She needed to calm down. Take it a day at a time. Yes, she'd like to be a mom one day, but only once her career was firmly established, so maybe five-to-ten years from now.

"So, you came here a few times then." His voice spun her back to the present.

"Cassie and I were good friends at high school, and like I said, your family seemed so nice and normal."

"Seemed is right."

She pushed his arm. It didn't move. "They *are* nice. I didn't learn to cook. I never really knew what time I'd have dinner because my mom was working jobs and studying nights and she never had time to teach me. And while I can look back now and appreciate that she did what she felt she had to do to get a better life, something about coming here, feeling the peace, learning to make cookies with your mom, really made me think that's what I'd want to do with my kids one day."

She blinked at the realization, as her thoughts tilted and turned, as if saying those words had allowed her heart to finally hear the truth. Her mom did love her, and had risen, phoenix-like, from the ashes of her marriage to be stronger and do all she could to help Hannah achieve her dreams. She owed her mom so much. But she also wouldn't want her kids to feel like they'd been sacrificed to their mother's career ambitions along the way.

He nudged her shoulder with his. "You okay?"

"Yes. Just thinking."

"Thinking about that time when we first met?"

She chuckled. "You know, for all your boasting about humble charm you can sound pretty arrogant sometimes."

"Boasting? Come on. I don't boast. I don't need to. I let others do the talking for me."

She knew he was teasing, but she loved this banter. "See? Arrogant."

"Just so you know I've never ever used the phrase 'humble

charm' to describe myself." He grinned. "I might've used cowboy charm once or twice."

Her laughter increased.

"So, you're saying I left no impression on you, huh?"

"And we're back to you needing to know how people feel about you. Again."

"Well, if you prefer, we can talk about how I felt when I first saw this supermodel friend of my sister in a swimsuit, like every teenage boy's fantasy woman."

Her cheeks heated. "Come on. I was sixteen."

"You were perfect," he said, his blue gaze drilling into her. "Still are."

Her mouth dried. She swallowed. She probably needed another dunk in the river to be able to talk again.

His lips curved. "What?"

She shook her head, and moved to study the river, finally finding enough mouth moisture to speak. "I...I had always felt so awkward, and I remember coming here, enjoying a swim and then Cassie's big brother came along, all handsome and cool."

He guffawed. "Please."

"No. I know it's probably not gonna help your giant ego, but I'll admit it, I was starstruck and then..." She swallowed. Okay, so her mouth had a tendency to run away like a train, but she didn't need to overshare.

"And then what?" he prompted.

"And then it was like you were paying attention to me, and it was so nice to feel liked instead of being a girl the boys avoided."

"Boys avoided you?"

She nodded. "I was smart and could beat most of them at sports. And I wasn't too pretty."

"Come on."

"Come on? I mean it. I didn't know much about makeup—it might surprise you but Mom didn't believe in it then—and I didn't have much of a clue about how to do my hair or dress nicely. It meant boys barely paid me attention except as a tomboy they tried to beat at sports, then go sulk when I beat them. High school boys were so lame. Then I came here, and met you, and it was so nice to think you liked me, even if it was just a silly fantasy."

He studied her, his blue eyes saying something she couldn't understand.

"What is it?"

"It," he swallowed. "It wasn't silly. I did like you. But I was going away so it didn't seem like there was any point when I'd be halfway across the continent." He shrugged. "Besides, you seemed so together and honestly it was kind of intimidating."

"Intimidating?"

"Hey, if I'm honest I still do find you intimidating some-times. You're so smart and strong, and pretty and quick-witted. I figured you had guys begging you for your number. That you still do."

She shook her head. "I've never had a boyfriend."

"What?"

"Right? Crazy, huh?" She rolled her eyes, her nose wrinkling. "My mom didn't encourage it, and then my studies and sports meant there was barely any time. And I guess a secret part of me always wondered what was wrong with me, especially when..." There she went. Oversharing. Again.

"Especially when what?" His voice was gentle.

"Especially when you never called."

A quick peek up showed him wince. "I thought it wasn't fair on you."

"I thought you didn't want me," she whispered.

He studied her as attraction arced between them. "Oh, I wanted you."

He shifted closer, reaching up to touch her hair, studying a strand like it was gold.

Her breath caught, as his knuckles caressed her chin, her

cheek, and he murmured "So soft" before his fingers slipped into her hair.

Every nerve ending was ablaze, and she dared place a hand on his solid chest, feeling the sculpted muscle under his T-shirt's thin fabric.

"I want you," he said quietly, his eyes dark with intent.

Her mouth dried as his gaze dipped to her lips. She'd wondered for months—years—what it would be like to have him kiss her, but now it seemed so close, so quick, so new, she didn't know what to say. Except, "Aren't you worried I might reinjure your nose?"

"I really don't want you thinking about my nose right now," he said, his fingers sliding to the back of her head.

Nerves filled her. She really hoped he'd had enough of his mom's garlic drink so he couldn't smell her breath, now they stood so close. Her hand ignored her internal memo to play it cool and lifted of its own accord from his shirt to his jaw, reveling in the tiny bristles there. "Do you want me thinking about how cute the dimple in your jaw is?"

"Don't tease a man," he murmured.

Very well. She pressed to her toes and leaned against him, her head tilted, her hands sliding to the back of his neck. She tugged his face down until his mouth was mere millimeters from hers.

"You sure?" he whispered.

She didn't reply, simply closing the gap between them and closing her eyes as his lips touched hers. Oh, what soul-soaring magic lay in his lips. She relaxed, her mouth clinging to his, molding against his, greedy for more. He gave a low-throated sigh, and pressed in hungrily, his lips warm, firm, as heated thrills raced up and down her body, and tugged low in her stomach. His arm slipped down to her waist, and he pulled her flush against his body, and she reveled in the feel of his strength, his muscles, his intensity. He kissed her, and she was sure their lips imparted eternal vows of devotion in shared breath.

Time stilled, then expanded, so their kiss might've lasted five seconds, a minute, an hour, she didn't know or care. Then she drew back, unsteady, mind spinning, lips swollen, hair a mess. She blinked, and the world drew into focus again.

He leaned his forehead against hers, as she caught her breath. "That was…" He closed his eyes.

Amazing? Terrible? Needing work? Garlic-flavored?

"The best kiss of my life."

Oh!

"And something I want to do every day for the rest of my life." He neared again, and while part of her screamed for his lips on hers again, another, too-practical part wondered what this would mean, and she hesitated.

"What is it?"

She didn't want to spoil this moment with practicalities, but surely the more they indulged in kisses the harder it would be when they had to pretend they weren't together. She tried to explain some of this and his gaze was so serious as he nodded.

"I shouldn't have kissed you."

"No! I'm so glad you did, but everything is so tricky with work, and—"

"I'm sorry."

"I'm not! Really, I'm not. I could kiss you forever."

His lips curved to one side, and she reached up and touched the side of his mouth.

He pressed a kiss to her palm. "We need to figure this out, huh?"

Longing tugged low. She wanted to throw herself in his arms and forget the world and their jobs and responsibilities and reputations and kiss him senseless. But she nodded instead.

He exhaled, grasped her hand, and drew her tight in a hug, so tight she could scarcely breathe. But it was more like he was gathering strength for what lay ahead. Just like she needed to do as well. So she clung on, soaking in the feel of him, the scent of him, savoring the taste of his kiss, as she willed this moment to never end. Then he released her. "We should go back."

She nodded, suddenly unable to speak. They should go back, face the real world, face reality, but she'd never forget this moment of utter bliss.

CHAPTER 15

His apartment was dark, cold, lonely. From his slouched position on the sofa, the lights of Calgary splayed beyond the uncurtained floor-to-ceiling window. A trace of herb-and-spiced pasta sauce—sourced from his mom—lingered in the air, drawing his thoughts back two days to Thanksgiving, to the ranch, to Hannah. His blood surged just thinking about his time alone with her. Again.

It was probably not healthy how much he wanted to relive that moment near the river. Who was he kidding? He *was* reliving that moment, any chance he got. In his mind, at least. In his dreams.

The delicate purple veins in Hannah's eyelids. The woven gold in her hair. The way her breath quickened as he slowly, oh so slowly, traced her oh-so-soft skin. Her lips, pink and full. That infinitesimal heart-surging pause of shared breath before she'd pressed her mouth to his, her lips melding and molding perfectly with his as if made for him. The fire erupting within. He'd always been considered even-keeled, cool and levelheaded, but she contained the power to make ice burn. To make him melt. To make his heart flame.

Since waving goodbye on Monday evening he'd had to fight for cool and calm. First among his sisters' tease. Then on Tuesday, when he'd met the rest of the team at the Saddledome for their first chance to practice together on home ice. As soon as that finished, he'd driven home to his apartment, showered, made a meal. Only to be disappointed when she called him and said she couldn't make dinner after all, because there'd been so much to do at the production meeting they had run way over time.

So instead of having another moment with her like he wanted, he'd ended up driving to her place and leaving a plastic container of leftovers outside her door, along with another bunch of flowers. Daisies, this time. They seemed more her than showy scentless roses, with their unpretentious happy natures, and soft clean fragrance.

He thought he'd been discreet, with his baseball cap and sunglasses, but wasn't completely reassured that the teenage kid who'd been near the elderly woman who let Franklin in hadn't taken a pic on his phone. Still, nobody else had to be any the wiser. Just like they wouldn't know about her visit to the ranch. And he knew he could trust her to stay professional when they met tomorrow for Thursday night's start to the regular season. Even if staying professional was the last thing he wanted.

He wanted to kiss her again. He wanted her hug. That humming sensation of her body against his. It was kind of scary how much he wanted her, to have her nearness, to soak in her laughter and wisdom and smile. He hadn't been joking the other day. He wanted to move to the ranch and be married and raise kids just like his mom cand dad. But then a niggle made him wonder how that would fit with a career woman like Hannah. And how the heck any of this could ever be possible, seeing they weren't exactly supposed to be together at all.

Franklin blew out a breath of frustration. Sure, he could see Mike's point that from a reporter position it'd look shady if she was known to be Franklin's girlfriend. How could she be trusted to report objectively? But another part of him wondered why the default had to be that she couldn't be trusted. Why couldn't people believe the best and see her as trustworthy and professional?

How much of any of it really needed to matter, anyway? It wasn't like anything she did could actually affect the game. It definitely wasn't like a situation where she worked for a betting company, where a relationship could be twisted to throw a game. The frustration was eating him up inside, and any time he tried to pray about it he felt like his prayers weren't pushing past the ceiling. He'd asked his parents to pray that a way would become clear. He knew they would. That they had already been, for sometimes when the edge of frustration felt too much he felt it suddenly ebb away, like someone had just that moment prayed.

His phone rang. Cassie. "Hey."

"Hey yourself," she said. "So, how are you feeling?"

"About what?" He knew his sister. And wasn't about to get tricked into saying things he'd be forced to defend or deny later.

"About tomorrow."

Well, that could mean a whole range of things. "I'm looking forward to finally playing at the Saddledome, if that's what you mean."

"Sure. That can be what I mean."

In the silence that followed, he could almost hear the click of her eyeballs as they rolled.

"It'll be good to see you all at the game," he tried again.

"And after," she reminded him.

He'd promised to take them to a meal, and had hopes he might somehow persuade Hannah to join them too. If only he could be sure it would stay confidential, and no camera-wielding peeps would burst their secret bubble.

"But actually, I meant about seeing you-know-who."

"I'm at home, Cassie. There's nobody else here so you don't need to speak in code."

"Hannah, then. Isn't she supposed to be doing your interview?"

"She's scheduled to do all the on-ice interviews, so it won't be just me."

"And do you think you'll be able to not kiss her?"

"Excuse me?"

"Come on. Everyone could tell that's what you two were doing the other day. Even her mom."

He winced. He'd kind of—foolishly—hoped she wouldn't put two and two together. Still, "I am an adult. I know how to control myself."

"Okay. Just thought I'd remind you that it won't just be a few relatives you're going to have to convince. It'll be everyone on TV."

"Thank you. I don't need lessons on protocol from my little sister."

"Not even two years younger, bro. But really, be careful. Don't mess with her heart. You heard her mom. Trust is hard for the women in that family, and it won't take much for them to write someone off."

"I don't know why you feel like you need to be telling me this," he grouched.

"Because someone needs to tell you straight. And I love you, and I love her, and I don't want to see either of your hearts break."

Before he could formulate a reply she hung up, and he stared at the phone, wondering when his sister had gotten so smart. And whether she was right in calling his attention to something he just blithely imagined would be fine. Clearly he needed to double down on his prayers and ask God to help them get through tomorrow night with nobody being any the wiser.

SWEAT SLICKED her palms as she made her way to the glassed-in box where the pregame skate was happening. She'd just concluded an interview with Bree, Mike's parents, and sister—up in the suite where the team's family often sat—and got footage about their pride in the new captain's first night in a game that counted. During her visit to the team's family box, she couldn't help but notice a bunch of wives and girlfriends, and Kristen's sneer. She tucked her hair—artfully styled by Mandi a short time ago— behind her ear a little further, reached the spot marked with a taped X, and turned to face Royce. "This okay?"

"Yeah." He squinted through the viewfinder, checking the composition of lighting and shadow, and she fought to not turn around. Calgary players were on the ice already, which meant Franklin was, and after their kiss on Monday she'd not seen him since. The Monday holiday meant twice as much work all week playing catch-up, and with the new pressure of rinkside and pre- and postgame interviews she'd barely had a moment free to blink. They'd talked on the phone—so much easier when he wasn't on a road trip with a roommate—and now, he was only mere feet away. He might as well have been miles. Because even if she did see him, she'd have to pretend he meant nothing more to her than any of the others. And after that earthquake of a kiss on Monday, just a smile from him would likely prove an aftershock.

Already she could feel her stomach tense, the players' shouts and calls bouncing off the ice. She wondered if he'd seen her yet, what he'd think, what he'd say. It was no surprise that Dirk had insisted that she interview Franklin in the first period break, regardless of the score. So she needed to talk to him now, to get that rush of giddy delight out of her system, so she could act the part of the professional she clearly wasn't. What kind of sports reporter carried on a clandestine relationship with a hockey player?

"That should do it," Royce stated.

"Good." She pivoted on her heels—fancy heels tonight, to match the suit she hoped wouldn't spark a million complaints. Honestly, the number of people who felt they needed to offer their opinions on what she wore was insane. Too fat, too thin, too young, too old, too high, too short, too tight, too loose, wrong color. And yes, she might not be channeling Beachside Barbie, but her knee-length skirt was short enough to show some leg. Jason had insisted and she had enough stupid pride to want to turn Franklin's head.

Her heart thudded. There. Scooping up pucks and sending them to Tom and Jake who kept blasting them at Kurt in the net.

She swallowed. Franklin looked good. Fierce, even. The red jersey with its flaming C stitched in gold was retro-inspired, probably because it looked so good, and was very similar to the last time they'd won the Stanley Cup. On skates and with his height and breadth, and with that focused look on his face, he looked the very picture of intimidation. Breath hitched. How could he have described her as the same?

A puck slammed into the glass near her head and she jumped.

"Whoa!" Royce stopped filming and moved closer. "That looked like it came from Alex."

Yes. It did. By now some of the players had recognized her, and skated closer.

"Good luck tonight," Tom said.

Her response of "Right back atcha" was met with "Don't need luck, we got skills" and Royce's laughter.

"Looking good, Hannah," Kurt called.

"I'm not the one that needs to look good. That's all on you guys tonight."

Kurt laughed, amid jeers of "got burned" and other chirps of a less savory nature.

Mike skated near, offering her a nod, his eyes serious. "Do well tonight, eh?"

She nodded, fairly certain he wasn't just talking about her reporting duties, but keeping herself professional in her demeanor. Well, she would. "You too."

Then Franklin skated near. His lips curved, but he said nothing. It was just as well as she had no words, they'd all drained away. Or been punched from reach by the banging in her ribs. He nodded. She did the same, then looked away. Exhaled unsteadily.

"So, who's on your radar?" Royce asked.

Only Franklin. She blinked, forced herself to focus. This was exactly why she'd needed to do this now and not be taken by surprise by his amazingness up close later. "Uh, I'm happy with anyone."

Royce got more footage and she managed to pull herself together enough to speak coherently to the goalie and a couple of others. Then the skaters went off the ice, and the pregame entertainment began, the music and lights bouncing around the stadium.

"You'll probably want to eat," Royce shouted.

No, she didn't. She felt sick with nerves. Maybe some water, but nothing to eat. Not when this was the first real test of her skills. Only it had nothing to do with her reporting.

The arena announcer began, the jumbotron showing the five-minute countdown, and the space filled with loud cheers from fans who hadn't seen a game here in months. The lights dimmed, and the opposing Vancouver players skated onto the ice. She knew most names: Zac Parotti, Chris Thomas, were just a few. But while they earned a few cheers they weren't who the red-clad spectators had come to see. The spotlights picked out Calgary's team as the announcer called their names: Mike

Vaughan, Kurt Matthews, Tom Chavez, Jake Hooper, Alex Kapaulenyuk. "And a big welcome to Cowtown, Calgary's own Franklin James!"

The other players tapped their sticks on the ice as Franklin skated, lifting a hand, before a similar welcome was performed for Chad.

Not that she paid attention to him. Franklin looked relaxed, chatting with Mike as they completed more shots on net. Cassie and the rest of the James family were here somewhere, but she was ignoring her phone, staying focused on work. And while she'd love to accept Franklin's invitation to have dinner with him and his family tonight, she'd declined, just as she had the past two nights, careful to not put themselves in a situation where their reputations might be compromised.

More official things, then the anthem while the starting sides lined up. Then the puck dropped and the game started.

It was weird watching the game, feeling fully invested, but knowing every minute that passed drew her closer to the moment of encounter. She was working, but not, merely waiting for the right time. So while she wanted to yell encouragement, she couldn't throw herself into things in the usual manner without being conscious she had to look a certain way and not like a sweaty superfan in a few ever-decreasing minutes.

Calgary was playing strong, Tom and Jake with multiple shots on the Vancouver net, giving Chris a good workout. She scribbled notes, making sure she paid attention to the players she was paid to interview soon. Which meant paying attention to Franklin.

He really seemed in his element, playing strong, fast, moving with Mike in blitz chess-like moves as if they'd been partnered together here for years. From this position here she couldn't see everything, but could certainly hear the crowd's appreciation as they stopped Vancouver pucks with their sticks, skates, and bodies.

The minutes ticked down, and her pulse ramped up. Two minutes, ninety seconds, sixty. Royce pointed to the spot and she moved into position, took a swig of water and straightened her jacket and skirt. Here went nothing.

Royce nodded, and pointed to the ice as the players moved off for the first break.

"Hey Franklin," she called.

He drew near—he'd been warned this was happening—and glanced at the camera before his gaze fixed on her. Butterflies soared, and she smiled, then dimmed it back. Professional, remember?

She glanced at Royce and he nodded. Steadying breath. Smile. Action. "Hey Franklin, thanks for joining us tonight. You're a homegrown Calgary player, playing for the team you cheered on as a boy in your first game here at the Saddledome. How's the experience been so far?" She passed him the microphone.

His lips twitched and he leaned in. "It's been great. The fans are obviously amazing, and it's good to see we've got momentum going our way in tonight's game."

She nodded, smiling. "And this is your first game in regular season after playing in Boston for many years. How welcoming has this team been for you so far?"

"They've been great, such a warm welcome, Mike especially. I'm really glad to be here."

"Well, we're really glad you're here too." Uh-oh. Had that been too much? "Well, thank you for doing this. Good luck in the game tonight."

"Thank you so much." He grinned, and she kept her smile fixed, not looking in his direction until Royce nodded, and she relaxed and stole a peek as he skated away. Only to catch Franklin glance back at her, his gaze full of heat as he quirked a tiny smile that drew a heart triple-thump and arrowed fresh fire within.

Her breath was shaky as she exhaled. Her cheeks were so warm her makeup might slide off any moment. God forbid anyone had seen that.

Royce cleared his throat.

She glanced at him. She needed a fan. This place might hold ice but she might as well be on a tropical island. "Yes?"

"What was that?"

"What do you mean?"

He pointed to Franklin. "I get paid to notice things, and I swear, for a moment there it looked like you two had a thing."

Oh no. What could she say? "Please. That would be ridiculous." At his frown she hurried on. "Now, who's next for us? Oh, look. Let's grab Tom Chavez."

Her pulse scampered as she did that interview, continuing to do her best to distract him. She could only hope her bombardment of questions suggested nerves because she was new at this, and not nerves due to anything else. She shouldn't have agreed to this. It felt wrong, underhanded, and she got the feeling that trying to hide a relationship with a hockey player was not something Jesus would do. Her forehead wrinkled. That didn't sound right, either.

"Hannah?"

She smoothed out her skirt, pasted a smile on her face. "Yep?"

"Are you okay? Do you need to eat something?"

Maybe she did. Then this lightheadedness might go away.

"I'll get you something. What do you want? Burger? Nachos? Hot dog?"

Oh, the huge range of healthy choices. Which would she be least likely to spill down her top? "How about some popcorn?" She couldn't go wrong with that, surely.

"Okay."

Her pulse rocketed as she watched Royce leave, praying she'd diverted his attention enough that he wouldn't revisit his earlier suspicions. For he'd been right. Anyone who didn't know Franklin would call that look a smolder. She could still feel the flames licking inside. She downed more water, managed to spill some on her jacket. Great. Good thing she was wearing black.

"Hey Hannah!"

She glanced up. Met a couple of leers from fans with beer guts and bald heads and attitude to match. One of them pursed his lips in a kissy motion, the other poked out his tongue. Mmm. Classy.

She pulled out her phone, ignoring their catcalls and their banging on the plexiglass, rubbing her arms to keep out a sudden chill. There might've been a recent renovation but like hockey arenas everywhere, it could also be a freezing cold barn. She had a bunch of missed calls and messages, including some from Cassie. She glanced across at where she was sitting with her parents and siblings. Given the parochial nature of the crowd, she perhaps should've arranged an interview with them, but hadn't wanted to push things on her very first night. Especially when someone might say something on camera that really didn't need to be said.

Royce returned, holding out a cup of popcorn. "Here you go."

"Thanks."

They discussed the setup for the next intermission interviews, as the banging on the glass nearby continued.

"You got some friends, eh?" Royce said, nodding to the goons behind her.

"Yeah." She rolled her eyes.

"Hey guys, can you knock it off?" Royce called.

Their crude gestures suggested otherwise. "Don't pay them attention," she muttered. "It only encourages them."

"I don't know. They were doing it even before I sat down."

"The game is about to start again," she said, pointing at the clock.

"We could go find someone else to interview," he said.

Like Franklin's family. They weren't too far away, and she could go there and return in time for the next intermission interviews with Chad, Kurt and Jake. "Give me a moment."

She called Cassie, who—miracle of miracles, given the noise —picked up, and said they'd love to do an interview. "We've already done one with the team media unit, but you know you'll always be our first choice for a reporter!" Cassie yelled.

"We'll be there in five."

That'd give them time to film the start of the next period and get some footage they could show on tomorrow night's edition of *Hockey Hour*.

A minute later she turned from collecting her faux leather bag with her notes and laptop when the music and lights signaled the start of the next period, as the players returned to the ice. She swiveled to watch the Calgary players, and sure enough, there was Franklin, and yes, he was studying her with that same small smile from earlier. When he saw her watching he nodded, then pivoted, as if satisfied.

Oh my goodness. Didn't the man know how many people watched his every move? They'd see him watching her, their gazes connecting, and it wouldn't take too much for people to start wondering. She'd need to tell him to avoid looking at her.

"Come on!" Royce yelled over the spectator noise.

She hurried up the concrete stairs, glad to escape the goon fans whose gestures and comments were certainly not family-friendly. But thick skins weren't developed by a lack of adversity. Although the rate things were going, she'd be boasting crocodile skin before too long.

The interview with Derek and Leonie, and Cassie and her sisters went well. Maybe Cassie had warned them not to say anything too personal, because there was nothing that seemed to ping on Royce's radar.

"Thanks so much," she said with a raised voice, as the crowd booed when Vancouver's Zac Parotti scored a goal. Fortunately for Franklin's family, it wasn't his shift on the blue line just then.

Leonie squeezed Hannah's hand. "So good to see you again."

Oh dear. Judging from Royce's raised brows this was exactly what she didn't need. "And you." Leonie looked like she was wanting a hug, which would've been totally awkward to try to explain. So with a mouthed "sorry" and a tap on her nonexistent watch, she gestured for Royce to leave while she blew a kiss of apology in Leonie's direction.

Royce, who clearly was paid to pay attention, was frowning when she finally met him in the concourse. "Don't try and deny it. There's something sketchy going on. You know them, don't you?"

"Well, so do you. We both met them, remember?"

He snorted. "Don't play games with me."

She was walking fast, in order to get back to their spot near the ice. "Look, I know Cassie James from school a million years ago."

"What? You mean you've known Franklin's sister for years?"

She nodded, not looking at him.

"Hannah, this is the kind of thing that people need to know. It's a conflict of interest."

"What—that I went to school with the sister of a now-famous hockey star? I don't think you have a case there."

"There is a case if something is going on." He studied her. "*Is* something?"

"Did they stick crazy sauce on your burger?" A question like that wasn't a lie, was it? "Come on. We'll be late if we don't get there before the crowds move again."

But she wasn't sure if her efforts had dissuaded him, and all through the next interviews with Chad, Kurt and Jake, she could feel Royce's eyes on her, watching her, in case she glanced a millisecond in Franklin's direction. Which got harder when the last period had him and Mike back near their spot, which meant seeing Franklin was unavoidable.

The action moved down the other end, and she kept her gaze trained on it, refusing to look at the man wearing the #10 jersey nearby. Which was ridiculous. How could she be an effective reporter when she was basically refusing to look at one member of the team? This wasn't good. She needed to own professionalism. Now.

She hauled in a breath, and glanced out at the ice, noting Franklin's nod as she finally looked his way. But she kept her gaze tracking, not daring to meet his eyes, not daring to get hooked by that gaze that contained too much heat and emotion. She wasn't supposed to do emotion. She was supposed to be a dispassionate reporter of sports, not involve herself in the story.

And she kept the smile from her dial the rest of the game, although she did permit herself some cheers and applause as Calgary scored two quick goals which put them in the lead. Then, when they won, she and Royce moved to the sidelines, and she conducted a couple of interviews before Royce hustled them to the locker room.

She swallowed. The locker room. This was new territory for her, and while female reporters had been permitted into men's locker rooms in pro sports for years, this particular female reporter hadn't. She glanced across, saw Natalie laughing with some of the staff outside the door. Natalie caught her eye, smiled. "Hey, how are you doing?"

But there was no time to answer as the doors were opened, and the media were permitted inside.

Hannah followed, wary, as she moved through to the noisy room where the players stood or sat in their stalls, in various stages of undress. Eyes up—nobody wanted to see what might be under those towels—she glanced around. Various players had mikes and cameras and phones thrust in their faces, recording their thoughts on the game. Someone jostled her, and she bumped into someone else, and turned to see Alex's leer. She jerked away, skin crawling, and glanced around for where Royce stood. He was filming Mike who was answering Natalie's question, and she needed to get there.

"Hey Hannah."

She turned, in time to catch Alex's drop of towel before she spun back, his harsh laughter behind her. Her skin turned hot then cold. Had he really just flashed her?

Thank God she hadn't actually seen anything.

"You okay?" Franklin's voice came from behind her.

She nodded, certain someone would see them talking here, and hurried to Royce's side. He glanced at her curiously, then across at Franklin, then Alex, who was still watching her, like he wanted to know he'd gotten a reaction. She tilted her chin, ignoring her nausea and pasted on composure as she tried to zero in on what Mike was saying.

"...and a win is always a good way to kick off the season," Mike said. His hair was sweat-soaked, his eyes looked tired. Vancouver was a physical team, and they'd played tough tonight, Parotti getting a lot of big hits on Mike's teammates.

"And are you pleased with your new pairing?" Anton asked.

Hannah had to ask a question soon, she couldn't keep coasting off other people's interviews. But judging from the media crowding around Mike she wouldn't get the chance to talk to him. She glanced around. Alex had gone—thank goodness. Franklin had his own league of reporters around him. Chad only had one, so she tapped Royce on the shoulder and moved to him. Smiled.

"Congratulations on your first regular season game for Calgary, and your first win. How did it feel to get an assist on that first goal?"

He looked at her, his gaze traveling down to her heels and

back, before he nodded, his expression pulling into what could only be called a leer.

Quick, she needed a redirect. "Anyway, tell us what was running through your mind when you helped set up that awesome saucer pass."

"Saucer pass, huh? Look who knows her stuff."

Her smile dropped away, her eyebrows raised. "I've played a game or two before."

"Uh-huh." He rubbed a white towel through his hair. "What was the question again?"

"What was going through your mind—"

"Oh yeah. Yeah, I wanted to score."

Well, duh. Some athletes made the stereotypes about knocks to the head and decreased intelligence make a lot of sense. "Okay, well, thanks for that."

"We all like to score around here," he said more loudly.

"I'm sure you do." Hannah glanced at Royce who shrugged and lowered his camera. Looked like that was their cue to go find someone—

"Franklin likes to score, too. Don't you, James?"

She stilled. Chad wasn't talking about goals anymore. She needed to get out of here. "I think we've got enough," she muttered to Royce.

"But we barely got anything," he complained. Then frowned. "Why are you looking like that?"

Like what? Worried? Anxious? Feeling like she'd been playing with fire and was about to get burned? She pivoted, almost crashing into Mike. Finally. Someone she could trust. "Hey Mike." Tears hovered at the back of her eyes. She blinked them back. Forced her voice to steady. Held out the microphone. "Congratulations on your first win as a captain. What are you planning to do to celebrate tonight?"

Mike's eyes creased. "I'm looking forward to some sleep," he admitted.

"He's gonna score," Chad yelled behind him.

Mike turned, his lips flattening, then he turned back to Hannah. "Some people are a bit excited. I hope you can cut that from the footage."

"You can be sure I will. He's in a strange mood, isn't he?"

Mike's compressed lips said words he couldn't say. She tried another tack. "So, I'm sure Bree and the kids were all excited to see you at your first game as captain." A Captain Obvious question, and one she already knew the answer to, given her interview before, but it was one the fans expected.

His shoulders dropped a little as he nodded. "And my parents, and my sister who flew here from Germany. It's pretty special to have this honor."

"And to have your first day as a win makes it even better. Congratulations again. Have a good evening. And get some rest, it's gonna be a deep season." She motioned for Royce to cut the video, and turned back to Mike again. "And say hi to Bree again for me. I hope she's feeling well."

"I will. And thanks."

She had to leave before anything else awkward happened again. Between her challenges with Franklin, and Alex and Chad's wrong and weird behavior, she was physically and mentally exhausted. Although she wouldn't be getting rest. Leaving only meant she'd be spending a good amount of time sorting through clips and writing copy and preparing for tomorrow.

But she was glad her job provided an excuse to leave, and that even if she wanted to—which truth be told she did—her work made it impossible to hang out with Cassie and her family as they celebrated the work of Calgary's favorite hockey son. Because tonight had proved just how precarious this tightrope of truth and lies and forbidden attraction could be.

Halloween decorations littered the streets as the team bus drove from the Edmonton airport. One more game on the latest road trip, then a few days off when he'd make Hannah see him. Well, not see him on game night like millions of others but the way he wanted. Alone.

Uneasiness clenched his gut. She'd want to see him, right? Nearly two weeks since their kiss and barely a peep from her since. He got that her work hours were insane, and that she was being careful about not stirring up suspicions. But come on. He was dying here. What kind of relationship was it if she never saw him and barely answered his calls? If things kept going this way there wouldn't be any relationship to keep secret.

Maybe that was what she wanted, and it was just her way of saying she didn't want him anymore. She'd been ticked about that hungry look he'd shot her in that game against Vancouver, and yeah, maybe it'd been a little intense, but he couldn't help it. She made him feel deeply and passionately, and it was wearing him down trying to hide it all the time. Since then she'd been reserved, her smiles dimmed, fixed, her eyes not really meeting his as she did that cool face thing whenever she interviewed him at the Saddledome. He worried that it was becoming obvious that she treated him differently, because she didn't do it with the others, the warmth he loved shining out in smiles and tease. Apart from when she spoke with Alex and Chad, who earned a poker face and coolness he completely understood.

He glanced across the aisle at them now, heads together, looking at Alex's phone, laughing. He shifted his head. They might be a team, and Mike was doing a good job as captain, but Alex and Chad weren't playing. Franklin, Tom, Kurt, and some of the others were trying to step up their commitment, bringing the fire and enthusiasm and team energy as he knew things weren't easy for his friend. Bree hadn't been well lately, and he suspected that was contributing to Mike's broken sleep and extra tension. He'd upped his prayers, and got his family praying too. He'd mentioned it last Tuesday to the online Bible study crew.

Mike hadn't exactly been pleased. "Dude, now's not the time."

"When is?" Franklin had countered. "These guys are your buddies, and care about you. And Bree."

"What's going on with Bree?" Josiah had asked.

"She's insanely tired all the time," Mike admitted. "The doctor doesn't seem too concerned but I'm worried about Bree's iron levels. She had a scare a few years ago and had to get medical attention, but that's another story. Anyway, it helped when her mom was here at Thanksgiving, but this pregnancy is really eating her energy levels."

Franklin had nodded. He'd thought that too the last time he'd had dinner there. It was no wonder Mike was under pressure when his wife's trademark vivacity had drained away to shadowed eyes and lethargy. He wasn't any expert, but it seemed more than what might be expected from a woman carrying twins.

"I'm sure the doctor is on top of things, but you could always get a second opinion," Ryan suggested.

"Maybe you need a nanny," Jai said. "Well, not you personally—"

The others had laughed, and even Mike had cracked a smile. "I'm pretty sure sometimes she thinks I do."

"Don't you just hate that?" Chris mock-complained. "I think it comes with the territory of being married. The wife is always right, which means I'm always in the wrong, and messing up one way or the other."

"Sounds like you need counseling, dude," Luc said. "Josiah's here, if you need to talk."

"Anytime, brother," Josiah said, with a twinkle in his eye that said he recognized the jest.

"Why don't you get someone in to help Bree?" Jai asked. "Allie's work at the museum means she has a cleaner and part-time nanny for little Banjo. And that's one kid."

Mike had nodded. "She's got a friend who's flying out soon who should be able to help, but to be honest, I'm not a hundred percent sure how I feel about it. My mom is a little concerned about it too."

"Why?"

"Sylvie's a little…alternative. Like, not a Christian, and really tattooed, and well, Mom is a little concerned about the influence she'd have on the kids, especially if she's with them so often."

"Tattoos don't make someone a bad person," Luc said, his bare forearms displaying his ink.

"Truth." Ryan nodded, his pushed-up sleeves revealing his own.

"It's more like some of her lifestyle choices I guess my mom and I have some reservations about."

"Is she a druggie?" Chris asked.

"No. At least, not that I think—no, of course not. Sylvie is

Bree's friend from TO, and a, well, sort of complicated character, shall we say."

"Don't be prejudiced, man," Ryan had said. "She can't be too bad if she's Bree's friend."

"I know. I'm not trying to be, it's just something is a little off, you know? Anyway, she's coming soon, she's got family in Red Deer, so we'll see how that works out."

"Red Deer?" Ryan asked. "I grew up near there."

"Yeah? Maybe you'll meet her one day. Seeing you're not prejudiced at all," Mike had snarked.

Whoa. Mike was never snarky. That was a red flag as big as Red Deer that Mike wasn't coping, as far as Franklin was concerned. And Josiah, too, judging by his next words.

"We'll be praying for you and Bree," Josiah said. "And this woman—what did you say her name was?"

"Sylvie."

"And Sylvie too."

Josiah had taken the opportunity to do exactly that exactly then, which Mike had appreciated, or so he'd told Franklin later.

But, as the bus slowed outside Edmonton's awesome arena, it didn't change the fact he'd do all he could to support his friend, line partner and captain, and make him proud tonight.

Later, his shoulders aching from teammates' thumpings, his cheeks sore from holding in his grin, his phone buzzed with a message. Ryan. Sorry I didn't catch you. You're going down next time.

Bus left early. Keep dreaming. He laughed to himself and pressed send.

"What are you laughing about?" Mike said, slipping into the plane seat next to him.

Franklin showed him the text conversation, which sparked another smile from Mike.

"Yeah, it's a good thing we weren't hanging around. A score like that didn't make us popular."

Security hadn't been quick enough to stop a few disgruntled fans from tossing jerseys on the ice. Ryan's #29 hadn't been one of them, but other Edmonton players had borne the brunt of rage. An 8-1 loss would do that. All of which had only made Franklin's evening better. And in less than an hour they'd have touched down and he'd sleep and see Hannah tomorrow.

"Two goals, huh? Someone's on fire."

"Says the someone who made those great passes. What was it you said? A great team is made of great guys working together to do great things?"

"Aww, someone pays attention."

"You know it."

Mike's grin poked out again, and he settled more deeply in the padded seat. "Good job, man."

"Thanks."

It might be what they paid him for, but defensemen weren't the usual goal-scorers. Of course, he'd always been open to attacking the net, and between Mike's precise passes and some sloppy Edmonton defense he'd managed to light it up twice. Twice! It had been a few years since he'd done that.

He'd explained to the reporters tonight that it had been due to recent slap shot practice. He hadn't explained that he'd spent a lot more time working on his skills because he was frustrated about other things. But at least he'd see her soon. Hannah had sent a good luck text earlier, and a praying hands emoji, a message he'd treasured given the drought in recent communication. He'd extra appreciated it knowing she had another Friday night gig tonight and likely been frantically prepping beforehand, so the fact she'd taken time out to think of him gave hope she'd see him tomorrow. He would've liked to see her tonight if it wasn't going to be past midnight by the time they left the airport. And after the past few days of road-tripping he really needed his own bed, and sleep.

He peeked across at Mike, who now sat with his eyes closed. Probably didn't need sleep as much as someone else.

He glanced at his phone. Then back at Mike. He had a dozen unanswered congratulatory texts, but the only person he wanted to message hadn't sent one yet. He'd kinda thought she would've by now. But hey, she'd had a late night too, so it shouldn't surprise him too much. He could just big-boy up and send her one anyway.

THANKS FOR PRAYING. YOUR PRAYERS WORKED!

He squinted at the screen. Did using exclamation marks make him seem lame or just friendly and excited? Man. Why did this woman twist him in knots all the time? He pressed send.

Then spent the next few minutes checking his phone, as he chatted with teammates and trainers and his coach.

Finally his phone flashed. CONGRATS.

A surge of gladness was followed by a dip at the one-word response—with no corresponding exclamation mark to signify friendliness or excitement. In fact, it read so flat it could come across as anything a stranger might write.

But no. That was stupid. She wasn't a stranger. She was the woman he'd shared the most soul-stirring kiss of his life with just less than two weeks ago. They were together. He needed to stop being insecure. He typed back CAN'T WAIT TO SEE YOU TOMORROW. WHEN IS GOOD FOR YOU?

His thumb hovered over the send key as he studied that last sentence. She'd be free. Doing *Hockey Hour* tonight meant she'd be freer tomorrow, not needing to prep or write copy. Maybe he should surprise her. He deleted those last five words and pressed send.

Her reply was swift and he wished he wasn't on a plane but

could just call her, like he would if he was at home. *Can't tomorrow. Working.*

Still? He exhaled. You'll still need dinner, right?

Sorry. My mom's birthday.

Man. He wondered if he should ask if he could tag along too, then figured Hannah would invite him if she wanted him to. And attending her mom's birthday probably suggested a seriousness he wasn't sure she felt yet, especially if they were keeping this on the down-low. That was, if there was any relationship at all.

His good mood from earlier dissipated, his heart shifting as he tried not to worry. So she had work. He could cope. He could sleep in, go to the ranch, see the folks. They'd love to see him, and there were always a million chores needing doing that would help distract him from the person who didn't seem to want to see—

His phone flashed. Sunday?

Heart knots loosened. Love to. Tell me where and when. Whatever made it easy for her, that made her feel comfortable, easy, like this could have a future.

Mike cleared his throat. Franklin's gaze swung up to meet him. "Who's that?"

His cheeks grew hot. No way did he want to lie to his friend but neither did he want to admit the truth to his captain.

The ease from earlier faded, Mike's eyes sharpening to points of blue. "Hannah?" he mouthed.

His chin jerked.

Mike shook his head, scrubbing a hand over his face, letting out a long breath.

Franklin's chest squeezed. So much for trying to make the man proud of him.

"You gonna call it off?"

No. "I don't want to get into this now."

"You're putting me in a really hard position," Mike muttered. "You need to talk to her."

He sure did. He had to know if there was anything here worth fighting for, or if things would just be better if they went the easy path and separated. "I'll see her Sunday."

Mike nodded, his eyes soft. "I like her, really I do. And you know Bree does too. I'm sorry this is hard. But if you don't get it sorted, it will come out. Secrets always do, and then it won't be fun for anyone."

"I'll see her Sunday," he repeated. "Pray for me."

"Haven't stopped," Mike said tiredly.

Franklin stretched out his arms above him, and rolled his neck to a song of creaks and pops. He glanced at his weary friend. "And I'll be praying for you too."

Mike's mouth creased. "Sylvie arrives tomorrow, so I get one night with my wife before we have company again."

"One night is better than none, though."

Which might be what he'd be facing, if he couldn't figure out how to make a relationship work. *Lord, I need Your help.* No way was he letting the perfect girl slip away again.

"And I will trust Him, I will trust Him with it all..."

Hannah closed her eyes and relaxed, letting the music wash over her. She still didn't know any of the songs well enough to risk singing along, but that didn't matter. She'd been learning from friends and the occasional podcast—like the one from that Sarah woman who'd written this song—that being a worshipper of God was less about the outward appearance and more about the heart. And God knew that Hannah's heart was a mess these days.

Her mom. Work. Franklin. Mostly Franklin. She knew she'd been unfair to him, using work as an excuse to get out of time with him. Time with him only meant a greater chance their secret would be found out, and her lies exposed. And while she'd never thought herself deceptive, recent weeks had shown just the depths of deception in her heart. She'd been lying to her work colleagues, lying to friends like Bree when she'd insisted she and Franklin were only friends, treating everyone so badly, including at her mom's catered birthday dinner last night which should've been a fun chance to build on the promising start of Thanksgiving, but instead descended into bitterness amid her mom's concerns about Franklin.

"If he was a real man he wouldn't be ashamed of you."

"He's not ashamed," she murmured, hoping her mother's friends in the dining room couldn't hear the hissed kitchen conversation. "You know why we can't tell people."

"And how long do you think you can continue this way? I haven't raised you to rely on a man, but if you're going to have a relationship don't you think you actually need to relate?"

And that was the problem. They weren't relating. Fear kept her silent, and away. And now they'd arranged to meet after church and she needed to figure out whether to keep going or pull the pin and walk away. And she didn't know how much longer she could keep carrying this burden for.

Emotion burned her throat, the backs of her eyes, and she lifted her glasses and rubbed her eyes. She wasn't sure how much the glasses protected her identity, but it made her feel a little more anonymous, especially without makeup and in jeans and a nondescript sweater. Glamorous, she ain't. But in this place that emphasized the inner heart over the outer, she knew her appearance didn't matter. And that maybe God could give her some pointers on what to do with the mess that writhed within.

"And I will trust Him, I will trust Him with it all..."

The musicians on the church stage sang the chorus again, and this time she felt more confident to mouth along. She closed her eyes. Shook her head. How much had she been trusting God with this? How much had she been trying to carry this on her own?

She exhaled heavily.

Felt a touch on her arm. Met Cassie's concerned look. "Are you okay?"

No. "Yes." She would be. As soon as she talked to Franklin. Maybe. But it would hurt, both him and her, but what choice did she have? Not if she was trying to live rightly, and put God's desire for "truth in inwards parts" into practice. *Lord, help me.*

Her gaze lifted, only to connect with the blue eyes of the man she was struggling to not think about. She lifted her lips in a sorry attempt at a smile and glanced away. The man was everywhere. Even interrupting her hard-fought attempts to focus on God. She needed God, not Franklin.

The song finished and she gratefully sank into her seat, doubly grateful that the lack of free chairs around her made any desire Franklin might have to sit next to her impossible, even if they hadn't already decided to avoid being seen together in public. She didn't need to be distracted by his scent, or the heat of his nearness, not when she was here to find peace with God. *God.* Not Franklin. Why was he here and not at Mike's church, anyway?

But despite her best efforts, the tendrils of her heart kept sneaking to thoughts of him, wrapping more confusion around her soul. By the time the sermon finished, she was growing desperate, heart questions urging her escape, even from Cassie's concern.

"But you don't want to come to lunch?"

To the ranch, where trying to find privacy to say what needed to be said would be impossible with the smirks and tease? Where else could she go with him that no one would see? "I'm really sorry, but I've got work," she lied.

See? Bad person. Lying to another friend. She should just admit the truth.

"You've always got work," Cassie complained. "I don't think that role is healthy—"

"Actually," she drew in a deep breath. "I really need to talk with your brother privately, and I—"

"Why didn't you just say so?" Cassie grinned, and tilted her chin. "Look, you can do so now. He's right behind you."

Of course he was. And while she might be dressed in anonymous-her clothes, that earlier glimpse showed him as handsome as ever.

She turned. Smiled. A smaller smile than usual, but she didn't want anyone here getting ideas. Even now she could see some kids waiting to take a selfie with him. She angled away so she wouldn't be in their photos.

"Hey Hannah," he finally was free to say.

"Hello."

His smile wavered, like he was unsure, and she ducked her head, suddenly wishing she didn't look quite so plain and ordinary today. If only this relationship could be real and not feel impossible.

"Are...are you still free for lunch?" he asked quietly.

She nodded, crossed her arms, glanced away.

"But not at the ranch," his sister said. "She needs to talk to—"

"Stay out of this, Cassie," he muttered.

Hannah glanced back. Even the fact the three of them stood here like this was likely giving people ideas. She rubbed her cold arms then bent to pick up her bag.

He sidled closer. She stepped back. His expression creased into hurt. "Want to come to my house?"

She toyed with it. His place had good security, and it meant she could say her piece and then leave. But then, people might know where he lived, so... "Come to mine."

What alternative was there? They sure couldn't run the risk

of meeting in a restaurant or even a park. Maybe they should've planned to hide among the tourists at Banff or Lake Louise.

"I'll bring food."

She nodded, still refusing to meet his eyes, then turned, offering Cassie a small smile of goodbye, which felt like a farewell of greater magnitude as she turned and hurried from the church auditorium.

She reached her car, keyed the ignition, drove away. She didn't care what food he got, her stomach was in such knots she could barely eat, even if Dirk hadn't been shy when he'd recently reminded her to be careful as the camera added pounds. Besides, after Franklin heard what she said, he wouldn't be staying too long anyway. Maybe she should tell him not to bother with food...

But then, the thought that this would be the last time she would talk to him made her hesitate as greedy hope imagined one last kiss. A second kiss, but a last one. How insane was that? Fresh emotion burned, and she flicked a tear away. This relationship had barely had a chance to breathe let alone grow into anything real.

But she knew it had to stop. Lack of sleep thanks to guilt was making her face break out in spots. And it wasn't fair to him to do this dance when clearly there was no future.

If only she could make him understand the same.

"I brought Chinese again, hope that's okay."

"Sure." She dragged him inside, glancing either side to make sure nobody was watching.

A click of a freshly opened door made her close hers with a thump. Good thing she wasn't paranoid or anything.

"Are you okay?" he asked, drawing closer.

She moved swiftly to the kitchen. After weeks of being apart she barely knew what to do with him. He was too big, too much, his presence, his scent almost overpowering in such close proximity. And while her brain might know what needed to be done, her senses and yes, her foolish heart, persisted in stubborn attraction that dared her to forget the world and just fling herself in his arms and lose herself in his kiss.

But she couldn't do that, so she concentrated on retrieving plates, glasses, forks.

"I've missed you."

The rasp in his voice stilled her movements, and the confusion in his eyes when she finally met his buckled her best intentions, and she sagged over the kitchen counter, head plunged in both hands.

"Hannah? What is it? Please, talk to me."

Then his hand was on her back, and she felt a different fluttery warming sensation, almost like he might've just prayed for her. The thought that he cared for her drew fresh moisture to her eyes, and she stifled a sob.

"Oh, sweetheart."

Before she could say anything else, he'd swept her into a hug, a strong, firm hug from which she never wanted to let go. It might be weak and non-Mom-approved of her, but clinging to him like this while she shuddered out tears drew a small measure of comfort. She rested her head against his chest, listening to the solid *thump, thump, thump* of his heart, wishing she could stay here forever, cocooned in his arms that felt a lot like love.

Love. That's what this really was about. For as much as she admired his handsome form and had thrilled to his kiss, choosing his best was what love was really about. Which meant sacrificing her own desires for what would benefit him. Even if he was bound to disagree with her.

He stroked her hair, reverently it seemed, and her clasp around his waist tightened. "It's been a big few weeks, huh?"

"Yes," she whispered.

"I watched the repeat of *Hockey Hour* yesterday. You were great."

"Thanks." She drew in another clogged breath. She needed a tissue to deal with this snot that she desperately hoped hadn't ended up on his clothes. But maybe that way he'd be so disgusted that he'd be happy to break up—

"Did you watch the game?" he asked.

"Against Edmonton?" She felt his nod. "I did. Well, a highlights pack anyway. You were great."

"Right?"

His humor lifted hers, and she finally pulled away, snatching a tissue as she wiped her nose before he could see her snot-smeared face, sneaking a peek to see—thank God—he didn't wear any of that on his clothes. Ugh. How gross was she?

"I'll just be a minute."

"Hey, I don't mind—"

She closed the door to the bathroom, studying her reflection. Nobody looking at that blotched face would recognize it as the bright smiling one decorating buses and billboards around the city. She barely recognized herself. One advantage of no makeup earlier was that she didn't need to clean that away. She dampened a washcloth in cool water, and pressed it on her eyes. What she'd give for slices of cucumber, or a spa day to deal with this.

She did the best she could with makeup and hair—certainly nothing on par with Mandi's efforts—and slipped via the sliding door into her bedroom where she swapped her plain shapeless sweater for a blouse that made her feel slightly better about herself. A girl might be about to break up with the best guy ever, but it probably didn't hurt for her to leave him with a good impression, if she could.

She finally made it back to the kitchen, only to see him

seated at the dining table, back to her, shoulders slumped, chin propped in his hand. Her heart twisted. "Hey."

He glanced up at her, rising like the gentleman he'd been raised and tugging out a chair. "You feeling better now?" He peered at her. "You look better."

Thank you, L'Oreal. "Is the food still hot? Sorry, I didn't think I'd be that long."

"It's okay."

She swallowed. He was always so gracious to her, so kind. She didn't deserve him.

They served themselves, and he grasped her hand briefly as he prayed. Conversation focused on food and church and his most recent games, and she was glad for his thoughtfulness that allowed her to find her composure. By the time they'd cleared plates and loaded the dishwasher, she felt almost herself again.

"Do you want a cup of tea?" she asked, hovering near the electric kettle.

His mouth curved. "As long as it's not any of those hippie herbal things my mom swears by."

"I refuse to keep them in the house."

Two cups of tea later and they sat on her sofa, opposite the silent TV. If this had been a normal day she'd have a game on, muted if necessary, in order to bone up for this week's program. But this wasn't normal, and Franklin deserved her full attention.

She placed her cup on the coffee table, next to his, and glanced at him.

His expression grew serious, and he grasped her hand. She let him hold it, savoring his strong fingers entwined around hers, trying her best to ignore the flutters of sensation each time his thumb passed across her skin. There was peace in this moment, peace that grew more fragile with each minute she did not speak. How could she—? What could she—?

"I," she swallowed. "I, oh, this is so hard, but—"

"You want to break up," he said, stealing her words.

A shaky breath escaped as she nodded. "I don't want to, but this sneaking around feels so wrong. I can't do it anymore."

A muscle ticked in his jaw, as his chin dipped.

Oh, thank God. He understood. "I...I've felt like I'm lying to everyone, and it's eating me up inside. It's not what God wants, I know that for sure."

His grip tightened fractionally then released. He shifted on the seat, elbows on knees, facing the floor. "I can't see how to make it work either." His Adam's apple dipped. "Mike has been on my case about it for weeks, too."

She'd suspected as much.

"He likes you, it's nothing personal, but he's just worried that it will affect you and your career, and will look bad for the team."

"I know."

He lifted shadowed eyes to her. "I don't want to let you go."

A heart couldn't literally break, could it? Because she was pretty sure she'd felt a cracking sensation heave through her chest. His features blurred. She blinked. Hard.

"You're like this vision of golden perfection to me. You always have been," his voice was ragged, "and I can't stand the thought of losing you again."

"But it can't work," she said softly.

"Not while you're working there."

She heard the unspoken question. Would she be willing to sacrifice her job for a future with this man? She could just imagine what her mother would have to say about that. But he couldn't sacrifice his job for her. Even swapping teams meant they were still in the same bind. She couldn't be a sports reporter if there was a perception of bias, and it wasn't fair to him to abandon all he'd worked for years to achieve, and leave the NHL.

"I don't know what else to do," she whispered brokenly. "I've prayed and I've prayed—"

"Me too." He glanced at her. "My folks have been praying too."

They had?

"They say hi, by the way."

"Hi back."

No smile.

Oh. "Did, um, they have anything to say? About the situation?"

His mouth tweaked. "If you're asking if they approve, then yes, they do. You know Mom and Dad love you. But they see the challenges too. And all they could say was that if it was of God then He would make a way."

Whoa. She leaned back against the chair, struck by the bigness of those words. Sure, some could see it as a simple "if it works out, it was meant to be" but it felt bigger than that. "Meant to be" sounded kind of lame. "Was of God" meant something deeper, like it was truly part of God's plans and purposes. Which meant regardless of what happened, it would be God's plan and purpose for her good. And for Franklin's.

His brow pleated. "What is it?"

She shook her head. "I don't know why I didn't see it like that before."

"See what before?"

"I keep praying and saying to God that I'm trusting Him, but I haven't been. Not really." She rubbed her forehead. "If I were, then I'd relax, because I'd know that He was in control and could work things out."

His eyes lit. "Are you saying you want to continue?"

"No. I mean, yes, obviously, but no."

His laughter sounded forced. "Yeah, nothing too obvious about that answer, Hannah."

She pressed her fingers into her scalp, begging the headache she could feel forming to stay away, as she tried to explain more clearly. "I feel like God is saying 'I've got this under control. You don't need to worry. Just do things My way,'" she pointed to the ceiling, "'God's way, and I'll take care of it. I'll take care of you.'"

"Yeah…?"

Maybe this wasn't news for him. "I don't know. It just feels like a weight is off. Like I can actually trust Him now, with you and with the future."

"What are you saying?" His brow creased. "Do you want to break up or not?"

"I think we have to," she murmured. "But if it's what God wants then He'll make a way for it to work out."

He groaned, placing his head in his hands again.

She bit her lip. "You know it's not what I want. I lo—" no, it was too early for that word "—like you, so much, Franklin. You've been like a dream come true."

He shook his head. "I don't want to end this."

"But you know it's right and what we have to do," she whispered.

He nodded, still not looking at her.

Finally, after what seemed an age, he sighed and shifted to face her. "I should go now, huh?"

She bit her lip to stop the sudden quiver. This was real. And it might be one thing to say you trusted God but it was another to actually follow Him when things were hard. She found enough strength to bend her head.

Another ragged breath escaped him, and he slowly pushed to his feet. Threw his hand in his hair. Glanced at her. "I refuse to believe this is over."

But it might be if God didn't open a way. Or—her chest panged—if this wasn't God's plan for them.

He held out a hand, and she grasped it, and he gently tugged her to her feet, drawing her near. "Can I have one last kiss?"

Oh, how her body screamed to say yes. But saying yes would

only prolong this longing, this yearning for what might never be, and stir the flames of something that God might wish to die. "I don't think that would be wise."

His lips flattened, as a small V formed between his brows. "A last hug then?"

Surely that couldn't hurt? She nodded, and a second later was swept into his arms, folded in his strength, while she did her best to keep from crying. This man, this beautiful man, was everything she treasured. And because of that, she kept reminding herself, she had to let him go. For God's sake. For Franklin's. And hers.

She squeezed him tight, then, a minute—an hour—later, walked him to her front door. She opened it, and he clutched her again in another final desperate hug goodbye, his face burrowed in her neck, which grew damp. Was that from tears? *Oh, Lord, help him know this decision was born of love.* God's love, as well as hers.

She closed her eyes, emotion pressing against her eyelids, as she savored the final seconds of his touch, reaching up to caress his hair, before sliding a hand down the rasp of his jaw. "It'll be okay," she murmured.

His eyes were red-rimmed, and if it had been possible for her heart to break any more it would have. His face angled, like he wanted to kiss her, and she leaned back.

And gasped as she saw the phones pointed their way.

CHAPTER 17

"_D_ude."

"What the"—expletive—"were you thinking?"

"No words."

"Were you insane?"

Other—less wholesome—words were pitched at him, describing his lack of intelligence, questioning his morals, ethics, and making him wish real hard he'd stayed away.

He hadn't been sure if he should show up or call in sick to practice today. Part of him was sick—sick with yearning for what could never be, sick with regret for how things had turned out. Another part of him—the naive part—hadn't realized how quickly things would escalate, as the photos from yesterday—yes, multiple pics, with him hugging her, looking red-eyed and teary, looking basically pathetic—had sprung straight to social media, or so Tom, Luc and Ryan had warned him in their messages early this morning.

Still another part of him, the analytical part that knew percentages and percentiles, was looking at this objectively and kind of amazed at how quickly the storm had flared into an inferno of nightmare proportions. And yet another part, the part with a heart, hurt and grieved at what all of this meant for Hannah, his family, Mike, and yes, himself.

He deserved pretty much every bullet his teammates were firing at him now.

He glanced at Mike's empty stall. Perhaps the worst part of this was that he hadn't realized the effect it would have on Mike. Mike had called him earlier, when the pictures of Franklin and Hannah had first started the rounds of gossip sites and social media.

"It's my fault," Mike had said. "I should've said something earlier, talked to her, or talked to management, but I didn't. And as the captain and your friend I have to take responsibility."

"No, you don't. It's on me. You warned me a million times, and I refused to listen."

"Yeah, well, great leader I am." Mike had cleared his throat. "Anyway, I'm going to talk to the coach and management this morning."

"I'll come too."

"Oh, I think they'll be calling you very soon." Mike blew out a breath. "You might want to have your agent on speed dial."

"My agent?"

"I'm sorry, man, but this may well end up being a suspendible offense like others have faced in the past."

Franklin had closed his eyes. Why hadn't he realized just how big the stakes were? "I'm so sorry, man."

"Tell that to the team."

Ouch. "Just so you know, we broke it off yesterday."

"Bree said you looked like you'd been crying."

He'd cringed.

"Sorry, I know this sucks."

Sure did. Big time.

He now glanced around the locker room, meeting expressions varying from sneers to sympathy. What a mammoth mistake this had been. He snatched up his phone, and moved to find Mike. No way was he going to let the man take the fall for him. And while Franklin's hurried phone call to his agent—who'd been just about to call him—had suggested a suspension was unlikely, although a fine and official reprimand might be due, he was man enough to own his mistakes and face what he was due. Whatever happened, he'd likely be getting off three thousand times more lightly than poor Hannah.

His heart clenched. He wished he could be there, take the shots no doubt being fired her way. He didn't need to hear Hannah's mom's feminist rhetoric to know the woman was often punished worse than the man, and he could bet the ranch that Hannah would be facing more than a fine and some angry words.

He pressed his lips together, praying for her for the millionth time, and wondered how she was going.

THIS WAS NOT GOING WELL. Hannah's gaze lowered to the conference table as the men talked in circles around her. Yes, she'd made an error in judgment. Yes, she'd owned up to her sins. Yes, she should've come to Dirk straight away with the fact that she knew Franklin and the potential for a conflict of interest. She'd told Jason about knowing Franklin, and back then he hadn't seemed concerned, but she hadn't shared about more recent developments. More fool her.

If it wasn't for this weirdest stubborn hope that God could somehow still work this out she would've followed her first instinct yesterday, when she'd seen that camera, and fled the country. That would've only made things worse. Instead, her panic had led her to call Jason and explain the situation, which had met with his stunned silence then several minutes of swearing, before he advised her to contact Dirk immediately.

She'd done that, and his response had been similar to Jason's, except with more moderate language, and several muttered expressed hopes that the photos wouldn't see the light of day. His words had fueled hope of her own, and she'd then called Cassie, and asked her and her family to pray, before contacting her agent. Lisa hadn't picked up, so she'd left a brief message, then called her mom.

"You're going to do what?" her mom had shrieked.

She explained. Mom had released her own non-God-approved word. "You would truly give up everything you've worked so hard for, just for a man?"

"It's not my choice, Mom. But according to what Jason thinks, it's likely the best scenario." She tried to spin it positively. "And it wouldn't be the first time I've had to alter direction."

"But that was an injury beyond your control! This is completely different. Oh, I'm so angry, but what should anyone expect? He's a man. You know they always let you down."

"He didn't let me down, Mom. He's been so—"

"You watch. He'll get off with a slap on the wrist while they cut your career off at the head. It's always the way. Men get off scot-free while the victims get the blame. You saw what happened with your father—"

"Mom, you've met Franklin, you know he's nothing like my father."

"He's a man," Mom interrupted. "He thinks with one thing, and it's not his brain."

"Franklin is not like that," she insisted. "And we've never done...that. We only kissed. Once." *Once.* How had all this erupted when they'd only shared *one* kiss?

"What's wrong with him?" Her mother's ability to pivot to new offense was remarkable. "You're beautiful and intelligent and wonderful and I'm so proud of you and...."

Surprise at her mother's compliments rendered her silent.

"Hannah?"

"I'm just not used to hearing you say things like that," she admitted, her voice small.

"Well, I *am* proud of you. I didn't work my butt off all those years so you'd be a failure."

Guilt strummed. "I'm doing my best to pay you back, Mom."

"I don't need to be paid back. I have a wonderful job that allows me to live comfortably, and I don't need anything except to see my daughter happy. Which is what I want for you. A good job and for you to be happy. Ugh! I am so mad and can't believe you have to wear the consequences of his selfishness."

And they were back to this. "I am equally to blame."

"He took advantage of you," her mother continued, as if she hadn't heard. "And I am disgusted. I can talk to my friends in legal circles and see if there is a way to get recompense—"

"Nothing is decided yet, Mom," she said wearily. "The meeting is tomorrow. This is just a heads-up in case you hear comments from others."

"Your father deceived us just the same. Pretending to be a gentleman when he was clearly a devil in disguise."

"Mom, you have to forgive him."

"Forgive him?" her mother cried. "I never will. After what he did—"

"But you keep letting him win." Frustration surged. "How has staying angry with him all these years helped you? You're always stressed, you're always angry, you don't let people in, you've never had another relationship even after your divorce, you barely let *me* in. I get you don't want to get hurt, but can't you see this anger is only hurting yourself? You can't blame the patriarchy for everything. You have to forgive him, Mom. Do that and it will set you free."

Her mother gasped. "You sound brainwashed by religion. You need to stop going to that church and being with people like that."

Hannah pressed her lips together. Sarah Maguire on her

podcast was right. She wasn't going to argue her mother to salvation or learning forgiveness. She'd have to keep praying and loving her into the kingdom.

"Not all men are bad, Mom. Franklin is one of the good ones. And I," her eyes filled with tears. "And I love him, Mom."

Maybe it was the sound of her daughter's shaky voice or just the fact she'd fully vented her spleen but her mother calmed down, even acting quite kind and motherly, before she again offered to contact her lawyer friend to help Hannah's situation.

Hannah had declined, but now, looking at the men of CNSTV still arguing around the table, she wondered whether she should've accepted after all.

The wrestling and wrangling over her part in this had gone on long enough, with nothing resolved.

This morning's early phone call with Lisa hadn't made things any clearer, her colorful language only slightly more tempered than Dirk's. "I can't begin to tell you how disappointed I am. You know they will likely spin a way to make this fit under the 'professional incompetence' clause of your contract."

"Yes."

Lisa had sighed. "I'll make some calls, but I'm afraid you need to prepare for the worst. We'll have to check to see if there's a clause about secret mandatory arbitration. If so, it means they can spin things to say they've done all they can and you weren't ready to play."

"What?"

"I know. It's not fair, but it's how the industry works. We'll see what happens, but I want you to prepared. You may have to consider giving up the lease on your apartment."

Her apartment? Oh no. If she lost her job, how could she afford to stay here? Where would she live? No way did she want to move back in with Mom again.

She peeked across the table, catching Jason's stone-faced

glare in her direction. Yep, she'd let him down, big time. He was right, she should've told him when things had progressed beyond mere friendship with Franklin. And as he'd said, and as Drew pointed out now, what she'd done was likely to be considered on par with Bob's sexist comments.

"As I keep saying, you can't cover the circus if you sleep with the elephants," Drew said, pointing at her.

"I never slept with him." But admitting she'd kissed Franklin only once seemed like information overshare. And right now, given all the overreaction, slightly humiliating.

The rounds of conversation continued, and every so often Will's phone would ping with a new message or picture, as more and more people found photos that "proved" she'd done wrong.

Some of these were forwarded on or passed around the room—she'd forgotten to charge her phone last night for the first time ever and it had died after her call with Lisa this morning—so she was forced to look at other people's phones as she tried to explain over and over the barely-there relationship she'd had with Franklin. Her fingers shook. She knew she looked like a liar.

How else could she explain that heated look between them someone had snapped at that hockey game? Her looking after him, him looking back at her. Or the Insta detectives who'd found a pic of Franklin and Hannah smiling—along with everyone else—at Thanksgiving on Poppy's private account, which one of Poppy's friends had screenshotted then last night shared to the world? Or another one taken at the front of her apartment showing Franklin glancing at the camera, with a woman behind. She squinted at that one. It looked like the first time he'd visited with Cassie. Hang on, that *was* Cassie.

She opened her mouth to explain, but another couple of images flashed up on the screen. Franklin and Hannah, smiling at each other at the steak house. Then another of them hugging, then getting into his truck leaving the restaurant, that day when he'd joked about pretending to have a relationship to convince everyone he didn't hate her after her stupid headbutt.

Hysteria bubbled up. And released in laughter choked with tears.

The conversation stopped, the men staring at her like she really was as crazy as suggested in that meme from long ago.

"Hannah?" Dirk frowned. "I really don't think this is a laughing matter."

"You're right. It's not. I'm sorry."

Dirk folded his arms, glanced at Jason, then Peter, then back at her. "I suppose it is obvious that you are relieved from your reporting duties here."

She nodded. She mightn't have slept with any elephants, but she couldn't cover any circus. Who could trust her now?

"And you are being put on personal leave starting immediately."

Well, that was better than immediate dismissal, at least. It was probably going to come soon anyway, but she bet Lisa would be fighting tooth and nail for her to somehow stay.

She glanced around the room. "Once again, I want to apologize to you all for how my actions have caused trouble for the station and for you all. It was not my intention, and I fully understand and accept the consequences." She pushed back her chair, glanced at Peter, then at Dirk. "On the off chance I'm not fired—"

Drew sniffed.

"—I want you to know that I would still appreciate a role here, but I know that you would have concerns about that. Anyway, I have appreciated my time here, and I'll go now and leave you to discuss what you think should happen next."

"Hannah," Jason said. "You know none of us wanted things to turn out like this."

A peek at Drew's smug satisfaction didn't exactly confirm that statement, but she let it slide. She nodded.

"You were good for the ratings, at least."

"Gee, thanks Will. Appreciate knowing that."

Jason's mouth tweaked.

She glanced at Dirk. "Thanks for giving me this opportunity. I'm grateful. Truly."

He nodded, and the others offered looks of sympathy or satisfaction as she collected her things and walked back to her desk. John offered a word of sympathy. Royce, watching tape in the video room, ignored her apology for her deceit, thanks for his help, and goodbye.

She cleaned out her desk, her hands and legs shaky, and passed Mandi, who gave her a hug. "You were fire, girl."

She offered a watery smile. Fire girl? That's for sure. She'd gone and burned down her career.

After handing in her accreditation she moved outside to her car. Heavy clouds spat raindrops at her, mimicking her tears, as she drove home, only to see a number of reporters milling outside the front of her apartment, while other people snapped selfies. How did they know where she lived?

She parked around the back, locked her car, then grabbed her door key, and ran inside, barely stopping to acknowledge Miss Petty before she took the elevator to her floor. Only to discover her apartment door was slightly ajar.

Weird. She might've been frazzled this morning but she *always* locked it.

Heart hammering, she pushed it wide. Then gasped. Someone had ransacked the place, and—"No!"

The words painted in large red letters on her living room wall screamed at her, punching into her brain, burning her heart, the hatred fierce and deadly. With a shaking hand she drew out her phone but it slipped from her grasp, landing with a clatter on the floor.

Kill the witch.

THEY KNEW where she lived too?

Franklin's pulse escalated as he considered his options. He couldn't return home. He'd talked to the coach and GM, owned his mistakes, and pleaded for Mike, and they'd agreed their new captain was culpable of nothing more than poor judgment. A statement had been released concerning Franklin, who was to be considered to have the "full support of the organization" with the request that he be given privacy at this time.

Privacy? If only.

Everywhere he'd gone today he could feel a hundred eyeballs following him. The team's official statement might have concluded with a "We won't be addressing this again" but that hadn't stopped reporters like Natalie and others calling him. How'd they discovered his number he didn't know, but he supposed reporters had a way of finding out such things. Management had said Hannah would probably get harassed along with him, and he'd prayed it wouldn't be the case. When he'd left practice and driven home it was to see unusual activity outside his apartment, so he'd driven instead to Hannah's, his suspicions proved correct when he saw her blue Mazda in the resident's parking lot. Maybe she was simply enjoying a day off, holed up inside watching Netflix, screening her calls. But he feared the worst. CSNTV weren't exactly leaders in supportive work practices, and the chances were high that she'd scored a lot worse punishment than him. And if the media—and the extreme fans—knew she was here, who knew what might happen? Especially as Hannah didn't have a doorman and good security...

He parked next to her car. Tried her phone again. She still didn't pick up. His nerves tightened. He pounded on the glass back door to the lobby, and the elderly woman he'd seen a time or two moved to open it.

"Oh." She peered up at him along her sharp nose. "You again."

"I need to see Hannah. Have you seen her? She's not answering her phone."

"She got in not five minutes ago."

"May I—?"

She drew the door wider and with muttered thanks he rushed past, catching her "All her friends are coming today" as he stabbed at the elevator. It was taking too long. He moved to the stairs and got a five-floor workout, puffing a little as he reached her floor. He didn't normally run that fast on the treadmill.

He moved to her door—why was it open?—and passed into the tiny entryway that served as her foyer. "Hannah? Are you —oh no!"

He rushed to where she was crouched, head on her knees, her phone beside her on the floor. He scooped her up in his arms. She was shaking, her breath unsteady, and as he clutched her to himself a dozen scenarios flashed. Had she been hurt? Worse? Then his gaze lifted to the words on the wall.

His chest squeezed. She'd just come in, or so her elderly neighbor had said. She hadn't disturbed the perpetrator, had she? "Hannah, honey, did you see who did this?"

She shook her head. He tugged out his phone. "Have you called the police?"

"My phone is dead," she whispered.

He dialed 911, giving a quick check of all the rooms as he gave the details, promising to stay with her until an officer was sent. What else could he do? His mind was awhirl as the threat silently shrieked. Who could've done that? Why? How? When? He could barely think. *God?*

He sucked in a deep breath. He needed to get her from this

room where those red words screamed. "Hey, come here." He gently tugged her to her feet and wrapped her in his hug more fully, making sure she was angled away from sight lines of the paint. "You're safe. I'm here. I'm not going anywhere."

He felt her head nod, the action driving a stake of fierce determination deep within. He'd get those responsible—or the police would—if it was the last thing he did.

He drew her into the kitchen, switched on the kettle. His mom probably had some hippie herbal concoction for moments like this but she wasn't here. All he knew was that Hannah did like real tea, and he'd read somewhere that sugar in hot tea was good for shock. He hoped it worked this time.

She was sipping it when the police came. Then after a flurry of introductions—"you're Franklin James, right? I'm a huge fan"—and photos and statements, she was advised to pack a bag and attend the police station, where her phone and laptop were taken for further evidence of the threats made against her.

Threats? Why had she never told him about the extent of the hatred against her? He knew why. She hadn't wanted to worry him. She had to grow a thick skin. This was *normal*. But the very fact anyone considered this normal punched deep anger in his soul. This wasn't right. And he hated how violence against women could be considered okay.

She was stoic throughout, the trembling fear of before gone as she answered methodically, and he did what he could, answering what little he knew, holding her hand when she let him. He didn't care that there'd been cameras when they'd left together in his car with police car lights flashing. He didn't care about hiding anything anymore. From what she'd said, he gathered she'd about lost her job anyway, so any relationship between them was likely now okay. And no way was he giving up on this woman. Not when she needed him more than ever.

It was midafternoon when they were released, and he settled her in his car again. The police had advised her to go somewhere safe, and given the media interest—who knew what they'd be saying now after seeing him, her and the police?—his place wasn't an option. "Where can I take you? Your mom's?"

She side-eyed him.

"Bree's?"

"I really don't want to be causing them any more trouble than I already have."

Neither did he. With all his claims of friendship, he needed to start proving it. "What about the ranch? You know Mom and Dad will look after you."

"But people know where they are, and might try to get there—"

"They can lock the gates." And his dad and Cassie were pretty good with shotguns. "You'll be safe."

She nodded, so he started driving that way. Then his phone rang.

Bree. He put it on speakerphone and kept driving. "Hey Franklin, have you seen Mike?"

"Not since this morning. Why?"

"He's gone to Alex's for a party—"

A party? Nothing had been said earlier. Or maybe Franklin wasn't one of the chosen ones.

"—and because some of the girls are upset about not being invited, I told Mike, which is why he's gone to speak to him. And now he's not answering his phone and I'm getting concerned."

Good thing he wasn't adding to her worry by dumping Hannah there too. "What can I do?"

"Would you mind—I know it's super inconvenient but would you mind going to see him? I get this twin thing with my brother when I know something is wrong and I feel the same way about Mike. I'm really worried."

"Now?" He glanced across at Hannah. Driving her to the ranch and back would take at least an hour.

"I don't mind," Hannah murmured. "I'll stay in the car."

"You sure?"

"Is someone there with you?" Bree asked.

"Hannah."

"How is she? How are you, Hannah?" Bree called.

"Fine," Hannah managed.

She wasn't really, but he didn't have time to go into everything with Bree now. He glanced at Hannah again, and at her nod, said, "Okay."

"Oh, thank you so much." Bree gave him the address, and Hannah punched it into his car's navigation system.

"We're going there now." He ended the call, turned the wheel sharply, pulling off the highway to the suburb where Alex lived.

"It's only two minutes from here," he said. "I'll be in and out to check on him. You'll be safe in the car. I'll give you the keys."

"Sure."

Tension filled the vehicle, and then he grasped her hand in his. "Hey God, we need Your help and protection, and so does Mike. Thanks for being with us."

"Amen."

A mite of the tension filling the vehicle ebbed away, aided by her small smile. "I won't take long, I promise."

"I'll keep praying."

He pulled up outside Alex's place, saw Mike's truck, gave Hannah his keys, kissed her forehead. "You're amazing."

"You know it."

He chuckled, still smiling as her call of "Go get 'em, Cowboy" chased him inside. There was no point in knocking. The music was thumping so loud the potted plants were trembling. The rooms were dim, smoke—from cigarettes and something else— clogged the air. He pushed past a couple of scantily-dressed women—maybe these were who the girlfriends were upset by— and moved through to the back room. No sign of any other teammates. Although he could hear two.

Mike's voice, raised louder, sharper, than Franklin had ever heard it. And Alex's roar. He twisted the door handle to enter when it suddenly opened to reveal a shirtless Chad, who instantly dropped a few swear words. Surprise, surprise.

"What the"—expletive—"happened to your shirt?" Chad asked.

Franklin glanced down. His chest wore the remnants of Hannah's tears before, along with mascara and lipstick smears. "Someone broke into Hannah's apartment today. Then decided to redecorate with a death threat on her wall."

"What?" Chad's eyes widened. He glanced at the room where Alex could be heard flinging a string of swear words at Mike. "Dude, no. That ain't what I signed up for. I'm outta here."

He exited, and Franklin's hands fisted, as he stepped inside.

HANNAH'S EYES REMAINED CLOSED, relishing the moment of quiet, and calm. Today had been insane. If only Franklin and Mike would hurry up. She rubbed her hands up her arms. It was getting cool sitting here without the heating. She should've worn a thicker jacket. Actually, there probably was one here somewhere in the bag she packed so quickly hours ago. She found it, pulled it on. Prayed for Franklin, Mike, Bree, and that whatever was wrong would quickly be made right.

The fear that had accompanied her earlier was slowly ebbing away, replaced by deep, deep anger. How dare anyone do that to her? How dare anyone treat *any* woman that way? As she looked at the cars she recognized a few from Mike and Bree's party, and revulsion grew for the man who owned this place. She should've said something about this man who hated women. The police had been glad she had kept detailed records of the abuse she'd received online but she hadn't done the same with Alex. Not the time he'd tried to touch her at Bree's party, when she'd had to knee him to make him stop. Not that flasher pervert moment in the locker room when she'd thought she simply needed to develop a thicker skin. She should've said something. Her mom would be ashamed of her. How many times had Hannah put her career above her self-respect?

A wave of nausea hit her and she opened the door and released her stomach contents. There wasn't much, as she'd barely eaten today, and she wiped her mouth with a tissue from the glove box. She hoped the smell of vomit wouldn't contaminate Franklin's pristine vehicle which until then had smelled so clean. Clean, sturdy, safe, built strong to bear loads and carry weight. Just like its owner.

She should've told him. His shoulders were broad enough to hold the truth.

She swiped at more stupid tears as another vehicle pulled into view. She recognized that flashy red number too. And the woman slamming its door. Kristen.

Kristen was muttering something, her fury evident in her high-heeled stomp which veered as she saw Hannah. "Are you kidding me? What are you doing here? Getting another of your stupid stories?"

"What?" She might've been suspended but her reporter nose still worked. "I don't know—"

"He hates you!" Kristen yelled.

That wasn't news.

"And it's all your fault!"

Up close Hannah could smell the liquor, see the smeared makeup, the red marks on her hands. Was that blood? Compassion stirred her heart. "Kristen, I don't know what he's blaming me for, but—"

"Everything!" Kristen threw her hands in her dyed hair. "He's so angry."

"I don't know what's happened, or what's wrong, but if I can help in any way—"

"*Everything* is wrong. He's done things, made me do things, and I—" Her eyes widened. "I didn't mean it. Not really."

"Mean what?"

Kristen shook her head. "You know he called me a zero today?"

"What?"

"He called me a zero. Just because I didn't have my makeup on. What kind of guy says that?"

"A cruel one." Now probably wasn't the time to tell her that her boyfriend had once flashed Hannah. "Any person who dismisses another because of their looks is shallow and vain. You're not your looks, Kristen. You're way more valuable than that."

"Right?" Kristen's fingers clenched. "I know I'm a ten."

Mmm. Clearly that pep talk hadn't sunk in.

"He's *evil*. You should hear what he says about others," Kristen hissed, "what he writes in his chat."

"What chat?"

Kristen squinted at her, then turned on her heel, stalking into the house still pulsating with sound.

Franklin had been way longer than two minutes. And Mike was still nowhere to be seen. And Kristen really wasn't in any fit condition to go have a conversation with an evil man. What was going on?

Should she go inside? Her earlier fears said no. But concern chased her to follow. If only she had her phone. Franklin had taken his.

A woman's screaming hurried her steps to the door. Hannah could hear raised voices, and seconds later, two women with less clothes than the cold weather warranted pushed past her. They fled to another vehicle, pulling away just as a police car drew in. Ooh boy. Things were going to get interesting. After a lifetime of no police interactions she was about to have two encounters in one day. Awesome.

Another scream. Franklin's yell. Her heart pounded and she raced inside, passing through a room of smoke and drugged-out people, into another where she paused. Time slowed into a collection of fractured images and sounds. Mike staggering to his feet. Kristen slapping Alex's face, nails drawing blood, as Franklin tried to hold her back. Her screams about death threats and "she's here!" Alex pivoting to see Hannah, his face contorting to a snarl worse than any horror hockey mask she'd seen. His lunge. Her spike of fear. Franklin's desperate reach toward her. Alex's beery breath and clutching hands. A surge of adrenaline as Hannah leaned back, then propelled forward, her momentum such that her knee connected with him at the same time as the top of her head.

His whimpering slump to the floor. More blood spatters. Pain in her head. Blood in her hair. Blood on her hands. Red-and-blue flashing lights. Kristen's screaming. Her own exhaustion. And Franklin's arms around her, his chest a drumroll, his ragged "I've got you," and that moment when she knew with him she was finally safe.

CHAPTER 18

"Well, good morning, Sleeping Beauty."

Hannah shoved a hand through her tangled hair. "I must look like a mess."

"You look like you slept. Anyway, no judgment here, right, Sylvie?"

The purple-haired woman wearing a skull and crossbones tee and plaid skirt lifted her mug. "None."

"Here. You look like you need a coffee, too."

Hannah nodded, slumping into the stool next to Sylvie as Bree moved to the espresso machine. She stole another peek at the woman beside her, as the machine's grind and whir filled the room. Spiderweb clips and a silver ring, black leggings webbed with silver thread. No wonder she was good with kids. Hannah could stare at her for hours.

"Here you go." Bree plunked the coffee on the counter, along with a little basket of sugar, spoons, and creamer.

She took a sip, closed her eyes, and sighed.

"You look like you needed that," Sylvie said.

"You got in so late last night it's not surprising you slept half the day away."

Hannah studied Bree. "Thanks so much for putting me up last night. Franklin was going to take me to the ranch but it was just going to take longer, and be more questions, and I was exhausted even before I went to the police station for the second time." She shook her head. "Can you believe it? A lifetime of no police run-ins then twice in one day."

"Look who's going bad," Sylvie murmured.

Hannah ignored her. "I never wanted to add to your stress, or be a burden."

Bree's eyes glistened as she clasped Hannah's hand. "Hey, it's okay. Mike's safe, I'm safe, the babies are safe, and most importantly, you're safe."

"But your blood pressure—"

"Will be fine, the doctor said. Especially now that Sylvie is here." She glanced across at her Goth-dressed friend.

Hannah managed a small smile but the woman's frown seemed etched on. How she and Bree had remained friends when they seemed polar opposites was a marvel to her. But who was she to judge when she'd barely proved worthy of friendship herself?

"Now, stop worrying about us, and let's get back to you. You say the police have your phone?"

She nodded. "And my laptop. They're going through the death threats, and—"

"Threats?" Sylvie interrupted. "Like, plural?"

Hannah needs a spanner to her head. Hannah swallowed. "Some people out there seem to get off on saying all kinds of horrible things. They think I'm ugly, call me fat, they hate my voice. They want me dead." She swallowed. "They want to rape me."

Sylvie's eyes rounded. "Are you kidding?"

"No. And it's all because I dared to be a woman reporting on sports on TV. There are a lot of sick men out there." One really sick one in particular. But Kristen's screamed accusations last night might see him locked away. *Please, God.*

"There's some sick women, too," Sylvie muttered. "But yeah. There are plenty of pathetic men, for sure. I only know one good dude, and he married this chick here." Sylvie pointed to Bree.

"Mike is the best," Bree said.

"He's pretty good." Almost as good as Franklin, who after completing his own interviews at the police station—again—had driven her here, given a brief report to a hugely relieved Bree, then held Hannah's hand until she'd dropped off to sleep. He'd said he'd stay at the ranch last night, before the team meeting this morning. If she was feeling this tired, he must be exhausted.

"Have you heard from Mike yet?" she asked.

"They'll be here soon. Him and Franklin."

Hannah nodded, unable to ignore the ping of relief to hear Franklin would be here too. Maybe one man had been caught, but she couldn't help but feel like there might be more out there trying to harm her.

"Hey, don't look like that. It's going to be okay," Bree assured her. "You're safe here. It's great security, and because it's gated, nobody can come here unless we know them."

She nodded. "I appreciate staying here more than you know."

With no phone, no laptop, and nobody knowing where she was, she might finally feel safe. Even her own mother didn't know where Hannah was. She'd called her mom and left a message late last night, only saying that she was safe, but going off-grid and staying quiet for a while. She suspected Mom would've insisted Hannah stay with her, and there was no way her own mental state would cope with listening to her rantings about Franklin. Not when Hannah *ached* to have him near.

She plunged her head in her hands. "I still don't know how

they found out where I lived." The police had mentioned something, but the stress of everything had blocked it from her mind.

Sylvie glanced at Bree. "You want to tell her?"

When Bree waved at her to continue, Sylvie nodded, and looked at Hannah. "It was there in the pictures. One of them was of Franklin outside your building, and in the background you could see the building number. The other one—where you and Franklin were kissing—"

"Hugging," she murmured.

"Whatever. That pic had your apartment number on the door." Sylvie shrugged. "It wouldn't take a genius to figure out where you lived."

"It's scary to think how someone might've been watching me." She shivered.

Sylvie laughed.

"What?"

"Well, what did you think people were doing? Every time you were on TV, people were watching you."

"But not stalking me. I don't think you really understand." Hannah glanced at Bree.

Bree nodded. "Hey Sylvie, do you mind checking on Ellison for me? She kicks off her blanket, and I don't want her to get cold."

"Sure." Sylvie's purple topknot had...spiderweb bows? Interesting.

"Hey," Bree said, when Sylvie had left. "She means well, just can be a little abrupt at times. Let me pray with you. I know it's all scary, but God is still here in the midst. We can trust Him, yeah?"

Hannah's mind flicked to the song sung in church the other day. She glanced at the clock. Had that really only been forty-eight hours ago? It felt like a lifetime.

Bree prayed, holding Hannah's hand, and peace flowed.

"And Lord, be with Mike and help him and Franklin and the team. Amen."

"Amen."

She glanced up, saw Sylvie had returned and was looking at them both strangely. Then Sylvie shrugged and resumed her seat on the stool again.

Hannah glanced at Bree. "Wait, I remember now. You were talking about the WAG group chat yesterday. What's happened with the girls?"

Bree winced. "It's been bananas. There's been so much gossip and speculation, and nobody really knows anything. That's why I'm so anxious to have Mike home soon. He'll know."

Bree's phone buzzed, and she glanced at it. Her brow creased, and she looked at Hannah.

"Who is it?"

"Cassie James." She read the message aloud. *"Franklin mentioned Hannah is staying with you. Is she okay?"* She passed the phone to her. "Do you want to reply?"

Hannah nodded, started to type, then pressed call instead. She moved to the living room, sinking into the plush sofa near a kiddie corner set up with a desk and crayons, as the phone rang. Maybe Cassie would know how he was do—

"Bree?"

"It's Hannah, actually."

"Oh my gosh! Are you okay? I can't *believe* all that happened. Franklin got in so late last night, we were all in bed, but then had to get up, and he told us, and—keep this to yourself but he might've gotten teary—"

Her heart clenched.

"—he was that worried about you. Oh, Hannah, are you okay?"

"I am now." Or she would be.

"I couldn't believe it. How anyone could ever have thought

Alex a worthy captain—it's no surprise his wife left him, with all the stuff he's been carrying on with. But I don't want to talk about him. Just you. You really are okay?"

"Yes. I'm at Bree's at the moment, and depending on what happens I might see if I can come out to the ranch soon."

"Oh, that'd be great! I know Mom and Dad were beside themselves too, and they just want you here, and safe, and well. We've all been praying nonstop."

Her eyes blurred. "Thank you."

"You know, I've never seen Franklin panicked like that. But then, I suppose it's only natural he's concerned about the woman he loves."

The woman he loves? Heart tingles. Oh…

"Did he, uh, say that?" she asked.

A beat passed. Two.

"Cassie?"

"Um, look, I probably wasn't supposed to say that, so can we pretend I didn't?"

"Yeah, I don't really think we can."

"Come on, Hannah. My brother will kill me if he knows I spilled the tea on how he really feels. I think he wanted to take you out somewhere romantic and tell you himself but—oh my gosh. I'm hanging up now." And the call ended.

She stared at the phone and chuckled.

"Was that laughter?" Bree asked Sylvie, as they joined her in the living room. "Did you hear laughter?"

"I heard genuine amusement, yes," Sylvie said with a straight face.

Okay, so maybe she could see what Bree appreciated in Sylvie.

"Amusement sounds promising," Bree said, placing a cup of herbal tea by her chair. "What did she have to say?"

"He loves me," she murmured. It still filled her with awe. She could cope with the uncertainties of the future if she knew he cared deeply in that way.

"Aww." Bree patted her heart. "Bless him."

Yes, Lord, bless him. No way was she going to admit to Bree he hadn't said that to her, but that his sister had accidentally over-shared about his feelings.

"He's a doll. And so sweet. And so handsome." Bree glanced at Sylvie. "You were dealing with Ellison last night so you didn't meet him, did you?"

A shake of the purple head.

"Well, just you wait. But remember, he's taken."

Sylvie rolled her eyes. "The good ones always are."

Bree cupped her mouth and stage-whispered, "I think she had a thing for my brother Brent at one stage."

"Look, can I help it if I can appreciate a finely crafted man? No, I cannot." Sylvie shrugged. "And I will not stop appreciating. Even if he is married. Except for Mike. That'd be weird."

"Yes, it would," Bree said firmly, but giving Hannah a wink to say not to worry, it was only Sylvie's way. "So, Franklin will be here soon. Did you want a shower? Get changed?"

"I'm okay," Hannah said. "He's seen me worse than this."

"I like when a woman is comfortable in her own skin," Sylvie said.

Said the woman wearing all kinds of statements in her hair and clothes.

"So, what are you going to do for a job now?" Sylvie asked.

Her job. With everything else that had happened she'd forgotten the million-dollar question. "I don't know." Her lips tweaked into a wry smile. "And I guess they won't have any way of contacting me, either."

"Your email still works though," Bree said. "You can always sign in from here."

Of course. Should've thought of that. "I don't think they'll have me back there, and honestly, I can understand why they shouldn't. It's a conflict of interest, and that's that."

"Do you want to keep reporting on sports?" Bree asked. "I'm sure someone somewhere would have an opening."

"Yeah, maybe in New Zealand."

"I don't know how much they know about hockey," Bree said. "I could ask Holly. She's Australian, so she might know."

"She's the one who married Brent, right?" Sylvie rolled her eyes.

"And you need to forgive her. It's been four years now."

Sylvie huffed out a breath. "Fine."

"Hey, speaking of Holly," Bree said, "did you ever ask her or Allie or the others about doing interviews with them?"

That seemed like a conversation from long ago. "No. I didn't get time. I was concentrating on the Calgary team members, then got busy with *Hockey Hour.*"

"Well, maybe you should. You could do that kind of thing freelance. And if you're doing those kinds of things, maybe you could start a podcast. Sarah Maguire—Dan Walton's wife, so she's Sarah Walton, now—she writes those songs for Heartsong Collective? Anyway, she's started one recently. You should check into how to start one."

Maybe she should. Technology these days meant she didn't need to be defined or limited to other people's rules and expectations.

"You could maybe add something about women in sports."

"Or how women are often pigeonholed and disempowered by toxic masculinity," added Sylvie.

Her mom would love that. "I'll look into it. Thanks for the suggestions. They're really good." She smiled at Sylvie, which earned a flick up of the lips in return.

Then the door opened, and Mike walked in, trailed by Franklin.

Hannah's heart leaped. Franklin's eyes were lasered onto

hers, and she couldn't move. She vaguely heard introductions in the background, but all she could see was Franklin. His breadth. His height. The way the haggard haunted cast to his features faded as relief washed over his face.

"You're okay?" he asked.

"She lost her job, and got her apartment trashed, so no, not really," Sylvie's voice said sarcastically.

"I will be," she managed.

"Can we—?" Franklin asked Mike, Bree, Hannah—she didn't know.

"Be our guest," Mike waved them to the study, and she took Franklin's proffered hand and followed him there.

He closed the door, and leaned against it, studying her. "Hannah, *are* you okay?"

"Yes." She drew nearer. Up close, she could see how this had impacted him. She'd never seen those shadows in his eyes before.

"Really?"

She traced a hand down his stubbled jaw. "Really."

He drew her close, hugging her tight, and she relished the moment of being held by such a man.

"I'm so glad you're okay," he murmured against her hair. "I could barely sleep last night. I kept seeing him trying to hurt you, and I'd wake up, and then remember you were safe, then try to sleep but only have the same nightmare again." His exhale was shaky. "I'm so sorry this went on so long. I wish I'd known so I could've helped you."

She tucked her head—still tender—in the crook of his neck and shoulder. "I should've told you. I'm sorry."

His clasp tightened. "I understand why you didn't, but I wish you never had to face any of that. I'm so sorry. I hate that this has happened."

She pulled back, leaning in the circle of his arms. "I'm so

tired of all the hate. And I don't want to talk about being sorry any more. I'd rather talk about—" She stopped.

He studied her, eyes deep, intent on her.

How could she ask him about what his sister had said?

"What would you rather talk about, Hannah?" he asked, his low voice holding an edge of growl.

"You. And me."

He nodded. "Well, that's a conversation I'm super happy to talk about. Especially because I know how I feel about you and me."

She fought a smile. "And how is that?"

His fingers grazed her cheek, her jaw, her chin, her lips. "I love you, Hannah Wade."

Butterflies escaped and danced through her chest. There was no point trying to hide her smile now.

His lips lifted. "So, what do you have to say about that?"

She swallowed, her gaze swerving bravely up to meet his. "I love you. And," she hurried on, conscious of the flame in his eye that word had brought, "and I think you should kiss me right now."

"Yes, ma'am."

His lips met hers in a glory of passion and sweetness, rainbows arcing through her as he drew her even nearer. Finally it didn't matter whether anyone else knew. Everyone else already did know, so they were free. Free to kiss, to be seen, to love. And boy, did this cowboy know how to kiss.

Her breath was unsteady, her eyes unfocused, when they finally came up for air.

"Whoa." She fanned herself. "I think I need an ice bath."

His head tilted. "How long do you think it takes to fly to Vegas and back?"

She blinked. Was he saying—?

"We could fly there after the game tonight." His lips curled on one side. "I'm not even really joking."

He wasn't? Oh my stars. "Well, you should be. You can't say things like that."

"Hey," he wrapped an arm around her, "I'm not taking any chances of losing you again. I mean it. You're stuck with me. Sorry, but not sorry."

She laughed, which seemed to be the cue for a knock on the door which was opened by Mike. "You guys all good in here?"

She nodded, her cheeks heating as she curled into Franklin's side. He wasn't joking. She could feel his protectiveness, that he'd do whatever it took. Even if it meant a quickie wedding in Las Vegas. She laughed again.

"What's so funny?" Mike asked, the creases deepening next to his eyes.

"Nothing."

"Yeah, I want to know what's funny, too," Franklin said, turning to her. "I mean, that was a genuine almost-proposal."

Mike coughed. "Did you just say what I think you said?"

"Look, I love this woman, and I want people to know that. So yeah, I'm prepared to do whatever it takes." Franklin studied her. "Would you marry me?"

A shriek came from behind them. "Did Franklin just say—?"

"If she passes, I'm available," Sylvie offered. "Just sayin'."

The room erupted into laughter, which woke a little baby, or so the crying from a room far away suggested. "I'll go," said Sylvie. "Clearly I'm not needed here," she grumbled, but Hannah caught the tiny smile wedged in the corner of her mouth.

Okay, she officially had revised her opinion on Sylvie. The woman was hilarious.

"Oh," Bree groaned. "I think I need to sit down."

"Come on, honey," Mike said, hurrying to wrap an arm around her and guide her back to the sofa. "Do you want anything? Want your feet up? A cup of tea?"

What a sweet man. If only Mom could see guys like this existed. But maybe, as she and Franklin grew closer over time, she'd see exactly that. She didn't need a quickie wedding—she had zero desire to hear her mom's thoughts on that!—but she'd take as much of Franklin's care and affectionate attention as he'd give. And regardless of the future, she knew she could trust God with her work, and the skills she'd learned at CNSTV would be useful for the next step in her career.

Once Bree was seated satisfactorily, and insisting everyone sat down, including Sylvie who brought little Ellison out for Bree to hold, she glanced at Mike. "I think you need to tell Hannah what you started to tell us about your morning."

"Oh." He scrubbed a hand over his face. "The morning after. Okay, brace yourselves. There's a bit to this. Talk about a mess."

"Just go one step at a time." Bree rubbed his back.

"Right, well, as you know, yesterday Alex organized a party with Chad and some 'girls,' and some of the team's girlfriends found out and told Bree who told me. So I went there, and found Alex and Chad doing all kinds of things the GM would be furious about if he knew. After my talk with the coach and management yesterday, I knew I had to get them involved, so I called them, then went back in, which is when Franklin arrived. Then Kristen arrived all upset, and she was furious to see who Alex had been, um, carousing with."

"Carousing?" Sylvie said.

"You gotta love a man who can use big words correctly," Bree said smugly.

Mike's strain eased as he smiled, and squeezed her hand. "Anyway, long story short, the police arrived because the neighbors had made a noise complaint, then they saw him try to attack Hannah, before she kneed him." Mike smiled. "Maybe it's unchristian to say it but that was about the highlight of my day."

Sylvie snickered.

"Yeah, and I think Alex forgot that I'm the woman who's good at giving headbutts," Hannah said.

The tension broke as laughter rolled around the room,

bringing little Ethan running in. "Mommy? Why is everyone laughing?"

Bree stroked his hair. "It's just something Hannah said, sweetheart."

His head tilted. "Hannah said sweetheart?"

"I wish she'd say sweetheart," Franklin grumbled.

Hannah shot him a look as the chuckles came again.

"Mommy?"

"Sylvie, would you mind—?"

"Sure."

As Sylvie took Ethan back to watching his kids' movie, Mike shifted back in his seat, and clasped Bree's hand. "Thank God for moments of joy in this world."

Franklin's grip on Hannah's hand tightened. "Amen."

Her look cut to his, and from his small smile and the intense look in his eyes, she had a fairly good idea what recent joyful moment he was thinking of. Yeah, she'd be up for a repeat of that soon too.

"I wasn't sure if they'd cancel the game tonight, but we're playing. Well, except for Alex and Chad who are sitting out." Mike's nose wrinkled. "When Kristen kept screaming all kinds of stuff, in front of the police and the guy from team management who arrived, I wasn't sure how much was true, but from what got said at our meeting today, it appears it was." He winced. "Alex has been involved in a private group chat where some of the players across different teams have been ranking wives and girlfriends and saying all kinds of obscene things."

"Oh my gosh." Bree's hand covered her mouth, her eyes wide. "Do you know who they've talked about?"

He shook his head. "Management are looking into it with the police. Kristen was saying all kinds of stuff last night, so it's gonna take some time to learn how much is true and how much is revenge talk." He glanced around. "Please don't repeat this."

Everyone nodded.

"She also said he'd been betting on games—"

Bree gasped.

"—and then," Mike glanced at Hannah, "that he was responsible for the death threats against you."

Hannah's mouth fell open. Franklin's arm tightened around her shoulder. So that hadn't just been part of yesterday's bad dream. "I knew he didn't like me, but to say those things?" She shook her head. "And was he responsible for my apartment getting trashed?"

"Ah, that was where Kristen went too far. Apparently that was her."

"What?"

"Yeah, it's insane, I know." Mike rubbed his forehead and exhaled. "I still can't believe it. The team manager told me today that the team will probably put Alex on waivers for the purpose of contract termination."

"Oh my gosh," Bree said, as Sylvie returned. "So goodbye Alex, huh?"

Mike shrugged. "We'll see. A lot was being said, and there's a lot more to unpack, I'm sure. But the crazy thing is she said all of this in front of the police who were wearing body cameras and filmed it all." His chuckle sounded strained. "So it's all there, on tape, and in our statements." He glanced at Hannah. "Have you heard from the police yet?"

"Not yet."

He nodded, his exhale long. "It's such a mess. I don't know how the team's PR will cope with this."

Sylvie laughed. All eyes swung to her and she shrugged. "Well, I think it's good."

Mike's eyebrows pushed up. "Excuse me?"

"Look, obviously this bad stuff was going on, so it's good that it finally came out, right?"

Bree nodded slowly. "And if it had to come out, it's good that it's now, when it's completely taken the focus away from Franklin and Hannah."

Oh. Yeah. So it was. She glanced at Franklin. He lifted her hand and kissed it.

This situation might feel awful, but there were glimmers of hope. And just like God had allowed these awful hidden sins to be exposed in order to bring light and truth and healing, she knew she could trust Him with all other aspects of her life. God hadn't let her down. He'd been with her all this time. Keeping her safe. Keeping her sane. She could trust Him with the future. She squeezed Franklin's hand.

"How are we ever going to come back from this?" Bree asked, her head on Mike's shoulder.

The question circled the room, meeting frowns and pleated brows. What was the answer? God had a good answer, for sure. *Lord?*

She closed her eyes, and a cavalcade of images rolled through her mind. Her heart beat faster. What if all her challenges had been leading up to this? God was into working all things for the good of those who love Him and were called to His purpose. What if God's purpose hadn't ever been for her to play in the Olympics, or to do sports reporting, but was something even bigger and more worthwhile? Her breath hitched.

"What's wrong?" Franklin asked.

She opened her eyes, met the concern in his, and reassured him with a smile. "I was just thinking." She glanced at Mike and Bree. "This is an awesome opportunity, really." She straightened in her seat. "You'll put a statement out, as I'm sure the club will too, that says something along the lines of violence against women and toxic masculinity is never okay."

Mike nodded. "The team guy was saying something similar." His mouth curved. "I should get the PR people to talk to you."

"I'm always happy to talk if people want me to."

Franklin pressed another kiss to her hand, and murmured, "Should we see about that trip to Vegas first?"

Amusement rippled, and she shook her head. "I don't need the protection of a wedding ring to know it's right to speak out. But I appreciate the sentiment. And," she added softly, turning so it was just for him, "maybe one day you could change my mind."

"I'll ask again tomorrow."

She laughed, but knew whatever happened, God was with her, making those paths straight. And with His love, and this man's, and these friends, she would walk into His purposes and plans.

Her chin tilted. Just watch her.

A VIDEO PUT *out with players and partners from the NHL:*

HANNAH WADE, to camera. "Objectifying women and reducing them to their bodies or what they wear or what they look like is not okay."

Franklin James, Calgary: "If you're a guy who hears that kind of talk, then tell your friends that's not okay."

Mike Vaughan, Calgary: "If you're a parent and you hear that kind of language, then tell your kids that's not okay."

Brent Karlsson, Detroit: "Toxic masculinity, misogyny, and deeply rooted hate is not okay."

Tyler Woletsky, New York: "Violence against women is never okay."

Jai Mullins, San Jose: "There is no place in our league for such attitudes and behavior."

Tim Carruthers, New York: "If you witness violent behavior, then speak up."

Luc Blanchard, Winnipeg: "If you want to see a change, then you gotta be willing to stand up and speak out."

Ryan Guillemette, Edmonton: "If you don't speak up, you're doing nothing to help bring change."

Chris Thomas, Vancouver: "Think about if your sister, mother, or daughter was one of those involved, and speak up and make a difference."

Beau Nash, Montreal: "Your life, and the lives of those around you, are valuable to God."

Dan Walton, Toronto: "Treat others with respect."

"Treat others with respect," Hannah said.

"Treat others with respect," Mike said.

The screen split into dozens of tiny screens as many more players and wives and coaches and team owners all joined the refrain: "Treat others with respect."

Finally the bold words in white filled the black screen: Treat others with respect.

Hannah paused the tape, glanced at the people seated around the conference room. "Well?"

Don Belisario studied her for a long moment, then dipped his chin as he began a slow clap. The other Calgary players—nearly all had featured in those boxes at the end—joined in. Mike gave her a thumbs-up, and Franklin grinned, placing a hand over his heart then pointing at her.

His perfect woman, using her skills to make the world a better place. CNSTV hadn't known what a treasure they'd cut loose all those weeks ago. Their loss. Calgary's—and the world's—and his gain.

"That was awesome," he told her later, stealing a kiss. "Have I ever told you you're amazing?"

"Mmm, once or twice."

"I'm gonna have to up my game. Once or twice a day, it is then."

"I'll be counting, Cowboy."

He grinned and leaned his forehead on hers. "So, have you had any more thoughts about a special trip somewhere?"

"Maybe. Or maybe a trip to a certain white chapel on a ranch I know, one day."

His eyes lit, as he drew in for another kiss. "Mmm. I like that idea." His eyebrows lifted. "Got any more surprises up your sleeve?"

She grinned. "You bet your sweet mama I do."

The End
Make sure you check out Sylvie and Ryan's story in
The Love Penalty

Thank you for reading *Fire and Ice,* the first book in the Northwest Ice romance series. I was thrilled so many readers enjoyed the Original Six series, so it was fun to establish a new Christian romance series set in some of the hockey cities of the north and west Canada and USA. I've been lucky enough to visit some of these places, and you can find pics on my website at www.carolynmillerauthor.com

Delving into the world of female sports reporting was eye-opening. Female sports reporters have long dealt with everything from misogyny, to innuendo, death threats, and yes, having hot dogs thrown at them. I do not wish to infer that this is a particular issue in Calgary (it's simply where the book was set), as this is something faced by female reporters across the globe. While conditions are improving, many women in sports-casting continue to face similar challenges.

The ranch near Calgary boasting its own movie set is real, and forms the basis for my new romance series based on Franklin's three sisters from the Three Creek Ranch. Find out more about Cassie's path to romance in *A Cameo for a Cowgirl.*

Mission Possible for Future Generations is a real missions

organization run by friends of mine that helps sponsor children in the Philippines. Find out more here.

Reviews help other readers find new-to-them authors, so if you can spare a moment to write a quick review at Goodreads / your place of purchase, I'd be very grateful.

Make sure you check out Ryan and Sylvie's story in the next book in the Northwest Ice romance series, *The Love Penalty*.

If you enjoy Christian contemporary romance you may want to check out the books in the Original Six hockey romance series, a sweet & swoony, slightly sporty Christian contemporary romance series.

The Breakup Project
Love on Ice
Checked Impressions
Hearts and Goals
Big Apple Atonement
Muskoka Blue

Romance fans who enjoy small town life may also enjoy reading the Muskoka Romance series, that starts with *Muskoka Shores*.

I'd love for you to check out my other books and to sign up for my newsletter at www.carolynmillerauthor.com where you can be the first to learn all my book and contest news, and discover more behind-the-book details and photos. Newsletter subscribers can also get an exclusive bonus book free, so grab your copy of *Originally Yours* here.

ABOUT THE AUTHOR

Carolyn Miller lives in the beautiful Southern Highlands of New South Wales, Australia, with her husband and four children. A long-time lover of romance, especially that of Jane Austen, Georgette Heyer and LM Montgomery, Carolyn loves to write contemporary and historical romance that draws readers into fictional worlds that show the truth of God's grace in our lives.

To find out more about Carolyn's books, and to subscribe to her newsletter, please visit www.carolynmillerauthor.com

You can also connect with her at

ALSO BY CAROLYN MILLER

<u>The Original Six hockey series</u>

The Breakup Project

Love on Ice

Checked Impressions

Hearts and Goals

Big Apple Atonement

Muskoka Blue

<u>Muskoka Romance series</u>

Muskoka Shores

Muskoka Christmas

Muskoka Hearts

Muskoka Spotlight

Muskoka Holiday Morsels

<u>Northwest Ice hockey series</u>

Fire and Ice

The Love Penalty

<u>Three Creeks Ranch Romance series</u>

A Cameo for a Cowgirl

<u>Trinity Lakes collection</u>

Love Somebody Like You

Tangled Up in Love

'More than Gold' from

the Across the Shores novella collection